THE DREADFUL CHARMS OF JENNA GETTY

ELLY SMITHTON

ECCENTRIC PEN PUBLISHING

For my mother, Linda, who read to me.

CONTENTS

PART ONE

CHAPTER ONE

FIREFLIES

December 2017

Jenna held her breath.

She eased her apartment door open an inch and listened. Nothing.

She poked her head into the dim hall, squinting through the slits of her ski mask, ignoring the flickering light bulb overhead, her senses keyed for other movement. She took one step forward and strained her ears for the sound of footsteps.

There was only the droning of Mrs. Tan's television across the way and muffled voices from apartment 311 at the end of the hall. On a cold Minnesota Wednesday, the residents of Ashton Place had nestled down for the night. The hallway was deserted.

Jenna opened the door wider, then whipped around as something hissed in the room behind her.

A nervous giggle escaped her. The radiator had her jumping out of her skin.

She glanced at the doorway that led to the bedrooms, hers and her mother's. But there was no one there.

There wouldn't be, Jenna knew. Her mom, Mae, had not had a good day, and the pain had come with a vengeance.

Jenna had given her mother the usual cocktail of meds, fed her as much chicken broth as she would take, and then watched her drift off to sleep.

She wouldn't wake for hours. There was no reason Jenna shouldn't go now.

Except that she wasn't supposed to set foot outside the apartment.

Ever.

Of course, Jenna had been sneaking out for over a month, but her mom hadn't caught her yet.

Not at this apartment, anyway.

Sweat beaded her skin where the ski mask clung to her face. Despite the heat in the building, she wore a navy-blue peacoat and long, knit gloves that covered her hands and arms.

She had to.

What she was doing was stupid. Reckless. She knew that. So she wore as many layers as possible to minimize the risk. Just in case.

But tonight, something was wrong. She jerked the sleeve of her coat up and pushed the glove down far enough to check.

The marks of her curse twisted along the back of her hand and arm. Two thin gray lines spiraled around a central black one, but the pattern etching her skin was raised—half tattoo and half scar. And the marks on her other arm were an exact match. *Charms*, her mother called the marks, though the curse was anything but charming.

The Charms were normally painless, but now they burned as if they were living things slithering beneath her skin, leaving a trail of fire. Jenna half expected to see the marks turn blood red.

Was she getting a fever?

She pulled the glove back down and shook her hands out, ignoring the pain.

She had to go now, or she'd miss him. And the fireflies.

She readjusted the ski mask and returned her attention to the hall outside. Still empty.

She slid out, silently closing and locking the door behind her. The wide central staircase was right next to their apartment, but she never went that way.

That was the staircase people *used*.

Instead, she turned left and crept along the mud-brown carpet, heading for the dingy emergency stairs on the far side of the building.

She passed by Mr. Cane's door, but her neighbor's apartment was, as usual, library quiet.

She slowed as she neared 311 at the end of the hall. Cigarette smoke thickened the air, and queasiness rippled through her.

She flattened herself against the rough plaster wall, listening. A television groaned inside, but there was no shouting. No rough movement. No heavy footsteps. Now was her chance.

She bolted past the door to 311 and into the staircase. She pelted down one flight of stairs and sighed in relief when she reached the landing without running into anyone. Here, her dread gave way to the buzz of anticipation.

She had chosen this spot carefully. The overhead light had gone out weeks ago, and no one had bothered to replace it.

Jenna wanted it dark.

The other great feature of the landing was the large bay window. From here, she had a much better view of the street and sidewalks below.

She held her breath so she wouldn't fog the glass, then pressed her nose against the window, peering out into the night.

A streetlight illuminated the sidewalk in front of the old brick dry cleaner directly across from her. And—she checked her phone—in three minutes he would be there, walking through that pool of light. Damian Vex. The guy she was stalking.

Jenna corrected herself. *Stalking* wasn't the right term. It was more like people watching—even if there was really only one person she was hoping to see.

Her habit had started innocently enough. She'd begun with her neighbors, observing them from her living room window.

The building had three floors with ten units per floor. After two months of watching the front door, Jenna had learned to recognize most of the people who lived in Ashton Place.

Mrs. Tan wore only shades of brown. Mr. Pick scratched at his nose whenever he thought no one was looking. And the Terrible Two would go limp as their mother held their hands, forcing her to drag them along the sidewalk as they screamed.

Her favorite resident, though, was her neighbor, Mr. Cane, who was about a zillion years old.

When she'd first moved in, Jenna would hear his door open and close, but from her window she never saw him on the street below. Naturally, she'd had to investigate.

She'd followed him.

Using his hand-carved cane, he left his apartment once each day to check the wall-mounted mailboxes in the lobby. A turtle could have outpaced him, but he hummed as he shuffled along, and she liked that.

Mr. Cane had groceries delivered every Monday, but other than that, she'd never seen or heard anyone visit. Which meant he was as isolated as she was. Maybe more.

She settled into her usual spot, sitting sideways on the window ledge. She had found this landing while following Mr. Cane, and it was here that she'd first noticed Damian Vex.

After that, the limited view from her living room wasn't enough. Her curiosity about Damian Vex was an itch that demanded scratching.

Damian Vex wasn't his real name, of course. She didn't know the actual names of the people she watched. But he had looked like a Damian Vex the first couple of times she'd seen him.

Tall, with a shock of dark hair that hung over one eye, he wore a vintage black leather jacket and a red scarf that contrasted with his pale skin. He'd caught her attention the moment she'd seen him.

Every night, he walked through the twilight with his hands jammed into his pockets, his back stiff with the Saint Paul cold. His eyes were always focused on something far ahead, and he radiated an air of mystery.

Jenna had named him dark, dangerous, Damian Vex.

Now she wondered how she'd been so mistaken.

In time, she realized that the curious glances people sent him rolled off like water on glass—not because he was arrogant—but because he was lost in thought.

So much for danger. The name Damian Vex was one of Jenna's less inspired ideas.

She remembered when she'd become certain her initial impression of him was...well, ludicrous. It was a cold and rainy evening late in October. Damian had trudged down the sidewalk, huddled beneath a small black umbrella.

A petite elderly woman in a raincoat and hat had come from the other direction. She'd clutched a handful of plastic grocery bags, but she stumbled and lost her grip, and a jumble of cans and boxes spilled onto the wet sidewalk.

As others hurried past, Damian handed her his umbrella and hopped to her aid, rounding up the wayward groceries without a second thought.

He stayed by her side, carrying the bags. She sheltered beneath his umbrella, and he strolled beside her as the rain inked his hair an even darker shade of black.

Jenna had watched until he was out of sight, an unaccustomed warmth seeping through her body. It had left her feeling...unsettled.

And then, a month ago, the fireflies appeared.

She knew it sounded crazy. Some part of her worried she *was* crazy. An image of her mother flashed into her head, but she forced it away.

She thrust her chin forward. The fireflies were real. She was sure of it.

That night, when Damian had walked beneath the streetlight, a cloud of them had shimmered to life around him.

Their glow was faint inside the pool of lamplight, but she'd seen it happen night after night.

Damian, though, was oblivious. He never so much as blinked when they emerged.

November turned to December, long past the season for fireflies. Still, they sparkled into being whenever he passed that spot. And they appeared for him and no one else.

It was uncanny.

Every night, more of the fireflies gathered. They surrounded him, flashing in and out like hundreds of tiny paparazzi taking photos.

She couldn't get it out of her mind. She couldn't get *him* out of her mind.

Jenna leaned into the window and strained her eyes to see into the distance. He was running late. Maybe he wouldn't be coming tonight after all. She got up and paced the staircase landing. Three grubby vinyl squares by three grubby vinyl squares.

Twice a day, she could count on seeing him—once early in the morning when he waited at the corner for the school bus and once late in the evening.

This morning, though, he hadn't been there.

A wave of heat rippled up and down her arms, distracting her from her thoughts. What was going on with her Charms? For the millionth time, she wanted to claw them off.

The door at the bottom of the stairs squeaked open, and Jenna froze. Most people preferred the bright central staircase over this grimy, narrow set of stairs at the end of the hall.

She turned to flee, but then she recognized Mr. Cane's throaty hum. He must have gone to his mailbox later than usual.

She hesitated.

If it were anyone else, she would have fled at once. But as slowly as Mr. Cane moved, he was the one person who posed no threat.

She didn't want to give the man a heart attack, though.

She snatched the ski mask off her head, making her auburn waves crackle into a static halo. Shoving the mask into her pocket, she rushed to smooth her hair.

She pulled out her cell phone and held it to her ear, bursting into Emmy-worthy laughter. Tonight, she'd play the role of ditzy teenager.

"Okay, so what are you wearing to the dance on Friday?" she asked her imaginary friend. She paused, pretending to listen to the other end of the conversation.

The thump of his cane was louder now, but he was taking forever. No surprise.

She glanced out the window and straightened as a tiny orange butterfly flitted by. It beat its delicate wings against the cold and then flew up and out of sight.

She frowned. How was a butterfly surviving in the dead of winter?

But then Damian turned the corner onto her block, and she forgot about the butterfly. She tipped forward to peek down the stairs. Was Mr. Cane moving slower than usual?

She spotted the top of his bald head as he trudged along. He leaned on his cane with one hand, grasping a half dozen pieces of mail in his other hand.

She launched back into her routine. "Oh, no. No way. I am not wearing pink. I'm a redhead. I'd look like a giant flamingo. No."

The humming stopped, and she paused again, twirling a curl around her finger for effect.

From the corner of her eye, she saw Mr. Cane stop and gape at her, both bushy eyebrows lifted in wonder.

She gave him an encouraging wave and angled herself on the window ledge so he had plenty of room to pass her on the landing.

Even so, a nervous thrill ran through her. Aside from her mother, it had been three years since she'd been this close to another person.

She looked away from him, playing up her dumb teenager act. "Are you serious? You think Henry Livingston is going to ask me?"

Then Jenna nearly broke character. Henry Livingston was the name of her fifth-grade crush. The boy she'd fixated on years ago, before the Charms had taken hold. Before she'd gone on the run with her mother. Before she'd left a normal life behind.

She did not allow herself to think about the past.

"Don't be stupid," she said aloud to her imaginary friend. She swiveled and peered through the window, checking on Damian's progress. He was close now. Then she glanced back at Mr. Cane.

A smile tugged at the corners of his mouth. His expression seemed to say, "Ah, youth," and he shook his head as he climbed past her.

Jenna could see the lines on his forehead, the white stubble on his chin. She could smell the chicken salad he must have had for dinner.

He nodded to her as he shuffled past, and she had to blink back a rush of emotions she didn't quite understand.

Distracted, she almost forgot about Damian, but she looked through the window just as he stepped into the lamplight. She leaned forward, waiting for the sparkle of fireflies to erupt.

Except this time, instead of fireflies, a woman appeared inside the circle of light.

Cold stabbed through Jenna, even as her Charms caught fire. The woman had flickered into existence from nowhere.

She wore a linen nightgown that was tissue thin, and her feet were bare on the icy sidewalk. Her thick ropes of hair whipped around her in a wind that touched only her.

And somehow Jenna knew. She *knew*. Whatever that thing was, it was not human.

Damian walked toward the creature, unseeing.

Then the woman began to glow from the inside, like some deep-sea animal. Dark patterns traced her body in a fine lace, the marks contrasting with the pale white light spilling from her skin.

Jenna flinched in recognition. The patterns looked eerily like the raised black scars that ran along the backs of her own arms and hands. Did the woman have Charms?

As if in answer, the lines of Jenna's curse blazed with scorching heat.

The woman—the creature—turned to face Damian.

He didn't miss a step. His head was down, shoulders hunched against the cold.

And the thing wasn't moving out of his path.

Jenna choked. Her cell phone clattered to the floor unnoticed as she jumped up and pressed her gloved palms to the glass.

The creature reached one arm toward Damian, pointing a long, thin finger.

Before she knew what she was doing, Jenna let loose a bloodcurdling scream.

Chapter Two

FOUND

The creature outside vanished like a television screen blinking off.

Damian looked up in confusion and slipped on the ice, landing hard. That would hurt, for sure. But at least he was alive. And alone.

Mr. Cane stumbled. He clutched his chest in surprise, and the mail in his hand spun through the air.

Jenna whirled to him and had to stop herself from reaching out. She clasped her hands over her mouth instead. "Sorry! I'm so sorry!" She scurried to gather his scattered envelopes.

"I thought you'd seen a ghost, child," Mr. Cane chuckled.

When she'd collected the whole pile, she held it out to him, careful to keep her shaking fingers far from his.

He squinted at her in the near-dark. "Are you all right?"

"Fine." Jenna nodded a few too many times and glanced over her shoulder. There was no sign of the strange woman.

Damian slipped again and again as he tried to regain his footing on the icy patch of concrete. All leg, he was like a clown on stilts. He pitched forward and then back, holding on to his balance with sheer willpower.

Despite herself, Jenna covered her mouth again, this time to hide a half-hysterical giggle. She turned to Mr. Cane. "I'm fine." She slapped a broad smile across her face.

Over the years, Jenna had honed her acting skills. She'd lied to countless teachers and classmates in her virtual classes, and once again, her talents were coming in handy. "I was jumping at shadows."

"Perhaps it's time you thought about heading to bed, my dear," he called down to her as he resumed his climb. "Rest is best in times of stress."

"I'll do that." She threw another look over her shoulder. "Sorry again if I startled you." As Mr. Cane disappeared up the stairs, she rushed back to the window.

She stood guard as Damian retreated down the sidewalk. If the creature reappeared, she'd...what? She wasn't sure. Luckily, she didn't have to figure it out. The woman was gone.

She eased herself away from the window. All her energy had gushed out when she'd screamed. Her limbs were as heavy as lead pipes, and her head was just as hollow.

What had she just seen? Fireflies were one thing. A glowing creature who flickered in and out of existence was another.

She shivered. She would wait until she was inside her apartment. *Then* she would panic.

With an effort, she picked up her cell phone and pulled the ski mask from her pocket. She sighed and tugged it over her head as she plodded up the stairs.

Looking down, she paused and scooped up an envelope she'd missed. She'd have to stick it under Mr. Cane's door.

At the top of the steps, she ducked behind the wall next to the door, checking that the coast was clear.

Cigarette smoke from apartment 311 filled the air, and raised voices echoed out into the stairway. That family's arguments were so loud, Jenna could often hear them from her living room, and she'd learned to match those voices with faces.

Dread coiled in the pit of her stomach. She didn't want to run into any of them, but the oldest son, Brent, would be the worst.

She hadn't needed to make up Brent's name because he had a habit of twisting his youngest brother's arm until the smaller boy screamed his name, begging him to stop.

Brent was around her own age—seventeen or eighteen—with a firm jaw and broad shoulders. Most people would consider him handsome.

Jenna was not most people.

She would never see him that way. His cruel streak made him repulsive, but it wasn't just that. The real problem was that she couldn't look at him without seeing someone else.

Michael had crossed her path three years ago, and he was the reason she'd sworn off every kind of social media and gaming platform. It was too dangerous. *She* was too dangerous.

She wished she could slice the memory of Michael out of her head, but she knew it wasn't possible. And Brent looked so much like him, it made her flesh crawl.

Both boys carried themselves like boxers, chin down and one shoulder forward, as if waiting to dodge the next blow. They both slicked back their short, wavy hair. And they both had crooked noses that had been broken before.

They were not the same person. But she felt sick even looking at Brent. Any time she left the apartment, her top priority was avoiding him.

The argument inside 311 wasn't dying down, so Jenna took her chance. She darted from her hiding place on silent feet and paused by Mr. Cane's door.

Kneeling, she tried to shove the letter under the door, but it wouldn't go. She pressed her cheek against the carpet, peering into the narrow gap along the floor. A thick orange throw rug blocked the opening, and she stood back up, frowning. There was a slim crack beside the doorknob, and she tried to wedge the envelope inside.

At that moment, Brent stepped out of his apartment. An unlit cigarette dangled from his lips.

He looked over at her, taking in her gloved hands at the doorknob and the ski mask hiding her features. He snared her with narrowing eyes.

She froze. She couldn't look away from that face.

"What do you think you're doing?" He advanced a step. "Did you think you could break in here without getting caught?"

She opened her mouth, backing away, but words burned to ash in her throat. She couldn't let Brent call the police, or worse, touch her. Her apartment was just next door, but it would take too long to fish out her key and get inside.

She was still frantically searching for a plan when he charged. She leaped away, scrambling down the hall.

Jenna had been taking classes in jujitsu and taekwondo since she was three years old. Her mother had insisted. It wasn't until years later, when Jenna developed the Charms, that she understood why.

And once she understood, she made sure to keep up her skills. She moved the coffee table once a day to practice her drills. And after doing the exercises for so long, she was in decent shape.

But she was no runner.

Brent was gaining on her. He would have caught her already, except for the rubber snow boots he was wearing.

His feet pounded behind her, but she didn't dare look back. When she reached the main staircase, she swung a hard right. She half ran, half slid down the steps and pelted for the front door in the lobby.

Brent shouted, his outstretched arm closing the space between them. The spot between her shoulder blades twinged.

He hadn't touched her, had he? She had a coat on, so the chances were tiny that she'd infected him, but.... A chance was still a chance.

The heavy glass door opened with a whoosh of freezing air, and a middle-aged woman with a waist like an inner tube blocked the entrance. She toddled inside, and Jenna danced sideways to avoid her. Her heart thumped in her ears as one of the woman's arms just missed brushing her.

Brent wasn't as lucky, and he became entangled with the woman.

Jenna's mind sped ahead of her. On the ledge beneath the rows of mailboxes were stacks of coupons, concert flyers, and advertisements. She snatched a handful of the papers as she ran past and scattered them behind her.

She bounded away, catching a glimpse of Brent as he stepped on the papers.

He went into a skid and crashed to the floor.

She widened her lead as she made for the basement stairs. She streaked down them and flung herself toward the laundry room at the bottom.

She looked around and cursed. The only way out was through the narrow hopper window above a row of dryers.

With Brent's shouts growing louder behind her, she clambered on top of one dryer and swung the window open, ready to scramble through.

Then she stopped. Brent was faster than she was. He would catch up if she tried to outrun him. Her only hope was to outsmart him.

She dropped back down to the floor, yanked open the dryer door, and threw herself inside.

She wedged her knees up beside her shoulders and pulled the door closed behind her just in time. Over the rolling thump of the tumbling clothes in the dryer next to her, Jenna heard Brent's boots as he rushed into the room.

She struggled to force her gasping lungs into submission. If he heard her, it was all over. Despite herself, her breath quickened.

Her limbs were dead weights, crushing her down, and her ski mask smothered her. She was suffocating under all her layers, being buried alive.

The curse was going to kill her, one way or another.

She clenched her fists and squeezed her eyes shut in the darkness. Beneath the fabric of her gloves, her Charms throbbed.

The silence was worse than the shouts. *Was he still there?*

Her eyes snapped open, and she nearly cried out as the dryer she was inside gave a loud, metallic groan. Brent had taken the bait and climbed up to get to the open window.

The dryer rocked as he shifted from foot to foot, and she hugged herself even tighter, afraid the top would cave in under his weight. Seconds ticked by.

Then he slammed his fist against the wall in frustration. He mumbled something unintelligible as he jumped back down, apparently believing she'd escaped through the window. Cursing, he stomped out of the room, and Jenna let out a slow breath.

She made herself count sixty Mississippis to make sure it wasn't a trick. That he was truly gone.

Itchy sweat trickled down her neck to the base of her throat, but the roll of the other dryers was the only sound in the darkness. Her deception had worked.

She eased the dryer door open and tumbled out into an empty room. She got to her feet, but without warning, her Charms began to sting. A wave of nausea hit her. She gritted her teeth against the pain, wobbling like a marionette with loose strings.

Her knees buckled, and she sucked in deep breaths, pulling off her ski mask and letting it drop to the floor. The nausea faded, but her Charms were still burning. She tugged down the edge of her glove to inspect them, and she froze.

One of the Strands that twisted along her arm had turned from gray to black.

What did that mean? She yanked the glove back up, covering the mark. She'd ask her mom when she woke up.

She shook her head to clear it. Her dizziness was passing. She took a deep breath and stood up.

And there in front of her was the glowing woman.

Jenna lost the breath she'd just regained. She stumbled backward until she came up against the dryer behind her.

Light pulsated through the woman, illuminating her skin everywhere it wasn't marked with raised black tattoos—*Charms,* Jenna thought again.

The woman's bare feet were planted hip-width apart on the concrete floor, and her face was unreadable. She lifted an arm and pointed at Jenna.

In her peripheral vision, Jenna spotted a long paisley umbrella with a hooked handle that someone had left beside a laundry basket. She lunged for it, holding it in front of her like a weapon.

"What do you want?" she demanded.

The creature's mouth moved soundlessly. It took a step toward her.

This time, Jenna didn't hesitate. She leaped on top of the dryer, umbrella in hand, and launched herself out the open window onto the frozen pavement.

She sprinted away, checking behind her to make sure the creature hadn't followed.

She saw nothing, but she kept moving, pounding through the slush toward the front of Ashton Place. She rounded the corner of the building, but unsure where she was going, she skidded to a halt.

Her heart drummed in her ears. She waited, ready to bolt, but the woman didn't appear.

Had her dizzy spell caused her oxygen level to drop, leading to a hallucination? Maybe she was running from nothing. She grimaced. That didn't explain the creature's appearance beneath the streetlight, though. Jenna hadn't been dizzy then.

Her pain ebbed, and she glanced around. The street was deserted.

It was the first time she'd been outside alone in over a year. She stood perfectly still.

The air felt cold and clean, rich with scent after so long inside the stale apartment. Without the stifling ski mask, the wind bit her bare face and whipped her hair around her shoulders. She reveled in it, closing her eyes.

When she opened them again, her heart picked up speed. What was she doing? She was not supposed to be here. She shook herself, starting toward the front doors of Ashton Place. Then she hesitated.

She was only yards from the streetlamp where she'd first seen the fireflies and the strange woman. She glanced around again, her nerves on edge, but the street remained quiet.

Her mind was buzzing with questions. How had the creature appeared and disappeared the way she had? Why had her skin glowed? And even more troubling, was the woman Charmed?

The marks had looked eerily like Jenna's own Charms. As far as she knew, she was the only person alive with her strange affliction. But the woman's appearance awoke a sliver of doubt. Was the creature somehow connected to her?

She needed to find out more. And she was already outside. She'd kick herself later if she didn't at least look. Summoning her acting skills, she ignored her misgivings and tried to appear normal, even though the paisley umbrella shook violently in her hands. If she acted confident, maybe she could force herself to feel that way. Squaring her shoulders, she crossed the street to the light.

She approached cautiously, but nothing and no one appeared. She inspected the brick wall of the dry cleaner and the light pole itself. Maybe there was a hidden projector that someone had rigged up to have a laugh at anyone watching. There had to be an explanation, but she didn't see any devices that would account for what she'd witnessed.

She craned her neck to study the light, not noticing the patch of ice on the sidewalk until she started to slip.

She caught herself, glancing around to confirm she was still alone. And that's when she noticed something on the ground. A lump of black among the gray-and-white slush. It drew her in with an odd gravity.

Her eyebrows lifted as she realized what it was.

A wallet. *Damian's* wallet, she'd be willing to bet. It must have come out of his pocket when he'd fallen.

She bent down beside it, frowning. If she left it there in the snow and ice, it would be ruined or stolen. She couldn't let that happen. She had to get it back to him.

No one was watching, so she snatched it from the sidewalk.

Stepping into the narrow alley that ran alongside the dry cleaner, she leaned her umbrella against the brick building and pulled out her phone for light.

Curiosity flared. She was not a stalker, she assured herself. Not really. But the only way to return the wallet was to look inside.

When she flipped it open, though, her expression soured. She was staring down at Damian's wallet-sized girlfriend.

Jenna knew he had a girlfriend. *Of course, he had a girlfriend.* A ballet-thin, blonde girlfriend, to be exact. They stood together every morning at the school bus stop.

In the picture, the girl looked a couple of years younger, and she smiled with a golden innocence Jenna would never have been able to pull off, even on her best day.

She glowered down at the photo. How long had they been going out?

Her face brightened, though, as her eyes found Damian's. She slid his driver's license from behind the plastic cover. Then her jaw sagged as she stumbled across his name.

Of course, she'd always known his name wasn't Damian Vex—she'd made that up, after all. But it was strange to learn his actual name—Lane McConnell. Huh.

She swallowed. Until now, he'd been a fantasy—not a real person.

Lane.

She studied the license again. He was tall—six feet, three inches. She'd never been able to tell, observing from above.

Also, they were the same age—he was probably a senior in high school, just like she was in her online classes. If things had been different, they might have been in school together. Weird.

She wondered why he had a license at all, since he was always taking the bus.

Regardless, she was pretty sure he'd want the license back. And soon. But how to do it?

She used her phone to map his street address. He lived a couple of blocks away, but for her, that might as well have been halfway around the world.

Still, she'd come this far.

The wallet slipped and bulged open. As it twisted, she glimpsed a two-dollar bill folded into one of the slots. *Who carried a two-dollar bill?* Curiouser and curiouser.

She tapped her finger on the flap of the wallet, considering. Her mother wouldn't be awake for hours, and Jenna would be back in no time. She bit her lip, working out the details.

She'd leave the wallet in Lane's mailbox. That way, she wouldn't have to speak to anyone. She racked her brain, but she couldn't think of a better plan.

Decision made, she jammed her phone and Lane's wallet into her pockets. She picked up the paisley umbrella and let out a long breath. She could do this.

Jenna walked slowly at first. She was used to watching the street from her perch at the window, but she was unprepared for how strange it would feel to be out in the world. This time of night, the block was empty. To her deprived senses, though, it was like a carnival.

The distant sirens were so much clearer and more alive than they were from inside her apartment, muted by panes of glass. It was alarming—and somehow exhilarating, too.

A late-night jogger in neon orange shoes zipped down the sidewalk in front of Ashton Place.

Jenna ducked behind the trunk of a tree, even though the jogger was across the street. She could hear him breathing, and puffs of cold air smoked, dragon-like, every time he exhaled. She froze, and even knowing she was overreacting, her own breath caught and held until he passed.

She clutched the umbrella to her body. The man was no danger to her. Not unless he was close enough to touch her. She tried not to picture it. Then she swallowed back bile, remembering what had happened last time.

Disgusted with herself, she pushed away from the tree trunk. The sooner she did this, the sooner she could get off the street. She hurried forward.

She narrowed her eyes, trying to focus. She had to stay alert. She was at the end of the block now, moving out of familiar territory, beyond what she could see from her window.

A car door slammed, and she nearly jumped out of her skin, gasping. *Stupid,*

stupid, stupid, she scolded herself, as she pressed forward. She wasn't sure, though, if she was telling herself she was stupid for jumping at every little thing or stupid for doing this in the first place.

She hunched her shoulders, almost running now. She'd come too far to turn back.

She reached Lane's block sooner than she expected, and she noticed with relief how quiet it was. Her pulse slowed a bit as she stopped to take it in.

Most of the homes were draped in Christmas lights. It was that kind of street—the kind where people gave out good candy at Halloween and decorated for every holiday and season.

And there was no one in sight. She moved slower now, scanning the buildings for street numbers.

She spotted his cozy brick house almost immediately. It was near the corner, with quaint window boxes filled with pinecones and evergreen trimmings. A colorful Christmas tree twinkled behind sheer curtains, and in front of her, a neatly shoveled sidewalk led to a short set of stairs and an arched door.

Then she pulled up short, wincing. Why hadn't she noticed before? The mailboxes didn't line the streets as she'd imagined. Instead, the black metal mailbox was mounted beside the front door.

She'd have to go all the way up on the porch to get rid of the wallet. Dread washed over her, and goosebumps popped up on her arms.

She set her jaw, trying to look at the bright side. She was seconds from being done. Then she'd get off the street, go home, and try to put this crazy night behind her.

Pulling the wallet from her pocket, she marched forward, counting her steps to distract herself from the idiotic thing she was doing. Nine steps along the walkway. Then five steps up the stairs. She'd make the drop and go.

But she paused when she noticed the mailbox. The name "Phillips" was stenciled on the front—not McConnell. Did she have the wrong address?

Hurriedly, she opened the wallet and double-checked, but the number was a match. Ready to be rid of the thing, she lifted the mailbox lid, but it protested with a loud, metallic squawk.

At that moment, a high-pitched bark erupted from behind the front door.

Heart in her throat, she scrambled back, wallet still in hand. The next thing she knew, the door was opening.

Speechless, she half ran, half fell down the stairs. She turned, poised to make her escape, but a voice caught her.

"Can I help you?"

She froze. She couldn't run off down the street with the wallet. Someone might raise an alarm, or worse, give chase.

She pivoted slowly, hoping against hope she'd see a stranger standing in the doorway. But her stomach flipped over as she glanced up and met his eyes.

Staring right back at her was Lane.

CHAPTER THREE

ANGEL

Jenna stared at him.

She couldn't think. Couldn't speak. Hurriedly, she shoved the wallet into the pocket of her peacoat before he could see it.

"Can I help you?" Lane repeated, raising an eyebrow. He gently pushed the yapping Yorkie behind him with his foot. He stepped out onto the porch, closing the door to muffle the nonstop barking.

She tilted her head and studied the air around Lane. There wasn't a firefly to be seen. He was just a normal teenage boy in rumpled flannel pajama bottoms, a hoodie, and a pair of house slippers.

And he looked even better up close.

Her cheeks heated. As shaken as she was, she couldn't make herself look away.

Six foot three was taller than she had realized. And from a distance, she'd never noticed the awkward cowlick that spiked his hair in the back. Unfortunately, it made him even more attractive.

Worse, his eyes were a distracting robin's egg–blue. And they were studying her quizzically.

Panic seized her. She backed away, even as she found her voice. "I was...you see...I was just going to—" Her foot stepped off the path and into the slush, throwing her off balance.

It was as if she watched herself in slow motion. Her arms pinwheeled as she tried to catch herself, but with nothing to grab on to, she went sprawling backward into the snow with a soft, wet thump.

She lay very still, wishing she could sink beneath the ground, never to be seen again.

"You all right there?" Lane moved down the steps toward her, hand held out. A smile played at the corners of his mouth.

With a huff, she sprang up and scurried away from him, clutching the paisley umbrella indignantly. She couldn't speak.

She was mortified that he'd seen her fall. Shocked to be standing there with him at all. Giddy at how amazing he looked. Terrified that he would come any closer. Livid that—even now!—he was trying not to laugh at her.

The thoughts flashed through her, each one fanning the flame of her emotions brighter until they burned like a raging inferno. The fear that had gripped her seconds ago was gone, and a new bravado flared up inside her. She no longer cared what he thought.

A wild impulse tickled her thoughts, and she seized on it. She would make him just as uncomfortable as he had made her. Laugh at her, would he?

She leveled her umbrella at him, holding it straight out like a rapier. She spoke with calm authority. "Stand back, Lane McConnell. You are in the presence of your guardian angel."

Now it was Lane's turn to go silent. "Uh, what was that?"

She overenunciated as she repeated her words. "I am your guardian angel."

"Okay...." He peered up and down the block, as if expecting a prankster to pop out from behind a bush. He smiled in confusion. "Come on. Who are you, really? How do you know my name?" He glanced around, trying to find the source of the joke. "Did Brie put you up to this?"

Brie.

Jenna seethed inwardly. That had to be the name of his girlfriend.

New venom laced her voice. "Listen. I am the answer to your prayers, okay? So show some respect." She thrust the umbrella at his stomach, and he stumbled back in surprise. "Don't make me use my superpowers on you."

Lane stared at her in stunned silence, as if seeing her for the first time. Then he threw his head back and laughed.

He put his hands in his hoodie pocket, regarding her with dawning interest. "Oh, you said *guardian* angel. I didn't realize our appointment was for today."

Jenna was struck dumb. *He was playing along.*

Lane crossed his arms. "I *am* going to need to see some identification, of course." He gestured to the spot where she'd fallen. "I hate to tell you this, but you don't even make a good snow angel." He looked at her with mock concern. "Shouldn't that be, like, Angels 101 or something? Maybe you need the remedial class." He leaned back against the stair rail, grinning.

Jenna planted the tip of her umbrella on the ground and pursed her lips. "You dare to taunt an angel?" She shook her head, feigning disappointment. "I suppose you don't deserve this, then." She held up his wallet.

Lane's face lit up. "Dude! Where did you find that? I've been looking all over for it!"

He moved toward her, but Jenna quickly raised the umbrella, blocking his approach.

"Not so fast. First of all—Dude?" She made a face. "I don't think so. You may call me Oh Heavenly One, or Miss Marvelousness, or maybe Angel Supreme—"

"That sounds like a fast-food sandwich."

"Shut it. Just shut it. I wasn't finished."

Lane whistled. "Awfully feisty for an angel. Are you allowed to tell me to shut it? I'd like to speak to your manager." He tilted his head, considering. "I would also accept a heartfelt apology and a bouquet of flowers."

Jenna ignored him. "The second reason you might not get your wallet back is that one of my angel informants told me you weren't in school today." She was rewarded by Lane's look of shock.

Of course, she'd noticed right away when he hadn't shown up at the bus stop as usual this morning. She'd been waiting for him, watching from her living room window. But he didn't need to know that. "You've been a very naughty boy," she scolded.

"Naughty?" He threw open his arms in exaggerated innocence. "I can assure you—I have been nothing but nice." He placed one hand over his heart. "In fact, I'm in danger of becoming boring, I'm so freaking good. I don't know where you get your informa—"

"Cut it. Save it for someone who cares."

He raised his eyebrows. "With all due respect, Dude, you appear to be suffering from what we humans call an attitude problem. I have to say, I expected better from an angel—or do they make special allowances upstairs for redheads?"

She shot him a withering glare.

"I know what happened. You were demoted for your devilish ways and now you've been sentenced to wait on me. That must be it. I'll have an Angel Supreme, please. Heavy on the pickles, hold the cheese." He waited for her to take the bait.

Instead, she tucked the wallet into her pocket. "Well, you're obviously not interested in getting this back. Sorry to have wasted your time."

She flipped her umbrella onto her shoulder like a ceremonial rifle and saluted him. "Best wishes and all that. I'll be on my way." She spun around, as if to go.

"Wait!"

She turned.

He crossed his arms over his chest, mischief dancing in his eyes. "How do you know I was naughty?"

Instead of answering, she strolled around him, keeping just out of arm's reach. She looked him up and down.

He endured her perusal in amused silence.

She returned to face him, leaning on her umbrella. "Well, for one thing, my inspection indicates good health. And yet, you didn't go to school today. Explain yourself."

He shook his head, amazed. "Who's your informant?" Then he caught his breath and narrowed his eyes. "Do you go to school with me?"

She frowned. "I'll do the questioning here. Besides, we at the Angel Academy have resources mere mortals cannot fathom. So what's your excuse for skipping school?"

"I'm sick." To illustrate his point, he launched into a fit of coughing, hamming it up until she rolled her eyes and lifted a hand to stop him.

"You're not a very convincing liar. Shouldn't that be, like, Humanity 101 or something?" Her mouth curved. "Maybe you need the remedial class."

A slow smile spread over his face. "Maybe you're right." He glanced over his shoulder at the arched door of his house. "But listen," he said in a hushed voice, "I had a good reason why I wasn't in school today. I needed to—"

"Reasons don't matter." She had no intention of letting him off the hook. "Lane McConnell, I hereby convict you of aggravated naughtiness."

"I appeal."

"No appeals."

"I protest."

"No protests. No talking."

Lane raised his hand.

She raised an eyebrow. "You're pushing it."

He put his hand back down.

Jenna continued. "I have evidence of another reprehensible deed. I, myself, am a convincing actress, so perhaps you didn't realize that my seeming 'fall' a moment ago was a test."

"Was that what that was?"

"Of course."

"Then it was very believable. I mean, it looked *exactly* like the real thing."

"Yes, yes. I'm amazing. The point is—that was a test, Mr. Moral Fiber, and you did not pass."

She paced up and down, delivering her argument to the jury. "There I was, for all you knew, a fragile young human girl. I pretended to trip. I've been told it happens to most humans." She wheeled on him. "But you...you were actually laughing at me in my moment of need."

"It was pretty funny, right?"

She tapped her toe on the slushy sidewalk. "Do I look amused to you?"

"Amused? No." He leaned back, studying her. "You look a little aggravated. Kind of flushed. And even with that devilish red hair, I have to admit you look lovely."

She opened her mouth, but no sound came out.

"Now you look flustered."

She scowled at him.

"I've got it—aggravated again. Ooh! I'm good at this game." He pointed at her. "Now you're angry. Angrier. Angrier...."

Jenna cracked a smile and Lane waved his fist in victory. "And *now* you look amused! Do I win a prize?"

She stared down her nose at him. "Your prize is that I don't turn and walk away." She pulled his wallet out of her pocket. "Your behavior today didn't do you any favors, but I've decided to take pity on you because of a good deed you performed."

"Good deed, huh?" He put his hand on his chest modestly. "I do so many. Which deed are you referring to?"

"You stopped to help a woman who had dropped her groceries in the rain."

Lane froze, a dazed look on his face. "How did you know about that?"

She smiled mysteriously.

"No, I'm serious. How could you know that?"

She took a step closer to him. "Lane, Lane. You need to work on your listening skills. I've been trying to tell you." She leaned in. "I am your guardian angel, Dude."

She chucked the wallet at him, and even though the throw went wide, he easily plucked it out of the air and slipped it inside his hoodie pocket.

His eyes never left her face. "What kind of prank is this, anyway?" He held up his hands. "Okay, I give up. Uncle! Just tell me what's going on."

She stepped toward him. "I'm sorry, Mr. McConnell, but that's for me to know and you—not to."

"Come on!" he sulked. "Tell me who you are!" Playfully, he reached out to grab her arm.

Jenna realized in a moment of blinding panic that she'd gotten too close. "Don't!"

She jerked backward so abruptly she dropped the umbrella and nearly landed in the snow again.

Her breath came fast, and her whole body shook. What had she been thinking? He had almost touched her.

"I wouldn't.... I would never...." Lane trailed off, and his words hung in the air.

They stared at each other.

Jenna took a deep breath. "I know," she told him. And somehow, she did.

She cursed her own stupidity. She didn't want her one conversation with him to end like this.

Trying to recapture the playfulness they'd shared just a moment ago, she said, "Bad idea, you know, to touch an angel."

"Really? I hadn't picked up on that."

"You see, we're very powerful. Dangerous."

"You? Dangerous? Why doesn't that surprise me?"

Jenna took courage from his gibe. She pressed on. "If you were to touch me—well, one of two things could happen. Either way, it would be bad for you."

"Do I want to know?"

"Probably not. But here's what I'll tell you. The last guy who tried...."

"Yeah?"

"They had to sweep him up with a broom."

"Ouch."

"It's true. I just saved your life. So you're welcome." She swept him a low bow.

He cocked his head. "What was the other thing that could happen?"

"What's that?"

"You said there were two things that could happen to someone who touched you. The first was some kind of angelic incineration. What was the other?"

She gambled. "You could fall hopelessly in love with me."

A slow smile spread over his face. "Is that so?"

Just then, the front door cracked open and a man with a graying beard stuck his head out. He eyed Jenna quizzically and looked back to Lane. "Everything okay out here?"

"Everything's great," Lane said, never taking his eyes off her.

"It's late, and you don't even have a coat on. You're sick, remember? Time to come inside."

"Just a little longer?" Lane asked. But at that moment the Yorkie squeezed through the open door and barreled down the stairs.

"Whoa there!" Lane scooped him up, and the man with the beard coughed meaningfully and stepped back inside.

Lane winced. "I'd better take Hercules in, but don't move. I'll only be a second." A tiny light flashed near his cheek. Then another near his hand.

Fireflies.

She had forgotten about the fireflies. Her eyes widened, but her words had fled.

Lane backed away, pointing his finger at her roguishly. "I'm going to get to the bottom of this."

There was no mistaking it. Dozens of fireflies blinked on and off all around him, but he didn't seem to notice.

Jenna just stared after him as he bounded up the stairs and reached for the door. The spell she'd been under was broken. She was way out of her depth.

He pointed at her. "Stay…. Stay…. Good angel."

She gave him a shaky smile.

And then he was gone, and so were the fireflies.

It was too much. As soon as the door clicked shut, Jenna fled.

She tore down the sidewalk as fast as she could, sprinting until she was gasping for breath. Then she realized how strange she must look, and she slowed to a frenzied walk.

Her brain fogged and her eyes blurred. The panic she'd been holding at bay flooded her. She stumbled forward, blind to everything but the snowy ground at her feet.

She didn't notice the car that followed her at a distance—the car that, only now, began to creep closer.

Chapter Four

CREEP

Jenna's thoughts whirled.

She hugged her arms to her body as she walked, trying to contain the powerful emotions that threatened to pour out.

She was confused by the fireflies. Mad at herself for letting Lane get too close. Stunned that it was over.

But the thing that frightened her most was the surge of joy bursting in her chest even now.

In all her imagined conversations with the fictional Damian Vex, talking had never been that easy—or that fun. Tonight, Damian had transformed into Lane McConnell, and Jenna was afraid of how much that had meant to her.

For one thing, any connection with him was impossible.

Her slightest touch would be enough to ruin both their lives. She shouldn't even think about putting someone in that position. Not again. Not ever.

She had learned her lesson and cut herself off from the world. After the last disaster, she'd even taken herself offline. She'd closed every social media account and deleted her gaming profiles. Those things were slippery slopes. And she'd already fallen once.

She knew there was no safe way to talk to Lane.

And even if it was possible, she was sure that for him their conversation was nothing out of the ordinary. His girlfriend, Brie, probably joked around with him like that all the time.

For Jenna, though, the conversation had been shocking. Unprecedented. As if she had spent her whole life reading subtitles and then discovered there was someone else in the world who spoke her language.

She wondered what had gone through his head when he'd discovered she was gone. Was he upset? Curious? Disappointed? Maybe he'd forgotten about her altogether once he was back inside his warm house.

She swallowed. She was better off not knowing.

Her chest felt tight with suppressed emotion. She had just left, and already she wanted to see him again.

As much as she tried to school her thoughts, they wriggled free and darted down the path that was forbidden to her. She imagined what would happen if she touched him.

Unfortunately, she knew what would happen.

He would desire her.

On the surface, the thought lit fires along her body. She could make him want her with one touch of her skin to his. Her Charms would do the rest.

It would be so simple. She could wait for him on the sidewalk, stumble into him by premeditated chance...and then lead him upstairs to her room. Her cheeks burned and she took a deep gulp of freezing air.

Of course, it wasn't simple at all. She could turn his desire on, but she couldn't turn it off.

For him, desire would be a thirst he couldn't quench. It would grow into an obsession. Into rage and jealousy. Into madness. It would eat at him until he would do anything—*anything*—to have her.

He would lose himself to the lust. In the end, he wouldn't be *himself* anymore. And there could be no turning back.

Except for the Charms covering her hands and arms, she looked just like everyone else. But Jenna knew better. She was far, far more dangerous. She ought to come with giant yellow hazard signs, caution tape, and flashing red lights.

She was a spark, ready to ignite. And anyone she touched would burn for it.

So she could never be with Lane. It was unthinkable. Unforgivable.

A nagging warning broke through her thoughts, jolting her back to the present.

Her shadow elongated as a pair of headlights caught her. From the sound of it, the car behind her was slowing. Maybe they were waiting so they could pull into their driveway. She walked faster, listening.

All she could hear, though, was the unrelenting crunch of icy slush as the car slid along behind her. *Shouldn't they have turned by now?*

Her muscles tensed. The more the car slowed, the faster her pulse raced. Something about this did not feel right.

And she had left her would-be weapon, the paisley umbrella, lying in the snow at Lane's house.

She cast her eyes to both sides and frowned as she considered her options. There was no easy escape route—and certainly no one she could call to for help. A few more steps, though, and she'd be at the end of the block, within sight of Ashton Place. She stretched her legs, heedless of the icy footing.

She turned left, hoping the car would continue across the intersection. But tires crunched, rounding the corner seconds later. She held her breath as the car pulled even with her.

Go away, go away, go away. Jenna willed it to move on. Instead, it crept along beside her, matching her frenzied pace. Unable to resist, she risked a sideways glance.

The car following her was a silver Mercedes, and the light from the dashboard cast an eerie glow over the driver. He was a middle-aged white man with a receding hairline and one large diamond earring. When he turned to look right at her, her attention caught on the white marks that ran from eyebrow to chin on one side of his face. It could have been a scar, but it looked more symmetrical than that—like a raised white tattoo.

Or Charms.

She'd gone her whole life without seeing anyone like herself, and now there'd been two incidents in one night. Or maybe, after seeing the glowing creature earlier, Jenna was leaping to conclusions or—worse—losing her mind. Had her mom shown signs of illness when she was seventeen?

She glanced at the man again, and a shiver ran up her spine at the look in his eyes.

Recognition. As if he knew not just who she was, but *what* she was. That look set alarm bells ringing in her head.

With an effort, she broke eye contact and stumbled to a halt. If he was going to come for her, she was going to be ready. Even without a weapon, she wasn't defenseless.

She dropped into a fighting stance, bending her knees to lower her center of gravity.

But the stranger turned away from her suddenly. He picked up speed and drove the silver Mercedes past without stopping. Jenna watched, transfixed, until the car disappeared from sight.

Who was he? She scrambled to explain it. They'd never crossed paths. She was sure of that.

Perhaps the man was a concerned stranger, worried that she was on the street alone this late at night. She bit her lip. If that was true, why hadn't he asked if she was okay?

Maybe he was some kind of perverted creep, then, prowling the night for girls. Now that was a definite possibility. Jenna nodded to herself. With his weird stare—he'd been checking her out. Funny when "perverted creep" was the comforting option.

Either way, she was lucky to have escaped. She looked around once more and then hurried down the sidewalk toward home.

She trudged up the front steps of her apartment building. She had never been so glad to be home in her life. Sighing in relief, she reached out to swing the front door open.

It wasn't until the hand closed around her arm that she knew she'd been caught.

Chapter Five

SHOT

Jenna swung into action.

She turned and jerked her arm in and around to the outside to free it from her attacker. Then she stepped back, ready to launch a counterattack. But she pulled up short when she looked up into the anxious eyes of her mother.

Mae wasn't looking at her, though. She stared into the distance, her mouth working. She wore a blue flannel nightgown, and her sandy brown hair with its one streak of white was wild from sleep. Her feet were bare on the icy concrete.

The nightgown. The bare feet. They made Jenna think of the glowing woman she'd seen earlier, and she suppressed a shiver.

Mae seized her arm again and tightened her grip painfully.

Jenna stepped sideways into her mother's line of vision, forcing her mom to meet her gaze.

Still, Mae looked right through her.

She put her free hand on top of her mother's and gave it a gentle squeeze.

Her mom was the only person she could touch safely. Jenna had inherited the Charms from that side of the family, so—thankfully—her mom was immune to the curse. According to Mae, Jenna's great-grandmother had been cursed in the same way, and the little they did know about the Charms had been passed down from her.

Mae mumbled to herself.

"What are you saying?" Jenna asked, even though she already knew the answer to her own question. Like she'd done hundreds of times before, her mom was repeating the word *four* over and over again.

She was obsessed with that number, and Jenna had never been able to figure out why. Nobody's birthday was on the fourth, and they'd never had a house or an apartment with that number.

She'd asked her mom about it, but Mae didn't like to talk about the episodes. Or maybe she didn't have an answer.

She'd changed so much since Jenna was a child. A doctor by training, Mae had been sharp as a razor. And not just sharp, but wise.

She knew it was possible that Jenna would inherit the Charms. So all those years she'd saved money, gathered false documents, and enrolled Jenna in jujitsu and taekwondo. She'd wanted to be prepared in case the worst happened.

And of course, it had.

One morning, at the age of twelve, Jenna awoke with the Charms fully developed on her hands and arms.

At first Jenna had hoped she could wear gloves—cover the Charms. But the curse didn't work that way. The Charms were just the symbol of a curse that affected her whole body. If she made skin-to-skin contact anywhere, she would infect someone.

She and her mother had to leave everything and everyone behind—including Jenna's dad.

It would have been too dangerous to stay. Jenna knew that. Her dad would not have been immune, and if he'd touched her.... It was too awful to imagine.

Working as a consultant, he was out of town more often than he was home. He'd left on a business trip the morning her Charms had appeared, and she'd never gotten to say goodbye.

On the phone with him, Mae had lied to buy them time. As far as he knew, they were still at home, going about life as usual. And Jenna had joined in, pretending nothing was wrong.

A week later, he'd returned from his trip, but by then they were long gone.

Mae had tried to explain it to him. She said Jenna was contagious with a rare disease—she was getting her help, and they'd be back as soon as she found a cure.

And it was true. Or at least, they thought it would be. Mae was confident she could find a way to heal her. She just needed time.

But her father hadn't understood. Of course, he hadn't. He was confused. Furious. He called the police, and then they couldn't risk any more calls home.

They ran.

In those first weeks, her mother tried medicines she thought might help. She even attempted minor surgery, but nothing worked to remove the Charms.

Weeks turned into a month, and then one night Mae stood in Jenna's doorway, her face ghostly white. She sat her down on the bed. And after that night, Jenna realized there would be no going back.

Ever.

Because her dad had died in a car accident. He was gone, and so was the life she'd had.

And deep down, she knew the accident had happened because of her. She could see it all play out in her mind's eye. Her dad had been out looking for them, distracted by anger and fear, and he'd lost control of the car. She couldn't get that image out of her head.

After her father died, Mae changed too, and the streak of white grew into her light brown hair almost overnight.

At first, her mother's spells were rare things. They lasted only a few minutes. She would sit and stare, transfixed, muttering to herself. When she woke, it was as if she'd dreamed. Sometimes she remembered fragments of what she'd seen, and sometimes not.

Mae hid or ignored what was happening to her. She went to work as a nurse using the name Getty, the false identity they'd assumed. While she worked, Jenna attended virtual classes. Life was weirdly normal.

Except that it wasn't.

The spells grew more frequent. Mae had trouble holding down jobs. She switched to a position she could do from home, working as a medical transcriptionist. And then that was impossible, too. She needed a job she could do on her own schedule, so she picked up general transcriptionist jobs when she could.

Even then, Jenna began to have to fill in. She'd transcribe the sessions for her mom, and then Mae would review what she'd done and upload them. As her mom got worse, Jenna substituted for her more and more. She fit her schoolwork around her mother's work schedule, ready to fill in whenever her mom couldn't do the job. And last year, that was almost all the time.

She was just glad she could do something. After all, if it wasn't for her, none of this would have happened.

Her dad would be alive.

Her mom would be sane.

She blinked to clear her head. She turned her mother around, taking her elbow to steer her through the front doors of Ashton Place. "It's going to be all right," she said with more confidence than she felt.

Mae didn't resist, letting Jenna guide her inside and up the stairs. Thankfully, they didn't meet anyone else.

The door to their apartment on the third floor was slightly ajar, so Jenna left her mom in the hall, going inside to check things out. Nothing seemed amiss, though, so she took her mother's hand and led her inside. With a sigh, she closed the door.

The noise jarred Mae from her stupor, and just that quickly, she was herself—as if a switch inside her brain had flipped. She whirled to face the door, her gaze piercing.

Jenna flinched. No matter how many times she saw her mom shift in and out of lucidity, the abrupt change always threw her.

Mae's eyes narrowed as she took in Jenna's coat and gloves, her back against the door. "You left the apartment, didn't you, Jenn?" She sucked in a sharp breath. "Were you touched?"

"No, Mom. I'm fine." Jenna refused to consider the possibility that Brent had brushed her coat with his fingers. Even if he had, it was a quick touch through a layer of clothes. Most people had to make direct contact with her skin for the curse to take hold. *Most* people.

Jenna didn't like to think about the others. In kindergarten, she'd gone to school with a kid who couldn't be in the same room with a peanut butter sandwich. And, according to Mae, there were people who could react just as strongly to Jenna's curse. People she could infect with the barest touch, even through clothes.

She lived in dread of those people.

She squirmed beneath her mother's gaze and worked fast to redirect the conversation. Her mom did not need to know about tonight. With her health already strained, it would only make things worse for them both. So she would bend the truth a bit.

"Sit down, Mom. Aren't your hands and feet cold?" She nudged her toward the couch. "I'll fix us some hot chocolate and explain."

Mae looked down at herself, frowning. Self-doubt flickered across her eyes. Then she pressed her lips into a thin line and turned her back on Jenna.

She wandered to the living room window, absently checking the half-dead peace lily she insisted on carrying from apartment to apartment. Then she sighed and pulled the pieced quilt from the back of the couch. She wrapped it around her shoulders as she sat.

Jenna finally relaxed as Mae made herself comfortable. The hot chocolate would help. She ducked into the kitchen and filled the small saucepan with milk. Once that was heating, she hung her coat in the closet.

Out of long habit, she peeled off her gloves without looking at the dark ridges that crisscrossed the backs of her hands and arms. Then she glanced at her mom.

Mae was staring into the distance again, although this time she wasn't having one of her spells. But Jenna could almost see the cloud of worry descending. She needed to snap her out of that mood.

She grabbed a half-empty bag of marshmallows from the kitchen counter and fished one out. Playfully, she tossed it across the room. "Heads up!"

The throw went wide, and Mae retrieved it from the other end of the couch. "I should have enrolled you in basketball," she said in a low voice. The shadow of a smile crossed her face.

Jenna was encouraged by her mom's teasing. "I'm just getting warmed up. Any year now, I'll be amazing." She popped a marshmallow into her own mouth and moved to the stove, stirring the chocolate chips into the pan.

With her back turned, she launched into her version of the truth. Lying was easier if she didn't have to look her mom in the eyes.

"So, here's what happened. After you went to sleep, I practiced piano." She congratulated herself on that detail. Her mother always ate up piano practice.

Actually, Jenna had never touched a piano in her life, but that's what they both called the full-sized keyboard Mae had bought her shortly after they started apartment hopping.

With the help of online videos and hours of time to kill, she'd become a fairly good player. Her passion, though, was composing. It was her outlet, and her audience of one, her mother, loved to hear her play.

She pulled down two ancient mugs from the cheap laminate cabinet and expanded on the lie. Specifics were key.

"I was practicing that new one. You know, the one that reminds you of classical guitar?" The kitchen was open to the living room, and when Jenna glanced over her shoulder, she could see the rigid set of her mom's shoulders.

She swallowed guiltily and pushed on. "Anyway, when I heard the door open, I realized you'd left, so I went after you. No harm done."

Mae was too quiet. *Had she detected the lie?*

Biting her lip, Jenna poured the hot chocolate and carried the mugs and the bag of marshmallows over.

"Thanks, Jenn," Mae whispered, as she took the mug.

She sat down beside her mom on the faded sofa. Her mother's wheels were turning, and that was never good.

Mae barely sipped her drink before she set it aside on the coffee table. "We need to make a change because now I'm putting you in danger."

"You're not—"

Mae cut her off. "I am, Jenn. You had to leave the apartment tonight to take care of me, and I won't have it." Her jaw tightened. "Maybe you should lock me in my room when I sleep."

"I'm not doing that! Don't be—" She was just about to say *crazy,* but she caught herself in time. "Ridiculous," she finished, half swallowing the word.

"It's not ridiculous. I won't risk you getting hurt because of me. I've kept you safe for the last five years. Let me do what I can to keep you that way."

Jenna set her mug down, trying to think of an argument that would work. Guilt stabbed her. She was the one who had left the apartment first. If she came clean, her mom might stop blaming herself.

On the other hand, would the truth be better? *You know what, Mom? I've been seeing these bizarre fireflies in the dead of winter, but tonight a glowing woman showed up instead. Oh, and also, a strange man in a Mercedes followed me home.*

There was no way she was saying any of that. She leaned forward, letting her hair hide her face as she pulled a marshmallow from the bag on the coffee table.

What could she tell her mom?

Suddenly, Mae clutched Jenna's head.

Too shocked to pull away, she let the marshmallow drop to the floor as her mom's fingers scrabbled across her scalp. It didn't hurt, but she cried out in surprise when her mom yanked out a hair.

Mae ignored Jenna. She sat forward on the couch and held the hair up to the light. It was a single strand, long and completely white.

"The second sign." Mae's hand shook, and the hair slipped to the floor. Her face turned as colorless as the hair, and her eyes went glassy, unseeing. The change came over her all at once.

But this was not one of her usual episodes. Inside her trances, Mae was like a sleepwalker, in no hurry to do anything.

This time, though, convulsions rippled through her, as if she stood at the epicenter of her own earthquake. She moaned and pitched forward into the coffee table, sending the nearly full mugs of hot chocolate tumbling to the carpet.

Jenna leaped to help her, but her mother threw her off, wailing loudly.

A chill climbed Jenna's spine. If she couldn't get her mom to stop, the neighbors would hear and call the police. Neither of them could afford that.

She ran for her mother's pills, but her mom only batted her away again.

And then she remembered.

The conversation had happened years ago, in the first apartment they'd rented after leaving home. Mae had sat her down and shown her a plastic tube containing a syringe. "This will work fast—I put together the formula myself. There may come a time when you'll need to use it on me, Jenn."

"You want *me* to give *you* a shot?" Jenna had asked. "Seriously?"

"Yes, seriously. If I'm ever out of control, or if I do something that really scares you."

"You mean like this conversation we're having right now?"

"Very funny." Mae had looked away from her. "If it happens, you'll know. Use it." And then she'd shown Jenna how to remove the safety cap, how to divide a thigh visually into three sections, how to aim for the invisible line in the middle section.

She'd never forgotten. And each time they'd moved, her mom had made sure to show her where she was putting the syringe.

Jenna vaulted over the couch and into the bathroom and swung the medicine cabinet open. She snatched the tube off the shelf and raced back to the living room.

She'd only have one chance to get it right. Dropping to her knees, she hiked up her mom's flannel nightgown to bare her thigh. Then she clenched her teeth and pushed the needle in.

Within seconds, the convulsions slowed, and Mae's eerie wailing stopped.

She removed the needle and took her mom's wrist, checking her heart rate. Mae was still panting, but her heart rate was slowing. Could the medicine be working that quickly, or had the shot worked by surprising her out of her agitation?

There was a soft knock.

Jenna cursed. She helped her mom onto the couch and rushed to the door. Then she crouched down and peeked through the gap along the floor. She recognized Mr. Cane's shoes and walking stick.

She forced a smile over her face and opened the door just far enough to poke her head through.

Mr. Cane's forehead wrinkled in concern. "Is everything all right? I thought I heard—"

"Oh yes," Jenna hurried to assure him. "Everything's fine. We were watching a movie. A sad, sad movie. And I got a little emotional. Teenage hormones," she added when he still looked skeptical.

"Well, I'm here if I can help." He turned to go, then hesitated. "Don't forget, no man is an island. No young woman either."

"I'll remember that," she said, giving him a thumbs-up. Before he could say anything else, she quickly closed the door.

She hurried back to Mae, relieved to see that her violent shaking had stopped. Gently, she took her by the elbow and helped her up. "Let's get you into bed."

She led her now-docile mom back to her bedroom and turned on the bedside lamp. She tucked her in under the pale blue covers and dragged the ladder-back chair from the corner of the room to the edge of the bed. Then she collapsed into the chair, massaging her temples. She'd watch until her mom was asleep.

Mae looked around the room, but her eyes couldn't seem to focus. "Is that you?" she whispered.

Jenna reached out and took her mom's hand. "It's me. You're going to be all right."

"Is that you?" Mae repeated. "Answer me." Her voice was ragged. She looked right through Jenna.

"I said I'm here, Mom."

"Say something." She struggled to sit up.

Jenna leaned forward, frowning.

Mae's voice was almost a sob. "Please, Fore. Is that you? Fore, are you there?"

For the third time that night, the glowing woman appeared.

CHAPTER SIX

KNOCK AND KEY

The chair toppled as Jenna sprang to her feet.

Without pausing to think, she launched into a side kick, swinging her leg out to hit the creature's chest. But her foot met only air, as if the woman were a hologram.

She stumbled back in surprise and then crouched into a fighting stance. She eyed the creature warily. "What are you?"

The woman regarded her with expressionless eyes. Her mouth moved silently, shaping a single word.

Jenna thought she could make it out—*Fore.*

She'd listened to her mom repeat that word for years. She'd always thought it was a number, but now she realized the truth. It was a name.

Ever since they'd gone on the run, Jenna had watched her mother's sanity deteriorate—or so she had believed. But unless the two of them were hallucinating in unison now, her mother had been seeing a part of reality that Jenna was now glimpsing for the first time.

It changed everything.

The creature bent and set the chair upright.

Jenna's eyes bulged. Seconds ago, the woman had been insubstantial. Now she—it?—was moving the furniture?

Fore glided across the room toward the foot of the bed, but Jenna stayed with her, keeping herself between the creature and her mom. "What do you want from us?" she demanded in a harsh whisper.

Fore...flickered. But it wasn't just the eerie light inside her—it was her whole body. She was there. And then she wasn't. And then she was there again. Fore's expression didn't change. She shook her head and held up her index finger.

Was she asking Jenna to wait?

She blinked out, and this time she didn't reappear.

Jenna whipped around, afraid the woman had gotten behind her, but there was no one. She looked at her mother.

Mae's eyes tracked a path from the foot of the bed to a place beside her, as if she was watching Fore walk toward her.

Jenna braced herself. How did you defend against something you couldn't see or touch?

"Fore?" Mae sat up. "Have you come back to me?" She stared feverishly into the creature's invisible eyes. "You promised you would keep Jenna safe, and I've done everything you asked."

She gripped the edge of the bed so hard her nails frayed the thin sheet. "I found the second sign on her." She leaned forward breathlessly, seemingly listening to Fore's response.

Was her mother able to hear the creature? Jenna edged closer, but Mae didn't notice.

Mae covered her mouth with her hands. "She's not ready. I won't—" She broke off, listening again.

Were they talking about Jenna? It was like overhearing one side of a phone conversation.

"It's too dangerous." Mae paused again, then pulled herself up onto her knees. "How can you be sure? If someone from the Council finds her Charms, they'll see her as an abomination. You know that as well as I do. They won't allow her to live."

Jenna's legs felt rubbery. *The Council?* Her mother had never mentioned a Council—or the fact that they would kill her if they found her. Why did she not know this?

Jenna thought her mom had told her everything she knew about the Charms. But she'd been holding back information—lying to her.

The thought cut deep.

Mae was not just the most important person in Jenna's life—with her father dead and her former friends abandoned, she was the *only* person in her life. Jenna trusted her completely.

Or she *had.* What else was her mother not telling her?

Mae curled into a ball, hugging her knees. Then she sagged back, falling onto the pillows. "Serene could still be looking for us," she whispered. "And Jenna doesn't even know I have a sister."

All the strength went out of Jenna. She sank onto the edge of the bed. *Her mother had a sister. A sister who was looking for them. Serene.*

Rage burned through her. She had family—an aunt. And her mother had concealed it from her.

Would an aunt be immune to Jenna's curse like her mother was? There could be another person who was safe from her touch. The thought was shocking. It doubled her world.

Mae jerked around to look at Fore. "What kind of help?"

She paused, then nodded, but her eyelids were growing heavy—the medicine was taking hold at last. Her breathing deepened. "Please. I need more time." It was little more than a whisper. Then her eyes closed, and she was asleep.

Fore reappeared so close to Jenna the woman's bare feet nearly touched her sneakers.

She leaned back, ready once again to defend herself.

But the creature moved to the other side of the room, hovering in front of the dresser. With an arm covered in black spirals, the creature lifted the lid of a small painted jewelry box Mae kept there. She reached inside and pulled out the brass pocket watch that had belonged to Jenna's father. It hadn't worked in years, but Mae had never thrown it away.

Fore glided back to Jenna. She held the watch by the chain, letting it sway hypnotically back and forth. She pushed it closer until, frowning in confusion, Jenna held out her hand.

Fore lowered the watch into her palm, but she didn't let go of the chain. For half a second, their eyes met. "Time," she said. Her voice had an odd cadence—hinting at music. "You must go."

"Go where?" she demanded.

But Fore had disappeared.

Jenna alternated between pacing the room and sitting rigidly in the chair.

Her mom was having a tough night. She was feverish and sweating one moment and shaking with chills the next. Even worse were the spasms that wracked her body. Through it all, though, she didn't regain consciousness.

Jenna kept vigil, waiting for her mom's symptoms to subside. She spun the pocket watch in her hands, while in her mind she turned over her mother's words.

There was a group called the Council who wanted to kill her. She had an Aunt Serene she hadn't known existed. According to her mom, she had the second sign on her now. And there was an otherworldly creature who was connected to them both.

Almost more incredible than any of that—her mother had been lying to her for years.

She clenched the watch in her fist, taking a deep breath to calm her racing heart.

For the first time in a long time, Jenna was angry. Seriously angry. At Fore for turning her life upside down and then vanishing. At her mom for lying. At herself for being so naïve. She was even angry that she couldn't *be* angry. Not right now. Not with her mom like this.

She wanted to rage. She wanted to scream and kick and demand answers. But it would have to wait.

Usually the pills knocked her mother out cold, but whatever had been in that injection was working differently.

Fear gnawed through the armor of Jenna's fury.

More than once, she started to call for an ambulance, but her mom had long ago forbidden it. And she knew better than to involve strangers in their lives. She had learned that the hard way. So she had no choice but to wait it out, watching.

She looked down at her mother. The lines of her face were soft in the lamplight.

Jenna had always wanted to be more like her.

Mae was everything she wasn't. Her sleek, sandy brown bob with its streak of white was the image of sophistication. She had dainty features and flawless skin.

But Jenna's auburn waves were constantly tangled, her nose was too large for her face, and her freckles were waging war against her, recruiting new members and expanding their territory.

More than any physical resemblance, though, she'd always wished she could *be* more like her mother. Mae was the calm one. The cautious one. She was smart and hardworking. Honest, too.

Or so she'd thought.

She swallowed the lump in her throat, toying with the pocket watch.

The creature, Fore, had wanted her to have it. But why? And why had she said it was time to go? Go where?

Jenna looked down. The two halves of the watch twisted back and forth in her fingers. She frowned and twisted further.

The back screwed off, revealing the gears of the watch—where someone had wedged a tiny brass key. Her jaw sagged. What did the key open?

She stood up, glancing around. All the furniture in the apartment had come with the rental. Their only possessions were what they could carry with them in the car. Did they own anything that required a lock?

Her gaze snagged on Mae's closet, and she strode over and swung the door wide.

Her mother had one large expandable suitcase she'd packed full of clothes a hundred times.

But she had a second vintage suitcase, too. It was a small hard blue rectangle with no wheels. On either side of the handle were two brass latches—with key-holes beside them.

She threw a glance over her shoulder. Mae was still sleeping.

Jenna crouched down and fitted the tiny key into the first lock. The latch sprang open with a loud thunk, and she winced, checking to see if the noise had disturbed her mom.

She was sound asleep, though, and Jenna turned the key more carefully in the second lock, holding the latch as it opened to keep it quiet.

She lifted the lid. A pile of papers took up most of the suitcase. She sifted through it and found their birth certificates and social security cards—the original ones and the fakes.

She set aside old vaccination records, tax documents, and her parents' marriage certificate. There was a prescription pad from her mom's days as a doctor and a photo album they used to keep on the shelf by the mantel in the house where she grew up.

A long, stretchy pocket ran across the back of the suitcase, and Jenna reached inside. She pulled out a handful of pictures and a letter. She'd seen most of the pictures before, but one seemed to leap out at her.

In the photo, her mom was in her twenties and wearing a business suit, her arm looped around the shoulders of a teenage girl.

Jenna's eyes widened. Now she knew her auburn hair and freckles had come to her naturally. That girl had to be her Aunt Serene.

If Jenna put on cargo pants and a tank top, they'd practically be twins. Did her mother see Serene every time she looked at her?

She flipped the picture over and read the label. "Mae and Serene, 1998," was written in her mom's handwriting. She turned it back over, doing the mental math. Her mom would have been twenty-five, and Serene looked much younger. Jenna hadn't even been born yet.

She studied the photo again. Her mother stood up straight, while Serene slouched against her, head tipped onto Mae's shoulder affectionately. The difference in clothing and posture made them seem more like mother and daughter than sisters.

Jenna put the picture aside and picked up the letter. It was tissue-soft with age, the creases worn as if her mom had folded and unfolded it many times. She started reading.

Dear Mae,

I'm worried you're so stubborn you'll throw this letter in the trash before you even let yourself look at it. But just in case you're actually reading this, I want you to know that I'm sorry for the way our last conversation ended. I wasn't myself, and I really am sorry. Also, can I get some credit for apologizing first, please? (Especially since you always say I never do.) See, I am maturing. Score! I can picture the look of amazement on your face right now. I may be nine years behind you, but I'm catching up at last!

So, here's the thing. I know you'll probably never understand why I left—that I had to leave—and that it never meant that I didn't love you or Mom anymore. But I couldn't keep living like that. There wasn't any room at home for me to grow. I felt locked away, honestly, and lonely. It just got to be too much. You've always wanted what was best for me, I know, but I had to find my own path, and I have. I'm very happy now, Maeby, and I hope you can be happy for me too. I'm dying to tell you in excruciating detail all that I'm doing and everything I'm learning. Your mind is made up. I know that. But I think you'd come around if you would just give these people a chance.

Anyway. I hope you and Ben are doing good in your new place. Are you still thinking about trying to get pregnant? OMG. I can't even imagine it. That would make me Aunt Serene, right? It is majorly blowing my mind. Let me know as soon as it happens, because I need plenty of time to practice being a grown-up. Miss you, Maeby. Call me soon. Love you always.

Serene (a.k.a. Chubs, a.k.a. The Dreaded Couch Hog, a.k.a. your little sis)

Jenna sat back on her heels. Her mom had held on to this letter. For years. Serene had tried to apologize for something—for leaving home?—but Mae had never accepted her apology. Never given her a chance.

Serene said she felt locked away and lonely, and Jenna could relate to that. All her life, she'd heard only one side of this story—her mother's. She hadn't even known there *was* another side.

Every bit of information she had about her family's past and about her Charms came from her mom. How much more could her aunt tell her?

At the bottom of the letter, Serene had scrawled a Chicago address and a telephone number.

Jenna avoided contact with other people. The times when she hadn't had ended in disaster. But her aunt was different. She was family. And she already knew about the Charms. It wasn't the same as contacting a stranger.

She needed answers. And the phone number at the bottom of the page was screaming her name. If she didn't call, curiosity would eat her alive.

She started toward the hall before she could stop and think. She tugged her phone from her back pocket, holding the letter in her other hand. It was older than she was, and that meant the phone number would have been a landline. There was almost no chance her aunt would be there, but she had to try before she could change her mind.

She took a breath and dialed.

A male voice answered. "Hello?"

Somehow, she hadn't expected that. "Yes, hello. Is...is Serene there?"

Silence filled the line. Finally, the man said, "Who?"

"Serene? Serene Dare?" she guessed, tacking on her mother's maiden name. "This...this is Jenna. Her niece."

Silence stretched again, and she had a sudden attack of doubt. What would she say if her aunt did come on the line? *"Hi, Aunt Serene, I'm not sure if you even know I exist, but could you please tell me what's really going on with my Charms? Because my mom has apparently been lying to me for years."*

"There's no one here by that name." The man's voice was abrupt, irritated.

Her fantasy conversation burst like a balloon. "Sorry to bother—"

He hung up.

Before the disappointment could sink in, she found the address on the letter and searched for it on her phone. The creature had told her she had to go somewhere. Had she meant for her to find her aunt?

Not that Jenna was keen on taking orders from a disappearing lady who glowed in the dark, but it wouldn't hurt to just look up the address.

The Chicago townhouse was a rental that had changed hands several times since the letter had been written over eighteen years ago, so that was no help. As a last-ditch effort, she searched online for Serene's name, but she had no luck there either.

She didn't know what she'd been expecting. She set her jaw. It would be better if she figured her situation out on her own.

She tucked the phone back into her pocket and stole into her mother's room to replace the letter and the key before she woke up.

Then she sank once more into the stiff chair. Her mom was sleeping more easily, and Jenna rubbed her eyes with her palms to ward off her own exhaustion.

She must have fallen asleep without realizing it, because three hours later her mother jerked upright in bed. Her body was rigid with a seizure.

"Cold water," she said, and Jenna scrambled to the kitchen to get it for her.

She hurried back and put the glass to her mom's lips, but Mae dashed it away, unseeing. Then she sank into an unquiet sleep.

The same thing happened two more times, until, when her mom called out again for cold water, Jenna ignored the request and took her mother's hand instead.

Night became predawn, and the first sounds of traffic reached her. The building's old pipes clanged and groaned as the residents of Ashton Place woke up.

She leaned forward and checked her mom's vitals. Her temperature and heart rate had returned to normal, and she was resting peacefully. At last.

Flopping back in the chair, Jenna ran her hands through her tangled hair. What would she say to her mom when she woke?

She shut her eyes. She'd gone past the point of exhaustion. Now she was wired. Twitchy.

When a knock sounded behind her, she almost leaped out of her skin. Then she froze as the realization struck her. Someone had knocked on their window.

Their *third-story* window.

Chapter Seven

COLLISION

The knock came again.

Jenna whipped around. She studied the closed blinds, but there was no sign of what was behind them.

Silently, she moved to the bedside lamp and clicked it off. Her mother didn't stir. She crept to the window and waited, letting her eyes adjust.

When the knock happened a third time, she yanked the pull cord and sent the blinds zipping up.

The dim streetlamp cast just enough light for her to see a tiny black-and-white chickadee. It perched on the windowsill, staring at her with its head cocked to the side. Then it leaned forward and pecked at the glass with three quick raps.

Jenna sucked in a breath as, behind the chickadee, a shadow detached from the dark and flew toward them.

Acting on instinct, she jerked the window open just high enough for the bird to hop inside. She slammed the window closed again, and a large crow swooped by, cawing as it changed direction and soared away.

She looked down at the chickadee, meeting its unwavering gaze. "You are one lucky little bird, you know that?"

Before she could let the bird out, though, it flew through the open bedroom door into the hall.

She cursed and followed it.

It sailed into the bathroom and alighted on the edge of their white plastic laundry basket. Then it hopped inside, nestling into a fuzzy sock.

Seizing the opportunity, Jenna grabbed a towel from the hook on the wall and tossed it on top of the basket, trapping the bird.

"Gotcha!" She peered at the chickadee through one of the small vent holes. It gazed back at her, unfazed.

If she opened a window to coax it outside, it could go rogue again, and she might not be able to catch it a second time.

She hurried to the front closet. Her own peacoat was still damp from her fall in the snow last night, so she grabbed her mom's old white puffer jacket and a fresh set of gloves.

Then she hesitated. She'd lost her ski mask in the laundry room yesterday. She didn't want to risk going outside with her skin exposed—especially not with so many people heading to work and school.

She rummaged through their duffle bag full of scarves and hats and came up with a white balaclava she could use instead.

It was a one-piece knit cap with an attached face covering. She pulled it over her head, grimacing. At least the material didn't fit tight like the ski mask. It was snug across her nose and cheeks, draping loosely to her collarbone.

Except for a narrow slit for her eyes, it covered everything—her hair, neck, and face.

She snatched her mom's keys from the bowl by the door. Then, as an afterthought, she grabbed her shades as well, pushing them on while she raced to the bathroom.

Now she was almost curse-proof, with every inch of her skin barricaded away.

When she caught sight of herself in the bathroom mirror, she drew up short. She was unrecognizable, even to herself. If she added a top hat, she'd be Frosty the Snowman.

The chickadee flapped its wings as she gently picked up the laundry basket and toted it to the door. She leaned into the hall and checked both ways, listening. The coast was clear.

She locked the door and hurried along the hall and down the side stairs, praying she wouldn't run into Brent again today. When she reached the back parking lot, she crouched down behind an empty van and eased the towel off.

The chickadee looked up at her from on top of a sock.

"Go on, now," she urged. "Fly away."

It lifted its wings in flight, and Jenna smiled and picked up the basket. Success.

But instead of soaring off into the sky, the bird flew maybe twenty feet and landed on the hood of Mae's blue Toyota Corolla.

Then Jenna's jaw went slack. Because there wasn't just a chickadee on the hood. There were dozens of birds flying from window to window and hopping along the roof and trunk.

She moved closer. There were cardinals, sparrows, finches, a duck, an owl, and others she couldn't name. A large crow—the one from earlier?—was there too, sitting stoically on the driver's side mirror.

She looked around. No one else in the parking lot was having this problem.

She sprinted to the car. "Shoo!" She waved her arms to scare the birds off.

They scattered briefly, flying up a few feet, then resettling on the Toyota.

A woman stood nearby, gawking. It was the lady Jenna had named Mrs. Tan because of the shades of brown she wore. Frowning, Mrs. Tan searched inside her leather purse.

Ice frosted Jenna's veins. If the woman got out her phone and took pictures, there was no telling what kind of attention it would draw.

She fumbled for her mother's key chain, found the right key, and unlocked the car. She flung the door open and tossed the laundry basket into the passenger seat. Then she slid inside and started the car. Surely, once she started moving, the birds would take off.

When Jenna was fifteen, she and her mom had been renting a mobile home in rural Alabama. Jenna would sneak out at night to drive on the dirt roads around the house, so she had *some* experience driving—although she'd been by herself on a dirt road, not out in traffic on a city street.

She put the car in gear and, thankfully, the birds took flight. Mrs. Tan frowned and got into her tan Ford, losing interest, and Jenna heaved a sigh of relief.

She planned to circle Ashton Place once and then park, but when she stopped the Toyota to ease onto the street, the same group of birds landed on her hood.

They pecked at her front window, then flew off, turning right. But the chickadee stayed behind. It took two hops to the right and cocked its head at her.

Jenna's eyes narrowed. Was the bird trying to show her something? It sounded bonkers, even to herself. But curiosity surged in her chest, kicking and screaming to be satisfied.

When the chickadee flew off to the right and joined the rest of the flock, Jenna followed it.

The birds stayed just ahead of her, and when she came to a red light, the entire group landed on her hood and waited. She looked around self-consciously, trying to see past the crow on her side mirror.

The odd thing—*one of the odd things*, she corrected herself—was that no one pointed, honked, or took out a phone to take a picture. Then it hit her.

No one else could see the birds.

Mrs. Tan hadn't been frowning at them. She'd been watching Jenna wave her arms like a lunatic, dressed like the Stay Puft Marshmallow Man.

So, this was—what? A hallucination? A vision?

Last night, Fore had told her it was time to go, and now she was going. Was this what she was supposed to do?

She ignored the bigger question—whether it was wise to follow the advice of a strange inhuman creature or to chase a bunch of possessed birds. Best if she didn't examine those thoughts too closely.

When the light changed from red to green, the flock took off, and she returned her focus to the road, following them.

Fortunately, daylight was dawning. But the local high school was up ahead, and the streets here were crowded. She began to doubt her choice.

She gripped the steering wheel hard. Trying to watch both the birds and the traffic wasn't easy. The flock turned a sharp left, and she veered into the turn lane just in time. She expected the birds to circle back and alight on her hood again, but they didn't appear.

She looked around. They were still there, watching her. But this time, they were perched on top of a large brick sign that marked the entrance to Coldwater High School.

All at once, she remembered her mother's repeated seizures in the night. Every time, she'd cried out for cold water.

Or that's what Jenna had thought. But what if she hadn't been asking for water at all? What if she'd been having a vision—a vision where she'd seen this sign? *Coldwater.*

Heat flashed into her cheeks. Fore had tormented her mother with that vision all night. Was she also responsible for these birds? She'd sent Jenna off on—almost literally—a wild goose chase. Why? If Fore had wanted her to come here, wasn't there a better way to tell her?

She sat glowering at the brick sign. When the cars behind her honked, she jumped.

She wrenched the wheel, making a U-turn and leaving the school behind. This time, the birds didn't follow.

What was the message here? That she was supposed to go to Coldwater High School?

That wasn't going to happen. She attended only virtual classes. With her cursed touch, attending a school in person was too big a risk.

At the stoplight, she sank back against the seat. It was too much to think about. She wanted nothing more than to go home, check on her mom, crawl into bed, and pull the covers over her head.

A police siren wailed to life behind her, and she jerked to attention. She had no license and no ID. The cops would think this was a stolen car. And then things would go from bad to…unthinkable. Her pulse leaped into her throat.

She swerved over onto the shoulder and stopped while her heart tried to pound through her chest. But the police car flashed by, and she let out a slow breath. They weren't after her.

She eased back onto the road, checking her rearview mirror. Three cars back, a silver Mercedes slipped into traffic behind her.

Jenna tensed. Was it the same Mercedes as last night—the man with the white tattoo?

She couldn't see the driver, but she wasn't taking any chances. She turned the corner, hoping to lose him, but the Mercedes followed, keeping pace.

Fear and curiosity competed in her chest. She had to know if it was him.

She slowed down, forcing the cars behind her to change lanes and go by, the drivers giving her dirty looks as they passed. When the Mercedes got close enough, she risked a glimpse in the mirror.

It was him. With his frowning mouth, marked face, and single diamond earring, it couldn't be anyone else.

What did he want with her? Maybe he was a member of the Council her mom had mentioned. Maybe he'd found out about her Charms somehow, and now he wanted to kill her. Or maybe he wanted to find out where she lived so he could kidnap her. Ashton Place was just ahead, but she refused to lead him there.

The light ahead turned yellow. If she sped through, she might be able to leave him behind.

Gritting her teeth, she stepped on the gas pedal, and her Toyota screeched forward. The Mercedes picked up speed.

But at that moment, she hit an icy patch on the road and slid sideways. She jerked the wheel, and the car fishtailed, skidding out of control.

She ran up onto the curb, and her car began to make an awful thumping noise. She slammed on the brakes, and the Mercedes roared by.

The man's steely gaze locked on her as he passed. He hit his brakes too, stopping the car farther up the street.

She held her breath as the seconds ticked by, but the man with the white tattoo didn't get out. After what seemed like an eternity, he restarted his car and drove away.

Hopefully, he wouldn't dare come back and assault her here on a city street in broad daylight.

She clenched her jaw and slid from the driver's seat. *What had she done to her mother's car?* The Corolla was up on the curb, and the front tire was flat. Her mom was going to freak out.

She was only about half a block from her apartment. Was it possible to drive the rest of the way home?

Footsteps pounded nearby, and she looked up as someone ran toward her.

She froze like a deer in headlights.

It was Lane.

Of course, it was Lane. She closed her eyes.

Of course, he had been at the bus stop when she crashed. Of course, he had been the one to watch her humiliating accident. And of course, he was here now to see her looking like the Stay Puft Marshmallow Man. Of course.

"Are you okay?" he called as he jogged up.

There were no fireflies this morning, but she still couldn't keep herself from staring.

He slowed to a walk and shook a lock of black hair away from his face. The cowlick at the back of his head stood straight up in the frosty morning air.

"Fine. I'm fine." She reached up to smooth her own hair, then remembered it was all tucked inside the balaclava.

She pretended to scratch her head instead as she held her breath, waiting for him to realize who she was. After the way she'd run off last night, he'd probably be furious.

"My name is Lane," he said. "If you're sure you're okay, I can take a look at your car."

She gaped at him, then swallowed and nodded once.

He hadn't recognized her.

She didn't know why she was surprised. She barely recognized *herself* beneath everything she was wearing.

Still, she pouted. She would recognize Lane anywhere, no matter how many jackets and scarves he had on. But to be fair, he hadn't spent months sitting at a window studying her.

She should correct him now. Admit that they'd met last night. The words rose in her throat and stuck there.

What would she say?

Hi! Remember me? I'm the difficult redhead who fell on my butt, pretended to be an angel, and then ditched you when your back was turned. And, yes, now I've wrecked my car, too. Thanks for asking.

Smooth.

Well, if he didn't recognize her, she wouldn't enlighten him. Besides, telling him who she was would just encourage him to ask questions. To get involved. It was the last thing she needed. She clamped her lips together and watched him silently.

He crouched down beside the tire, surveying the mess with a look on his face like someone had given him a pony.

He whistled low under his breath. "If I had to guess, I'd say you knocked the tire off the bead. It might be able to hold air though. They can check for you at a shop. If that *is* what's wrong, ask that they rotate this one to the rear just to be safe."

He looked up at her at last. "I've never seen you around. Are you new to the neighborhood?"

"Yes, I'm new here," she lied smoothly. Then her thoughts stuttered as the force of his blue-eyed gaze hit her. "I'm a newbie." She stalled, forcing a smile, even though he couldn't see it through the balaclava. "I'm super new."

She sounded like a toddler. What was wrong with her? This boy was frying her brain cells.

"I'm Lane," he said again. He stood and brushed off his jeans. "I can put your spare on for you if you've got one."

She waved him away. "No need." She scrambled into the driver's seat. "I'll just...pop the trunk and get started."

He was staring at her. "Shouldn't you—"

She knew her mother opened the trunk by pushing a button. Somewhere. *Did the car have to be on?* She waved Lane away again, but he didn't move. *Why wouldn't he stop looking at her?*

She turned the key to the "ON" position and poked at a couple of buttons, hoping the trunk would miraculously open. From the car's speaker, a syrupy-sweet Robo-voice asked, "*What would you like to do?*"

He lifted an eyebrow. "Have you driven this car before?"

"*What was that?*" the voice responded.

Jenna jerked the keys from the ignition. She leaped out, slamming the door behind her. "Listen. Do you think that because I'm a female, I can't change a tire?"

"Not remotely." He nodded toward the bus stop where his slender blonde girlfriend was watching them with narrowed eyes. "Brie can change a tire as well as I can."

Brie. Jenna had forgotten about the girlfriend. "Well, if Brie can do it, I'm sure I can figure it out."

"I'm sure you can, too. But right here," he pointed, "the car could roll off the jack and onto you."

He took a step toward her. "Let me push it into the cafe parking lot where it's flat. I mean, I like pancakes as much as the next guy, but that doesn't mean I want you to become one."

Jenna pursed her lips. "I can drive over there myself, thank you."

"You can, but I'd be happier if you'd let me look underneath before you start it up."

"So, I won't start it. I'll push it over there and then check it all out."

"You plan to steer and push at the same time?" He shook his head. "Not safe...or even temporally possible, really. Unless you happen to be a time traveler. But *we* can do it. Together."

"I...." Jenna frowned. "Won't you miss your bus?" Her eyes slid past Lane to where Brie was waiting.

"Nah. Even if the bus pulled up right now, I could have that tire swapped before everybody got on board."

She let out a long breath. "Fine." She climbed into the driver's seat. She was on a collision course with Lane McConnell. She needed to get this over with. Then she'd be rid of him and his stupidly blue, brain-canceling eyes.

He showed her how to put the car in neutral. Then she steered as he pushed the car into an empty part of the cafe parking lot.

"Teamwork!" He held up a hand for her to high-five him as she got out, but she pretended not to see, heading to the trunk to get the spare tire.

He shrugged and stepped up beside her.

She panicked. There was nowhere to insert her key. Then she remembered she could open the trunk with a button on the key itself. She scowled as she popped it open. Why was there an inverse relationship between her intelligence level and her proximity to this boy?

Lane whistled in appreciation. "You carry a full-size spare? I'm impressed." He nodded in approval as he lifted it out and set it aside. "Now, if you'll just hold the car up for a minute, I'll switch out the tires."

Jenna stared at him.

"Kidding!" He pulled out the jack and grinned, then kneeled and began prying off the hubcap.

"What can I do?" she asked.

He paused, considering. "Do you know any tap steps?"

She crossed her arms.

"Show tunes?"

"I'm ignoring you now."

He loosened the lug nuts and set the jack under the car. "You can keep me company. That's all."

"I'm a little out of practice," she admitted. She squatted down to see what he was doing.

He looked over at her, his eyes warm. "Just be normal."

She snorted. "Yeah. That's not possible."

"Did I say normal? I meant *ab*normal. Normal people suck. They're dull. Predictable." He turned the handle, raising the car off the ground.

She smiled behind her balaclava. Then she glanced down the street again and caught Brie's glare.

Her smile evaporated. "If you can't change the tire before your bus comes, I can get it from here."

"If I can't change the tire?" He was clearly affronted. He unscrewed a lug nut as he scolded her. "Listen, I get along better with cars than I do with people. I could change this tire with my eyes closed and my hands tied behind my back."

"Maybe you should. The way you're doing it now is so normal it's dull. Predictable even."

He stopped and eyed her curiously. "What did you say your name was?"

"I didn't. In the spirit of unpredictability, I think you should guess it."

"Touché."

"Not even close. I'm not French."

"Ha, Ha. Very funny." He pulled the last lug nut off and removed the old tire. "Do you give up?"

"I'm thinking." He hefted the spare tire into place and tightened the lug nuts. "Give me a clue."

"There's at least one vowel in my name."

"Mmm. Thank you. That really narrows it down." He lowered the jack, tilting his head as he considered. "Maybe...Suzanne?"

She gasped. "How did you know?"

He sat back on his heels, stunned. "Your name is Suzanne?"

"Yes, and I love to tap dance and sing show tunes, all while lifting heavy vehicles."

"Right."

"One guess left."

He did a final tighten of the lug nuts, pressed the hubcap into place, and stood to survey his work. He shrugged. "I give up. No—wait, I know. Is your name Rumpelstiltskin?"

"You are so close. I mean really, really close." She took a breath, then hesitated, almost changing her mind. But she decided it didn't matter. This would be their last conversation. She could tell him her real name. "I'm Jenna."

He swung his fist in frustration. "I was going to say Jenna. It was a toss-up. I thought, either Rumpelstiltskin or Jenna. They're so similar."

"It's true. I answer to either name."

"Good to know, Rumpelstiltskin." Lane lifted her old tire and put it in the trunk, slamming the lid.

"At a glance, everything looks okay underneath. But I want to start it up and make sure it's running all right. Can I have your keys?"

"Heads up." She chucked the keys at him, and the throw went wide.

He leaped to the side and caught them. He turned to her, his head cocked in curiosity. "Are you sure we've never met? You seem so...familiar."

She laughed too loudly, backing away. "No, no. Nope. I'm a newbie, remember?"

"If you say so." He shook his head and ducked into the car.

It roared to life, and she heaved a sigh of relief because, A) he hadn't caught her lie, and B) with the car working, her mother might not kill her.

He climbed out and tossed her the keys. Then he coughed and shuffled his feet. "Well, this is awkward, but we haven't talked about payment yet."

She stiffened. She didn't have any cash on her.

"Lucky for you, all I'm charging today is your firstborn child."

She relaxed, and her mouth twitched. "Shoot. I don't have my firstborn on me right now."

"You'll have to owe me."

"I will."

They looked at each other.

"So, I—" she said.

"Are you—" he said at the same time.

Then Brie yelled for Lane as the bus rounded the corner. He didn't notice.

Jenna raised her eyebrows and pointed toward the bus.

He whipped around. "Crap." He turned to her. "See you, Rumpelstiltskin." And he sprinted off down the sidewalk.

"See you. From my window," she said. But he was already gone.

She slid back into the Corolla. As she put the key into the ignition, her phone vibrated.

Usually, she ignored her phone when it buzzed—it could only be spam. Aside from her mother, no one knew she was alive.

But what if her mom had woken up and found her missing? She grimaced. That would be a disaster.

She reached around and fished her phone out of her back pocket.

There was a text message waiting for her. She opened it and read, *Jenna, this is your Aunt Serene. Please, can I call you?*

Her hands went numb. For a full minute, she couldn't do more than stare at the screen.

She should never have made that call last night. She knew that. She wasn't supposed to contact anyone.

For years, she and her mom had painted over their old identities, crisscrossing the country to keep everyone off their trail. They'd forged papers, lied to countless employers and teachers. They'd built a fortress out of deceit.

But Jenna had never guessed that her mom was lying to *her*, too.

Also, there was a Council trying to kill her, a man following her, and a creature giving her cryptic messages. There were eerie birds and fireflies...and her mother's frightening episode last night.

It was too much.

She needed answers, and she wouldn't get them from her mom.

She texted back. *Yes. Call me.*

Chapter Eight

A WALK IN THE PARK

When her cell phone buzzed, Jenna pounced before she could lose her nerve. "Hello?" Her voice came out scratchy.

"Jenna? This is your Aunt Serene. Thank god you called. Can you talk right now? Are you someplace private where we can talk?"

"I can talk."

"Good. Jenna, you have no idea how long I've been looking for you. Since forever, really. So when I missed your call last night, I almost had a heart attack. Ian answered the phone, and I guess he thought you were a scammer or something and hung up. When he told me about it later, I nearly died. I mean, I was one step away from the pearly gates. I've never been so shocked in my life."

Apparently, Aunt Serene was a talker. But Jenna was glad to have someone else carry the conversation. She was speechless.

"Jenna, I need to see you." Her aunt's voice grew serious. "Listen, I'm not going to say anything bad about your mother. I know you love her. *I* love her. That's why I've been trying for so long to find you. Your mom needs help, Jenna. And unless Maeby has completely changed her stripes in the last twenty years, I'm sure she's too proud to ask for it."

That was true. Her mom did not like asking for help. Jenna opened her mouth to agree, but Serene was already forging on.

"Okay, so don't freak out. I don't want you to freak out. I know I should have called first, but the thing is, I really need to meet with you in person. It's...it's important. And I know someone who works at the phone company, so I pulled a few strings to get your call traced. When I saw you were in Saint Paul, I thought to myself, 'I could be there by the morning.' So I got on the road from Chicago last night, and I'm here in the city now. I know that sounds super creepy and I'm sorry, but I just couldn't risk losing you again. You can understand that." Serene came up for air. "Are you freaking out?" she demanded.

Jenna was in shock, but after the way her day had started, this was manageable. She wasn't sure how to explain the problem, though. *Sorry, Aunt Serene, but I avoid people because my touch is insanely dangerous.*

"I'm not freaking out," she hedged, "but I'm not sure an in-person meeting is the best idea."

"Is this because you have Charms? You do, don't you? I knew it," she said, not waiting for Jenna's response. "Listen to me. I do not want you to worry about that. I'm your aunt, remember? Not some random stranger on the street. I grew up hearing about the Charms the way other kids heard about the Three Little Pigs or whatever, okay? So believe me, I know enough to be careful. Is there anything special you should tell me, though?"

"Um...we shouldn't touch. I guess."

"Ah, I see."

"Unless you think that because we're related it wouldn't matter...." Jenna broke off, unused to talking about her Charms.

"It's interesting that you say that. Honestly, I'm not sure. Probably better to be safe than sorry, though. Right? Listen, I want to hear all the details. But you should know that, even though your mother isn't speaking to me, I can guess what's going on with you guys. Your mom.... Jenna, she's not well, is she?"

She blinked. "No, she's not."

"Jenna, she's...." For the first time, Serene was tongue-tied. "I have to talk to you, but I want to tell you face to face."

A hard knot of dread coiled in the pit of Jenna's stomach. *What was so bad that her aunt couldn't say it over the phone?*

Jenna had a strict No People policy, but this situation was different.

For one thing, Aunt Serene might be able to help. The curse ran through that side of the family, so Serene was already in on the secret of the Charms. And maybe she'd be more willing to talk than Jenna's mom had been.

"Can you meet me now?" Jenna asked, before her aunt could launch into another monologue.

Serene agreed immediately. They both pulled up maps on their phones and found a park just a few blocks away from where Jenna was. They could meet there without worrying about a crowd—or Mae. It was as easy as that.

Jenna drove slowly, unsure what to tell her aunt. Hopefully, Serene would take the lead.

A Jeep Wrangler was already parked in one of the spaces when Jenna arrived. The window was cracked, and a beagle poked its head out and barked. The guy in the driver's seat was probably around twenty-five, with long blond hair in a ponytail. He shushed the dog and then went back to eating his lunch. He didn't even glance at Jenna, but she kept driving.

Luckily, all the parking spots were open at the other end of the park. She pulled in, looking around.

It was a well-maintained neighborhood park with a track and picnic tables. A young mother and her two toddlers were in the playground area, but they were the only other people around. And with the sun out and shining, the park was positively picturesque.

But Jenna was too wired to sit. She got out and tugged off her balaclava and shades. She tossed them into the car and slammed the door. She wanted to look normal for her first meeting with her aunt.

She walked back and forth on the track, keeping an anxious eye peeled. A red-tailed hawk swooped overhead, and for a second she worried the eerie flock from this morning had returned. Then she scolded herself. Not every bird was a sign. She didn't want to make a fool of herself in front of her aunt.

At that moment, a large white SUV pulled into a spot near Jenna's car. A woman rolled down the tinted passenger window. Her wavy hair was a darker shade of red than Jenna's, but Jenna spotted the resemblance between them at once.

It was oddly pleasing. Her own nose wouldn't be so bad if it eventually looked like that. The woman's features reminded her of Mae, too—with her large eyes and full lips. She was unmistakably Aunt Serene.

Serene's hand flew to her mouth, and her eyes welled with tears. "Jenna?" she asked, her voice trembling. At Jenna's nod, she turned to the man in the driver's seat. "Oh my god, Ian, it's really her."

The man nodded. He wore jeans and a stretchy shirt beneath a gray sport coat. He barely glanced at Jenna. Instead, he cracked a raw egg into his mouth and tossed the shell out the window.

Serene returned her gaze to Jenna, shaking her head. "I can't believe I'm looking at you after all these years. Get in!" She gestured toward the back of the SUV. When Jenna didn't respond, Serene blinked and exchanged a quick look with the driver.

Jenna's eyes flicked back and forth between the two of them. She didn't want the man to listen in on her conversation. "Could we maybe take a walk instead—just us?"

Serene nodded eagerly and hopped out of the car. "Of course, we can do that. I don't know what I was thinking."

She wore a gray cable-knit scarf that was looped twice around her neck. Over her brown leggings, she had on knee-high leather boots with faux laces, and she carried a small multicolored purse slung cross-body over her shoulder. Her over-size rose sweater was thick enough to double as a coat on a day as unseasonably warm as this one.

Serene reached into the SUV and lifted out a white paper bag and a disposable tray with a couple of cups of coffee. "Let's grab a picnic table first. I stopped and got us breakfast. I don't know about you, but I'm starving."

Jenna's stomach gurgled in response as the smell of bacon hit her. "That would be great."

Serene smiled and then gasped, half turning around. "I just realized I didn't introduce you two. Jenna, this is my friend Ian, and Ian," her voice took on a scolding note, "this is my niece Jenna, who you so rudely hung up on last night."

"Sorry about that," he muttered.

"It all worked out in the end," Serene said, waving it away. "Ian, wait in the car while we chat?" At his nod, her smile returned.

She motioned toward a green metal picnic table bolted down to a concrete pad near the center of the park. "I can't believe it's actually you!" She glanced sideways at Jenna. "I am dying to give you a big bear hug right now, even though I know I can't." Her smile turned misty. "I always hoped I'd have the chance to know you as a child, but you've already grown into a beautiful young woman. How is it possible it's been that long?"

Jenna squirmed and shrugged, overwhelmed. It was all so surreal. Until a few hours ago, she hadn't known her aunt existed. Now she was brimming with questions, but she couldn't have squeezed out a syllable if Serene had let her.

"I see Mae in you, you know. You have her hazel eyes and her fabulous cheekbones. I'm so jealous." She tilted her head. "How did you ever find me, though? Don't get me wrong—I'm glad you did. But I wondered how." She gave her a teasing look. "Maeby doesn't know you called, does she?"

"No," Jenna admitted, finding her voice at last. "I found a letter you'd written to her before I was born, and you put your number on it. I wanted to.... Well, I thought I would call and see if you were still there."

"So she kept that letter all these years," Serene said softly. She blinked back tears and glanced away. "You don't know how much that means to me."

They walked in silence once more, passing the playground where the young mother was helping her two small girls take turns on the slide. She struggled to hold on to the hand of the youngest as she steadied the older girl's balance on the ladder.

Then the smaller girl broke away and took off running, ignoring her mom's shouts. She laughed as she toddled toward Jenna and Serene.

Jenna stumbled to a halt, but Serene's voice was warm and confident. "Go back to your mom and your sister, sweetie."

Obediently, the girl reversed course, still laughing as she ran back to her family.

The mother waved her thanks, and Serene's face turned wistful as she watched them.

"So, in the letter, it sounds like you and my mom had a fight. You never did work it out?"

Serene shook her head, starting toward the picnic table once again. "Jenna, your mom is one of the most amazing women I've ever known. Growing up, she was more like a mother than a sister—because of the age difference and because of our own mother's...quirks."

She glanced again at Jenna. "But your mom can be too single-minded sometimes. I'm sure you know that. Forgiveness is not her strong suit." They reached the picnic table, and Serene turned to her abruptly. "I want you to give me a chance to start over."

"Of course," Jenna reassured her. She'd experienced her mother's single-mindedness firsthand. "You have a clean slate with me."

She sighed in relief. "I was hoping you'd say that. Now, let's eat before it gets cold. Sit here across from me."

"It's probably better if I sit over here," Jenna said, her cheeks heating. She moved to the far end of the table where their feet couldn't accidentally touch.

Surprise flickered over Serene's face once more. Then she nodded and waved her agreement. "Of course. Sorry about that. You'll have to keep reminding me."

Jenna sat, her stomach grumbling loudly, and Serene pushed a paper-wrapped sandwich and one of the coffee cups over to her.

She unwrapped the sandwich—a bacon, egg, and cheese biscuit—and took a big bite. She hadn't realized how hungry she was.

Her aunt sipped her coffee, her brows knitted together as she studied Jenna. "I notice you don't take your gloves off to eat. Is it—you can tell me to take a hike if I'm being nosy—but is it because you have Charms on your hands?"

The food in her mouth suddenly felt too thick. She swallowed heavily, nodding.

"Can I see them?" Serene asked. "Don't worry—I won't touch."

Jenna scanned the area, self-conscious. The little family and the guy in the Jeep were nowhere near. Still, she felt exposed when she tugged off her glove and bunched up her white jacket sleeve.

She hated the sight of the three dark, twisting ridges that wound along the backs of her hands and arms. But her aunt regarded the marks with eager curiosity and not a hint of disgust.

She breathed out slowly. "Your Charms are just like the ones my grandmother had—if you can believe my mother's description. I never saw them, of course. Granny was murdered long before I was born."

"Murdered?" Jenna glanced up with a start.

"You didn't know?" When she shook her head, Serene sighed. "I wondered what Mae told you—and what she didn't."

She took another sip of her coffee, lost in thought. "So, if my theory is correct and your Charms work like Granny's, that means your touch causes someone to desire you. Am I right?"

Jenna could only nod.

"And you know this for sure?"

Jenna's breath caught, and she had to force herself to meet her aunt's eyes. She nodded once more. "His name was Michael," she whispered. "Michael Stevens." She looked away.

"It's okay." Serene reached her hand toward both of Jenna's—almost, but not quite close enough to pat them. "It wasn't your fault."

Her aunt meant well, she knew, but Serene was wrong about that. It *was* her fault, and she could never make it right.

She changed the subject. "You said my great-grandmother was murdered. What happened?"

Serene pursed her lips. "Her name was Vera. And, well, she touched two different men—accidentally, of course—and they both went mental. Insanely jealous. Both of them. And Vera was caught between them and killed."

"That's awful," Jenna breathed. She could picture it all too easily. One mistake, and her own life would end the same way. She picked the remainder of the biscuit into pieces, her appetite gone.

"It's horrible," Serene agreed. "But it could never have happened if the Council hadn't betrayed her. I blame them."

Jenna's ears perked up. "The Council? My mother mentioned them once, but I don't know anything about them. I always thought the Charms were only in our family."

Serene set her coffee cup down. Her face had gone white. "You don't know about the Council?"

"Just that my mom said they would think of me as an abomination. That they might try to kill me."

"You better believe they would." Her jaw squared in anger, and she drew her hands into fists. "They're monsters, Jenna. The Council controls a group of Charmed people, and most of them live in a place called Haven. It's where your great-grandmother was from. Now, the group that lives in Haven is smaller than ever, but don't underestimate the Council's power. They use the ones who are born with Charms to protect themselves and grow their wealth. It's all they care about." She stopped and took a sip of coffee, obviously trying to calm herself. "Sorry. I get angry just thinking about it."

"It's okay. I want to know everything."

She nodded. "So, like I said, your great-grandmother was raised in Haven. Vera would have been an Artifex. Do you know what that is?"

At Jenna's blank look, Serene blew out her breath. "It's hard to explain, but it's probably the most important position inside the Council. Vera was powerful. But when her Charms appeared, they didn't look right. Something went...wrong. And anyone who touched her wanted her. They went crazy, you know?"

Jenna nodded. "She was like me."

"Yes. Like you." Serene crossed her arms. "And instead of helping her—instead of protecting her like they should have—the Council threw her out."

"You mean they banished her or something?"

"Exactly. Left her to fend for herself in the outside world. I'm sure they believed it was a death sentence. And it was. Eventually. But they never guessed she'd survive long enough to reproduce, or I bet they would have killed her outright." She gave a bitter little laugh.

"And that's why they'll kill me if they find me?"

Serene's face turned deadly serious. "We can't let that happen." She leaned forward. "I will do everything I can to protect you. We all will."

Jenna frowned. "Who's *we*?"

"A few of us are working to make things better for people like you. We call ourselves the Unbound because we're not sworn to the oaths the people inside of Haven take." She flipped her hair back over her shoulder. "The oaths are a joke, anyway. They don't serve anyone but the Council."

She took a deep breath and continued. "Anyway, all of us in the Unbound have the Charms somewhere in our bloodlines—we have people we love, like you, who we want to protect. But we believe that the way the Council operates is wrong. That what they did to Vera was wrong, and that what they'd do to you is wrong, too. The whole way they live their lives—hiding their gifts and hoarding their wealth. That isn't right either." She put her coffee cup down with a sharp thud. "People who've been given gifts should use those gifts to help others, don't you think?"

Jenna nodded.

Her eyes glowed with passion. "I've been working to make things better for years now. It's why your mom and I got into that fight so long ago. She's no fan of the Council, believe me, but she doesn't want to do anything to stop them either. She wants to sit and wait, hoping things will improve." Her eyes filled. "But Jenna, time is running out."

Jenna went still, sensing something important coming. Her stomach flipped over with a dread she couldn't name, and her voice was scratchy when she spoke. "What do you mean?"

Serene's face was drawn. "It's why I wanted to meet with you in person. I'm sorry. I'm so sorry to tell you this. But your mom.... Jenna, your mom is dying."

Chapter Nine

A Normal Life

Jenna sat very still, but inside, she was falling. Falling and hitting the ground hard—with all the air knocked out of her.

Her mom was not just the center of her world, she *was* her world. Life without her was...unthinkable. "What do you mean, she's dying?"

"Does she have seizures? Moments when she's in a kind of trance or when she says strange things?"

"Yes." Jenna's voice was hollow, carefully scraped of feeling.

"How often?" Serene asked. "Once a week?"

"No." Jenna clasped her hands together beneath the picnic table to keep them from shaking. "It happens every day now. Usually more than once."

Serene sucked in a breath and turned an even whiter shade of pale. "I didn't realize it was that bad."

Jenna couldn't sit still any longer. She swung her legs over the bench and strode to the other side of the table, towering over Serene. "Mom is a trained doctor with years of experience. Wouldn't she know if she was dying?"

Serene looked up at her, eyes full of pity. "She does know. But I'm sure she hoped she could fix it before she ever had to tell you. She's been overconfident, thinking she could heal herself with medicine. The problem is, it's not a medical illness. It's a magical illness. The only thing that will cure it is biomagy."

"Biomagy," Jenna repeated. She stood there frozen. If she moved, she might shatter.

"Yes, the Charms are what we call biomagic. They're bound up with biology. Charmed people don't have power over swords or jewelry or hurricanes or anything. It's more like a DNA hack that affects their bodies. And right now, the magic is taking Mae over like a cancer."

Serene got up, looking at Jenna intently. "Have you noticed your mom taking medicines—maybe even a lot of them—trying to slow the sickness down?"

She nodded stiffly.

Serene hesitated. "Your mom never mentioned any of this?" A thought seemed to strike her. "What has she told you about her own gift?"

"Her gift? I…. No. My mom doesn't have Charms. They're in our bloodline, but they skipped her." Jenna stopped short at the look on her aunt's face.

Serene sank onto the seat of the picnic table again. "Unbelievable. You don't even know your mom has Charms."

Jenna shook her head. "You're wrong. I would have seen the marks—the tattoo."

"Not necessarily. The marks vary with the gift." She threw her hands up. "See, this was what I was afraid of. She hasn't told you anything."

"What should she have told me?"

Serene tapped her fingers, then blew out her breath in frustration. "Let's start at the beginning. Your mom is a Seer—or that's what the Council would call her, anyway. It's a super rare gift. Basically, your mom has an extra sense. She sees visions—glimpses of other times."

"Since when?" Jenna asked.

"Since forever. Or at least since she was a teenager." She gazed off into the distance, remembering. "But when Maeby was young, the visions didn't happen often, and they were easy to explain away. She looked like she was daydreaming. The Seer gift intensifies with age, though. And with trauma."

"You mean like when we left home? When my dad died?"

She gave an abrupt nod. "It probably pushed her over the edge. But here's what makes me mad. If Mae had grown up living in Haven, the Council would have extended her life. A Seer loses connection to this time and place, and eventually it's fatal, but if your mom could have had access to Healers, this wouldn't be happening."

"Can we get a Healer, then?" Jenna sat forward on the bench.

Serene sighed heavily. "Mae would never risk going to the Council. She'd be too afraid they'd find out about you. Besides, from what you've told me, she's too far along for a Healer, anyway."

A wave of nausea rolled through Jenna. If it wasn't for her, her mother could have gotten help. She wouldn't be dying.

Serene turned sideways on the bench to face her. "I wish I could tell you something different, Jenna. But if Mae is having seizures every day, she doesn't have long. Our mother died the same way. She had the Seer gift, too."

"It's not a gift. It's a curse." Jenna rubbed the spot between her eyes, forcing back the tears that threatened to spill.

Serene slapped her hand down on the table. "Listen to me. Are you listening?"

She waited until Jenna nodded. "I need you to shift your mindset. You're looking for pitfalls, not possibilities. Stop assuming the worst. I didn't come here to tell you your mother is dying, okay? I came here to give you hope. I don't have the gifts you and your mom have, but I've studied the Charms for years. My friends in the Unbound—they're already experimenting with a procedure that could cure your mom."

Jenna's head snapped up. "What kind of procedure?"

"It's nothing you'll find in a hospital, that's for sure. You have to have the help of Charmed people to heal a biomagical illness. Mae needs other mages. She's never accepted that."

She waved her hand, dismissing that train of thought. "Like with surgery—you need doctors, the procedure itself, and medicines. Well, our doctors are mages, and we know the procedure we need to use, but we're still working on finding the right medicine. We're close, though. I can feel it."

Jenna rubbed her temples, thinking. "You say the Council is powerful. Wouldn't they know something about this? Mom can't—or won't—go herself, but why can't *you* go and ask them?"

Serene spit out a sarcastic laugh. "Oh, they'd love that. Listen, I'm in more danger from the Council than you are. They're rounding up members of the Unbound, and they know I'm one of them—along with Ian and all my friends. That's why your mom hasn't let me come near you. She didn't want the Council sniffing around. But I've stayed safe this long because I know what I'm doing."

She sat back. "You bring up a good point, though. The Council still doesn't know you exist, right?"

"I think so. Except...." Jenna hesitated.

Serene's mouth tightened. "Except what?"

"Except there's a man here in the city who followed me. Twice."

Serene stiffened. "Tell me what happened."

Jenna described the man with the diamond earring and the white tattoo—the strange way he'd looked at her and the Mercedes he drove.

Serene nodded her head as she talked. "That mark means he's a member of the Vigil—an enforcer for the Council. He could be watching you, waiting to see if you violate any of their laws. But because of the oaths he swore, he shouldn't be able to make a move against you unless he has proof." She leveled a finger at Jenna. "Don't do anything to give him a reason to question you. And in the meantime, Ian and I will find out more about him. Was it just the one man you noticed?"

Jenna paused. She didn't want her aunt to think she was crazy. "Yes," she said slowly, trying to decide how much to say about Fore.

But Serene caught the hesitation in her voice. She cocked her head, waiting.

"Well, last night I also saw a woman with marks—Charms probably—all over her body. She sort of...glowed...and she called herself Fore—"

Serene started so violently she knocked over her coffee. Her hand shook as she righted the cup. "Fore? The Foremother appeared to you?"

"The...Foremother?"

Serene leaned so far forward she was in danger of tipping over. "Do you have any idea how significant that is?"

"Um, not really. Is it bad?"

Serene stood up in a kind of daze. "Bad? Jenna, it's a miracle!" Then she wagged her finger. "See—you assumed the worst. Mindset, remember? No, this is amazing news. The Foremother's the one who founded Haven. No one knows who or what she is exactly, but she's more than human. I can tell you that. And she's the reason Haven has thrived, hidden away for hundreds of years."

She leaned toward Jenna. "But here's the thing—no one has seen her for two generations. She just up and disappeared." Serene made a poof gesture with her hands. "And the Council has had a hard time explaining why." She clenched her fists in excitement. "If Fore appeared to you, it may be a sign that the Council is out of favor with her. Maybe she's choosing to connect herself with our family.

With the Unbound."

She sat down again, although she was nearly vibrating off the seat with energy. "With Fore on our side, we won't need to ask the Council about medicine. Fore knows more than all the books in the Council library put together. With her help, I know we can get the cure ready in time to save Mae."

Inside Jenna's chest, hope flared like a sparkler.

Serene leveled her gaze at Jenna with laser intensity. "Tell me every detail."

So she did. She hurried through all the parts involving Lane, trying not to blush. She told her aunt about seeing Fore in the streetlight and then again in the basement laundry room. Then she described how she'd appeared in Mae's bedroom and how the creature had given her the key that led to their meeting. She even told her about the way her mother had called out the words *cold water* and how a flock of birds showed her a brick sign that said the same thing.

"What do you think it means?" she asked.

Excitement radiated from Serene in waves. "It means she's trying to guide you, and you need to let her. The fireflies. The birds. Those were absolutely sent by her. It's how she guided the Council for most of its history—not with words, but with symbols. She chose you, Jenna. And she led you to me. This validates everything I've been working toward. Don't you see? She wants to help us both."

"How? What do I do?"

She pursed her lips, thinking. "I'm not sure exactly what she intends, but it's clear she wants you to connect with that school."

At the other end of the park, the beagle barked loudly. The blond man put him on a leash and began running the track.

The noise jolted Serene into action. In a rush, she cleared the picnic table, stuffing their uneaten food into the white paper bag and putting the coffee cups back in the tray. "Do everything you can to curry Fore's favor, and see if you can get her to talk to you again. Follow where she leads." She strode toward the SUV, and Jenna hurried after her.

"She's already pointed you in one direction—to that school. Maybe there's something there she wants you to retrieve. Something hidden. I don't know. But if your mother saw the school in a vision and then Fore's messengers guided you there, it's important."

Jenna struggled to keep pace, her head reeling as Serene charged ahead.

"We're on the cusp of something huge here. It could change the whole direction of my research. And now that you've told me about seeing Fore, I know we can find the cure. But listen to me." She stopped, waiting until Jenna looked her in the eyes. "The most important thing now is to protect your mom from stress. She's at a fragile stage, and we don't want to trigger a seizure she might not come out of."

Jenna winced. It was true. Her mom had withered both physically and mentally. It took very little to set her off.

Serene pressed on. "Tell me your thoughts. Do you think it will stress your mom out if she knows you talked to me? I want to see her so badly, but I'm worried. What do you think?"

"I know what you mean. If she thinks you could draw the attention of the Council, she'll worry I'm in danger. She'll make us move again, and I don't think she's strong enough for that. Maybe I shouldn't say anything about you until the cure is ready."

"You're probably right, Jenna. So how good are your acting skills?"

"Um, not bad."

"Good. I know it will be hard to pretend that nothing's changed, but I agree with you. I think it's for the best."

Jenna nodded silently as they neared their cars.

"Here's what I want you to do in the meantime." With one hand, Serene reached into her brightly colored purse and pulled out a small, unmarked pill bottle. "Unfortunately, these won't cure her, but they should make her symptoms a little better. They might give her more time. Grind up one pill a day and mix the powder in with Mae's coffee."

Jenna hesitated. "What kind of pills are they?"

"One of my friends in the Unbound came up with this formula, and we've already tested it." Serene stopped and handed Jenna the coffee tray. "Watch." She shook a pill out onto her palm and then tossed it back. Then she picked up her coffee, washing the pill down. "See? It's like an aspirin. You and I can take them all day long. They're not at all dangerous, but they should be strong enough to stop your mom from having seizures until the cure is ready." She dropped the pill bottle into Jenna's gloved hand. "Keep this safe."

"I will." She tucked it carefully into her pocket.

"I promise you we're going to find an answer for Maeby." Serene strode purposefully toward the cars once more. "Now, watch for signs from Fore, and focus on finding a way into that school." She glanced at Jenna. "The number you called before was a landline, but I'll stay in the area in case you need me. If you see that man or Fore, call me at the number I used to text you, okay?"

"Got it," Jenna said as they reached the cars.

Serene turned to her, hesitating. "There's one more thing I think you should know. If I can get this cure working for your mother, I think it will work for you, too."

Jenna's mind couldn't process the words. "You mean—"

"I mean we could remove your Charms. You could have a normal life again."

Serene smiled at Jenna's stunned expression. Then she opened her car door and clambered inside, exchanging a swift look with Ian. She rolled the window down. "I loved seeing you today. Keep me posted."

Jenna nodded and waved her off, walking to her own car in a daze. If they could discover the medicine that would make this cure a reality, she could save her mother and herself in one stroke. She *had* to find a way. Whatever it took. She'd follow every sign Fore sent her.

And right now, all the signs pointed toward the school—Coldwater High. She needed to get inside. But how could she do that without putting herself and everyone there in danger?

She swung open the door of the Corolla and nearly sat on the balaclava and shades she'd left behind on the seat.

Then an idea struck her.

This time yesterday, she would never have considered it.

But this time yesterday, she hadn't met a creature with powers beyond her comprehension. She hadn't known her mother was dying. And she'd thought she was doomed to live in isolation, cursed by the Charms etched into her skin.

What a difference a day could make.

Jenna snatched up the balaclava and shades as her mind raced ahead, planning for tomorrow.

PART TWO

Chapter Ten

ZINNIA

Three Weeks Later

Mae's eyes drilled into the back of Jenna's skull.

The air was thick with her disapproval, but Jenna ignored it and pulled the sandwich bread down from the kitchen cabinet. She had to keep her hands moving so her mom wouldn't see them shaking.

"Are you certain this is what you want?" Mae asked for possibly the thousandth time. "Absolutely certain?"

Jenna cut a glance at her mom as she went to the fridge for raspberry jam.

Her mother hovered in the kitchen doorway, her back rigid. She gripped her coffee mug the way she'd held on to the metal bar on the first upside-down roller coaster they'd ridden together when Jenna was ten. Mae had been stressed that day. This morning, though, she was pressing her lips so thin they made a minus sign on her face.

Jenna needed to keep her mother stress-free. But at the same time, if she had any hope of finding a cure, she also needed to go through with this plan.

This super-stressful plan.

At least the pills Aunt Serene had given her seemed to be working. Dissolved in coffee, they were tasteless—she'd tried one herself to be sure. But as soon as she'd started giving them to her mother, Mae's sleep and appetite had improved. Even better, she hadn't had a single episode.

The pills would have to be enough to get her mom through the stress of today.

"I've thought about this a lot," Jenna said. "Just be happy for me." She was doing her best to act cheerful—even as her stomach lurched. She held the open jar of raspberry jam as far away as she could, avoiding the scent of food.

It was the first day of second semester at Coldwater High School, and despite her mother's repeated protests, Jenna had made up her mind to go.

Every sign the creature Fore had given her pointed to this school. The flock of birds had literally led her there. Lane—with his swarm of fireflies—went there, too. Her mother had called out the name of the school during one of her visions. And Fore had told Jenna directly, "*Time. You must go.*" It seemed obvious now.

If Serene was right, Fore's cooperation could be the key to a cure—one that would get rid of her hated Charms and save her mother's life. But since that night three weeks ago, the creature had made herself scarce. There were no more birds. No strange appearances. Even the fireflies had disappeared. It was as if Fore was waiting for her to do her part now.

Well, the wait would end today.

She'd go to the school and figure out what Fore wanted. Then she'd be out of there. She'd go back to her virtual classes and tell her mom she'd changed her mind about Coldwater High. It was simple.

The last three weeks had been tricky, though. Jenna had to walk a fine line with her mom now.

Her chest tightened again at the thought of her mother's betrayal. She'd been keeping secrets. Lying to her. There was no way to un-know that.

She wanted to call her mom on it and demand answers, but she bit her lip instead and focused on the peanut butter she was spreading. That confrontation could wait. It would have to. Her mother was dying.

No matter how angry she felt, she wouldn't risk her mom's life by venting. In her head, she heard her aunt's warning that stress could be fatal.

Mae didn't remember the events of that evening three weeks ago. She'd slept far into the next day, waking confused but composed. But Jenna remembered every second. And she hadn't said a word.

The knife clattered from her fingers, and she wiped the smear of peanut butter from the counter with unsteady hands. She stepped to the side so her mom wouldn't see her jitters. She had to do this, for both their sakes.

The plan had crystallized in her head that day in the park when she'd looked down at her balaclava and shades lying on the seat of the car. She'd suddenly remembered a patient her mother had talked about years ago—a young woman with a severe case of photosensitivity, an allergic reaction to UV light.

Her mother had mentioned that the patient had to cover her whole body with protective clothing, even when she was exposed to UV rays from fluorescent lighting. The kind you might find in a school.

It was that detail that had gotten Jenna's attention that day in the park. It was her ticket into the school.

Of course, she hadn't been inside a school building since she was twelve. Once she had Charms twisting up and down her hands and arms, she would have had to wear a hazmat suit to keep anyone from touching her, and even a hat was against school rules. Her days in a classroom were over.

But now, if everyone believed she'd been diagnosed with an extreme case of photosensitivity, they couldn't question what she wore. She would look...odd. That was true. But no one could stop her from putting on as many layers as she wanted. And she could go to Coldwater High in relative safety.

Three weeks ago, when she'd opened her mom's blue suitcase, she'd found a pad of prescription forms amid the paperwork. So all she had to do was get her mom to resume her old identity as an MD for one minute and fill out a medical excuse.

Convincing Mae, though, had not been easy.

"What's gotten into you?" she'd said, pacing the length of the couch back and forth in front of Jenna. "You only have one semester of school left before you graduate. Why do this now?"

"If I'm wearing a balaclava and a ton of clothes, there's really no risk."

Mae barked out a sarcastic laugh.

Jenna barreled forward. "I'll be eighteen soon. I'll need a job. But my virtual instructors don't know me well enough to be references. Meeting teachers in person could open doors for my future." It sounded like something a mom would want to hear.

Mae fisted her hands on her hips. "Do you remember what school is like?" She leaned forward. "Crowded cafeteria tables. Packed hallways. What if the worst *does* happen?"

"It won't. I'll be careful."

"Jenna Lynn Getty, are you even listening to me?" Mae's eyes bore into her. "What about Michael Stevens?"

She flinched.

"Answer me. Have you forgotten about Michael?"

Anger blazed quick and hot before Jenna could tamp it down. She stood up, facing her mother. "I could never forget him, Mom! Not if I lived for a thousand years." She bolted for her room.

"Jenn, wait."

The strain in her mother's voice brought her up short. With an effort, she reined in the tidal wave of fury and remorse that threatened to swamp her. She couldn't let this escalate. She turned around.

"I'm sorry." Mae sagged onto the couch. "I'm so sorry. You're right. I shouldn't have said that. You live with it every day. I was just angry—scared. Come back and we'll talk about this. Please."

Her mom looked wrung out. Frail. It was easy to forget how fragile her health really was.

She sank down onto the edge of the couch beside her mom. A new angle occurred to her, and she chose her words carefully. "I depend on you for everything. Have you ever thought about that? What would I do if something happened to you?"

Mae swallowed hard and looked away.

Jenna pressed her advantage. "I'd be totally and completely alone." She let the silence linger until her mother finally met her gaze.

"You're sure you want this?"

"More than anything."

Mae nodded once, and the conversation had ended.

Until the next day. It had taken several tries before her mom agreed to write the medical excuse and register her. Reluctantly, Mae met with the school administrators and emailed the teachers, so at least *they* wouldn't flinch at Jenna's strange attire. Of course, there was no way to warn the students.

She tried not to imagine how that was going to go.

She almost dropped the butter knife again when Mae's voice startled her from her thoughts.

"If you're doing this, you should get there early," she said tightly. She turned her back on Jenna and went to the living room window to check on her stunted peace lily.

Jenna could always tell how upset her mom was by counting the number of times she went to that plant. It was her mom's version of a hot bath or yoga music.

Her mother would be fine, Jenna told herself. This was one day of stress, and then it would all be over.

She called out, forcing her voice to stay chipper. "Almost ready." She stuffed her sandwich into a baggie and zipped it into the largest pocket of her backpack, alongside a bag of chips.

Then she went to the closet to put on her navy peacoat. She struggled to get the coat on over all her layers of clothes. Wordlessly, Mae handed Jenna her own oversize white jacket instead.

Jenna headed to the bathroom for one last check, grateful she was cold-natured. Otherwise, she'd die of a heatstroke before the end of the school day. She closed the door behind her and leaned in toward the mirror, tilting her head forward. Crap.

Sure enough, there was another white hair poking straight up, even though she'd already gotten rid of two of them this morning. They were growing unnaturally fast.

Thankfully, her mom had been too distracted to notice. After the way Mae had freaked out three weeks ago over that first hair, Jenna had been careful not to let it happen again.

She plucked it and flushed it down the toilet. She took the long gloves out of her backpack and tugged them on. She pulled on her balaclava, tucking her hair inside. Then she pushed the shades onto her face and grimaced.

She looked like a comic book villain.

It's only for one day, she told herself.

Besides, Lane had seen her dressed this way when he'd changed her tire, and he hadn't treated her any differently. But Lane was...not like anyone else. She imagined seeing him at school. Then she scolded herself for doing it.

She had a mission to accomplish today. Everything else was a distraction. Especially Lane.

She hurried out of the bathroom. Maybe she could slip past her mom on her way out. She didn't want anything to tempt her into a change of heart.

But Mae intercepted her at the door, holding the car keys hostage.

"I don't like the thought of you driving," her mom grumbled.

"The car was your idea. You said you didn't want me taking the bus."

"I know what I said. But I still don't like it." She sighed and handed the keys over.

It was part of their agreement. If Jenna *insisted* on going through with this, Mae argued, she had to take the car in case she needed to make a quick escape. So together, at night, they'd practiced driving the route to school until Mae was reasonably sure Jenna wouldn't crash.

Jenna never mentioned the flat tire she'd already gotten or the strange man in the silver Mercedes who had followed her. She hadn't caught sight of him again, and she hoped he was gone for good. What her mom didn't know wouldn't hurt her.

Mae reached into the pocket of her cardigan and thrust something at her. "Put this in your pocket."

Jenna turned the small canister over in her hands, reading the label. "Pepper spray? Are you kidding me?" She tried to hand it back. "I'm not taking that into a school."

"Yes, you are. You should be glad it's pepper spray. I thought about giving you a gun."

"Mom! Seriously? I would never shoot anybody."

"Which is why you're getting pepper spray." She rolled her eyes. "Just take the spray. I'm not forcing you to use it, but I won't be able to relax unless you have it."

"You won't be able to relax anyway. I know you."

"Then you know I'm not taking no for an answer. Promise me you'll keep it on you."

Jenna wrinkled her nose. "I promise." She slid the pepper spray into her coat pocket. "Happy now?"

"Ecstatic." Mae kissed her cheek through the fabric of the balaclava. "If someone touches your skin, get out of there any way you can."

Jenna pulled away before the fear in her mother's voice dissolved every bit of her courage. "Everything's going to be fine," she said, then privately congratulated herself on the finest acting she'd ever done.

Mae frowned and opened the door. She checked to make sure the coast was clear and waved Jenna off, watching as she hurried down the hall and out of sight.

On the way to school, Jenna had to force herself to loosen her death grip on the steering wheel. She glanced around her, on high alert, but there was no flock of strange birds. There was no silver Mercedes either.

Coldwater High was less than ten minutes from the apartment, but her heartbeat quickened with each passing mile.

Long before she was ready, she pulled into the school driveway. She nabbed a space toward the back of the student parking lot and stopped the car. Then she sat as still as possible, trying to let her shaking subside.

People got out of cars nearby and walked past, but she stalled. Her sense of dread grew as she watched the other students. She did not belong here. What had she been thinking? She glanced over at the colossal concrete school building, wishing it didn't look so much like a prison.

A high voice yelled, "Give it back, Brent!"

Jenna whipped around. A small group was passing right in front of her car, and she slid lower in her seat as she recognized her neighbor, Brent, in the center of the circle. The last time Brent had seen her, she'd been wearing her navy peacoat and a ski mask. But even though she was dressed in white today, she was afraid he would recognize her.

As always, Brent's crooked nose, boxer's build, and short, wavy hair summoned up the image of that other one—Michael. The last person she wanted to think about today.

Brent held a donut high above his head while a smaller boy trailed after him.

"That's supposed to be my breakfast, Brent!"

"We're friends, Dillon. And friends share with friends." Brent stopped in his tracks, and goosebumps lifted beneath the fabric of Jenna's gloves. Why was he stopping?

He pivoted, eyes searching.

She froze. If he saw her, there was no place she could run this time.

But before he could turn all the way around, Dillon batted at his arm in a fit of temper. It drew Brent's attention and made the others laugh. He took a huge bite of the donut, and a wicked grin sliced across his face. "I've had better." He ruffled the smaller boy's hair and walked away, dropping the donut. Dillon scrambled, catching it just before it hit the asphalt.

Jenna's eyes narrowed. She yanked the car door open and got out, feet crunching in the light snow. Her angry breath fogged the air. But then she made herself unclench her fists. The group was already past, and the small boy was cramming what was left of the donut into his mouth, running to catch up with his so-called friends.

She had to focus on why she was here. Although now that she was out of the car, she couldn't seem to make her feet move.

Her mother had told her to report to the cafeteria, get breakfast, and then wait for the bell. But her stomach protested at the thought of food. She would not be eating today.

She stood there gawking at the school until a voice behind her made her spin. "You okay?"

The girl in front of her was about her age, with dark brown skin and a heart-shaped face. Her long locks were twisted up into a ponytail on top of her head. Her hands were in the pockets of her plum-colored coat, and her eyes took in everything at once.

Jenna realized the girl was waiting for something. *What was it she had asked?* She squinted, trying to focus, and then it came to her. She wanted to know if Jenna was okay. "I'm fine," she said, uncomfortable beneath the girl's close gaze.

"Now, that's a lie," the girl said without venom. "Question is, are you lying to me or to yourself?"

She blinked. "Both, probably."

A wide smile broke over the girl's face. "And there's the truth. Walk with me." She motioned for Jenna to follow.

"That's all right. I don't need any help, thanks."

"Another lie." She cocked her head thoughtfully. "Are you or are you not aware that there are two thousand people who go to this school?"

Jenna's jaw sagged. She shook her head.

"And are you or are you not aware that at least half of them are waiting in the cafeteria at this very moment?" The girl eyed her patiently, seeming to expect an answer.

"Not. Aware," Jenna admitted.

She nodded, smiling. "That's what I thought." She thrust her mittened hands back into her coat pockets. "Now, me. I'm bypassing all that mess and heading to a room with just six other people. Plus—possibly—yourself. *If* you'd like to join me. I'll let you take a moment to consider."

An orange butterfly the size of a dinner plate fluttered through the icy air and landed on the side of the girl's head like an outrageous hair clip. It flapped its delicate wings, but the girl didn't notice, gazing steadily at Jenna with her perceptive eyes.

In a flash, Jenna remembered the butterfly she'd seen the day Fore had first appeared—on another brutally cold day. Neither butterfly should have been able to fly—or to even move in this weather. Fore had to be responsible.

Her heart beat faster. This meant she was on the right path, and this girl was the key.

"I'm coming," Jenna told her.

"Good." The orange butterfly lifted away, and the girl started walking. "I didn't take you for a fool, and I'm always glad to be proven right."

Jenna scurried to grab her backpack from the car and catch up.

The girl walked briskly, not even glancing at Jenna. "I haven't seen you before, so unless I'm losing my touch, I'd guess this is your first day. Am I right again?"

"You are."

"Thought so. I had you pegged the moment I saw you. Trust me, if you'd picked the cafeteria, you'd be tossing your cookies right about now. Stop me if I'm wrong."

"That sounds...accurate." Despite her nerves, a smile tugged at the corners of Jenna's mouth. There was something about this girl that she instinctively liked.

"I'm Zinnia, by the way. Zinnia Inkosazana Carter, and yes, that is my real name."

Jenna didn't know how to respond to that. Her confusion must have shown because Zinnia laughed.

"My parents wanted me to have a unique name—a name I had to live up to. Or that's what they always tell me."

Jenna considered that. "I like it."

"I do, too." Zinnia started walking again. "But don't tell my parents I said that."

She hurried after her. "My name is Jenna Getty."

They were nearing the building now, but instead of turning the corner and heading to the front doors, Zinnia led her to a heavy blue side door and banged on it. "Some people go through life never noticing the sunshine until it rains," Zinnia said. "You should know—right now you're standing in the sun. This is your lucky day."

The door opened with a blast of warmth. The jumbled sound of horns, wind instruments, and drums spilled out, and a broad-shouldered student held the band room door wide. "I thought you'd forgotten about me today, Zinnia."

He had the deepest voice Jenna had ever heard.

Zinnia eyed him haughtily. "Have we met?"

"We meet every night in your dreams, and you know it."

"Those would be your dreams, Devonte."

"You're cold, Zinnia Carter. But I could warm you up." He closed the door behind them. "You gonna stay here with me and practice?"

"Nope. Got a TOTEL meeting." She jerked her thumb toward Jenna. "New inductee."

He hooted and glanced at Jenna. "Good luck with that. You're gonna need it."

Jenna's forehead furrowed in confusion.

Devonte turned to Zinnia. "You know where to find me, Ms. Carter."

"Keep dreaming, Devonte." She herded Jenna forward into the band room. "I could eat that man up with a spoon," she whispered. "But don't tell him I said that."

They picked their way around students practicing alone or in clusters, but no one even looked up at them. So far, so good. They moved out of the band room and into a long hall.

Zinnia studied her. "It's not my business, but you know the teachers are gonna make you take all that off, right?"

Jenna reached into her pocket and pulled out a folded square of paper. "I have a medical excuse that says they can't make me."

Zinnia raised her eyebrows in surprise. "Well, all right then! Rebel in the house." She turned and headed for the corner stairs. "Theater room's up here," she said when they reached the top. "But first, I'm going to show you just how lucky you were to run into me today."

They traveled along a hall lined with royal blue lockers, and with every step they took, a sound like a massive hive of bees grew louder and louder. At the end of the hall, they stepped out onto a second-story mezzanine that overlooked the cafeteria below them.

Jenna's eyes widened. Even from this distance, the sight of more than a thousand students staggered her.

Zinnia leaned against the railing, watching her with one raised eyebrow. "Had enough?"

"More than enough." She backed away from the edge.

"It's important you understand your options." Zinnia pushed off from the rail and strolled toward another heavy blue door. "Here we are." She was reaching for the handle when she paused. For the first time, she seemed hesitant.

"I should probably warn you. Kelsea is...." She frowned. "I mean, she's not really...." Zinnia sighed and shrugged. "The truth is, Kelsea's a raging lunatic. And also one of the best people I know." She smiled slyly. "But don't tell her I said that."

She pulled the door open and motioned Jenna forward. "After you."

CHAPTER ELEVEN

TOTEL COMMITMENT

Whatever Jenna had been expecting, it was not this.

At the far end of the room was a stage. In the middle of the stage was a throne. And on the throne was a short young woman regarding her imperiously. Upside down.

The girl sat—*was "sat" the right word?*—in the throne with her legs straight up in the air where her back should have been. Her head hung over the edge of the seat, and her cloud of wavy hair floated down toward the floor.

The eyes behind her wire-framed glasses were unblinking, and none of her clothes matched, as if she'd gotten dressed with the lights off. She had smooth, dark brown skin, and her fingers were laced comfortably over her stomach, as if she sat this way all the time.

That was the first thing Jenna noticed.

The second thing she noticed was the room itself. It was massive, with black walls and no desks. It was mostly just empty gray carpet. Around the edges, though, were assorted furniture pieces, platforms, painted flats, shelves full of props, an old upright piano, and several heavy costume racks.

And there were other people in the room, too.

Nearby, a wiry boy with light brown skin lay flat on the floor, asleep. He wore long shorts and a Hawaiian shirt. He rolled onto his side, waking briefly to check his lime green watch. Then he went back to snoring, unbothered by their arrival.

Jenna had to do a double take when she noticed the dark-haired girl dressed all in black. She sat at the top of a six-foot scaffold in one corner, and at first Jenna thought she had Charms. Black marks snaked up and down the girl's light brown arms. But then she pulled the cap off a Sharpie with her teeth and went back to inking the bare skin of her hand.

Just like the boy in the Hawaiian shirt, she wore a lime green watch, but it slipped off her wrist as she drew. She slapped it back on and inked around it, making it part of the enormous tarantula she was drawing. She didn't look up at Jenna, and her downcast eyes matched her sullen expression.

Beside the scaffold, another girl sat cross-legged on the floor. She wore a billowy, ankle-length skirt and a powder-blue blouse that blended in with the tufted couch she was leaning against.

Everything about her was round: her eyes, her face, her figure—even her hair curled in loose honey-colored spirals. And she was scratching the head of a fuzzy brown-and-white guinea pig she had nestled in her lap. She smiled shyly at Jenna, her cheeks flushing pink.

The room was silent.

Nothing in her past had prepared Jenna for…this.

She'd been so certain she was supposed to follow Zinnia. Had she misinterpreted Fore's sign? What had she just walked into?

Aunt Serene had said there could be an object she needed to retrieve from the school, and this space was chock full of stuff. Maybe that's why she was here. But if something was hidden in here, she had no clue how to find it.

A commanding voice rang out across the room. "You're late."

Zinnia stepped forward, unfazed. "A throne, Kelsea? Really? Isn't that a little over the top, even for you?"

Kelsea righted herself in one fluid movement. "Not at all. I'm certain I was a queen in a past life. The throne still suits me."

Zinnia snorted. "I've got a new recruit," she said, gesturing at Jenna.

Kelsea narrowed her eyes. "Indeed."

Jenna spoke up quickly, waving her hands in denial, "Oh, no. I'm not a new recruit. I—"

But Kelsea wasn't listening. She was already in motion. She pulled a whistle from around her neck and blew it. Then she raised her voice. "Okay, people. Everybody, front and center!"

Two boys Jenna hadn't seen before clambered out from behind a nearby rack of costumes. One was scrawny, and the other was massive.

"The twins," Zinnia noted as they passed.

The short one had light brown skin and looked like he belonged in elementary, not high school. He had on skinny jeans and a black T-shirt with a picture of a game controller on the front.

The other boy was tall, blond, and broad-shouldered. He could have been a linebacker—or maybe one of those guys who tossed giant logs end over end for fun. He wore tan cargo pants with multiple pockets, and he had a canvas army surplus backpack he carried over both shoulders.

The two boys couldn't have been more different. *Twins?* she wondered.

"They're not blood, obviously," Zinnia said, answering her unspoken question, "but they might as well be. They're inseparable, those two."

The shorter twin caught sight of Jenna. He grinned and put his hands in his pockets, making a beeline for her. The larger twin tagged along reluctantly.

The short boy thrust his hand out. He came so close she took an automatic step backward.

"I'm Jose," he said. "Nice to meet you."

Zinnia's arm shot out. She grabbed his wrist and twisted his hand over.

He had a round metal buzzer nestled inside his palm.

"I've told you before, Jose. No pranks. I won't have your nonsense in here." She flung his hand away in disgust.

His smile vanished. "Thanks a lot, Zinnia! You spoiled my joke." He stomped off in a huff, and the taller boy trailed sheepishly after him.

"Jose is one of the Gonzalez siblings," Zinnia said, as if that explained everything. She heaved a sigh as she herded Jenna toward where the group was gathering.

All at once it clicked in Jenna's head. The sullen girl dressed in black, the sleeping boy in the Hawaiian shirt, and this boy—Jose—they were siblings. Their faces were eerily similar, even though they dressed nothing alike.

A closet door swung open as Zinnia and Jenna walked by, and a boy wearing a black-and-white embroidered sweater and parachute pants stepped out. He had dark olive skin, and Jenna had a hard time guessing his ethnicity. Maybe he was part Asian and part African American?

He stopped short when he saw her. "Wouldn't you know it? Somebody new shows up and I've already come out of the closet."

Jenna's mouth opened, but she was speechless.

He fluttered his lashes at her. "Laughter's not a crime, sweetie."

"She'd laugh if it was a joke, Markese," Zinnia said.

He breezed by them. "Only the truth is funny."

"What did you say this group was?" Jenna asked.

"We're called TOTEL, but we start most meetings in Thinking Stations. That's what you're seeing." Zinnia strolled to join the others.

"Thinking Stations. What does that even mean?" Jenna had no choice but to follow. She eyed the gathering students warily.

"Kelsea's theory is that looking at the world in a new way…well, helps you look at the world in a new way. It sparks ideas. Or it's supposed to, anyway. So we find strange places to be, different angles to see from." Zinnia shrugged. "It's also possible that Kelsea just thinks it's fun."

"Okay. That's…interesting, but what I mean is, what kind of group is this? The Drama Club?"

"What gave you that idea?"

Everything. Everything had given her that idea. Her brow furrowed. "If you're not the Drama Club, what are you? Is TOTEL—"

Another of Kelsea's eardrum-piercing whistles cut her off. "What's wrong with you people? We're running out of time! Let's get going."

The others sat in a large circle in the middle of the room, and Zinnia joined them. Awkwardly, Jenna did the same. She edged as far away as possible, though. Direct contact was the last thing she needed.

She wished Fore would send her a sign right about now. Since the enormous butterfly had appeared in the parking lot, the only weird thing she'd seen was this group of people. She glanced around, studying them.

Beside her, Zinnia was speaking in a low voice to Markese. On Jenna's other side, the girl dressed in black was holding on to the forearm of the curly-haired girl with the guinea pig. She'd already drawn the word "DOC" on the other girl's skin, and now she was embellishing her artwork with intricate curves that made Jenna think of an ornate wrought-iron fence.

"That tickles, Lita," the curly-haired girl said.

But the other girl only grunted and kept drawing.

Now that she was closer, Jenna could see that the girl in black had the word "LITA" penned on her own forearm—her name, she realized.

And Doc must be the name of the curly-haired girl.

Lita had embellished her own name with an elaborate spiderweb, and she'd covered her arms and ankles with dozens of other drawings: black roses, weeping eyes, and strange moths.

Jenna raised her eyebrows and looked away.

The boy in the Hawaiian shirt and shorts sidled between Doc and Jose and sprawled on the floor, right in the center of the circle. The guinea pig in Doc's lap made high-pitched whistling noises at him until Doc shifted the little creature, fished in her purse, and fed him a carrot.

The boy must have sensed Jenna watching him, though, because he rolled over onto his side and stared openly at her with his head propped on his hand and a puzzled expression on his face.

He also had his name inked onto his forearm. "NARDO," Jenna read, and Lita had decorated his name with large hibiscus flowers like the ones on his Hawaiian shirt.

Uncomfortable being stared at, she quickly looked away.

Across the circle, the twins sat together. Jose, the other Gonzalez sibling, was thrashing back and forth, playing a video game on his Nintendo DS.

The larger boy watched him play, only occasionally glancing down to check his work as he crocheted what looked like a half-finished hacky sack. A long strand of yarn stretched from his crochet hook to a side pocket of his canvas sack.

Beside him, Kelsea had stacked a pile of textbooks in front of her. She rummaged now in her backpack and produced a wooden gavel. With relish, she pounded it against the textbooks, making everyone flinch. "This TOTEL meeting will come to order."

"Kelsea loves that gavel," Zinnia whispered behind her hand. "She's had it since she was ten."

Oblivious, the twins stayed focused on their own activities until Kelsea reached over and hammered the gavel on the carpet between them. "Jose and Hampton, either you put that stuff away now, or I will use this gavel in a way you won't like."

They scowled, and Jose tucked his DS out of Kelsea's reach while Hampton shoved his crochet hook and yarn back inside his pack. Nardo sat up, and across the circle, Lita capped her Sharpie. All eyes were on Kelsea.

"Time for the pledge," she chirped. She counted down with her fingers, and then at her signal, everyone in the circle chanted the words together.

"I will seek the truth, defend the defenseless, right the wrong, and stand up for fairies."

"Amen," Markese called out as suppressed laughter bubbled up around the circle.

Kelsea clenched her fists, spluttering. "No, no, no. How many times do I have to tell you people? It's *fairNESS,* not *fairies.* I will stand up for *FAIRNESS.*"

"And also for fairies." A smile hovered at the corners of Markese's mouth.

Kelsea threw her hands up in the air. "Fine. I will also stand up for fairies, Markese. Are you satisfied?" She rolled her eyes. "Let's keep moving."

She smacked the gavel against her pile of books again for good measure. "Thinking Stations, report!" she commanded. "Any breakthroughs today?" She looked eagerly around the circle, but no one spoke up.

"Come on, people," she groaned. "We're still looking for our shiny, sparkly, exceptionally stupendous idea. I'm calling a TOTEL meeting every morning until we've got something to work with. It's time for Operation: Let's Get Inspired."

The people in the circle shrugged and murmured in reluctant agreement.

Kelsea brightened. "Moving on to other business, today we have a new member who's going to critique our rehearsal."

It took Jenna a moment to realize that Kelsea was talking about her. She had a powerful impulse to get up and walk out, but she thought again of the orange butterfly that had landed on Zinnia. Fore had guided her here, and there was something in this room she needed to find. She had to be patient.

She waved vaguely.

"This is Jenna Getty," Zinnia jumped in to explain. "I met her in the parking lot this morning and thought she'd be a good fit for us. Today's her first day, so play nice."

The silence stretched, and Jenna wondered if they expected her to make a speech.

Kelsea peered at her over the top of her wire glasses. "Why are you dressed like that? Are you just religious, or do you have scars or a disease, or what?"

Zinnia moaned and covered her face with her hands. "You are so wrong for that, Kelsea. See, this is why we can't keep new members. You either scare them away or you piss them off."

"Amen," Markese said again.

Kelsea was unmoved. "I only said what everyone else was thinking, Zinnia. No need to freak." She turned to Jenna. "It's nothing personal."

"Actually, I'm happy to tell you why I'm wearing all this." It was the perfect opportunity to try out her lie. She cleared her throat and spoke so they could all hear. "I have a rare kind of photosensitivity, and I have to keep my skin out of the light."

A spark of inspiration struck. "Also, my skin is covered in blisters, so please don't touch me because that would be extremely painful." Hopefully, that little speech would keep them all at a distance. "Does that make sense?" she asked when no one said anything.

"Indeed," Kelsea answered for everyone. "Can you fill her in while we get set?" she asked Zinnia.

"Yeah, fine, I got this," Zinnia said.

Jenna's eyes widened. She'd expected disgust, or at least pity. But no one was even looking at her.

There was a wild scramble as people moved furniture and fetched props.

She wondered if she could make some excuse to Zinnia and use the distraction to search the room, but Markese planted himself on her other side, hemming her in.

"Are we dishing dirt here, girls? Count me in."

"Not dirt, Markese. Data," Zinnia said. "The problem is where to start."

"Best start with Kelsea," he advised. "Everything does."

"Now that's the truth." She turned to Jenna. "TOTEL is Kelsea's brainchild. She's the one who got Ms. Chester to let us meet here in the mornings—even though we're most definitely NOT the Drama Club," she said pointedly. "So I guess you'd say Kelsea's our president."

"But don't you call her that," Markese warned. "She likes to be called…," he put up air quotes, "*Presidempress*." He shook his head at Jenna. "Don't ask, girl. Don't even ask."

Zinnia considered. "It's Kelsea's brand of crazy. Think of it as free entertainment. Every once in a while, it's charming." She looked at Jenna. "But don't tell her I said that."

Markese pointed his finger at Jenna. "Hold up. I'm getting a vibe here. Let me guess." He squinted at her. "You're a water sign, aren't you? A Pisces. I have a sense about these things."

"I'm an Aries, actually."

He sucked in a breath. "Oh, my lord. Fire sign." He turned to Zinnia. "Keep an eye on this one."

Then he pulled out his cell phone. "Group shot! This is going on my Instagram. Smile and say *Tease!*" He held the phone out at arm's length and leaned in so close Jenna flinched behind the fabric of her balaclava.

He snapped the photo, and she breathed again as Markese leaned away.

"Lights and sound are ready, Kelsea."

Jenna turned around and looked behind her. The girl in black, Lita, sat inside a darkened light booth in the back of the room. The glow from her laptop illuminated her morose expression.

Markese and Zinnia exchanged glances.

"How Lita can make every sentence sound like a sigh, I will never know," Markese said. "One time she wished me happy birthday, and I almost cried."

"Hush, Markese. She's doing the best she can." Zinnia caught Jenna's eye. "Lita is a whiz with anything electronic. Kelsea calls her our techspert."

"And that's her younger brother, Jose, over there by the throne." Markese pointed out the smaller of the so-called twins. He shook his head slowly, watching Jose. "Girl, pray for a growth spurt."

"Stop it, Markese," Zinnia said. "And that," she gestured to the tall blond boy beside him, "is Hampton." They all watched as Hampton easily hefted the throne and carried it offstage.

"He's strong," Jenna observed.

"And, I'm sad to say, straight as an arrow." Markese turned to Jenna. "Girl, pray for a miracle."

She raised an eyebrow, but her curiosity got the better of her. Doc was onstage, tucking her guinea pig into a cylindrical case she wore strapped across her body. "What's the deal with the guinea pig?" she asked.

"Is that what she's got today?" Zinnia leaned forward for a closer look. "I love the girl, but if you knew some of the creatures she has carted into this room.... Don't get me started."

"She promised us no more snakes, Zinnia." Markese turned conspiratorially to Jenna. "Doc's always got an animal hidden away on her. Always. Nardo used to call her Dr. Dolittle, but over the years it got shortened to Doc."

She nodded. "Got it." She took a breath and tried again. "But what I still don't understand is what TOTEL is supposed—"

Kelsea's whistle sounded once more. She aimed her glare straight at the three of them. "All right, Gossip Girls, time's up." She raised her voice. "Places, people!"

Markese got to his feet and looked down at Jenna. "You should have left when you had the chance." He stepped up onto the stage.

"Don't pay him any mind," Zinnia said soothingly.

But Jenna was already trying to figure out a way to explore the room. "Aren't you in this?" she asked, hoping she might be left alone for a few minutes.

"I was smart enough to volunteer to be assistant director. And with Kelsea around, that means all I have to do is sit and watch."

"But don't tell Kelsea you said that," Jenna added.

She nodded approvingly. "You got it."

At that moment, Jenna jerked to attention as a tiny orange butterfly the size of a dime fluttered past her face.

"You okay?" Zinnia asked.

"Fine." She jumped up. "But my...my leg is cramping. I need to walk around." She hurried after the butterfly.

She watched to see if this butterfly would guide her to an object like Aunt Serene had suggested, but it stayed aloft. If there was a pattern to its movement, she couldn't see it.

Behind her, she heard Kelsea yell at Jose. "Exactly what were you planning to do with those sausage links? You just got ketchup all over the stage!"

"I'm playing a zombie, right?" Jose defended himself. "The ketchup is blood, and the sausages are brains. It'll be a cool effect when I eat them."

Outraged, Kelsea blasted the boy, but Jenna tuned her out. The butterfly flitted over to the scaffold in the corner and flew even higher.

She trailed it, stepping up onto the tufted powder-blue sofa. Then she grabbed a rung of the scaffold's ladder and climbed.

She reached the top rung, and for a moment she thought she'd lost the thing. But there it was, perched on the steel deck. Doing nothing.

It hadn't led her to anything.

And then a thought occurred to her. Maybe the butterfly wasn't leading her *to* something. Maybe *it* was the thing she was supposed to find. She needed to catch it.

Careful not to frighten it, she let go and balanced with her weight forward, reaching with cupped hands. But the motion startled the butterfly, and it flitted straight up and back over Jenna's head. Cursing, she leaped for it, trying to cage it loosely in the fingers of one hand.

Before she could stop herself, she was toppling backward off the ladder. Her hand clenched into a fist as panic seized her, and she cried out. She fell backward onto the powder-blue sofa.

She let out her breath in relief. She wasn't injured. But she looked at her clenched fist and winced. There was no way the butterfly could have survived.

She uncurled her fingers, expecting to see its mangled orange body, but there was nothing there. She blinked. Somehow, the butterfly had gotten away.

Footsteps pounded toward her.

She sat up abruptly as Kelsea and the other TOTEL members raced over. Crap! She couldn't let them help her up. "Don't touch!" She held up both of her hands, and they halted in their tracks, uncertain. Jenna stood up. "It's okay. I'm not hurt."

"What did you think you were doing?" Kelsea demanded.

"I...." She glanced at the circle of confused faces. What could she say that wouldn't sound crazy? "I wanted to try out Thinking Stations," she said quickly.

Kelsea rolled her eyes. "We do that at the *beginning* of meetings, Jenna Getty."

Zinnia piped up. "We've got extra cleaning to do, and we're at three minutes to the bell, Kelsea. Let's table the discussion until tomorrow."

Jenna closed her eyes and gave a silent thanks for Zinnia.

"Three minutes? Well, bat barf." Kelsea wheeled on Jose and Hampton. "You two clean that mess up before Ms. Chester sees it. Everybody else, room reset!"

They all scrambled to put the room back in order and pack up to go.

Kelsea swung toward Jenna. "I need to see your schedule."

Jenna frowned but complied, retrieving her schedule from her backpack.

Kelsea studied it, nodding.

A plump teacher wearing a colorful scarf walked in, and Kelsea hurried to meet her at the door with a smile. "Ms. Chester, we've got a new student today. I'll need passes."

Ms. Chester flipped through her papers and didn't even look up. "Fill them out and I'll sign them," she said absently. "You know where to find them."

"Indeed." Kelsea opened a drawer in the corner desk. She pulled out a pad of passes and scrawled the needed information. She handed the pad off to Ms. Chester, who signed one pass after another, barely glancing down.

"Are you meeting again tomorrow, dear?"

"Indeed." Kelsea swung around and addressed the group. "Same time and place tomorrow, people. Come with thinking caps preloaded."

She ripped off the passes one by one and handed them out to the others. "Check out your room assignments, and talk to me if there's a problem." Then she rounded on Jenna, thrusting the schedule back at her. "When the bell rings, stay put. One of us will come and get you."

Jenna took the paper from Kelsea before the truth dawned on her. They were going to escort her from class to class.

She grimaced. It had been one thing to choose these people when her only other option was a crowd of more than a thousand students. It was another thing to make plans to see them later, as if they were friends.

"I'm fine," she told Kelsea and Zinnia. "I don't need—"

Zinnia held up her hand. "Sorry, but I have to cut you off. You've exceeded our daily limit on lying."

"You've got first period?" Kelsea asked her.

"Got it." Zinnia pursed her lips at Jenna. "The truth is, you need all the help you can get. Am I wrong?"

"Everybody in!" Kelsea called.

Jenna stood apart as the group drew into a tight circle, hands stretching into the middle.

Kelsea raised her voice again. "TOTEL commitment in three-two-one...."

"TOTEL commitment!" the group chorused, lifting their hands in unison.

The group dispersed, and Kelsea wheeled around. "So, Jenna Getty, are you in?" The small orange butterfly flew out from behind the girl and perched on her shoulder.

Jenna's eyes widened, and she sighed in resignation. Apparently, she wasn't done here yet, and Fore wanted to make sure she knew it.

"Uh, yeah. Yes. I'm in." *For today,* she added silently, shouldering her backpack.

Kelsea beamed. "Excellent. I'll see you after third period." She pivoted on her heel and marched away, shouting instructions.

The bell chimed, and Jenna narrowed her eyes suspiciously at Zinnia. "What is this group?"

"I didn't tell you?" Her eyes sparkled with mischief as she strolled to the heavy hall door. She grinned and swung the door open. "This is the Take Over the Earth League—TOTEL for short. And you, Jenna Getty, are our newest member. I told you this was your lucky day."

They stepped out into a crowded hallway that was straight out of Jenna's nightmares.

Chapter Twelve

TOUCHED

There was nowhere for Jenna to hide.

Her appearance caused a murmur of horrified excitement that rippled up and down the hall. People stared, as if she had a neon "Freak!" sign blinking above her head.

Whispers snaked across mouths. Heads turned and didn't look away. Elbows nudged. Eyes narrowed.

And her face burned beneath the fabric of the balaclava.

"Don't let them bother you." Concern creased Zinnia's forehead. "You're not going to hurl, are you?"

Jenna gritted her teeth. "I can do this." She'd hug the wall on one side, and Zinnia would keep anyone from bumping into her on the other side.

She pulled a binder out of her backpack and held it in front of her like a shield. Then she slung the backpack over her shoulders. Hopefully, it would work as a buffer against the person walking behind her.

She nodded at Zinnia, and they plunged into the river of students.

The one advantage of her strange appearance was that people gave her extra room, as if they were afraid of catching something. She and Zinnia pressed forward inside a tiny bubble of open space.

The hallways seemed to stretch on forever, and after several turns, she was hopelessly lost. Panic threatened to drown her, but at that moment Zinnia herded her past a distracted teacher and through a doorway.

She blinked as she stumbled into the first real classroom she'd seen in five years. It was familiar in so many ways: the rows of worn desks, the newly waxed floors, the smell of sneakers and pencil shavings. Those things were reassuring.

But the faces that turned toward her wore expressions that ranged from worried to hostile.

She brushed all of it off. She was here for one reason, and it wasn't to make friends.

Zinnia raised an eyebrow. "You good?"

"Sure." She couldn't quite meet her eyes.

Zinnia took pity on her and ignored the lie. "Markese will be here to get you when the bell rings. Hang on to your insides until then." And then she was gone, leaving Jenna to fend for herself.

It was the first day of a new semester, so students were jostling to claim seats.

She hurried toward an open desk in the back corner, ignoring the whispers that raced around the room like wildfire as her classmates noticed her.

Afterward, she remembered only two things about that class, and neither one had anything to do with economics.

The first thing she remembered was the way everyone stared at her during roll call. Her throat caught as she tried to say "here," and the other students exchanged horrified glances until her coughing fit subsided.

They probably thought she had the plague.

The other thing she remembered was the look of disgust on one girl's face as she stole a glance at her gloved hands. She didn't blame the girl for that look. If she knew how dangerous Jenna *really* was, her disgust would have changed to terror.

The rest of first period passed in a haze. Absorbed in her own thoughts, she jumped when the bell rang. She had a page full of notes she didn't remember taking.

For a moment, she considered striking out alone for her next class, but then she thought about the crowded hallway and resigned herself to waiting for Markese.

She drummed her fingers on the desk. Fore hadn't sent her a single sign during first period. Was she doing something wrong?

Just then, Markese popped into the room. "Hello, hello Cinderella. Your fairy godmother's here to whisk you away, but if we run in to any handsome princes, I call dibs."

A smile pulled at her lips—at least until she followed Markese back into the packed hallway. But this time around was easier, if only because she knew what to expect.

She changed classes without any disasters, and second period was as uneventful as first period. She weathered the whispers and the suspicious glances, ignoring all of it. But why was there still no sign from Fore? She wanted to see...something—an orange butterfly, a bird at the window. Anything.

The day was half over, and dread began to creep through her. What if she had to come here again tomorrow? It was an unsettling thought.

Doc poked her head around the doorjamb, her honey-brown spirals bouncing. Her voice was gentle as she asked, "How are things going?"

"I'm surviving." Jenna stood up and stuffed her notebook into her backpack.

Doc paused in the doorway. "I...um...I wondered if maybe you'd like to join me and my dad for lunch instead of going to the cafeteria. He's a teacher, and I usually eat with him. We could turn the classroom lights off for you." She shuffled her feet. "But if you don't want to, I understand."

The girl was so friendly. *Too friendly*, Jenna thought. She'd be inviting her to slumber parties before lunch was over.

She should definitely refuse.

But she hadn't thought about the fact that she couldn't eat without removing her balaclava. With Doc, there'd be less of a chance of a stray touch than in the cafeteria. "Thanks," Jenna said. "I'll take you up on that."

"Oh yeah?" Doc made the word "yeah" sound like "yah." Her curls bounced as she nodded. "Great! It's this way."

Jenna followed her through the maze of halls until they reached the end of a long corridor.

Doc turned the fluorescent lights off as she entered the classroom. "That's safer for you, isn't it?" She waved Jenna over to the corner where there was a rug and a couple of big pillows. "Be right there. I need to feed my little ones first."

She ducked inside the closet and removed a cage that held her guinea pig. Then she fed the excited fuzzball salad greens from her lunchbox.

Jenna peeled off her balaclava and unzipped the pouch in her backpack with her peanut butter and jelly sandwich. Her stomach growled, and she took a huge bite as she looked up.

Doc had a gigantic millipede crawling up one arm, and Jenna froze. Finally,

Fore was trying to show her something.

Then the girl scooped the millipede up and set it down in a shallow bowl.

"You see the millipede, too?" Jenna blurted.

Doc sat back on her heels, eyeing her strangely. "Of course." She paused. "Are you sure you're okay?"

She shook herself. This was not a sign from Fore. It was just another of Doc's animals. "Um, I meant to say...why do you have it? Here at school."

Her worried expression vanished. "Oh, that." She took tiny banana slices out of a Tupperware container and set them alongside the millipede. "Well, my pets make me feel less nervous. I can even carry Milly with me, and the other teachers never know." She stroked Milly fondly. Then she scratched the guinea pig under the chin.

Jenna shook her head. "It's like *Animal Planet* in here."

"You should see my house," Doc laughed. "At last count there were three cats, a parrot, two mice, three goats, a dog, five chickens, four guinea pigs, a lizard, a frog, two snakes, and—oh, an aquarium." She squinted up at the ceiling, puzzled. "I know I'm leaving somebody out...."

Just then, a tall man with a mustache walked in carrying a stack of papers.

Doc spoke up. "This is my dad, Mr. Lindgren. He's a teacher here."

But Jenna barely heard her. Her throat tightened. Doc's father looked almost nothing like her own dad. He'd been shorter, with curly brown hair and a square jaw. But there was something about Mr. Lindgren—something about the way he looked at Doc—that brought her own father powerfully into her mind.

Her breath quickened, and she scrambled to her feet, clutching her backpack. "I'm sorry, but I have to find a bathroom."

She ignored their surprised faces and rushed past them into the hall. With one hand, she yanked on her balaclava. Then she broke into a run, pounding along the waxed floors until she came across a bathroom.

She darted inside one of the beige stalls and locked the door behind her. Her back against the door, she put her hands on her knees and gasped for breath, fighting to regain control.

When she'd left home five years ago, she'd missed her father so much she'd prowled that first apartment like a tiger in a cage. She'd tried to tell herself that the separation was no different from when her dad went on business trips. Except this time, she and her mom had done the leaving. She'd paced a U-shaped path around her bed until the carpet looked as beaten as she felt.

But then, overnight, everything had changed. Her mom told her that her father had died in a car accident. And suddenly, Jenna couldn't move at all.

Mae would come to check on her, and she'd blink away the fog, wondering how half a day had passed while she sat in her too-stiff desk chair, seeing nothing.

Her blood had turned to sand. Raising her head, standing up, even moving her fingers meant lifting a heavy weight. It was easier to sit in stillness and silence. Or to sleep—when sleep would come.

They moved apartments, and then they moved again. The chairs were different. The beds were different. She was the same. She crawled under the covers and hibernated.

And slowly—very slowly—the weight had lifted. She woke up. When her mother asked how she was doing, she found she could answer.

Fine. She was fine. That awful four-letter word beginning with *F*.

Her breath caught as she heard someone come into the bathroom. Doc's gentle voice whispered, "Jenna? Are you okay?"

"I'm fine," she said. "Don't worry about me."

"It's just that I thought maybe with your health and everything—"

"Nope. I'm good."

Doc was silent. "Well, at least take this hall pass. I don't want you to get in trouble if a teacher or a monitor comes in." She held the blue paper up above the top of the stall door, and Jenna took it, careful to keep their fingers from touching.

She waited for Doc to leave, but there was only silence.

"Did I say something wrong?" Doc asked miserably.

"No, you...." Jenna berated herself. This was why she stayed away from other people. All she ever did was hurt them. She tried to explain. "You didn't do anything. But your dad.... He reminded me of my dad.... And my dad is dead."

It was strange to say it like that. She'd never told anyone. There hadn't been anyone to tell. She swallowed.

"Oh," Doc breathed. "I'm so sorry."

"I'll be fine, but I'd like to stay here a while longer."

"Okay, but if you change your mind, you're welcome back." Doc rummaged through her purse. "I'll come get you before the bell and take you to your next class. But call if you need me." Above the door, she held up another scrap of paper. In pretty, looping handwriting, she'd written down her name and phone number.

Jenna took it. "Thanks," she mumbled as Doc's footsteps faded away. Even though she'd never use it, it was nice to think she had one phone number besides her mom's. Or Aunt Serene's.

Aunt Serene. It struck her. This was the perfect chance to call. And she could use the distraction right now. She pulled out her cell phone and dialed.

Serene picked up almost at once. "Jenna! What have you found?"

Jenna launched into a description of everything she'd seen so far—the giant orange butterfly, the smaller orange butterfly, and even the strange group of students from TOTEL.

"This is exciting! Fore is cooperating with someone for the first time in ages. Can you come to the park right after school? I want to hear more, and I'll see if my friends have any ideas about the butterflies. But this is fantastic, Jenna. Keep up the good work!"

Her shoulders slumped. Her aunt was so proud, and she'd ruin that if she told her how much she hated this. She injected her voice with false cheer. "See you after school." Then she hung up.

She raised her eyes to the ceiling. "Fore?" she whispered. "If you can hear me, I'd love another sign. The sooner the better. If we could wrap this up by the end of the day, that would be great."

But the bathroom was silent, and she spent the rest of lunch brooding, too worked up to eat.

Doc returned a few minutes before the bell. Thankfully, she didn't say a word about their conversation earlier. She only asked, "You have Ms. Ortiz next?"

At Jenna's nod, she led the way out of the bathroom and into the hall. "This route is longer, but it's not as crowded." They left the main hallway, turning a corner to climb a back staircase. A brash male voice made Doc jump, and they stumbled to a halt.

"Should I text her with your phone, Dillon?"

On the landing, a group of guys stood in a loose circle around one person—Brent. Jenna winced as she recognized him. Just like this morning, he held something out of reach of the shortest boy, Dillon—the same one he'd stolen the donut from in the parking lot.

Jenna's anger surged, and she pressed her lips together to keep herself from saying something. Did Brent think this game would be funny again?

Apparently, he did. He held Dillon's phone above his head and spoke slowly as he keyed in a text message with his thumbs. "*Celia U R so hot.*"

Laughter and catcalls rippled around the circle.

"Don't, Brent," Dillon said, his face tight with humiliation.

Doc edged backward, whispering, "We should go."

But Jenna couldn't tear her eyes away.

Dillon's protests only egged Brent on. "*Luv U sexy!* Kissy face emoji. Heart emoji."

The group roared, and Jenna's expression darkened.

Brent lowered the phone slightly, looking at the circle of guys for support. "Should I press *send*?" he asked. "What do you think?"

She lashed out before she had time to consider. "*I* think you wouldn't be interested in Dillon's love life if you had one of your own."

Brent's attention swung to her. Fury and...something else...flashed across his features.

Had he recognized her as the person he'd chased three weeks ago at Ashton Place? She was dressed differently, but similarly enough that he might be suspicious.

But he was apparently too distracted by her insult to make the connection. Instead, he threw up his hand in exaggerated horror. "*What* is *that* thing?"

The other boys laughed, and Brent handed Dillon back his phone, never taking his eyes off Jenna. He took a step forward, emboldened, and pointed at her. "This chick is so ugly she has to cover her face."

She felt her cheeks redden beneath the balaclava, but she met Brent's gaze defiantly.

He smacked the small boy on the back. "Good news, Dillon. If she's that ugly, she might actually do you."

Doc motioned urgently. "Come on. We'll go the other way."

They turned to leave, but one of Brent's friends came up behind them. He stood with his feet spread, arms crossed over his chest.

They ground to a halt.

"You can't go yet!" Brent called. "You didn't kiss your boyfriend goodbye!"

The guys cracked up, and dread washed over Jenna.

"One kiss to show how much you love him. That's all he needs." Brent planted his hands on both of Dillon's shoulders.

She was outnumbered and hemmed in. She couldn't fight them all. If it came to force, she'd never avoid being touched.

She glanced at Doc beside her, silent and scared. Maybe she could talk her way out of this. "We just want to go to class. Let us get by."

"The mummy speaks!" Brent said to a chorus of laughter. "No problem. You can go. You just have to give Dillon a little kiss first. That's the price of passage."

The bell rang, and she hoped they'd abandon their game and go to class. But nobody moved.

The buzz of approaching students grew louder, but the boys stood their ground. A thin girl started down the stairs but reversed direction when she saw the guys blocking the landing.

Dillon piped up. "I don't want her to kiss me! I don't know what she looks like under all that stuff."

Brent swatted him. "You should be on your knees thanking me, Dillon. This may be your one and only chance to make out with a real girl." He eyed her up and down. "But you're right. She might be too ugly even for you. You need to take a look at the goods first, right Dillon?"

"Yeah. I want to see what she looks like," Dillon agreed, stepping away from Brent and crossing his arms over his chest.

Jenna blinked in surprise.

Brent smirked at her. "Let's see your face."

Her skin caught fire with suppressed rage. If she showed Brent her face, maybe he'd let the two of them pass. But the idea sickened her. Everything inside her rebelled against giving in to any of his demands.

If she did this, what would he ask her to do next? He might want her to kiss Dillon—and her Charms would infect him at once.

Brent leered. "Take off the mask, and you both can go."

One of the boys began to chant, "Take it off—take it off," and the others joined in.

She tried again. "The bell rang, so please let us by. We have to go to class!"

"You know what to do," Brent shook his head. "Show us your face."

There wasn't any way out. She closed her eyes and moved her hands up to pull the balaclava off. Better to get this over with.

"You must be hard of hearing. She asked you to let her by."

Jenna knew that voice.

His voice.

Lane.

Her eyes flew open, and her jaw dropped behind the fabric of the balaclava.

She watched in stunned silence as Lane's long legs and impossibly blue eyes came into view from above. He stopped near the top of the steps, leaning against the rail.

Brent spun to face him. "What did you say to me?"

"Oh, so you *are* hard of hearing." He nodded his head in sympathy. "That's a relief. I thought you were just stupid."

Jenna choked back a laugh.

For two heartbeats, Brent was shocked into silence. No one in the stairwell dared move or breathe.

"Are you calling me stupid?"

"Well, I don't mean to be rude, but if you have to ask...." He shrugged his shoulders.

With an enraged growl, Brent charged.

Lane watched him come, unmoving, and Jenna took an involuntary step forward. But there was nothing she could do.

Brent stormed up the stairs, but the second he came into range, Lane flashed out one of his long legs and kicked him square in the chest.

The force was just enough to throw him off balance. He flailed and tumbled back down the stairs, curling up on the landing. He lay there groaning and cursing Lane.

Dillon scrambled to his side and propped up his head. The other boys gathered around him.

"After you, ladies," Lane said with a debonair sweep of his arm.

Doc was the first to respond. She scurried around the group on the landing.

Jenna followed, her eyes full of Lane. She veered away from Brent, but as she darted by, he twisted violently toward her. She cried out.

And his hand wrapped around her ankle.

Chapter Thirteen

ALARM

Her body reacted as if a snake had bitten her.

She tore her ankle free and stumbled away, fighting the urge to retch. She whirled to look at him.

He stared back at her, an odd expression on his face.

She raced to identify it. *Shock? Bewilderment?* She couldn't quite read it.

Her heartbeat pounded in her ears, and it was an effort to think. She narrowed her eyes. She had only seconds to make the right decision.

Had he touched her skin?

No. His hand had wrapped around the bottom of her jeans. Even so, her stomach turned over as she remembered the feel of his heavy fingers on her ankle.

He could be one of those people who was ultra-sensitive to her curse. But then, wouldn't he be launching himself toward her right now? He wasn't doing anything but staring.

Everything was fine. It had to be.

The world filled back in, and sound returned suddenly, as if she'd surfaced from a deep pool.

"Come on, Jenna!" Doc motioned wildly, eyeing the boys gathered around Brent.

She'd all but forgotten them. She looked up, and reality slammed into her.

At the top of the stairs, Lane was studying her with one eyebrow quirked. Somehow, he had been there. He'd shown up when she needed him. Again.

She focused on his bright red scarf and hastened up the steps. Still, she could swear Brent's eyes burned into her as she fled.

When she reached the top, Doc and Lane stepped into the hallway traffic, and she followed, trailing behind.

Lane didn't say anything to her about their last meeting when he'd helped her change her tire. Maybe he didn't recognize her, or maybe Doc hadn't stopped talking long enough for him to speak.

"That was so great—what you did back there," Doc said, breathless with enthusiasm. "Thank you so much."

"You're welc—"

"You could have ignored us like everybody else, but you didn't."

"It was no big—"

"So, do you know karate? When you kicked him, it looked like you knew karate."

"Oh no. I know nothing," he said, finally able to squeeze in a sentence. "But I had the advantage of height. Now, if I meet that guy in the hallway, I'm dead meat," he said cheerfully. Then, as if to prove his point, he slipped on the newly waxed floor, catching his balance just in time.

"You are so funny!" Doc laughed. She stopped beside the next classroom door. "Well, thanks for walking us."

"Huh. I think I'm in here too." He fished a schedule out of his pocket and double-checked it against the room number. "Yep. Spanish."

Jenna froze. He was *in* one of her classes? This was not good. How was she supposed to focus on finding signs from Fore with him around?

Doc wrinkled her forehead, confused. "Your class is here? But I thought you were headed downstairs before you ran into us."

"My locker's downstairs. I was going to grab my notebook, but...I'll just have to wing it."

"You can borrow one of mine," Jenna said. Then she cursed herself. Other people could loan him paper. Why had she volunteered?

"Awesome." He turned to her, smiling. "We met a few weeks ago, Rumpelstiltskin. Do you remember me?"

Did *she* remember *him*? Uh, yeah. Yes, she did.

She feigned nonchalance. "Oh, that's right. I knew you looked familiar."

"I'm Lane," he told them both. "Lane McConnell."

She nodded as if it was only now coming back to her, when in fact she knew every detail of his driver's license by heart.

"Thank you so much again for helping us, Lane," Doc told him.

"No problem. That's the most excitement I've had in weeks. I can't wait to tell Brie. Seriously, she's threatening to kill me if I open my mouth about coin collecting again."

Doc giggled. "Coin collecting? That is too funny!"

But Jenna was watching his face, and she didn't think he'd been joking. She was torn between being charmed at this new bit of trivia and annoyed at his casual mention of his girlfriend, Brie.

Doc glanced at her watch. "Well, I should go. See you tomorrow morning," she said to Jenna. She waved goodbye and swung into the flow of passing students.

Lane motioned toward the door. "Shall we?"

A guilty thrill ran through Jenna, but she squelched it and stepped into the classroom.

"I'll let you pick out our seats," he said. "After all, you are my school-supply sugar mama now."

She ignored that, scanning the room. She gestured to the first open desk she saw. "You can take this spot." She unearthed an extra notebook and pen from her backpack and put them on the desk. "See you later," she said without making eye contact. She headed for a desk at the back of the room.

She set her backpack down and was about to sit when Lane snatched the backpack away, shouldering it.

He pointed. "There are two desks together over there. Let's nab those."

She opened her mouth to protest, but he was already striding away. She swallowed hard and followed.

Sinking into the seat behind him, she waited for him to notice the swell of whispers and mutters she'd caused, but he was oblivious. It was oddly comforting.

The bell rang, and the teacher began her spiel. Not even five feet tall, Ms. Ortiz had a fringe of wild white hair around her face, but she radiated energy despite her age. She made quick work of her introduction and jumped straight into the first activity.

"Pair up with someone near you and have a conversation to review your Spanish. You have a few minutes to chat while I make the seating chart."

Lane spun to face Jenna. "Okay if we team up?" he asked in Spanish.

"Um, isn't there somebody else you could…." She trailed off as she realized that everybody else was already talking, leaving only the two of them.

"Sure," she choked out. But suddenly, she couldn't cobble together a coherent sentence, even though she'd had four years of Spanish online. In her other classes, she'd never had to deal with eyes that were a brain-numbing shade of blue.

She groped for a topic, but ideas puffed away like smoke. "You collect coins?" she finally asked in Spanish. Then she gave herself a mental kick. Would he think she was making fun of him?

But the question seemed to excite him. He launched into broken Spanish, throwing in English words here and there when he couldn't find the Spanish equivalents.

"I've been collecting since I was five—ever since my granddad got me started. He loved old coins, antiques, vintage cars, anything like that. Things from the past have stories to tell, he always said. And I agree."

She tilted her head to the side, forgetting to speak in Spanish. "So, you like old stuff?"

"Guilty."

She pointed discreetly at Ms. Ortiz. "Should I try to get her number?"

He laughed, Spanish practice completely forgotten. "I'm too late. She's wearing a wedding ring." Then he leaned forward, looking serious. "Okay, I've confessed to coin collecting. So now you have to tell me about one of your guilty pleasures. What do you do for fun?"

"Fun?" Her mind was blank.

"Yeah. When you're not trapped in stairwells or stranded on the sides of roads, what do you do with your free time? What do you enjoy?"

She prepared a lie in her head. She'd make up a story about friends or shopping or sports. Something.

But when she looked at Lane, he seemed genuinely interested. Her cheeks warmed, and the lie died on her tongue.

"Music," she said quietly. "I taught myself how to play keyboard, and I love it." Then she snapped her mouth closed, embarrassed. Why was she telling him this?

He leaned forward, surveying her with new respect. "That is wicked cool. I've always wished I could play guitar, or any instrument, really. I sing a little, but I've never had lessons, so I don't think it counts. But playing keyboard is awesome! That takes actual skill."

"I guess." She was surprised by his enthusiasm.

"I'm going to change your name from Rumpelstiltskin to Mozart."

She looked down her nose at him. "You will not."

"No. You're right. You don't look like a Mozart." He sat back, squinting his eyes thoughtfully. "Mo is much better. Nice to meet you, Mo." He held his hand out for her to shake it.

She ignored him. "If you call me Mo, I'm going to call you Shirley."

He frowned. "Why Shirley?"

"Because there are no famous coin collectors, Shirley!"

"That's fair." He nodded sagely. "But now I'm intrigued, Mo. I need to know more about you. Where are you from?"

A flicker of apprehension ran up her spine. She didn't want to talk about her past. At all.

"I've moved around so often I'm not really from anywhere," she hedged.

"I can relate." He looked at her sympathetically. "Now, me, I've always lived within thirty miles of here, but I've moved at least seven or eight times inside the Twin Cities. The whole thing—starting over, leaving your friends. It's exhausting, don't you think?"

"It is," she agreed, startled. She'd imagined Lane growing up in the little brick house—the very picture of stability. But it sounded like he'd bounced around a lot. Like her.

"It's my first year at this school, my second semester."

She struggled to process this information. He was almost as new as she was. "Do you like it here?" she asked.

"Well, it sucks to change schools your senior year. Everyone already knows each other, so it's hard to meet people. But they've been okay." His jaw hardened. "Don't judge this place too hard because of those jerks on the stairs."

He looked at her, and his expression softened. "Speaking of that, are you going to be all right?"

"Yeah, I'll be fine. Thanks."

"If they bother you again, let someone know, okay? You don't deserve to be treated that way."

"I appreciate that."

"Some people are threatened by anyone who looks a little...different," he finished awkwardly.

"You mean my shoes?" she asked, deadpan.

He froze. She finally had him at a loss for words.

"I'm kidding," she laughed, letting him off the hook. "I know I look different." She took a deep breath. "And you're probably wondering why."

She told him her invented story—about the light sensitivity and the blisters that caused her to cover her skin. She avoided his painfully sincere eyes as she spoke, staring fixedly at his red scarf instead. Since when was lying difficult for her?

Just as she finished her explanation, Ms. Ortiz got to their desks, seating chart in hand. "Who do I have here?"

She was thankful for the interruption. "I'm Jenna Getty and this is Lane McConnell."

Ms. Ortiz paused only a second longer than she needed to, looking Jenna up and down. She scribbled their names on her clipboard. "These will be your assigned seats, Lane and Jenna." Then she moved on to the last set of desks.

"Jenna?" Lane whispered. "Who's Jenna? I thought you told me your name was Mo. Or was it Rumpelstiltskin? I'm so confused."

Behind her mask, she pursed her lips to keep from smiling. "Shut up, Shirley."

By the end of third period, Jenna worried that Lane was a bigger threat to her than Brent. Brent, she wanted to avoid. Lane, though, was a temptation she had to fight to resist.

She couldn't make herself look away. After sitting behind him for only one class, she knew the texture of his red scarf (ribbed), the cut of his shoulders (square), and the exact shade of his hair (piano key black).

She was supposed to be watching for signs from Fore. But Lane was like a black hole, sucking every single one of her thoughts toward him.

He stood up and turned to her when the bell rang. "If you want, I can walk you to your next class. This place can be confusing. Where are you headed?"

She sat there rooted in place. Did it *mean* something that he wanted to walk with her? Her heart lifted dangerously. Not that she could go with him. Of course, she couldn't.

But, hypothetically, was he asking?

No, she scolded herself. He was just a nice guy. That's all it was.

She looked up and realized he was still waiting for an answer. "Oh, my next class. It's art. I have art," she stammered. "But you see I.... Thank you, I would like that. The walking. But, um, someone is supposed to come get me, I think."

She was rambling, but she didn't know how to stop. "Maybe you can walk me to class another time. Not that you'll need to because I'll know where to go and all, but maybe...." She clamped her lips together to shut herself up.

Before Lane could respond, someone seized his arm from behind and spun him around.

Small as she was, Kelsea had the uncanny ability to tower over people. She examined Lane through her wire-frame glasses. "Is this the one?" she demanded, glancing sideways at Doc, who had edged up beside her.

"That's him," she whispered.

Then Kelsea pumped Lane's hand up and down hard enough to make him wince.

"Congratulations," she beamed. "I am personally extending an invitation for you to join TOTEL."

"That's great," Lane smiled through his pain. "But who are you?"

"Kelsea," Doc and Jenna answered at the same time.

She plowed on. "Doc told me about the way you stepped up today. And that kind of leadership is just what we're looking for." She clapped him heartily on the shoulder, startling him. "Our next meeting is tomorrow morning at seven a.m. in the drama room. We'll see you there."

"Wait, what? TOTEL?" Lane shook his head, backing away. "I'm not interested in joining any clubs right—"

"He'll be there."

Everyone in the room turned to see who had spoken.

Jenna flinched in recognition, and jealousy snaked through her. Brie stood silhouetted in the doorway.

Just as Jenna had feared, she was even more beautiful up close. She was tall, with gleaming blonde hair and porcelain skin. Her lemon-yellow pullover and black leggings showed off her slim form to perfection. She could have graced the cover of a fashion magazine.

"Brie, what are you doing here?" Lane asked.

"I thought I'd catch you before your next class." She crossed her arms and fixed him with a stern gaze. "I think you should go tomorrow. See if you like it."

"Wait, what?" He ran a nervous hand through his hair. "Okay, first, what about you? I won't leave you to go join some club. Not gonna happen."

Jenna fidgeted, feeling like she was trespassing on a private moment. It was as if she wasn't there anymore. None of them were. It was only Lane and Brie, their eyes locked together as something passed wordlessly between them.

Brie sighed in defeat and turned to Kelsea. "Would it be okay if I came along?"

Jenna stopped breathing.

"The more the merrier." Kelsea shrugged, then pointed a commanding finger at Lane. "Tomorrow morning. Drama room. Be there or *beware*." Then she turned on her heel and marched out.

She said something to Jenna as she left, but Jenna didn't hear her. All she could hear was the noise inside her own head—alarm bells blaring in warning.

Chapter Fourteen

PEPPER SPRAY

Jenna arrived at the park a full ten minutes earlier than she'd told her aunt. She'd rushed out of Coldwater High like the building was on fire, and she'd raced the entire way to the park.

She felt justified, though. The sooner she got there, the sooner Aunt Serene could tell her she never needed to set foot in a school again.

Maybe one of her aunt's colleagues would understand Fore's cryptic symbolism and know how to proceed. Or maybe the Unbound had some secret textbook in their possession—*Flying Insects and How to Decode Them.* Or *The Insect Lover's Guide to Portents and Prophecies.* There had to be something.

She'd gotten through the day safely, but she felt strung out. Agitated. Like a can of soda someone had been shaking for hours. And if she wasn't careful, she was going to go off.

She circled the park, noticing with wry humor that the same guy was there again today—the guy with the blond ponytail and the beagle. He didn't look up as he jammed out inside his car.

She parked at the opposite end of the track, in the same spot as last time. There was a family with a baby stroller in the playground area. Near the center of the park, a teenage girl with blue hair sat at the green picnic table talking on her cell phone. And across from her, two young men with baseball gloves tossed a ball back and forth.

It wasn't as deserted as the last time she'd been there, but after navigating crowded classrooms and halls, it felt blissfully empty.

Also, no one was looking at her, and she wanted to keep it that way. She peeled off her balaclava and flung it onto the passenger seat alongside her shades. Then she shrugged out of her white jacket, looking at it with disgust. She was still burning up from wearing it indoors all day.

She was about to put it down when she noticed the weight of something in the jacket pocket. It was the pepper spray her mom had given her that morning. She'd forgotten all about it. She thought about setting it aside, but she'd promised to keep it with her. Dutifully, she shoved the small canister into her jeans pocket.

Then she texted her mom a lie about staying late to get help from a teacher. That should buy her some time.

She stepped out of the car and into the ridiculous cold. It was like shedding an identity, and for once, the temperature didn't bother her. All she cared about was being rid of her bizarre clothing and feeling normal for just a few minutes.

There'd been a light snow the day before, and she hopped up and down, appreciating the crunch of snow underfoot, while she tried to drive blood back into her cramped legs. How did people go to school and sit at desks day after day? And that was the least of it.

The sneering looks, the laughter, the pointing—those things were bad, it was true. But she could ignore them. Brent, though, was a problem. And the people in TOTEL were a problem too, just in a different way. They thought they could recruit her—be her friend. If they knew what she really was, though, they'd barricade the door against her.

And then there was Lane.

Part of her wanted to see him again. The delusional part. But there was no future there. And the thought of watching him exchange lovesick glances with Brie at the TOTEL meeting tomorrow morning made her stomach turn.

She prayed her aunt had found another solution.

Her phone buzzed, and she tapped to answer when she saw her aunt's name come up on the screen. She exploded onto the phone.

"I'm already here at the park, Aunt Serene. Please tell me you know what to do next, because I'm honestly feeling like I'm about to have a heart attack. Could I have a heart attack at age seventeen? Oh, and I didn't tell you that this boy named Brent who also lives in my building touched me today, and I don't know what I should do. So I guess what I'm getting at is, did you figure out the butterflies?"

There was a brief silence before Serene answered. "Jenna, love, I want you to take a deep breath right now. Then stay calm and tell me about the touch."

Jenna paced back and forth on the track while she filled her aunt in on the Brent situation.

When she wound to a stop, Serene said, "I hear you, but think about it. *If* your Charms affected him—and that's a big *if*—this boy Brent doesn't have a quick fuse, or he would have already acted. He wouldn't have been able to help himself. But after the touch, you didn't see him again."

"No," she agreed slowly.

"So listen to me. As long as he doesn't get too close, I would ignore him. Now, if he'd touched your skin and not your jeans, we'd be having a different conversation."

Jenna pressed her lips closed. Of course, Aunt Serene was right, but she had never witnessed Brent's cruel streak. She released a long breath, trying to let it go. Brent was not the most important matter at hand.

"What do you think Fore was telling us?" she asked. "Why did she want me in that school?"

Serene paused. "You're not going to like this. Should we wait and have this conversation when I get there?"

Jenna halted. "No. Tell me now. What won't I like?"

"I'll tell you, but don't freak out. Are you freaking out?"

"I'm still deciding."

Serene sighed. "Well, it seems obvious, doesn't it? Butterflies are a common symbol. They signal change. Transformation. Birth."

There was a long silence.

"If you're about to tell me I could be pregnant, I'm hanging up."

"No, Jenna. Listen. I think the Foremother chose the butterfly because she doesn't want you at home all the time, trapped—if you'll pardon the metaphor—in your cocoon. I think you're the key to a larger change that's coming. Why else would she have led you to me? She wants power to change hands, and it all has to start with you. She sent the butterflies to signal that you're on the right path. And Jenna, that means you have to go back."

"Back," she repeated. She switched the phone to her other ear, trying to process what her aunt was saying. "I have to go back?"

"Yes. Until Fore sends a sign telling you something different."

She couldn't speak. Numb, she left the track and ducked under the limbs of a nearby Scotch pine. The ground here was free of snow, and she crawled forward under the shelter of branches until she reached the trunk. Then she leaned back against the tree, exhausted.

"Are you still there?" Serene asked. "I'm only a couple of minutes away now, and we'll talk about it. But please don't forget what's at stake. Don't forget your mother."

She dropped her head into her hands. "I haven't forgotten."

"So, focus. You need to find out more about that TOTEL group. The butterflies were linked to them. Maybe one of them is more than they appear."

"They seemed pretty normal to me." Jenna paused. "Scratch that. Not *normal*, but none of them had Charms or anything."

At that moment, a giant hornet buzzed close, and Jenna's jaw dropped open. The thing was prehistoric. It was so huge, it looked as if it had swallowed three or four other hornets. And it hovered inches from her face. It had shiny onyx eyes and alternating red-and-black bands that circled its body. And its stinger was massive and sharp. She'd never seen anything like it.

Was this another sign from Fore? Was she supposed to follow it?

Her aunt had been saying something, but Jenna hadn't heard a word. "Aunt Serene, I think—"

She dropped the cell phone and nearly jumped out of her skin as a black cat darted by. It leaped up, batting at the hornet, but the insect was too quick.

It flew behind Jenna and, seconds later, a sharp pain stabbed her between the shoulder blades. She arched forward, clawing at her back to dislodge the thing.

Before she could reach it, though, it zipped away. She ducked under the limbs of the pine and crawled after it on her hands and knees. Was Fore attacking her?

She parted the branches and squinted into the sunlight. There was no sign of the hornet.

In the open area near her, the two young men were still playing catch. The girl with blue hair had joined them, and their laughter rang through the park. Nearby, the beagle howled and then barked ferociously.

Was the dog reacting to the laughter, or had a hornet stung him, too? The man with the blond ponytail started his car and rolled up the windows, silencing the dog. He pulled away, and the black cat sashayed forward and sat down beside Jenna, staring at her with eerie intelligence.

"What?" she asked it.

It inclined its head as if motioning to something, and she followed its gaze.

A car slid, shark-silent, into a parking spot on the street. A silver Mercedes.

She went cold all over. She knew that car.

The driver's door swung open, and the man with the white tattoo stepped out. He strode forward, scanning the park and moving with slithery grace. His diamond earring glittered in the sunlight as he tilted his head—almost sniffing the air.

The black cat fled, scurrying to safety beneath a parked car.

All of a sudden, Jenna remembered her cell phone. She'd dropped it when the cat made her jump. And then the hornet had stung her, and she'd forgotten Aunt Serene entirely.

She had to warn her.

If the man was part of the Council, he'd be searching for members of the Unbound. Her aunt needed to stay away from here.

Careful not to draw attention, she scurried backward and snatched up her cell phone. Then she crept back to her spot just inside the shelter of branches, watching the man.

"Aunt Serene, are you still there?" she whispered.

"Oh, thank goodness! I didn't know what happened to you."

The man stalked slowly around the park, looking for something.

Keeping her voice low, she said, "I'm okay, but the man in the silver Mercedes is in the park now. Please don't come here, Aunt Serene. Gotta go!" She hung up and thrust the cell phone into her pocket.

The man's unblinking gaze swung in her direction, and she dropped flat. But it was too late. Somehow, he'd caught sight of her through the branches.

He started forward, closing ground with every stride, and she scrambled out from under the confining limbs of the pine.

But he was already so close she didn't think she could outrun him. "Don't touch me!" she screamed as she backed away. She got her feet under her, lowering herself into a defensive stance.

The group that had been playing ball stopped their game, turning to look. Ball in hand, the girl with blue hair met Jenna's eyes, and a frown creased her forehead.

Jenna shifted her gaze back to the man with the white tattoo. He was near enough now for her to read the wary expression on his face as he approached. She was certain—the man knew what she was.

Then there was a blur of movement, and the man was falling. A baseball rolled across the ground toward her. The baseball that had just struck the man on the temple.

She glanced up.

"You're welcome," the girl with blue hair called, giving her a little wave.

The two young men who'd been playing ball exchanged shocked glances. "Did you see that throw?" the taller one asked. He shook his head in amazement, and both boys ran to check on the man.

The blue-haired girl motioned for her to get going, and Jenna mouthed her thanks.

This was her opportunity. The boys were crouched over the fallen man, blocking his view. She should run to her car and floor it for home. She knew that.

But a wild thought occurred to her, and she hesitated.

She wouldn't get a chance like this again. Because, if she was right, the man with the white tattoo hadn't bothered to lock his car.

Before she could talk herself out of it, she raced toward the street. She rounded the silver Mercedes and skidded to a stop when she reached the driver's side.

A quick glance over her shoulder confirmed that he was waking up, but he hadn't spotted her yet. She squatted down beside the car door and tried the handle, gasping with pleasure when it opened.

She crawled inside and yanked open the glove box. Quickly, she rifled through the contents until she found what she was looking for—the registration.

She stuffed it into her jeans pocket. If she was lucky, he'd never even notice it was gone. And once she gave her aunt the man's name, they could figure out what kind of threat they were dealing with.

She peered through the car window. The man was only now getting to his feet, trying to extricate himself from the two younger men. She slid out and shut the door as quietly as possible.

She hazarded another glance back. The man was stalking back to his car on high alert, and she ducked out of sight. There was no way to get to her own car without being seen. She'd have to hide and wait.

She cursed, staying low and creeping from car to car, putting as much distance as she could between them. Then she darted between two parked cars and used their cover to shield her from the man's gaze.

She paused behind a red Chevy as the Mercedes engine roared to life, and she watched the car glide out onto the street.

The black cat meowed loudly, and she jumped. She turned just in time to see it crawl from beneath the red Chevy, and she had the urge to shush the thing. Then her hackles rose.

Because the silver Mercedes had come to a stop.

Suddenly, the man with the white tattoo swung the car into a U-turn and headed in her direction.

She cursed. How had the man spotted her? Again?

She pounded away from the park and crossed the street. But the man had a car, and she didn't. He was gaining on her. Fast.

She clenched her hands into fists. She'd have to make being on foot an advantage.

She cut across the lawn of the brick house on her left, sprinting for the back yard. Then she scaled a chain-link fence and landed lightly behind another house on the next street over.

Her plan would work if the man didn't figure out what she was doing and leave his car.

She ducked behind a thick tree trunk and spared a second to dial her aunt's number. Then she took off again, phone to ear. She had to make sure her aunt had gotten the message to stay away. But Aunt Serene didn't answer.

When she shoved the phone back into her pocket, it bumped the pepper spray she'd tucked into her jeans earlier.

Seizing on an idea, she dropped to one knee behind a holly bush and dug the canister out, twisting the cap to unlock it. Then she bolted from her hiding place and raced away, armed.

Carefully, she alternated between sneaking from yard to yard and dashing across open streets, her eyes always scanning for the silver Mercedes.

She tried to head for home, but despite her efforts, she got turned around. She wasn't used to navigating.

If she could find a hidden spot, she'd pull up a map on her phone and orient herself. She whirled, looking for a likely place. The black cat streaked in front of her, heading across the street.

She blinked. Was the cat one of Fore's creatures? She'd thought the same thing about the hornet just a few minutes ago, but now she wasn't so sure.

She tried not to overthink it. The hornet had stung her. The cat had batted at the hornet. Jenna decided she was on Team Cat.

She followed the animal as it darted alongside a white vinyl house and then into the back yard. There, it squeezed through a narrow opening in the neighbor's fence.

She scrambled over the fence, afraid she'd lose it. But the black cat was waiting for her on the other side, swishing its tail lazily. Then it sped across the yard and into a thick stand of bushes.

Somewhat dubious, she ran after it and plunged into the hedge, pushing aside branches and wedging herself as far in as possible. She crouched down, squinting as she searched for the cat. It was dark.

A branch slapped her back where the hornet had stung her, and she winced. Maybe the hornet's sting had been a sign after all. If so, she thought she knew what it meant. *Stay out of trees. And bushes.*

Inside the house, a small dog barked, no doubt at either her or the cat—maybe both. She gritted her teeth.

She was about to take off again when she heard the sound.

Footsteps on snow.

The cat had abandoned her, and the man had tracked her down. She held her breath as the steps came closer.

A hand parted the branches right beside her and she sprang to life. She did the only thing she could. She thrust the can of pepper spray in front of her and pushed down on the trigger.

The hand jerked back, and she heard a violent fit of coughing.

She coughed a bit herself as a draft of wind carried some of the pepper spray toward her. She gathered herself to run.

"You," he said.

She stopped dead. No.

He went into another fit of coughing. "You're...," he tried again.

Oh no, no, no, no, no, no, no.

"You're an angel all right," he said, choking.

Lane.

Chapter Fifteen

THREE QUESTIONS

Jenna scrambled out of the hedge. She clenched her hands together and leaned over Lane. "Are you okay?"

He kneeled in the snow, choking. His face had turned cherry red, and his eyes streamed tears.

She wanted to rewind time and undo what she'd just done. And also, maybe, strangle that cat.

She couldn't believe all her maneuvering had landed her in *his* back yard. It would be funny, except that it wasn't. It really wasn't.

Another fit of coughing wracked him.

"Should I call for help?"

"It's too late."

She sucked in a frightened breath and dropped to her knees beside him. The can of pepper spray rolled away in the snow.

"Promise me something."

"Yes?"

"Don't let me into heaven. The angels are hell." His laughter turned into a wheeze.

She jumped to her feet with a shriek. "That was not funny you...you...mortal!" She picked up a pinecone and hurled it at him.

He dodged the missile easily and continued to half chuckle, half choke. He plucked the can of pepper spray out of the snow and tucked it into his jacket pocket. "I'm confiscating this, even though you have the world's worst aim. Thank goodness."

She threw another pinecone at him, but it didn't come close to grazing him.

He lay back down on the ground and wiped his face with his red scarf. "Are you aware that you had your eyes shut?"

"I did?"

"If you want to use me for target practice, open your eyes next time."

She crossed her arms in front of her. "I wasn't targeting you."

"Hmm. That may be true. You did nearly murder the bush." He turned to the hedge and shook his finger at it. "Let that be a lesson to you!"

He looked at her sideways as he got to his feet and brushed the snow from his clothes. "You know, Angel, if you wanted to woo me, you could have brought flowers. Peonies are nice, or maybe—"

"I wasn't wooing you!" she snapped. And then it hit her. He'd called her Angel. Not Mo, not Rumpelstiltskin, and certainly not Jenna. He hadn't recognized her. *Again.*

He didn't seem to realize that the girl standing in front of him now was the same girl he'd saved on the stairway—the same one he'd talked to in Spanish. Without her balaclava and shades, apparently she looked like a different person.

She considered coming clean. A few words would clear up the misunderstanding. But then he'd wonder why she hadn't spoken up earlier.

Besides, the goal was to keep people as far away as possible. For everyone's sake. If she confided in Lane, it would only invite questions. It was a horrible idea.

He finished wiping the snow from his clothes. "Well, if you aren't wooing me and you aren't on a secret mission to kill the world's shrubbery, why *are* you here? I'm going to need an explanation. But I need to wash my face first, so let's go inside."

She stiffened. An explanation? Inside?

He held up his hands, signaling innocence. "I'm not plotting revenge. I promise. But the last time we met, you bolted as soon as I went in. I won't make that mistake again."

As far as Lane knew, the last time he'd seen her was the first time they'd met—when she'd said she was his guardian angel. Then she'd gotten overwhelmed by the fireflies and the feelings flaring inside her—and she'd left without ever saying goodbye.

She gazed longingly at the sidewalk, weighing whether she should make a break for it.

He noticed. "You disappear off the face of the earth for a month. Then today I see you jump over my backyard fence and hide in the bushes, and when I walk over to see if you're okay, you try to shoot me with a can of pepper spray."

"I wasn't trying to—"

He cut her off with a cough. "Whatever you were trying to do, I think I deserve an explanation." He shrugged. "Either that, or you can grant me three wishes."

She crossed her arms again. "I'm an angel, not a genie."

"Explanation it is, then. Follow me." He turned on his heel and headed for the back door.

She wanted to flee, but his coughing bit into her conscience. Besides, Fore had singled Lane out—first with fireflies and now with the black cat. Here was an opportunity to learn more. It would be a crime to squander it. With a mix of worry and curiosity, she trudged after him.

She needed a plausible explanation, though. And fast. There had to be a lie that would work. She just had to conjure it up.

He swung the back door open, holding it wide. "After you."

She scooted past, staying as far from him as she could manage. Then she hurried through the mudroom and into the cream and mint-colored kitchen. The house was quiet. Hopefully, that meant it was empty.

The little Yorkie that had barked at her came nosing over, wagging his tail and sniffing at her feet. She bent down to let him smell her hand and nearly yelped when he licked her. She rubbed behind his ears, grateful that animals didn't react to her touch the way humans did.

Lane came in, taking in the two of them together. He hung his black jacket and red scarf on the rack by the door. "Let her be, Hercules. Come here, boy."

But Hercules just rolled over for Jenna to rub his belly.

He shook his head in disbelief. "Traitor dog." He picked up Hercules and deposited him in the mudroom.

Then he motioned for Jenna to follow him into the hall. "Can I have your word as an angel that you're done attacking me for the day?" He peered over his shoulder at her.

"Perhaps," she said, her nose in the air. "*If* you behave."

"My definition of behave or yours?"

"Definitely mine."

He grinned. "It was worth a try."

She felt her cheeks heat as he led her into his bedroom. She looked everywhere but at his rumpled bed in the corner.

He coughed again, and she had to move further into the room as he slipped past her, opening his closet. He pulled a button-down shirt from a hanger and backed into the hall, pointing at her.

"Now, I'm going to wash off the pepper spray, but if you're not here when I come back, Hercules and I will hunt you down."

"Oh, please. I own that dog."

Lane scowled at her until she sighed in defeat.

"Fine. I promise."

He nodded and left, leaving her to indulge her curiosity.

Unfortunately, his room was practically bare. There were no posters on the walls, no gaming consoles, skateboards, or mounted baseballs.

It was painted a blue-gray color with dark brown furniture that looked a zillion years old. Bed and dresser. A hamper spilling clothes. All very standard.

There was a desk on one wall, and on top were some worn books and graphic novels, a pad of paper, a plain wooden box, a fancy velvet case that displayed his coin collection, a magnifying lamp, a model car, and a picture of an elderly couple.

Other than that, there was a disappointing amount of material to feed her snooping.

Then she noticed the paisley umbrella tucked into a corner. She'd forgotten it—left it here on her last visit when she'd been using it more as a weapon than an umbrella. She was surprised Lane hadn't thrown it out, but she was glad to have it back. She'd return it to the laundry room where she'd found it.

She picked it up and searched awkwardly for a place to sit. The bed was out. And the only chair was draped with a piece of clothing she didn't want to inspect too closely.

She crossed the floor and threw open the window. Then she perched on the sill, appreciating the cool air—not to mention the potential escape route.

Lane rushed back into the room, his shirt only half buttoned. He gaped at her.

"Dude, seriously. Were you about to climb out the window?"

Her eyes fastened on his chest and her mouth went dry. "I...." She needed her mind to work. Unfortunately, her mind was sitting in the front row of the theater, eating popcorn.

"No," she tried again. Then the lie came to her. "I thought the fresh air would help with the pepper spray." Valiantly, she studied a clover-shaped spot on his ceiling as he finished buttoning his shirt.

He eyed her suspiciously, then let it drop. He gestured to the paisley umbrella. "I kept that, hoping it would lure you back here. And it worked!" He plopped down on the bed, facing her. Then he leaned forward in anticipation. "So now that you're here, talk to me."

She struggled to breathe normally. He wanted an explanation, of course, but she didn't have one. Still, she had to say *something*. She seized on her surroundings for inspiration. "Are those your grandparents in that picture?"

He stared at her.

"You show up out of nowhere and attack me, and then you want to chat about my grandparents?"

She crossed one leg over the other, braving her way through. "That is correct."

He barked a laugh. "Oh no. That's not how this is going to work." A gleam sparked in his eyes. "But I will meet you halfway."

He spread out on his side and propped up on his elbow, putting his head in his hand. "The game works like this: I answer a question of yours, and then you have to answer one of mine."

She narrowed her eyes. If she was clever, she could use her turns to find out why Fore had chosen this boy. She just had to make sure she didn't give too much away in the bargain. "You get three questions," she told him.

"You said you weren't a genie!"

"That's wishes, dumbo, not questions." She pointed the paisley umbrella at him. "Angels can answer only three questions." She tapped her foot as she waited.

He considered. "Okay. I'll bite." He swung back up and sat cross-legged, glancing at the picture on his desk.

"To answer your first question, yes, those are my grandparents. They basically raised me. They'd help anyone, and they loved each other like crazy."

He got up and went to his desk, opening the plain wooden box that sat on top. He pulled out a dollar bill. "Look at this," he said, handing it to her.

As she carefully reached for it, she realized it was actually a two-dollar bill. She remembered seeing one in Lane's wallet the night she'd found it. She looked up at him, confused.

"Turn it over."

She flipped the bill to the other side. There was a message written there in elegant cursive. She read it aloud. *"Our love, my love, can't be undone. For we are two and also one."*

"My granddad gave it to my grandmother when they were first married. It symbolizes two people who would always be joined."

Jenna looked away. "That's so romantic."

"That was my granddad." He smiled, taking the bill back from her. "My grand-mother died when I was eight, and after that, he carried the bill in his wallet."

He placed it reverently inside the wooden box and closed the lid. "I keep a two-dollar bill in my wallet, too, in memory of them."

He sat down on the bed. "When I was fourteen, my granddad died from a heart attack. So the people I'm living with now are the Phillipses. They're foster parents."

Jenna blinked. That was way more than she had bargained for. She tried to take it all in. Foster parents. "So, your parents are...."

"Is that your second question?" He smiled mischievously.

"No!" she said, holding up a hand to forestall him. Then she said more quietly, "I'm sorry about your grandparents, though."

"I appreciate that." He glanced away, and when he looked back at her, his face had cleared. He shifted on the bed, rubbing his hands together in eagerness. "Okay, my turn."

She braced herself and waited for him to ask why she was in his yard with a can of pepper spray.

"What's your name?"

She had not seen that one coming. Of course, he already knew her name. He just didn't *know* he knew.

She blustered her way through. "According to the Office of Angel Affairs, names are categorized as classified information and so—"

He flopped back onto the bed, flinging out his arms. "I knew it! You're cheating!"

"No, wait—I really can't answer that. I can't explain, but it's the truth." She hesitated. "You can keep calling me Angel, though. I kind of like it."

He sat up. "Oh, you do?"

She scowled. "Maybe."

"That's good to know, Angel. It must be awfully hard, Angel, when you have to keep your true identity a secret. Isn't that right, Angel?"

She buried her head in her hands. "What have I done?"

"I'll tell you what you've done, Angel. It's—"

"Shush. Okay, my turn." The fireflies had always appeared while she watched him walking down her street at night. But she'd never been able to figure out where he was coming from. She cocked her head. "Where do you go every evening?"

He spoke slowly. "I don't understand how you know so much about me."

"Is that *your* second question?"

"No!" he blurted. "Just an observation. So, Mr. Phillips—my foster dad—he found out I was interested in classic cars, and he got me a job with a friend who owns an auto shop. I go in after the shop is officially closed, and he shows me what needs to be done. There's one car—a 1960 Ford Falcon, six-cylinder—that I'm working on little by little. I'm saving up to buy it." He shrugged. "Does that answer your question?"

"Yes, actually." She was fascinated. It didn't tell her a thing about his connection to Fore, but she was still glad she'd asked.

He leaned forward. "My turn again. Question two, right?"

She nodded, and dread pooled in her stomach. She hadn't thought up her lie yet.

"What's your phone number?"

Her jaw literally dropped open. "What?"

"What's your phone number? You know, the particular combination of numbers that will let me talk to you using a magic little machine like this." He held up his cell phone, giving her an exaggerated demonstration.

"That's not a *fair* question!"

"Why not?"

"Because it's—"

"Personal? Like asking about your grandparents or where you go in the evening?"

She looked down her nose at him. "I never stipulated—"

"I know angels aren't known for their techie skills, but I'll walk you through this. You're going to call me, and then I'll have your number, and you'll have mine. Ready?" He waited, watching her expectantly.

He had her trapped. She couldn't think of one good reason not to give it to him.

She swallowed. "Ready." Her voice was little more than a whisper.

Half in a trance, she plugged the numbers into her phone as he said them, entering his name into her contacts. With a warring sense of elation and dread, she called him.

His phone rang, and she hung up.

He smiled like a cat with a mouse.

"Happy now?"

"Oh, yes." If possible, his smile grew wider.

She needed to take control of this conversation. "My turn again. Question three." Her mind stalled.

She could ask him whether he'd seen anything strange lately—like a glowing woman. Or maybe she should find out if he had a history with fireflies. Had he spent his summers catching them in jars? She could ask about that.

He was waiting on her, one eyebrow quirked in amusement.

The question came tumbling out of her mouth. "Have you thought about me since the last time we met?"

Even as she said it, she wished it back. She bit her lip, suspended between mortification and anticipation.

He gave her his slow smile. "Wrong question. You should have asked whether I've been able to *stop* thinking about you."

What did that mean? Did it mean...? But that wasn't possible. He wasn't *interested* in her. Was he?

She couldn't do this. She stood up and started for the door, but Lane jumped to his feet, standing in her way.

The smile fled from his face. "Whoa. Hold on. I'm sorry, okay? I didn't mean to make you uncomfortable." He ran a hand through his hair. "Forget I said that. I'm an idiot, okay? Now, will you sit down?"

They stared at each other for what felt like a small eternity.

Then she let out a slow breath and returned to her perch on the windowsill. She must have misunderstood. He already had a gorgeous girlfriend—Brie.

The back door squeaked as it opened, and Hercules gave a joyful bark of greeting.

Jenna stiffened.

"Crap. Somebody's home." He backed away, pointing at her. "I just need to let them know you're here, and then we'll talk, okay?"

"Sure," she said.

"Don't forget. You still owe me an answer."

"I do," she agreed numbly.

He nodded and ducked out the door.

The second he was gone, she launched herself through the open window and into the yard.

She couldn't allow herself to become even more entangled in Lane's life—to meet his foster parents like a normal person. She was *not* a normal person. Everything was moving too fast. She had to get out.

She started running as soon as her feet hit the ground. She scanned the street, but there was no sign of the man with the white tattoo. At least she had the paisley umbrella to use as a weapon if she needed it.

When she rounded the corner, she slowed to a walk. Then she slid into the shadow of a tree next to the sidewalk. She dialed her aunt again, but the phone just rang and rang, not even switching over to voicemail.

She frowned. Was everything okay?

She reached into her pocket and took out the registration she'd stolen from the Mercedes earlier. It told her the man's name—Thairyn Hinsen—and his address. But the car was registered in Missouri, not Minnesota. No help there.

She chewed on her lip and shoved the paper back into her pocket. Hopefully, her aunt would call soon.

She needed to return to the park and get her own car, so she pulled up a map on her phone. If she wasn't taking a crazy, zig-zagging route, the park wasn't far.

She set off at a brisk pace, already working out the lie she'd tell her mom to explain why she was coming home so late.

She'd only gone a few steps when her phone started buzzing. She looked down, hoping it was Aunt Serene. Then she wrinkled her nose.

It was Lane. She'd almost forgotten he had her number now. She cringed and picked up. "Hello?"

"I should have known better than to leave you alone," he said dryly.

"That's true." A smile tugged at the corner of her mouth. "You are not the fastest learner."

He barked a grudging laugh. "At least you answered your phone. That's something." There was a pause. "I didn't mean to scare you off."

She took a deep breath. "I'm sorry I left like that. It was just...time to go."

"Okay, I get that. But you are obligated by law to stay on the phone with me. After all, you still owe me another answer. Fair is fair."

"Fine," she grumbled. "What's your question?"

"Why were you in my back yard hiding in the bushes with a can of pepper spray?"

And there it was.

She closed her eyes. How could she explain without sounding like a lunatic?

"It's...complicated," she hedged. She blew out her breath in frustration. "The simple answer is that a man in a Mercedes was chasing me."

There was a heavy silence. "Are you serious, Angel?"

"Yes, but don't worry about it. He was in a car, and I was on foot, so I could cut across yards." She made a calming gesture with her hands, even though he couldn't see it. "I'm sure he's given up by now. And I got away the other times too."

"Other times?!" he practically shouted. "You've had some guy in a Mercedes chase you before? More than once?"

"Well, it sounds bad when you put it like that."

"Yeah, it sounds bad. It *is* bad. Is this guy someone you know?"

"Oh, yes. I mean.... No." She shook her head. "No, I don't know him, but I've seen him before." Her voice got smaller. "The other times.... When he was following me."

"Angel! You should have told me right away! I figured you were playing a prank. I didn't know you were caught up in something serious." His voice was firm. "We need to call the police."

"No!" she said sharply. "No, we are not doing that. Let me handle this."

"You don't seem to understand that you're in real danger. I can't believe you're out there alone right now. I should have walked you home, at least."

"I'm fine," she insisted.

"You're not. You need to report this. Give a description to the police. You know...what does he look like...what color was the Mercedes...that kind of thing. Maybe this guy is a repeat offender, and they can bring him in."

She ground her teeth. "It's not like that. You don't understand—"

"That's true. I don't. What are you not telling me?"

She almost laughed aloud at that. If he had any idea what she wasn't telling him, he'd be done with her.

The silence stretched between them, and Lane finally gave a lingering sigh. "Think about it, at least. Please? But do me a favor. Stay on the line with me until you get home. I want to make sure that guy isn't out there looking for you."

She glanced around again. "I think I'm good."

"Come on. Just this once. And then I won't bother you again if you don't want me to."

She raised an eyebrow, skeptical. "Just this once? Really?"

"Really, really. Just this once. Or twice at the most. Although they do say the third time's the charm. Now, personally, I try to be charming at *all* times, but I'm resigned to one phone call if that's what you want. Put me on trial."

She took a deep breath. She had to admit, after the day she'd had, it felt good to have him on the line. "Okay," she agreed. "We'll talk. Just this once."

"Just this once," he confirmed, sounding relieved. "Twice at the most."

Chapter Sixteen

WORLD'S CUTEST COUPLE

The next morning Jenna did an encore performance for her mom, pretending she was thrilled to go back to Coldwater High.

But dread gnawed at her as she pulled on her gloves, oversize jacket, balaclava, and shades.

She had to go to the TOTEL meeting if she wanted to avoid the crowded cafeteria. But going to the meeting meant seeing Lane. And Brie. Together.

It was too much to take on an empty stomach.

She scolded herself. This wasn't a big deal. She'd be a fly on the wall—eyes open and mouth shut. And as soon as she got what she needed from Fore, she'd get out of that school and never go back.

She wished her Aunt Serene hadn't been so certain about their plan. Jenna had texted her several times last night, but she'd gotten no response. Hopefully, there was a good explanation. One that didn't involve the man with the white tattoo—Thairyn Hinsen.

She drove to school, keeping one eye peeled for the silver Mercedes, but there was no sign of it. If there was a pattern to the man's appearances, she couldn't decipher it.

When she arrived in the parking lot, she tried her aunt again, but the phone went straight to voicemail. Lost in thought, she jumped when Zinnia knocked on the passenger window.

She'd pulled her locks up into a bun, and amethyst earrings dangled from her ears. "Ready to take over the earth?" she asked as Jenna slid from the car.

"Not really," she admitted.

Zinnia nodded in approval of her honesty.

Jenna slung her backpack over her shoulder and glanced around, looking for the giant orange butterfly, but it was nowhere to be found. She walked alongside Zinnia. "Can I ask you a question?"

"I hope so."

"It's just—why are you even in this club? Kelsea's...a little much."

"Do you want the real answer or the realer answer?"

"I don't know. Maybe both?"

"The thing about Kelsea is, she's not always right. And you might not like what she has to say. But she'll tell it to you straight, and that's rare—so rare it's almost nonexistent. She's strange, I know, but she's not fake. That's the real answer."

"And the realer answer?"

Zinnia shrugged. "She's got my back. Always has. It's who she is." She stopped at the band room entrance and pounded on the door.

While they waited, the nape of Jenna's neck crawled as if someone was watching her. She swung around.

Brent was leaning against a nearby car, eyes fixed on her.

She shivered and turned away, ignoring him.

Then Devonte swung the door wide, grinning at Zinnia. "Like a bee to honey. You can't stay away from me, can you, Zinnia Carter?"

"Best watch yourself before you get stung." She raised her chin to a haughty angle and brushed past Devonte, not even glancing his way. But when they were out of earshot, she whispered, "Don't worry. I know what I'm doing."

They wound through the band hall and then climbed the back stairs to the theater room. As Zinnia pushed the door open, Jenna braced to see Lane and Brie. But they weren't there. The morning would certainly be less stressful if they didn't show up.

She reminded herself why she was there and glanced around, searching for signs from Fore.

In the light booth, Lita and Doc were hunched over a laptop. And, just like yesterday, Nardo was asleep in the middle of the floor, dressed in his signature long shorts and Hawaiian shirt. Was the boy aware that it was winter?

Markese was stretched out beside him, his feet near Nardo's head. He was wearing balloon pants and a black-and-white striped vest. He held a pillow over his face.

"Where's Kelsea?" Zinnia asked, looking confused.

Markese slid the pillow to the side, uncovering one eye. "I'm working on my beauty sleep here."

"Markese. Tell me where Kelsea went."

He pretended to doze off.

"Come on, Markese. We all know you don't need beauty sleep. You're already gorgeous."

He gasped with pleasure, sitting up. "Zinnia, you are a woman of taste. Have I told you that?"

"Every time I tell you how cute you are. Now, about Kelsea?"

"Oh, that," he said, waving his hand dismissively. "Jose and Hampton didn't show up, so she's gone to find them."

"Oh no."

"Oh yes." Markese settled himself down for his nap. "Now, it's time for Operation: Let's Get Some Shuteye." He pulled the pillow back over his face.

Zinnia shook her head. "I'd better go find the twins before Kelsea does. We can't afford to lose any more members." She headed for the door.

Jenna thought she might finally get to explore the room, but then she heard Zinnia speak up behind her.

"Good. You're both here. Have Jenna give you a tour."

She whipped around. Zinnia was gone, and Lane and Brie were standing in the doorway.

"Mo," Lane said, waving.

"Shirley."

Lane's hair was rumpled, as if he'd only just crawled out of bed, and the cowlick on the back of his head stood straight up. His red scarf was uneven, and the hoodie he wore beneath the black jacket was twisted to one side.

Brie, though, was dressed in a crisp sunflower-yellow top. She shone with flawless beauty, even this early in the morning.

Jenna ground her teeth.

Brie's lip curled. "This is the meeting?"

"If this is a napping club, sign me up," Lane said, grinning.

"Oh, hello!" Doc popped out of the lighting booth, saving Jenna from having to deal with the newcomers. Doc had yet another guinea pig tucked into the crook of her arm.

Lane yelped and leaped away. "Is that a rat?"

"Relax," Brie said. She put a calming hand on his arm.

Jenna's eyes narrowed at the easy familiarity between them.

"It's a guinea pig, right?" Brie asked Doc. When she nodded, Brie reached forward and petted the guinea pig's head.

"He's called Piglet," Doc said, handing him over.

"See, Lane? You can touch him. He's cute." She held the guinea pig up to her cheek.

"There's almost nothing I can think of that's worse than a rodent. It's repulsive. No offense," he told Doc.

"Oh, I understand." She took Piglet from Brie. "I'll keep him in his carrier when you're here. No worries." She placed Piglet gently inside the cylindrical bag she wore over her shoulder. "Come with me. I'll show you around before we start the TOTEL meeting."

"TOTEL? What is that?" Brie asked.

Doc nodded, smiling. "We're the Take Over the Earth League—TOTEL for short."

Brie looked dubious. "Why do you need to take over the earth?"

"Because it's a mess," Doc said. "Haven't you always thought the world would be a better place if you were running it?"

Brie nodded. "I guess so."

"Well, here's your chance. But the world can wait a day. Let's do the tour. Where do you want to start?"

"What's in there?" Brie asked, nodding to the darkened tech room.

Doc poked her head inside, making her honey-brown curls bounce. "Lita, do you mind if we look around in here?"

Lita sighed. "It doesn't matter what I want. It never does." She was dressed all in black again today, and she ignored Doc and Brie as she took out a Sharpie and drew thorny vines up and down her fingers.

Lane and Jenna lingered outside the lighting booth.

Jenna cleared her throat awkwardly. If she didn't count the boys sleeping on the floor, she and Lane were alone. Unfortunately, the image of him in his bedroom yesterday with his shirt half buttoned was lighting up all the billboards inside her mind. She had to get some air.

"I...uh...I think I lost something in here, and I need to look for it." She backed away, congratulating herself on her cleverness. She'd get some distance and check out the room at the same time.

"I'll help you look," he volunteered. "What did you lose?"

She winced. Of course, he wanted to help. "I lost...a pen. My favorite pen. But I can look for it myself. Don't worry about it." She walked away.

"It'll be fun," he said, following her. "This place is awesome."

She had no choice but to stroll along beside him as they surveyed the perimeter of the room.

He pointed to the upright piano wedged against the wall as they passed it. "You can play that thing, can't you?"

She grimaced and ran her gloved fingers soundlessly over the keys. "I'm not sure," she hedged. "I've only ever played on a keyboard." Unable to resist, she put her hands in position, imagining the chords.

"Play something."

She jerked her hands back and searched for an excuse. "People are sleeping."

"He won't mind," Lane told her.

"I need to find my favorite pen, though." She hurried past the piano, stopping in front of a tall metal shelf full of props. She pretended to search the shelf for her pen, picking up prop after prop and feeling around with her gloved hands.

"This must be a special pen," Lane said, joining in the search.

"It is." She thought fast. "My...uh...my pen pal person gave it to me." *Pen pal person? What did that even mean?*

"Really?"

"Not just a pen pal. He's my boyfriend. In Singapore," she added. She hoped her dark shades would keep Lane from reading the panic in her eyes.

He grinned. "Oh, I see." He went back to rummaging on the top shelf. Then his face lit up. "No way!" He pulled down a tattered stuffed lion. "Brie!" he shouted. "You've got to see this."

Markese sat up, throwing aside his pillow in a fit of pique. "Does nobody around here respect the sanctity of beauty sleep?" Then he spotted Lane, and his demeanor flipped. "Hello, hello. Who do we have here?"

Nardo shook his head, watching. Then he lay back down. He put his arm over his eyes as Markese floated over to Lane.

Markese held out his hand, palm down. "Charmed, I'm sure."

Lane looked as if he didn't know whether to shake Markese's hand or kiss it. He gave him a fist bump instead, grinning. "I'm Lane."

Brie walked over, trailed by Doc and Lita. "What do you want?"

Lita noticed Lane for the first time. "Another new person?" She sighed. "It's never-ending."

Lane had hidden the lion behind his back, and now he pulled it out and showed it to Brie.

She gasped. "It looks just like Mr. Grizzle! I can't believe you remembered!" She gave Lane a quick hug and took the lion from him.

Jenna wrinkled her nose. This was what she'd been afraid of. Disgusting levels of sweetness.

"Who's Mr. Grizzle?" Doc asked.

"A stuffed animal Lane gave me about a million years ago." Brie turned the lion over in wonder. "Except for the stain where I spilled juice on his paw, this could be him."

Lane looked down at her. "You used to sleep with him every night, remember?"

Jenna wanted to gag.

"That is too cute," Markese said. "Fate brought you together." He pulled out his phone. "This is going on my Instagram. You guys move closer together," he directed, pointing.

Lane stepped in close and put his arm around Brie.

"Now smile and say *Squeeze*!" Markese told them, adjusting his phone.

Lane squeezed Brie's waist and the two of them smiled at the cell phone. The phone flashed brightly in the dark room.

"Caption: World's Cutest Couple," Jenna muttered under her breath.

But she must have spoken louder than she'd thought because Brie jerked away from Lane. They both looked at her oddly.

"What did you say?" Brie demanded.

She frowned. "I said...you two make a cute couple."

Brie gave an outraged shriek and Jenna flinched.

Lane burst out laughing.

"That's disgusting!" Brie yelled.

Disgusting? She couldn't understand where she'd gone wrong.

"Come on, Brie," Lane soothed. "She didn't know."

"She should have!" Brie glared daggers at Jenna. "He's my brother, moron, not my boyfriend."

Markese put his hand over his mouth, and the other TOTEL members exchanged worried looks.

"Whoa, Brie!" Lane steered her away from the group. "Let's go cool off over here."

Jenna's mind was still spinning. *Brother?*

She tried to recall each time she'd seen them together. They walked to the bus stop every day—like siblings coming from the same house, she realized. Lane would reach out to steady her on the ice, or he'd bend his head down to listen carefully. Like a protective older brother.

Now that she thought about it, she'd never seen them kiss or do anything remotely romantic.

And she remembered seeing Brie's picture in Lane's wallet. She'd noticed then how young she looked and concluded that they'd been together a long time.

She was the biggest idiot on the planet.

With the threads of her own jealousy, she'd spun a relationship out of thin air. She'd also made a fool of herself and probably alienated them for good.

Then, all at once, it struck her.

Brie was not Lane's girlfriend.

Maybe he didn't even *have* a girlfriend. The idea was staggering.

She fought to rein in the happiness that spiraled through her body. *If her aunt could find a cure for her Charms....*

She quashed the thought, fighting to remember that she was still a threat to Lane and everyone else. The Charms were still there.

And even if they weren't, would it really make a difference? All she'd ever done was wreck the people she loved. If Lane was smart, he'd stay far away from her, whether she had Charms or not.

But when she looked across the room at him, a thrill ran up her spine. A spark devouring a fuse.

She needed to tamp that feeling down, to smother it. But as hard as she tried, hope—awful, dangerous hope—flared to life inside her.

Chapter Seventeen

ROCK

"That was outrageous, right?" Markese asked, interrupting Jenna's thoughts.

Doc shook her head. "I'm sure Brie is just having a bad day."

Markese looked unconvinced.

Doc turned to Jenna, handing her a hall pass. "Speaking of bad days, my dad wanted you to have this in case you need to be by yourself again at lunch."

"Thanks," she said, torn between embarrassment and gratitude.

"Can you hook me up with one of those?" Markese asked Doc.

Before Doc could answer, Lane joined the group. "Are we plotting world domination over here?"

Jenna looked up, worried he was upset with her, but he smiled reassuringly. She glanced over at Brie. The girl gave her one last enraged glare and disappeared into the light booth with Lita and Nardo. Apparently, she wasn't as forgiving as her brother.

"Tell me about this Take Over the Earth League," Lane said to the circle. "Do you guys have superpowers or something?" He cocked his head. "Wait, are you the heroes or the villains?"

"Villains," Markese said, at the same time Doc said, "Heroes."

Lane nodded. "Smart. I've always thought the heroes and the villains should cooperate more." He put his hands in his pockets. "Seriously, though. What is TOTEL about?"

Markese spoke up. "TOTEL is basically Kelsea's scheme to improve things, but her ideas never work. Now, me? I'm in the club for the naps and the snacks."

"Naps and snacks sound good," Lane said.

"Kelsea's plans do work sometimes, Markese," Doc corrected him. "What about the time we gave out donuts to everyone who attended a meeting? We packed the room."

Markese tipped his head onto Doc's shoulder, his eyes glittering with nostalgia. "And I got to hand them out. I was the belle of the ball."

Doc nodded. "Kelsea thought the school board should give out money for good attendance, so she gave out donuts at our meetings to prove it would work."

"Oh, it worked," Markese said. "Until she tried to force everybody to sign a petition saying we'd attend classes in the summer." He shook his head. "Even donuts couldn't save that sorry suggestion."

Doc rushed to Kelsea's defense. "She says summer break is only necessary for farmers. And I guess she's right. We really don't need it."

"That's bull," Markese huffed. "I need summer breaks to invest time where it really matters—on social media. My YouTube channel doesn't post itself."

At that moment, Jose and Hampton burst through the drama room door and darted into the circle.

"Kelsea's right behind us. Say we've been here the whole time," Jose panted.

Then he noticed Lane. He grinned, taking his hand from his pocket and extending it for a handshake. "I'm Jose."

Before anyone could stop him, Lane took Jose's hand. With a yelp, he jerked his hand back, shaking it.

Jose burst into laughter and revealed the buzzer in his palm.

Lane scowled, unamused.

They all looked up as Kelsea strode through the door, followed by Zinnia. With laser-like focus, Kelsea zeroed in on the two boys. She ignored Zinnia's pleas for calm and stalked over. "Where have you been?"

"What are you talking about, Kelsea?" Jose said smoothly. "We've been here the whole time, right guys?" He looked at the rest of them for support.

"We were here," Hampton echoed him, somehow looking small in the face of Kelsea's wrath.

Kelsea narrowed her eyes. "Indeed. Then what were you just discussing?"

Markese took pity on them. "Jose was telling Lane and Jenna about Schoolwide Siesta."

Jose didn't miss a beat. "Yes, Schoolwide Siesta was the best. See, Lita hacked into the PA system, and I got on the loudspeaker and announced it was siesta time. I told everyone to take a twenty-minute nap. It was pretty amaz—"

Jose's eyes widened, and he took a step back, colliding with Hampton's chest. "Who's the tall goddess in the light booth?"

Kelsea glanced behind her and crossed her arms. "That's Brie, one of our new members, and you'd better not run her off."

"I think I'm in love."

Jenna felt Lane stiffen beside her.

Kelsea snapped her fingers in Jose's face. "Hey. Hey. Eyes over here." She stepped into his sightline. "I'm giving you and Hampton the benefit of the doubt and letting you back in the League, but don't screw it up. Got it?"

"Yeah, yeah. I've got it." Jose licked his palm and slicked his hair down, looking at Brie. "We'll do whatever you want."

Kelsea nodded and pulled out her whistle, blasting it.

Markese grabbed his ears. "Kelsea, girl, we're all right here. You'd better start saving for hearing aids for all of us. And I want mine diamond encrusted."

People moved into the circle, sitting on the floor, but Jose waited, his eyes on Brie. When she was settled, he got down on one knee in front of her. "My name is Jose Gonzalez, and you're the most beautiful girl I've ever seen. Could I have the honor of sitting beside you?"

She regarded him coolly. "Jose, is it? Listen to me." She spoke slowly, so he'd be sure to understand. "I would rather spend the rest of my life as a dung beetle than spend one second sitting beside you. Message received?"

"Loud and clear." He turned to find a different spot, but before sitting, he wheeled back around to Brie. "Is it okay if I keep trying, though?"

She raised an eyebrow. "You can try all you want. The answer won't change."

Jose grinned and gave Hampton a double thumbs-up. "Still in the game."

Lane caught and held Brie's gaze, and something unspoken passed between them.

Jenna could read anger in the hard line of his jaw. "Are you okay?" she asked.

"I'm good." He shook himself and turned away. He obviously didn't want to talk about whatever was bothering him, so she didn't press it.

Kelsea set up her gavel and then cued the TOTEL Pledge.

Everyone chanted in unison. *"I will seek the truth, defend the defenseless, right the wrong, and stand up for fairies."*

Lane gave Jenna a confused look as Markese stood up, applauding, but Jenna just shrugged her shoulders.

Kelsea pressed her lips together, choosing to ignore the outburst, and Zinnia tugged on the edge of Markese's vest until he sat back down.

"So," Kelsea said, "we're ditching our last project, thanks to Jose and Hampton, who ruined it." She threw them a menacing glare.

"This is Operation: Let's Get Inspired. We're on the verge of discovering our shiny, sparkly, exceptionally stupendous idea. I can feel it. So what have you got?"

No one spoke.

"What's wrong with you people?" Kelsea clambered to her feet. "Okay, new strategy. No more Thinking Stations until we clear this mental block. Everybody up. We're doing a Moving Meditation."

All the others groaned and stood up. Jenna followed along, exchanging glances again with Lane.

"Go!" Kelsea shouted.

Suddenly, everyone began moving randomly, each on their own path.

Nardo climbed up on the scaffold and watched, but Kelsea didn't notice.

Jose pinged around like a loose pinball. He circled Hampton and then Brie at top speed.

Doc cradled Piglet's carrier close to her body as she walked, and Lita barely covered any ground, staring down at her sneakers.

Zinnia and Markese strolled side by side until Kelsea reprimanded them. "No partners!" she shouted.

Lane's eyes were wide in mock horror as he passed Jenna. She smiled briefly, but then returned her attention to the room, trying to avoid a crash. It was like human bumper cars.

"Now freeze!" Kelsea commanded, blowing her whistle. Everyone stopped in their tracks. Kelsea pointed at Zinnia. "Go, Zinn. What's your idea?"

Zinnia shook her head. "I don't know, Kelsea. Let's bring back the schoolwide dating survey. That was fun. Remember? We made a couple of good matches."

"But did it help us take over the world?"

"Love makes the world go 'round," Markese suggested.

"Potty rot. And wait your turn, Markese," Kelsea scolded. "No, it's not the right idea. Everybody, walk!"

The room unfroze, and Jenna's level of panic increased. What would she say if Kelsea called on her?

Seconds later, Kelsea had everybody freeze again. She pointed at Hampton this time.

He unslung the army surplus bag from his back and set it on the floor. "I wrote down an idea last week," he said, as he began pulling things from the sack. "Something about cafeteria food."

Jenna's eyes got bigger with each item he took out. Besides his crochet hook and yarn, there was a hand-crank flashlight, seed packets, a bag of Doritos, a first aid kit, a yo-yo, iodine tablets, duct tape, an emergency blanket, origami paper, and a lighter.

Lane, who had stopped near Jenna, whispered, "How much more could be in there? Is Hampton actually Mary Poppins in disguise?"

"Or Hermione Granger," she whispered back.

"I don't even carry a backpack," Lane said. "Besides my wallet, I only have one thing on me. This." He pulled a can of pepper spray from the inside pocket of his jacket. "Until this moment, I forgot I had it."

Her eyes widened as she recognized the canister she'd used on him the night before.

Before Jenna could give herself away, Kelsea's voice blasted them. "What do you have there, Lane McConnell?" She marched over and snatched the can from him. "I'm impounding this," she said, putting it in her own bag. "This is a weapon-free meeting, I'll have you know."

Lane exchanged glances with Jenna, then shrugged his shoulders.

Hampton was still taking item after item out of his sack. He pulled out a length of rope and then a drone. He was reaching in again when Kelsea stopped him. "Everyone's too bored to listen to your idea now, Hampton. Put your stuff away. Everybody, walk!"

Hampton nodded stoically and piled his things back in the bag as everyone else resumed their zig-zagging walks.

Seconds later, Kelsea halted them. "Brie, go."

"I just got here," she said, glowering.

"Tell us how to take over the earth," Kelsea prompted. "Or, since you're new, you can tell us about your skill set. Maybe we can use that."

Brie raised her eyebrows. "I don't have any skills." She pointed at Lane. "My brother sings, though."

He put his hands up. "Just around the house." Then he pointed at Jenna. "Mo plays piano. What about that?"

Jenna gave Lane the evil eye, wishing her shades didn't ruin the effect.

"Indeed." Kelsea regarded her speculatively. Then she let it drop. "Everybody, walk!"

The next time they stopped, Kelsea pointed at Doc.

Doc shifted from foot to foot, uncomfortable with the attention. "I'm not an idea person."

"All people are idea people," Kelsea insisted.

"But I—"

"No excuses. Come up with something!"

Doc's breath hitched, and she stood there frozen, a deer in headlights. The silence stretched uncomfortably.

Jenna felt her skin go hot with anger, and she lashed out before she could stop herself. "I'll tell you my idea, Kelsea. I think the problem here is your leadership. All of your plans have been too small. You aren't the Take Over the *Earth* League. You're the Take Over the *School* League."

No one breathed.

For the first time, Jenna could hear the small sound of Ms. Chester's clock ticking behind her. Like a bomb about to go off.

All eyes were nailed to Kelsea—waiting for the explosion.

And even though she knew it was coming, Jenna flinched when the small girl erupted.

"Bat barf!" she bellowed, stomping off across the room.

The others closed into a loose huddle around Jenna, as if to protect her from the coming storm.

"Turd burgers!" Kelsea circled the floor like a rabid animal.

"Bat barf and turd burgers?" Jenna whispered.

"That's Kelsea's way of cursing," Zinnia whispered back. "She made up her own phrases to pack more of a punch."

"They're pretty foul." Doc's nose wrinkled in distaste.

Markese leaned in. "I think they're adorable. My favorite is—"

"Tick testicles!"

"How did she know?" Markese asked coyly.

Then Kelsea stopped pacing and swung to face them. Her gaze narrowed on Jenna, and she pushed her wire-framed glasses up on her nose. "So, Jenna Getty, you're brand new, but you have the audacity to question everything we've done." Her voice was savage.

Jenna swallowed but held her ground as Kelsea stalked toward her.

"You have no respect for tradition. No concern for procedure. No obedience to authority." Kelsea halted in front of her. "I could kiss you."

Jenna's eyebrows climbed wildly. "Please don't."

Lane stifled a laugh.

Kelsea clapped her hands together. "I can see it now. We've been too focused on what happens here inside these walls. But this school is small potatoes."

She spread her arms wide. "This is our shiny, sparkly, exceptionally stupendous idea, people! And what better way to change the world than through music? As of today, we're starting a rock band."

Kelsea pointed. "Jenna Getty, you're on keyboard. And Lane, you're our lead singer. Who else can play something?"

"I play trumpet," Zinnia volunteered doubtfully.

Brie stepped forward, excited. "I want to play drums," she said. "Although I don't know how."

"Not a problem," Kelsea assured her. "Knowledge is not a prerequisite. Only perseverance."

Markese tapped Kelsea on the shoulder. "I call dibs on branding and publicity."

"Fine, fine," she said, her wheels turning. "We'll figure out the details later." She pointed again to Lane and Jenna. "You two get on the piano and work out some tunes."

Lane eyed Jenna with a crooked smile.

"All right, people, this is Operation: Let's Get Lyrical! Join forces and start working on song lyrics. Now, I've got calls to make. Doc! You're with me." She swung into action, leaving everyone else to form clusters around the room.

In a daze, Jenna followed Lane to the old upright piano.

He shoved a fake potted palm tree out of the way and scooted a wooden stool closer to the piano bench.

Jenna sat down heavily. "You're actually going to do this?"

"Could be fun," he said, looking far too cheerful.

She threw her hands in the air. "It could be a humiliating failure, and everyone will say the whole stupid idea was my fault."

"Nah." He dismissed all her worries with one syllable. "Did you see how enthused Brie was about playing the drums, though?" His face lit up. "I haven't seen her like that in years. And there must be online videos that teach drumming."

Jenna wanted to snarl a skeptical comment, but watching online videos was how she'd learned to play the keyboard. She crossed her arms and stewed.

Then she shrieked.

Behind Lane, something had moved inside the potted plant.

A long green stem grew straight up between the plastic palm fronds, unfurling new leaves. It grew so quickly, it was like watching one of those time-lapse videos where everything happens in fast forward.

No plant could grow like that.

All at once, she became aware that everyone had gone silent. They were staring at her, wondering why she'd screamed.

No one was looking at the plant—because they couldn't see it.

She coughed. "I thought I saw a mouse."

Lane yelped and hopped up on the stool, peering down anxiously.

Everybody else turned accusingly to Doc.

But her eyes were wide with innocence. "Pinky and the Brain are at home in their cage. Only Piglet is here today."

Jenna tried to calm the group. "Sorry. There was no mouse. I think I was jumping at shadows. Not enough sleep last night."

Everyone went back to their conversations, but Lane still seemed reluctant to come down from the stool.

"I'll double check," she told him.

He shuddered. "Go right ahead."

She pretended to study the floor, looking for a nonexistent mouse. Then she stole a glance upward. The plant was now over seven feet tall.

She reached her hand out to touch one of the leaves, but her fingers went straight through it. She backed away. It had to be a sign from Fore, but what did it mean?

"Did you see anything?" he asked.

She wanted to laugh. Yes, she had, but she just shook her head. "You can come down now," she told him. And she sank onto the piano bench, numb.

Kelsea blew her whistle. "Okay, people! Attention! Doc texted her dad, and he says it's all right if we have band practice at their place on Saturday morning. Anybody have a problem with that?"

Jenna went rigid.

Kelsea turned to where she and Lane were sitting. "New people, are you coming?"

Lane exchanged a look with Brie, silently asking what she wanted.

"So long as I'm the drummer, I'll be there," she said.

"Then count me in," Lane added.

"Indeed." Kelsea shifted her gaze. "Jenna Getty, are you in or out?"

In her peripheral vision, Jenna watched as the imaginary plant formed a bud that exploded into an enormous crimson flower. Unseen by Lane, the giant bloom stretched over his head like a parasol.

"Jenna Getty!" Kelsea barked, drawing her attention. "I need an answer. Are you in or out?"

"I...I have to...." She tried to think of an excuse to get out of it. But the flower distracted her. It was withering.

She got to her feet, unsure how to stop it. The whole flower shriveled until it was a hard, dry shadow of itself. What was she meant to do?

"In or out, Jenna Getty?" Kelsea repeated.

Her brain refused to supply a plausible lie. "Um...in. I'm in."

"Good." Kelsea nodded and returned to her conversation with Doc.

Then Lane cried out, grabbing his head. "Something just hit me." He searched the floor and picked up a small black object.

"It's a rock," he said wonderingly. "Where did that come from?" He peered up at the high ceiling, frowning.

Jenna's mouth was dry. "Can I have it? I collect rocks," she lied.

"It's yours." He set it on the piano bench.

She picked it up, rolling it in her fingers. It was solid—real. Small, hard, and almost perfectly round.

But it wasn't a rock.

She clenched her fist around it.

It was a seed.

Chapter Eighteen

Almost an Igloo

Jenna trudged up the back stairs of Ashton Place, wondering why she wasn't ecstatic. Compared with day one, day two had been a resounding success.

The halls were less confusing, the other students had gotten over their initial shock at seeing her, and the whole experience wasn't as overwhelming. All good things.

Also, she'd only seen Brent once today. After she'd caught him watching her on her way into school, she hadn't run into him again. So that was great, too.

She paused at the top of the stairs, peering around the corner to make sure he wasn't coming. Thankfully, he hadn't made the connection that the person he'd chased weeks ago—the one in the ski mask and navy peacoat—was the same person he'd seen in a balaclava and white puffer jacket. And she wanted to keep it that way. The last thing she needed was for him to realize they were neighbors.

With no one in sight, she skimmed down the hall on silent feet.

Mr. Cane opened his door just as she was passing.

She yanked the shades and balaclava off her face and waved awkwardly.

"Ah, hello," he said to her, leaning on his cane with both hands. "Nothing worth screaming about today, I trust."

Actually, she *had* screamed today when the strange plant had started to grow. But he didn't need to know that.

She forced a laugh. "No, no. It's all good," she lied. Then she waved again and slipped inside her apartment, locking the door behind her.

She called out to her mom to let her know she was home. She stripped off the hated shades, balaclava, and coat and went to check on her.

Mae was sitting up in bed, her laptop balanced on her thighs. And that, Jenna acknowledged, was another reason to celebrate.

She'd been putting Aunt Serene's pills in her mother's coffee every morning, and the medicine had worked a miracle. Her mom hadn't had a single episode, and her energy had returned almost to normal. She'd even taken back the responsibility for her own job duties— work Jenna had been doing for the last year.

Mae put her laptop aside, eager to hear about Jenna's day. And, unlike the web of lies Jenna had woven yesterday, this time she truthfully reported that everything had gone smoothly. Mae's relief was palpable.

Jenna carried her backpack to her own bedroom, locked the door, and sat down on the bed. She unzipped the backpack and carefully pulled out the large black seed.

She rolled it between her fingers. Here was hard, physical evidence of success. Fore had given her something at last. It had to be important.

If only she knew what to do with it.

She tucked the seed into her pocket for the time being. She needed to talk to her aunt.

Aunt Serene, though, wasn't answering her phone. Jenna had tried the Chicago landline on the off chance that she'd returned home, but the phone just rang and rang. There wasn't even the option to leave a message.

Could the man with the white tattoo have found her and turned her over to the Council?

No. She was overreacting. Her aunt's phone had just died, or.... She swallowed. Maybe Aunt Serene was ghosting her. She couldn't blame her. Jenna was a bad luck charm, and maybe Serene had finally noticed.

But until Jenna knew something for sure, she had to keep moving forward. And that meant she needed to know more about Thairyn Hinsen—the man with the white tattoo.

She took out the registration for the silver Mercedes, opened her laptop, and searched for his name. But it returned no hits. Weird.

She searched for his address next, but all she could retrieve was a long-outdated street view of a Missouri farmhouse. Not helpful. She thrust the laptop away, thinking.

The phone in her pocket buzzed. A text. She whipped the phone out, hoping it was her aunt at last.

Guardian angel needed. STAT. Life-altering dilemma. Call ASAP.

Lane. She should ignore him.

Except this morning Fore had literally dropped the seed right on him. He was involved, whether she wanted him to be or not. She sighed and pulled up a playlist on her laptop, turning the music up loud enough so Mae wouldn't hear her talking.

She called Lane. "What's the life-altering dilemma?" she challenged as soon as he answered.

"Thank goodness it's you," he said. "I am in serious need of help." Then his voice shifted gears. Lazily, he asked, "So, what are you up to?"

"What's the dilemma?" she repeated firmly.

"All right. All right. I'm getting to that. But first, tell me how you're doing. How's heaven?"

"Heavenly. Are we done here?"

"We're just getting started. Relax and chat with me."

"Relax? You texted me about a life-altering dilemma."

"Oh, that. Yeah. So...I'm trying to decide on my afternoon snack. Do I want string cheese or popcorn? What's your advice, Angel?"

She pursed her lips. "How is that a life-altering dilemma?"

"Dude, seriously? My afternoon snack affects my health, and my health affects my life. Hence: life-altering. What do they teach you angels nowadays? Is it all halo polishing and feather dusting?"

She let her pointed silence communicate her displeasure.

"Okay. Busted. I confess. I already picked the string cheese, and it was delicious." He cleared his throat. "No, the snack dilemma was just a clever ruse. My real question is: do you want to video chat with me?"

Her stomach clenched and her mind flashed to Michael Stevens. It was an effort to keep her tone light. "Video chatting is strictly forbidden by the Office of Angel Affairs."

"Seriously? You don't strike me as a rule-follower. Where's the red-headed rebel I met the other day?"

"She died of boredom when you called to discuss string cheese. The new me does not do video chats." She rolled over, thrusting the Mercedes registration paper out of her way.

"Why don't you come over, then?" he said, excited. "We can stay on the phone while you walk in case the creeper guy shows up. Or I can come to you if you tell me where you live. What do you think?"

"I think you—"

She sat bolt upright, snatching up the registration paper. "You work in a mechanic shop, right? So, do you know cars?"

"Do I know cars?" he asked, affronted. "Does the sun rise in the east? Does the ocean meet the shore? Does string cheese make a delicious afternoon snack?"

"Shush," she told him. "I need your help with something."

"Absolutely."

She tapped her finger on the paper. "Let's say that, hypothetically, I possess a vehicle registration that doesn't belong to me. It shows the name and address of the car's owner, but the address is out of state."

"Interesting." He paused. "Is the hypothetical vehicle a Mercedes that's been following you around?"

"That's beside the point. Anyway, the paper also lists a VIN number. Could I use that to find out something else, like, for example, an alternate address?"

"My buddies from the Street Rod Association know a lot of the guys who work on cars around town. With the VIN number, I might be able to find out where he has the car serviced. It would be a start."

"That would be great. I really appreciate it."

"Bring me the registration and I'll get right on it."

She narrowed her eyes. "*Or* I can just tell you the number over the phone."

"*Or* you can bring me the paper, and I can show you something cool while you're here."

"*Or* I can tell you—"

"I'm happy to have this conversation all night," Lane interrupted. "*Or* you can come over."

"You're not bluffing, are you?"

"Knock on my window when you get here. And don't forget my bouquet of flowers."

"I'm hanging up now," she said and clicked the phone off. But going to Lane's house was easier said than done. She'd have to make an excuse to her mom. And she'd need to dress like Angel and not Jenna. *And* she couldn't mention anything that had happened at school, or he'd figure out that Angel and Jenna were the same person. She'd have to stay on her toes.

She slipped out of her room, leaving the balaclava and shades behind, since Angel didn't wear them. Then she went to the hall closet and got out her navy-blue peacoat and a different set of gloves, pulling them on as she hurried to the bathroom. She leaned into the mirror and plucked another white hair that had grown in since this morning.

Heading back to the hall, she tipped her head inside Mae's doorway. "I have to go out for a minute and do an experiment for biology. I'm supposed to count how many bird species I see."

Mae looked at her steadily. "You're not enrolled in biology."

Crap.

"It's a partnership between art and biology," she said quickly. "And I'm doing the artwork. I shouldn't be long," she said, backing away.

"Be careful!" her mother said, eyeing her closely. Her lips tightened. "Of the birds."

Jenna turned on her heel and hurried to the door. She hustled the entire way to Lane's house, alert for anything out of the ordinary. But there was nothing to give her alarm.

When she got there, she squeezed behind a row of bushes and crouched beneath his window. She reached up and knocked.

A few seconds later, Lane propped the window open and leaned out. "No flowers?" he asked in mock indignation. Then he shrugged. "That's okay. You can serenade me instead."

She glared at him.

"Or not. Here. I made this for you. It'll put you in a better mood." He tossed something at her, and she caught it against her chest.

"What is it?"

"A weapon. I know how much you like them. It's a ninja throwing star."

She frowned. "It's paper. How is that a weapon?"

"Did you expect me to learn metalsmithing overnight? Angel, has anyone ever told you that you're very hard to please?"

She raised an eyebrow. "Is this the cool thing you said you wanted to show me?"

"No. It gets better. One second." He moved out of sight and then returned wearing his black leather jacket, red scarf, and a knit cap.

He pushed the window wider and jumped down beside her, pulling it shut behind him. "Doors. They're so last year. Don't you think?"

She threw the ninja star at him, but it missed the mark. He picked it up and handed it back. "It's the gift that keeps on giving." He strode off before she could take another shot. She tucked the tightly folded paper into her pocket and trailed after him.

His long legs carried him to the opposite corner of the back yard from where she'd climbed the fence yesterday. Just past a large pine tree, there was an enormous pile of snow hidden out of sight of the house. The mound was almost as tall as Lane was, and it took her a moment before she noticed that there was an entry hole. "An igloo?" she asked.

"Almost an igloo. It's called a quinzee. Instead of building it with blocks of ice, you hollow out a pile of snow." He gestured her forward. "Come in—it's a lot warmer inside." He bent to crawl through the entry.

She hesitated. "There's room for us both in there?"

"Don't worry. I haven't forgotten the no-touch rule. Your angelic incineration thing. There's plenty of room. You'll see." He disappeared inside.

She leaned down and poked her head through the arched doorway. The quinzee was at least six or seven feet in diameter. She could make this work.

She crawled through and looked around, marveling. Lane had lit a couple of candles, so the lighting was soft, and the air smelled of lavender.

And she was surrounded by snow. It was otherworldly.

"Have a seat." He gestured to a large foam pad he'd put on the ground. Then he settled down across from her on his own foam pad.

She sat and crossed her legs. "You built this yourself?"

"It wasn't hard. You build the snow as high and wide as you can, basically. Then you find a bunch of sticks around a foot long and poke them all the way into the walls. When you hollow the pile out, you know when to stop when you hit the end of a stick. Simple."

"That's mildly impressive."

He beamed. "It's my homage to the Winter Carnival."

"What is that?"

He gawked at her. "Seriously? The Winter Carnival. You've never been?"

When she shook her head, he leaned forward. "You have to go! There are ice and snow sculptures, sledding, food trucks, music, and a huge scavenger hunt. There are parades and the largest puzzle competition in the country. It's running for two weeks this year because of the Twin Cities hosting the Super Bowl, and there'll even be a seventy-foot ice palace made of 4,000 blocks of ice. It's amazing!"

He cocked his head sideways. "You know, if you've never been, maybe we could—"

"Why don't we get down to business," she said, cutting him off. This was veering into dangerous territory.

She yanked the registration paper from her pocket and thrust it toward him. "I brought this so you could take a picture of it."

He held up both hands. "Whoa. You just got here. We can't talk business yet. I need to be wined and dined a little, thank you very much. Slow down and take in the ambiance, Angel. Where's your sense of romance?"

"My sense of romance?" she demanded.

"Yes. Your sense of romance. Do you even have one?"

"You couldn't handle my sense of romance."

"Try me."

She held both hands up in warning. "Okay, but I want you to remember that you asked for this."

"Bring it on." He scooted his mat closer.

Instantly, she shifted character, curling her legs to one side and tilting her head. She imitated the half-smile worn by porcelain dolls, staring at him with wide, fixed eyes. "Hello, Lane," she said in a syrupy-sweet voice.

"That's...kind of creeping me out, actually."

"I thought you wanted me to be more romantic." She giggled, winding a strand of hair around one finger. Then she sighed dreamily. "Let's spend all day just gazing at each other."

He gaped at her. "Okay, that's enough. I admit it. You were right, and I was wrong."

She kept her face frozen in doll-like sweetness. "I thought you said you wanted romance." She batted her lashes at him.

"Stop. Seriously. Stop." He scooted his mat away from her. "You're going to give me nightmares."

She broke character, leaning back on her hands and smiling wickedly.

He shook himself. "Never. Ever. Do that again."

"Can we get down to business now?"

"You're no fun," he pouted. "Let's at least do the three questions game. Then I'll take a picture of your registration paper. Deal?"

She heaved a sigh. "Deal."

"Also—and this does not count as one of my questions—you do realize that your sense of romance is seriously warped, right?"

She laughed sarcastically. "That's fitting."

"Because you've never had a romance?"

"Because I never should," she said, glancing up at him. "I'm a complete disaster."

He looked grave. "That's not true, Angel. You—"

"Do you want your three questions or not?" she snapped.

He regarded her silently for a moment, then let it go. "Who goes first?"

"Me. This will be a rapid-fire round. Short answers only. Ready?"

"Fire away."

She knew she should probe for something useful, but he had thrown her off balance with his talk of romance. She glanced around at the walls of ice and said the first thing that came to mind. "What's your favorite flavor of ice cream?"

"Butterscotch."

She moaned, tilting her head back. "I should have known. That is so 1950s of you."

"Thank you for that compliment." He leaned forward. "Favorite flower."

"Dandelions. When they have the top like a little white puff ball."

"The kind where you blow on them and they scatter in the wind? Those aren't flowers. They're weeds."

"I don't care. That's what I'm picking."

"Why, though?"

She looked away. "Because you can wish on them."

He nodded, studying her. "Five seconds ago, I would have said my favorite flowers were peonies, but suddenly I'm partial to dandelions. Go figure." He pointed to her. "Your turn."

She considered. "What do you want to be? After high school, I mean."

"What do I want to be?" He put his head in his hand, thinking. A serious expression stole over his face. "I want to be happy. I want to be useful. I want to be there for the people I love."

She blinked. "Oh."

"Or, if you were looking for the easy answer, I want to be a mechanic." He smiled winningly. "You?"

The question caught her off guard. She'd thought about it. Of course, she'd thought about it. But not in any real way. She'd always assumed she'd have to do something virtual. Something that involved working on her computer and never setting foot outside her apartment.

"I want to be...harmless." The word was out of her mouth before she had time to think about it. But she realized it was true. She was so tired of hurting the people around her. She glanced away, uncomfortable beneath his gaze.

He watched her steadily, all joking gone. "That's not possible, you know. For anyone. We all mess up. Make mistakes. You're only human."

"But I'm not." The shadow of a smile slid over her lips. "I'm an angel."

"Of course, you are," he said. His tone was soft. "No wonder you hold yourself to impossible standards."

She was in over her head again. "Last question. Will you please take a picture of this registration now?"

A familiar voice cut across the yard. "Lane, are you in that stupid quinzee?"

She froze. She'd already faced Brie's hostility once today. So far, Lane hadn't realized that she was both Angel *and* Jenna. She might not be as lucky with his sister.

Seconds later, Brie poked her head through the entrance. "I've been looking for you everywhere. I need—who's that?" Her sharp gaze swept Jenna from head to toe, and her brows knitted in confusion, as if trying to place her.

"This is my friend, Angel," he told her. Then he looked at Jenna. "Brie's my sister."

She didn't speak, afraid Brie would recognize her voice. She waved instead, hoping no one asked her anything.

Blessedly, Brie returned her attention to Lane. "The Phillipses won't let me go to Kayla's house until I finish that stupid algebra assignment. Will you please let your friend know that you promised you'd help me?"

He scowled. "All right, all right. Give me a minute."

Brie backed out of the entrance, giving Jenna a look of loathing that should have melted a hole in the snow behind her.

"Does your sister hate everybody?" she whispered when Brie was gone.

"She's had a rough time of it." Lane looked down, rolling the end of his red scarf back and forth in his fingers. "You remember I told you we lived with my grandparents until they both died?"

"I remember."

"Well, after that, the court gave custody back to my mother and...it wasn't good. Especially for Brie." His shoulders slumped. "I should have seen what my mom was doing—lying right and left. I should have protected Brie better."

"Now who's holding himself to impossible standards?" she asked quietly.

He looked up at her. "Don't judge Brie too harshly, okay?"

She thought of the picture in Lane's wallet where a younger version of Brie smiled sunnily for the camera. But a picture could tell its own lies.

She swallowed and nodded. "I'll try."

He let the scarf drop and reached forward. "Here, give me the registration."

She handed it to him carefully, and he pulled out his phone and snapped the picture. "I'll see what I can find out."

She took the paper back, tucking it into her pocket. "Your sister is waiting for you. I should get going."

Then Lane aimed his cell phone at her.

She froze. "What do you think you're doing?"

"I'm taking a picture so I can see you whenever I want."

She crossed her arms over her chest and glared at him. "Put that away!"

"Perfect!" He gave her a thumbs-up. "Angry is your best look. Now turn to the side and chew me out."

She hurled the ninja star at him and missed.

"Ooh, action poses—I like it."

"I'm leaving."

He thrust the phone hastily into his jacket pocket and held up his hands. "Gone! It's gone. Don't leave."

But she was already backing out of the quinzee.

"Hey! I didn't get my third question."

She stopped.

"This is a serious one, Angel. Will you please call the police? I'm worried you're trying to deal with this Mercedes guy by yourself, and I don't like it."

"There's nothing to worry about," she told him a little too brightly. "I'll see you tomorrow, okay?"

"You will?" He looked both puzzled and excited. "Do we have a date I don't know about?"

She momentarily turned to stone.

Angel was not supposed to see him tomorrow. *Jenna* was the one who'd see him in class. She scrambled for a way out.

"Don't be presumptuous, Earth Boy." She pinned him with her most imperious gaze. "You won't see *me*, but *I* will see you. As your guardian angel, I'm always watching. So I'll see you tonight. I'll see you tomorrow. I'll see you whenever I want." She paused, hoping he would buy the lie.

He shook his head in amazement. "Wow. Now that is intriguing." He leaned toward her. "I didn't realize you were *always* watching. I'll have to remember to wave tonight when I'm in the shower. Enjoy the show."

She opened her mouth to give him a piece of her mind, then thought better of it and huffed her way out of the quinzee, ignoring his soft laughter.

She stood up, grateful for the brittle air that cooled her flaming cheeks. Without looking back, she turned and pelted down the sidewalk for home, trying to outrun Lane's last words and her own wicked imagination.

Chapter Nineteen

ALEXVANDER

Saturday morning, Jenna flexed her hands on the steering wheel, trying to work blood back into her numb fingers.

She'd zipped her white jacket all the way up and added extra layers underneath. But even with all that and her balaclava on, she was still freezing. She asked herself again why she'd left her comfortable apartment to go to Doc's house.

But she knew exactly why she was going. She patted her jeans pocket again, making sure the seed was still inside. Fore had given her the seed—like a stamp of approval—when she'd said she would come here. So here she was, driving through the frozen countryside.

Fore was leading her by the nose, throwing out a trail of breadcrumbs and expecting her to follow. And she was sick of it.

She'd had no word from her aunt. She didn't know what to do with the stupid seed. And apparently her mother's life depended on the whim of a magical jellyfish woman who couldn't just show up and have a conversation like a normal person.

It was infuriating.

But she didn't have any better ideas. So, she was going to treat the day as an experiment.

So far at Coldwater High School the only signs Fore had sent her had come during TOTEL meetings in the drama room.

But was Fore pointing her toward something in that room or toward one of the TOTEL members? If Jenna got a sign today at Doc's house, she'd know for sure.

Doc lived in the country about a half hour away. It was so far, she would never have gone to Coldwater High except for her dad's teaching job. But, at length,

Jenna reached the gravel drive Doc had described and turned in.

Three black-and-white goats roamed a field beside a large, weathered barn and a smaller shed. There was also a red chicken coop with five plump chickens pecking behind wire mesh.

Ahead of her, Doc came out a side door of the brick and wood split-level house. She waved, pointing to a place where Jenna could park next to their sky-blue Subaru Outback.

Jenna pulled in. As she got out of her car, a beat-up army green camper van rumbled down the driveway with Kelsea at the wheel.

She laid on the horn, and an old-fashioned AH-OOO-GAH sound blared out. The van exhaled a thick cloud of exhaust as Kelsea mercifully shut the thing off. Then she leaped down from the driver's seat and beamed.

Today she had on turquoise tights and combat boots, and beneath her gold-colored coat was a dress like a patchwork quilt. She spread her arms wide, displaying the van proudly. "Meet AlexVander!"

Doc's brow furrowed, and she peered around to the passenger side, looking for a newcomer. But it was Lane and Brie who clambered out.

Lane waved to Jenna, and Brie pointedly ignored her.

Doc eyed the two of them, confused. "Alexander?" she asked.

"Not Alexander. AlexVANder," Kelsea said. "It's the van's name."

"I told her it was corny." Markese scoffed as he climbed out. "But nobody listens to me."

Kelsea started to respond, but Markese held up one hand to forestall her. "No. Something heinous is about to happen. I can feel it. I tried to tell you about my alligator dream this morning, but you didn't listen. And then a black cat ran out in front of us when we were leaving. Should've called this whole thing off. But it doesn't matter what I say. Nobody cares."

"Shush, Markese. Nothing heinous is going to happen," Zinnia said, climbing down after him. "I told you, I looked it up on my phone, and it says an alligator dream can be a sign of opportunity."

"And my auntie says it's a sign of spiritual danger, especially when there's more than one alligator, so don't make me tell you where you can stick your phone, Zinnia."

"But you're wearing your lucky necklace. You'll be all right." She patted him on the shoulder.

He sniffed and hunched into his coat against the cold. "There's only so much luck can do. All the necklaces in the world won't stop an alligator dream."

"Enough about your alligator dream, Markese!" Kelsea snapped. She swung to the group. "What's wrong with you people? Attention must be paid right now to our excellent new tour bus." She stamped her foot. "This is your cue to ooh and ahh, people."

"Ooh," Lane said in his best game-show voice.

"Ahh," Jenna chimed in.

"That's more like it," Kelsea said. "And our musical instruments are loaded in the back. Everything's portable, so we can take this show on the road. I've even got headsets with microphones to communicate backstage. It's the whole package." She bowed as if expecting applause.

Doc walked around AlexVander, her eyes wide. "How did you get all this, Kelsea?"

She grinned smugly. "My Uncle Ronnie owns the Smooth Sounds music shop on Snelling Avenue. I told him about our new band, and I promised we would credit his store at every one of our shows."

Zinnia coughed. "And..." she prompted.

Kelsea's smile faltered. "He said he would loan us the instruments and even throw in his old van if I promised to never, ever mention him or his shop." She crossed her arms, glaring at them. "I got what we needed, didn't I?"

"You did good, Kelsea," Zinnia soothed.

A dark purple Honda Fit with a rusted undercarriage came into view. Inside were the Gonzalez siblings, Lita and Nardo and Jose, plus Hampton. The car chugged down the gravel driveway toward them, and Doc waved Lita into a parking spot.

Jose sprang from the backseat of the purple Honda, heading straight for Brie. He had slicked back his spiky hair with handfuls of gel. And instead of his normal skinny jeans and T-shirt, he wore khakis and a suit jacket—only his old sneakers detracted from his look.

Nardo slid from the car behind Jose, shaking his head. He had on his usual

Hawaiian shirt with long shorts. Except for the lime green watch on one wrist, his arms were bare. He had no coat or gloves, and Jenna didn't know how he wasn't already frozen solid.

Then Hampton climbed out, pulling his canvas backpack over his shoulder. He came around and closed the car door that Jose and Nardo had left wide open. Then he leaned against it with his arms crossed disapprovingly over his chest.

Lita remained in the driver's seat. She checked her own lime green watch and then took out her Sharpie to draw on her hand, refusing to get out until her brother was finished making a spectacle of himself.

Jose bowed and presented Brie with a platter of churros formed into hearts. "Sweets for my sweet."

She made no move to take the platter. "What are those?"

"Churros. They're like donuts. I know you'll like them. And I can cook for you later, too. I have everything prepared at home if you'll join me. What do you say?"

Brie raised an eyebrow. "Let me see if I can clear this up for you. If you were the last guy on Earth, I wouldn't go out with you. If the planet exploded and I found out you were the last person in the galaxy, I still wouldn't date you. And if, in the entire universe, there was only you and a foul-smelling, flea-infested goat boy, I would pick the goat boy. Got it?"

"You are as poetic as you are beautiful."

"Stand over there." She pointed toward the house. "Way over there." But she smiled as Jose trotted away, still carrying his platter of churros.

As Lane watched Jose go, his eyebrows drew so close together they made a single line on his forehead.

Kelsea pulled the whistle from around her neck and blew it to get everyone's attention.

Markese jumped and muttered something under his breath about hearing aids, but Zinnia swatted him silent.

"Big news, people!" Kelsea announced. "We've got our first show on the thirty-first, a little over three weeks from now. So, let's make good use of our time today."

"Three weeks?" Markese said, appalled. "You think we can be ready in three weeks?"

"Where are we performing?" Brie asked at the same time.

Kelsea ignored Markese and answered Brie. "It's a stage in Minneapolis that's attached to a bowling alley."

Lane and Brie shared an excited glance, and Jenna's eyes widened in surprise. To her, Kelsea's announcement was more like a hurricane warning—the kind that meant you ought to leave town.

Kelsea held up her cell phone. "Also, clear your calendars for January twenty-fifth at 5:30. We're going to the Winter Carnival to pass out flyers and get the word out about our concert. A ton of people will funnel into Rice Park after the opening night parade. I expect everybody to be there."

"Remember what I told you about my skin condition?" Jenna asked.

"Indeed."

"So I can't go to this Winter Carnival thing. It'll be too hard to keep people from touching me."

"We'll figure something out." Kelsea wagged her finger. "Plan to be there, Jenna Getty. Now then...." She turned back to the group. "We're on a tight deadline, people, so no more questions. Everybody in!"

Everyone gathered in a circle with hands extending toward the middle. Jenna hovered just outside the group, shifting from foot to foot.

Kelsea raised her voice again. "TOTEL commitment in three-two-one...."

Everyone but Jenna lifted their hands toward the sky, chanting, "TOTEL commitment!"

A smile on her face, Kelsea took the keys from her pocket and tossed them to Markese. "Can you pull AlexVander over by the barn?"

"Oh, sure. Ask the person who had an alligator dream last night. The van will probably catch fire as soon as I start it up, but why would that matter to anybody?" He continued grumbling as he climbed inside and drove off.

"Follow me, people," Kelsea announced to the group. "You've got until we get to the barn to figure out what your role in the band will be."

There was a mad scramble of dibs, rock-paper-scissors, and shouted orders from Kelsea as everyone trailed after the camper van.

As Jose passed Brie, he thrust the platter of churros into her hands and then raced after Hampton. She shrugged but kept the pastries, ignoring Lane's scowl.

Jenna went to her car, pretending she needed something from the trunk. She tried to call her aunt again, but once more, there was no answer. She put her phone away and hurried to catch up with the others.

Lane and Brie walked side by side at the back of the pack. As Jenna got closer, she realized they were arguing.

"I'm going to tell him not to talk to you again."

"Lane, I'm the one who told him it was okay to hit on me. It's kind of cute, actually."

"It doesn't matter."

"It *does* matter. I don't need you to fight my battles. You have to stop protecting me sometime."

His voice was subdued. "Because I've done such a wonderful job."

She sucked her teeth. "You know what Granddad always said. The past has passed, and the future isn't promised. You've got to get over it, because none of it was your fault, and you're not making it any better by dwelling on it."

Brie's statement was met with stony silence.

Jenna wondered if she should fake a cough to alert them that she was there, but then Lane spoke up.

"I don't trust him."

"You don't trust anybody when it comes to me."

A stick cracked beneath Jenna's foot, and Brie spun around, pinning her with a glare. "Did you get a good earful?" She looked back and forth between Jenna and Lane. "Why don't you both get your own lives and stay out of mine!" She flounced away.

"I'm so sorry," Jenna said, turning to Lane. "I didn't mean to—"

He shrugged. "I'm the one who got her going." Then he smiled crookedly. "Beating on the drums today should get some of it out of her system."

Jenna nodded, and they both headed for the barn.

One disaster at a time.

Kelsea jogged back and fell into step beside them. "Here's the update. So I'm the band manager, obviously."

"Why obviously?" Lane asked, but Kelsea plowed on.

"I already promised Brie she could play drums, and Zinnia's on trumpet. Doc's agreed to learn a little guitar, and except for you two, everybody else will be working behind the scenes."

"Minor question," Jenna said. "What music are we playing?"

Kelsea looked at her as if she were crazed. "I'm the manager. You guys are the creatives. Create something." And she jogged away.

Lane shook his head. "Turd burgers."

When they walked into the barn, the propane heater was going, so it was warmer than Jenna had expected. And the smell of hay and animals was strong but pleasant.

There were a couple of stalls and a loft at the back of the space. The front half was set up with a table saw, drill press, and other tools she couldn't name. Along one wall was a workbench and counter, and above it someone had hung dozens of old license plates along with antique wagon wheels, coils of rope, and rusty farm equipment.

Doc had collected a variety of chairs—everything from beach chairs to a wooden rocker—and placed them around the room.

Lita was busy pulling up online videos for Brie and Doc in one corner, and Nardo climbed into the loft after Markese and Zinnia.

Someone had already unloaded the keyboard from the back of the van, setting it near an outlet. Jenna headed for it, and Lane followed.

"Oh." She scratched her head through the cloth of the balaclava. "You should join one of the other groups. I work better by myself."

"Me too," he said. "That's why I think we'll make a great team."

She frowned. "I'm serious, though. I like to work alone."

"That's because you've never worked alone with me. Come on. You still owe me your firstborn child, remember? But I'll accept working together today instead." He gave her a winning smile, and she sighed in defeat.

Lane grabbed chairs for them both while she finished setting up the keyboard. He turned his chair backward and sat down, crossing his arms on the back of the seat. He waited expectantly.

She plugged in the keyboard and played some chords to break the silence. After a few awkward moments, though, she burst out, "I have no idea what to do now. Do you?"

"Not a clue," he admitted. Then he got a gleam in his eye. "We should do something so terrible Kelsea puts someone else in charge of coming up with the songs."

She tilted her head, suddenly inspired. "What would you think about a rock version of 'Mary Had a Little Lamb'?"

"That's it," he said, snapping his fingers. "But let's change it just enough that she thinks we're being serious."

"I could play it in a minor key," she suggested. "That would give it an eerie sound." She played the tune slowly.

"Wow. It's like the lamb is dead." He nodded. "You're an evil genius, Mo."

Behind the fabric of her balaclava, she suppressed a smile.

"We should change the lyrics too," he urged. "We could do a sci-fi theme and call it 'Mary had a Hologram.'"

"Or would people respond more to 'Mary had an Instagram'?"

"OMG," he said. "I love them both."

They spent the next hour twisting every nursery rhyme they knew. They were cracking themselves up over "Twinkle, Twinkle" when Kelsea sailed over.

"Let's hear it," she demanded.

The laughter died on their lips. They exchanged glances, and Lane got into character.

"We're working on one now that's really deep," he told her. "It's called, 'Twinkle, twinkle little star. You are more than who you are.' What do you think?"

They held their breath, awaiting her outrage. But she only clapped him on the shoulder. "I knew I picked the right people."

They turned shocked eyes on each other.

"Turd burgers," Jenna whispered.

"Now come share that genius juice with Jose and Hampton," Kelsea said. "They're painting AlexVander, and they could use creative feedback."

"Painting?" Jenna asked as she and Lane followed her outside.

"Indeed. It's free advertising. Lita's going to build our website, and once we figure out our name today, we'll paint that on, too."

They rounded the corner, and Jenna and Lane both stopped short.

"What do you think?" Kelsea asked.

"Wow," Jenna said.

"Wow," Lane echoed. "It's...certainly a showstopper."

She nodded in satisfaction and strode away.

Near two heating lamps, Hampton and Jose had spread a blue tarp over the snow. It was littered with paint cans, and they huddled over them, talking and pointing.

The twins had been busy. Already, they'd painted swirls and abstract patterns all over the van, covering the army green paint with a kaleidoscope of colors no one could miss. It was as if a rainbow had sprung up over AlexVander—and then vomited.

"What are you guys doing?" Jenna asked, walking over. Lane followed more reluctantly, shooting an irritated glance at Jose.

"We figured out a cool way to paint the top of the van," Jose said.

Hampton swung his canvas bag to the ground and dug around until he found his drone and a roll of duct tape. He tore off a length of the tape while Jose grabbed a brush from the canary yellow paint can.

Hampton taped the handle of the brush to the drone so that the bristles pointed down. Then Jose held the drone aloft and Hampton used the remote to get it flying. He maneuvered the drone over the van.

"Do a lightning bolt," Jose prodded. "It could stand for Zeus, or Harry Potter, or Shazam, or—"

"The Flash." Slowly, Hampton made the drone hover over the roof, and then, using the video feed, he began to paint the lightning bolt.

"That's pretty good," Lane said, peering over his shoulder.

Hampton flew the drone back and forth, stopping periodically for Jose to dip the bristles into the paint. When they finished, there was a recognizable bolt of lightning on the roof, and they whooped in celebration.

Then Hampton went back to painting the doors of the van while Lane and Jenna watched. Jose returned to the cans of paint, crouching down.

Suddenly, a small mouse scooted across the tarp, moving straight toward Lane. He yelped, hopping up and down.

Hampton spun around, dropped his paintbrush, and scooped Lane up in his arms. He cradled him as easily as if he were a small child.

Jose burst into laughter, and Jenna marched over and picked up the wind-up mouse where it had collided with the barn.

She rounded on Jose, hands on hips. "That wasn't funny."

His smile melted. "You guys are no fun."

Still in Hampton's arms, Lane looked at his savior sheepishly. "Um, you can put me down now," Lane told him. His cheeks were as red as his scarf.

Hampton set him down, and Lane stepped quickly away. "Thanks, dude."

Jenna was getting ready to unleash on Jose again when Markese marched out of the barn.

He went straight to the van. Avoiding the paint, he climbed into the passenger seat and slammed the door shut. Then he manually rolled the window down an inch. "Jose, tell Kelsea I need a word." He rolled the window up and sat back, holding on to his necklace and muttering to himself.

Kelsea appeared, followed by Zinnia. They went over to the van and waited for him to crack the window. "What's wrong, Markese?"

"Oh, nothing. Nothing at all. Everything is sunshine and roses. It's not like you led me into a death trap."

"Death trap?" Zinnia prodded gently. "It was a spider web."

"It wasn't just a spider web. It was an alligator dream, followed by a black cat, followed by a spider web. That is a Trifecta of Evil. I should've had you leave me home this morning after I dreamed about the alligator last night. I don't know what I was thinking. That was three signs in a row, Kelsea. Something bad is coming. Something heinous. You need to take me on home."

"Nobody's going anywhere, Markese. Come back out."

"I don't think so."

"Markese, I was the one who walked into the spider web," Zinnia said. "If you come out, I'll do it again, and you can get the whole thing on video. Think how fun it will be to vlog about it tonight."

Markese rolled the window up, ignoring them all.

It suddenly struck Jenna. Maybe she wasn't the only person Fore was trying to communicate with. Was the black cat Markese saw this morning the same one that had appeared to her? If Fore had made the spider web, what did that mean? Or was Markese finding signs where there were none?

Doc and the others joined the group. "Dad texted me that he has apple cider set out for us in the den." Then Doc noticed Markese. "Are you...is everybody leaving?"

"Kelsea and I will handle Markese," Zinnia told her. "You all go ahead in."

Jose and Hampton cheered and raced for the house, and everyone else followed.

Lane fell into step beside Jenna as they walked. He tried to strike up a conversation, but she was no longer listening.

Nardo was about ten yards in front of her, trailing along behind Lita and Doc. And every time he took a step, clover grew up through the snow, making perfect green footsteps in a sea of white.

She put her own shoe inside one of Nardo's green prints, feeling the springy softness of the clover. Then she stepped outside the footprint, and her shoe crunched on frozen snow.

Fore.

She narrowed her eyes and followed the footprints.

CHAPTER TWENTY

SOMETHING HEINOUS

Nardo's trail of bright green footprints led all the way to Doc's house. And no one else had noticed.

What was Fore telling her?

At least now she knew it wasn't the drama room that was important. It was the group. Or maybe it was just Nardo.

Beside her, Lane's conversation broke off mid-word as he stepped on a patch of ice and went into a skid.

She instinctively reached out to steady him, but then snatched her hand away in time.

He regained his balance and grinned sheepishly. "Pretend you didn't see that."

"See what?" She was pretending not to see all kinds of things lately.

She opened the door to the house, and Lane came in after her. They stopped in the mudroom to take off their shoes and Lane's jacket. Then they went through a second door into the den.

Jose, Hampton, and Lita sprawled on the sofa, and Brie lounged in the recliner, scrolling on her phone. Jenna wasn't sure where Nardo had gone.

A Saint Bernard that was the size of a small pony bounded over. The dog had long black patches that ran from his eyes to his jowls, and his floppy brown ears were tipped in black as well.

"Pudge, sit," Doc said. He sat obediently at Doc's side, leaning out to sniff Jenna and Lane.

Doc handed them napkins and two steaming mugs of apple cider, and Jenna took hers carefully, making sure she didn't touch Doc's fingers. They found a place by the windows where they could sit on the floor.

The den was covered in dark brown paneling, so at first Jenna didn't spot the branch-like structure where a huge bird was perched. When it unfolded its wings and took flight, she nearly spilled her hot cider.

The bird landed on Doc's shoulder, and she pulled a treat from her pocket and fed it to him. "Everybody, this is Gandalf the Grey. He's an African grey parrot."

Except for his bright red tail feathers, he was the color of smoke, with ruffles covering his neck and chest. He looked a lot like an earless owl, with white rings that circled his eyes. He whistled and tugged at a strand of Doc's curly hair.

"Gandalf was a rescue from a family who didn't know what they were getting into," she explained. "He got bored and ate the molding around their doors and windows."

"That thing?" Brie asked, looking up from her phone.

"It's true," she said, running her hand down his back. "And they can live to be seventy, so it's a big commitment. But I've been working with him, and he might talk to us if he's in the mood." She held up another treat. "What do you have to say, Gandalf?"

The bird squawked, then said, "You shall not pass!"

Jose and Hampton clapped in appreciation, and Doc fed the bird another treat.

Jose jumped up. "Will he do it for me?" he asked, coming to stand near Gandalf.

"Fool of a Took!" Gandalf told him.

"You trained your parrot to insult people?" Jose asked. "That's awesome!"

"Maybe it just knows a fool when it sees one," Brie said, rolling her eyes.

But Jose's smile widened at her attention. He scurried to the couch and squeezed in between Lita and Brie.

Lita sighed and excused herself for the restroom, shooting an annoyed look at her brother.

Kelsea stormed in. "Doc, we need cider fast, before we freeze to death."

Zinnia came next, stoic as ever, followed by Markese, who was pouting.

"We wouldn't be frozen now if we'd canceled this madness. So whose fault is it that you're cold?"

"Yours," Kelsea and Zinnia both told him.

Doc went to get the cider, and Gandalf flapped away from her shoulder, settling on his perch. Pudge lifted his colossal head, then let it fall back onto his paws, yawning. Hampton, Jose, and Brie made room on the sofa for Zinnia and Markese.

As Doc pressed steaming mugs into the newcomers' hands, Kelsea strode to the desk beside the door and sat cross-legged on top of it. She pulled her gavel out of her purse and thumped it on the desk. "I call this TOTEL meeting to order."

They ran through the pledge, and Markese was so distracted he forgot to substitute "fairies" for "fairness." He shook his head ominously.

"This is Operation: Let's Name the Band," Kelsea said. "I'm giving you one minute to brainstorm."

Everyone began talking among themselves, while Gandalf the Grey made flushing sounds from his perch.

Lane turned to Jenna. "Give me your napkin."

With a quizzical look, she handed it over. He folded his napkin and hers together. "This is Gandalf the White," he said. He produced a paper bird that looked more like a turkey than a parrot.

She laughed. "Does he speak, too?"

"Of course. But only in Pig Latin."

Kelsea's voice rose over the noise. "Quiet!" she yelled.

"Quiet!" Gandalf the Grey echoed.

"Ietquay!" Lane made the napkin whisper.

Kelsea slid off the desk and stood up. "When I point to you, tell me your idea for a band name." She pointed to Jose.

"The Earlobes."

"Terrible," Kelsea said. "Hampton, go."

He looked at Jose in a panic. "Uh, the...Cheeks."

"No more body parts," Kelsea huffed.

She pointed to Zinnia, who was next in line on the couch. "What have you got, Zinn?"

"One second. I'm plugging some things into a band name generator online."

"You can't do that!" she said, aghast.

"Why not?"

"It's soulless!"

"We're the Itchy Infinity," Zinnia said, holding up her phone.

Everyone murmured in appreciation, but Kelsea stamped her foot. "We're tabling this discussion until later."

"I think everyone likes that one, Kelsea," Zinnia told her.

"Yes, but half of you are drunk on paint fumes and cider."

"It's nonalcoholic," Doc said, confused.

The room erupted in debate, and Lita and Nardo came back in.

Jenna watched closely as Nardo crossed in front of her, but he was no longer leaving footprints. He went to stand in front of Gandalf the Grey.

Gandalf started hopping up and down, whistling. Nardo imitated him, flapping his arms and jumping up and down. Pudge raised his head, watching Nardo. Then he stood up and barked.

Kelsea blew her whistle, and everyone stopped talking. But Nardo kept going, and the animals got even more worked up. Pudge barked louder, and Gandalf called out, "Fly, you fools!"

Kelsea frowned at Doc over the cacophony. "Can't you get them to be quiet?"

She stood up, troubled. "I don't know what's wrong. They've never done this before."

She motioned for Pudge to calm down while she held up a treat for Gandalf. But both animals were so focused on Nardo, they didn't notice.

"What's going on?" she said, puzzled.

Jenna stated the obvious. "Maybe it would help if Nardo wasn't messing with them."

Nardo stopped playing with the animals, turning to Jenna with a shocked look. The room went deathly silent.

She felt her face redden as everyone continued to stare at her.

Then Lita bolted from her seat and ran out of the room. Jose went after her, and Markese put his hand over his mouth. A heavy hush filled the air.

"What...what did I say?" Jenna asked. She stole a look at Lane, but he seemed as confused as she was.

Zinnia spoke slowly. "We don't mention Nardo in front of Lita."

That didn't make sense. She glanced sideways at Nardo.

He had moved closer to her and was crouching down, so he was at eye level.

"Why can't we mention Nardo?"

"Jenna Getty," Kelsea said, putting her hands on her hips. "Even I know better than to mention Nardo. Lita still gets upset, even though he's been dead for over two years."

Chapter Twenty-One

ANOTHER

Jenna's throat constricted. Her eyes slid to Nardo's.

He gave her a doleful look and nodded slowly. Then his mouth moved, shaping words, but no sound came out. He gestured, and her eyes caught on his lime green watch. A watch similar to the one Lita always wore.

All at once, she realized the truth. The watches weren't similar. They were the same. Because Lita was wearing Nardo's watch—in memory of her dead brother.

She couldn't catch her breath.

Markese nudged Zinnia and whispered, "Didn't I tell you something heinous was about to happen? Didn't I?"

She ignored him and sat forward, her eyes on Jenna. "That was a mistake—yes. But an honest one. You didn't know."

Doc hurried to reassure her as well. "I'm sure Lita will be fine." She looked at the others. "Jose will talk with her. We all will."

"I'll see if I can help," Brie put in, giving Jenna a withering glance as she left to find Lita.

"Here's what I can't figure out," Kelsea said. "How did she know about Nardo?" She spoke as if Jenna wasn't sitting right there.

"We must have mentioned his name, and she just...misunderstood." Doc's face crumpled with worry as she glanced at Jenna.

Jenna's mind whirled. How *had* she known his name? Then she remembered her very first TOTEL meeting. Lita had been drawing Doc's name on the girl's arm. Lita had inked her first name on her own forearm as well. Then, when Jenna had looked over at Nardo, she'd seen his name written the same way and assumed Lita had drawn it there. Her breath caught.

She stood, feeling the weight of everyone's eyes. "I'm so sorry. Please tell Lita. And Jose, too. I have to…." She rushed from the room, avoiding Nardo's gaze. She slowed just long enough to shove her feet into her sneakers, and then she was outside, gasping for breath in the welcome cold.

She glanced behind her.

Nardo had followed, a dazed expression on his face.

Panic gripped her, and she ran.

Was this another of Fore's tricks? A message of some kind?

Fireflies she could handle. Birds, butterflies, ginormous plants, and patches of clover—no problem. But this was different. This was a person. A dead person. It was too much.

She stumbled to a halt near the barn and turned to look behind her. Nardo was gone.

She put her hands on her knees, sucking in air. Then she stood. She had to go before he came back. There was no way she was staying to practice music with a dead guy. She spun and hurried toward her car.

How had she not known? It was so clear now. Nardo had never changed clothes, not even in the freezing weather. No one had ever introduced her to him or told her his name. And Nardo had never taken part in the conversation. In fact, he'd never spoken a word.

She shuddered. She'd spent days hanging out with a ghost and never noticed. It was beyond creepy. And what would she do at the next TOTEL meeting? She couldn't face Nardo. Or Lita. Or any of the rest of them.

And they probably didn't want to see her, either.

She looked up as Lane called her name. "Don't worry. I'm leaving." She blew past him, eyes down.

He hurried after her, trying to keep pace with her rapid steps. "Why are you leaving, Mo? Nobody wants you to leave."

"That's not true. And anyway, I'm not going back in there. I made a complete fool of myself."

"I do that all the time," he told her. "It's practically my life's work."

She refused to look at him. "It's not funny. I hurt Lita, bringing up her dead brother like that."

"She'll get over it. It was a slip of the tongue. We've all done it."

As they neared the house and her Corolla, she glanced around warily, but Nardo was still absent. She made a beeline for her car door, but Lane stood in the way.

"Will you wait a second, please? There's no reason to be upset. It was just one stupid sentence. You probably overheard somebody mention Nardo's name, and then today you made a joke, not realizing. It's no big deal."

He didn't get it. It wasn't just that she'd made a joke about a dead boy. It was that the dead boy *had been there*. "I need to leave," she insisted.

"I'm worried about letting you drive when you're this worked up, Mo. Take a minute and calm down."

That wasn't possible, but he didn't need to know that. She could bluff her way out.

"You're right," she said, channeling the demeanor of a yogi. "I overreacted." She took a deep breath in and out. "But I already feel a lot better, and I'm okay to drive. Really. It's totally safe."

He furrowed his brows and tapped his foot. Then he pivoted. "Speaking of safety, I meant to check the tire we changed." He walked around to the passenger side, crouching down to inspect his handiwork. "Is the car riding okay?"

This was a delay tactic. She knew that. But she used the opportunity to climb into the driver's seat.

Before she could pull out, though, he knocked on her passenger window, frowning.

She rolled the window down. "The tire has been great, Lane. I promise. It will—"

He held an object out to her. A small black box. "You know this is on here, right?"

"No," she said, taking the thing. "What is it?"

His frown deepened. "It's a GPS tracker."

She shook her head. "A tracker?"

"So someone can see where you go." He leaned in through the open window. "Do you think your mom put it on there for safety? In case you're hurt, or the car is stolen?"

Her mouth went dry. This was not her mother's doing. She knew that.

Then it hit her. Maybe this was why Thairyn Hinsen hadn't been following her. Maybe he hadn't needed to. He knew exactly where she was.

She set the black box on the seat beside her, avoiding Lane's eyes. "I'll ask my mom about it," she lied. "Thanks for your help. Speaking of my mom, though, I need to get home."

Reluctantly, he backed away. "All right then. See you on Monday," he called, waving her off.

In a daze, she headed back up the Lindgrens' driveway. She waited until she was out of sight of the house, then she pulled over and dialed up her aunt. She had a million things she was desperate to ask, but the phone rang endlessly, and she threw it down on the seat in frustration.

She was tired of waiting. Tired of being hunted.

Then her mouth twitched with an idea.

She picked up her phone again and pulled up a map of the area. She needed a pond or a lake nearby. And somewhere she could park without being seen. Thankfully, Minnesota deserved its reputation as the Land of 10,000 Lakes, and she found a likely place not far away. She started the car.

Her mom wouldn't be expecting her for a couple of hours yet. And though she'd given Lane the VIN number so he could help her find Thairyn's address, she wasn't sure she could wait that long. If the man in the silver Mercedes had taken her aunt, every minute counted.

She drove to the frozen pond and parked on a side road. Then she scrambled out and made her way to the edge of the ice. Checking that no one else was around, she hurled the little black box as far as she could. It landed on the frozen surface and slid a good distance, coming to a stop far out on the ice.

If someone was watching her movements, it would appear as if her car was suddenly out in the middle of a pond. She'd see what her tracker would make of that. She backed away, settling down behind a large bush to watch. She was the hunter now.

After nearly an hour, she considered abandoning the experiment due to impending frostbite. But then a car pulled up. It wasn't a silver Mercedes, though—it was a black Jeep. It looked familiar, but she couldn't place it. And she couldn't see the driver from so far away.

The Jeep waited there for several minutes, but no one got out. And when it pulled away, Jenna made a quick decision. This wasn't Thairyn Hinsen's car, but what if he was inside? Or what if the driver was working for him? There had to be a connection.

She bolted toward her Corolla, quickly slid in and turned the key, then followed the Jeep at a distance.

Soon, she was on a two-lane highway surrounded by fields and patches of dense woods on both sides. More than once, she had to let the Jeep get out of sight, so it wasn't obvious she was following.

Distracted by a distinctive bright red silo on her right, she almost didn't notice when the Jeep turned off the highway and onto a dirt road. She pulled to the side, letting it get even further ahead. Then she turned after it, driving cautiously through the thickening woods. Maple, oak, and ash trees towered over her on both sides, and she crept along a path hardly wider than the car itself.

She glanced at the map on her phone. The road dead-ended ahead at some deep woods, and she could see a couple of scattered ponds on the map. There were no other houses around.

She found a place where the path widened enough to pull over. From here, she'd go on foot.

Using trees and brush for cover, she crept closer until, at a turn in the bend, she spotted a dark wooden house. It had a garage on one side and a screened-in porch on the back, but the entire building was deteriorating. There were shingles missing from the roof and wood rotting on the door jamb.

Music blared from somewhere inside, and she slipped closer, using every bit of stealth she possessed. When she ran out of trees to hide behind, she darted to the garage and peered through the window.

She was hoping to see Thairyn's silver Mercedes parked alongside the Jeep, but it wasn't there. That didn't mean the driver of the Jeep hadn't been following her, though. If so, she should find out more about her stalker while she was here.

She edged around the house in a half-crouch. At each window she checked, her view was blocked by dark brown curtains.

One window, though, was strange. Unlike the others, there was a layer of frost trapped between the panes of glass—as if the room behind the drapes was humid enough to make the window sweat and refreeze. As she drew nearer, she could hear high-pitched noises—squeaks, or maybe chirps—coming from inside. A shiver worked its way up her spine, but she kept going.

On the other side of the house, she had a bit of luck. One set of curtains wasn't drawn completely closed. Holding her breath so she wouldn't fog the glass, she peered inside. No one was in the room, so she leaned closer.

The main part of the house was large and open. The walls and the wooden floors were both a dingy brown, and the ceiling showed signs of mold. Near the fireplace, there was a worn plaid sofa and a scarred coffee table. Another corner housed a twin bed with a metal frame. And across from her was a small kitchen with cracked laminate countertops.

The only thing that stood out was a set of shelves on one wall that held six large aquariums and several cages. But it was too far away for her to see what animals were inside.

Everything else seemed normal. Neglected, but normal.

What had she expected to find? Thairyn, huddled over a master plan, plotting? Her aunt, bound and gagged, as she silently begged to be saved? She slumped against the wall.

At that moment, her phone rang at full volume, and her heart leaped into her throat.

Toenails scrabbled on wood and then a beagle's head appeared in the window, barking furiously. Inside the house, someone clicked the loud music off. Footsteps creaked on the wooden floor as someone came to investigate.

She dove for the woods, fumbling to silence her phone. Hesitating at the edge of the trees, she glanced back.

A man in his twenties with long blond hair stepped outside. He was as different from Thairyn Hinsen as you could get. He had hippie hair and baggy clothes, and Jenna couldn't even picture the two men talking to each other, much less working together.

She plunged into the undergrowth and ran.

What had she been thinking? She'd spent her afternoon trespassing—spying on a random stranger. Nothing connected her to this place. It was just bad luck that this guy had stopped at the pond earlier.

When she reached her car, she jumped inside, did a three-point turnaround, and peeled out onto the narrow path, praying she wouldn't meet anyone coming in the other direction. She glanced in the rearview mirror, but no one was following her. Relieved, she turned onto the main road, glad to put this embarrassing fiasco behind her.

She pulled out her phone as she tried to catch her breath. She had two texts and a missed call from Lane. The phone was still in her hand when it went off once more. The call switched to Bluetooth, ringing over the car's speakers.

Lane. Again.

Had he found out something about the VIN number already? She pressed her lips together. If he had Thairyn's address, she couldn't afford to ignore him.

She took a second to compose herself. She had to remember not to mention anything that had happened that morning. No TOTEL-related conversation was allowed. Lane was calling Angel—not Jenna—and she needed to keep her stories straight. She pressed to connect the call.

"Hi there," she said, trying to disguise the fact that she was out of breath.

There was a brief pause. "What's wrong?" he asked suspiciously.

"Nothing. Why do you ask?"

"Because you're panting like you're on the run from a murderer. Are you on the run from a murderer?"

"No. No murderers. I'm totally safe."

"Really?"

"Yep."

"Really, really?"

"Really, really," she assured him.

There was another pause. "But...," he prompted her.

"But...I might have just accidentally become a stalker."

"Huh. Not sure what that means. Should I be concerned or jealous?"

"Neither. Never mind. It's not important. The main thing is, there's no danger."

He sighed heavily, unconvinced. "Okay, Angel. I hope you're not lying to me, because I have something to tell you. But I'm worried about what you'll do."

"What did you find out?" she demanded, sitting up straight.

He held the phone away from his mouth. "I'll be right there, Brie. Give me one second!" Then his voice returned to normal. "Sorry. I snuck away from a meeting to call you."

She swallowed. Lane must still be at the TOTEL meeting at Doc's house. But she wasn't supposed to know that. It was getting harder and harder to juggle her two personas. "What do you need to tell me?" she pressed, steering the conversation back into safe territory.

"Promise me you won't do anything dangerous. Do you promise?"

"Of course," she said a little too quickly.

He grunted. "Angel, I mean it. Don't lie to me about this. I really, really don't like to be lied to. You promise you won't do anything unsafe?"

The lie was harder the second time. She injected her voice with sincerity. "I promise." Her hands tightened on the steering wheel. "Now, what is it?"

He sighed again. "I just got a call from a buddy who works at a shop in town. Thairyn Hinsen has been taking his car in to be serviced there, and there's an address on file that's different from the one on the registration."

"What is it?" She pulled over and got out her phone, ready to plug in the address.

He paused again and spoke more slowly. "To be clear, the reason I'm telling you this is because I'm trusting you to do the sensible thing and go to the police."

"That's what I was thinking," she said smoothly. "So what's the address?"

As he read it out loud, she put it into her phone and took a screenshot. Maybe she could salvage this day after all. If she could do her stalking at the right place this time, she'd get some answers at last.

"Now," Lane said, brightening. "I did a favor for you, so it's your turn to do one for me. I want you to come over later and assist me."

"What? That's blackmail!"

"I prefer to see it as mutual aid."

She drummed her fingers on the steering wheel. "Exactly *how* do you think I'm going to assist you?"

"Easy. I just want you to be with me."

She froze. "To *be* with you?"

"Not—" He groaned. "Don't go there. I'm being serious, Angel. Not *serious* as in...." He grunted in exasperation, and she could almost see him running his hand through his heavy black hair. "I want to be with you, okay? I want us to hang out. Together."

She stopped breathing. "You don't mean *hang out*, do you? I mean, you don't want to...."

He waited.

It hit her all at once. "Are you asking me on a date?"

"Of course, I'm asking you on a date! Again. Like when I tried to ask you to the Winter Carnival. But that's beside the point. I want to see you sooner than that. I want to see you today."

She couldn't speak. No one had ever asked her out. No one ever *should* ask her out. Her mind spun.

The seconds ticked by.

"Didn't you read the *Lane McConnell Handbook for Guardian Angels*?" he joked, filling the awkward silence. "It says on page one: '*This human will repeatedly ask you for a date.*'"

But she didn't laugh. Her throat felt tight, like invisible hands were strangling her. She'd let herself get too close. Again. And this time, she had to make it right. Her voice was hoarse when she spoke. "I...I can't."

"Okay. If today isn't good, we could do tomorrow—"

"There isn't a good day. There won't be a good day."

He went silent.

Her heart thudded erratically. Even if her aunt found a cure for her Charms, she couldn't go on a date. She was a disaster. And she'd only drag Lane down with her. The inevitable fallout was too painful to think about. She could hurt him a little now or a lot later. It was obvious what she needed to do. Still, she had to force the words out. "I can't go out with you. Ever."

He stayed silent.

She felt pressure building at the back of her eyes. "I'm sorry."

"No. I appreciate your honesty." His voice was stilted. "Does this mean I shouldn't call you anymore?"

Her breath hitched. "It's probably better if you don't."

"Okay," he said thickly. "I won't bother you again." He paused as if he wanted to say more, then quickly added, "Be safe out there, Angel." And he hung up.

She leaned her head back against the seat, blinking rapidly. She'd done the right thing—she knew that. But then, why did she feel sick to her stomach?

She couldn't allow herself to think about this now. She needed a distraction. Sitting up, she took a long, shaky breath and eased back onto the highway—heading for Thairyn Hinsen's house.

The man with the white tattoo lived only about twelve minutes outside city limits. Even so, his home was isolated, no neighbors nearby, on a remote two-lane road. The ride there passed in a blur, and she shook her head as she got closer, trying to clear it.

According to her phone, the address was just ahead, before a curve in the road. She slowed the car, pressing her face almost into the glass as she studied the one-story brick ranch that came into view.

The house sat back from the road with woods on three sides. There was no sign of anyone in the yard, but that didn't mean he wasn't home. The silver Mercedes could be parked in the garage. She'd have to proceed with caution.

She drove past the house and went around the bend before pulling over to the side of the road.

If he was monitoring the tracker, Thairyn would think she was miles away. But he'd discover the deception soon enough when the tracker never moved from that spot. She wouldn't have another chance like this one.

Her body hummed with energy as she got out of the car and darted once more into the cover of the woods. She'd had her fill of hiding in bushes today, but she didn't have any other choice. She needed to find out why this man was following her—and if he had her aunt.

She skimmed around the inner edge of the tree line. Then she moved toward the back yard where the woods came closest to the house. Peering out from between the branches of a fir tree, she didn't see any movement, so she headed in for a closer look.

She scurried to the back wall and crouched low beside the HVAC unit. Then she paused to catch her breath, straining to hear over the sound of her pounding heart. But there was only silence.

Cautiously, she inched up the wall and looked through the nearest window into a study. A quick glance reassured her that there was no one in the room. What was less comforting, though, were the rifles, crossbows, and knives displayed on the walls. She swallowed.

Squinting, she tried to read the papers on the desk in the corner, but she couldn't make out anything from here. There was nothing to do but keep moving. She rounded the corner, listening for voices as she sidled along the east wall of the house.

At the next set of windows, the curtains were closed, but she noticed a gap between the drapes. She edged closer to peek inside, and that's when she saw a girl's face in the gap, watching her intently.

She jerked backward, ready to run, but the girl didn't raise the alarm. Instead, she pushed the curtains wide, and Jenna got a good look at her for the first time.

She was a frail-looking child of around five or six. Her bare scalp was covered by a crocheted black cap that looked almost like lace, and she wore a faded olive dress that swallowed her slight form. In the crook of one arm, she clutched a stuffed owl to her side.

Her face was thin, and her eyes were immense—like a pygmy lemur Jenna had seen at the zoo once. But it was the shadowed, mournful expression in those eyes that made Jenna's heart clench.

Then she gasped, her gut twisting in horror. One of the girl's wrists was bound to a post on the wooden bed with a length of tights. She could walk only a couple of feet from the bed, and her arm was bent at an odd angle as she stood by the window.

The knots holding her captive were tight from where the girl had strained against them. Why Thairyn was holding her hostage, Jenna didn't know, but there was one thing she did know for certain: she couldn't leave her here.

She smoothed her expression, trying not to startle the child. Then she put her finger to her lips and motioned for her to open the window.

Squeezing her owl tighter, the child used her free arm to unlatch the sash and raise the window.

"Hi," Jenna said softly. She leaned closer, but the girl flinched back, crushing the owl to her body.

Jenna stopped, remembering that she was still wearing her shades and balaclava. Of course, she looked scary. She pulled them off and tucked them away in her jacket pockets. She kept her voice low. "I'm Jenna. What's your name?"

The girl pursed her lips, uncertain. Then she whispered, "My name is Raloria, and this is Owly." She made the owl's wing flap hello.

"It's nice to meet you both." Jenna gave her an encouraging smile. "Are you alone right now?"

Raloria tilted her head, thinking. Then her face brightened. "Owly is here with me."

"Ah." Jenna glanced behind the girl at the closed bedroom door. "What about Thairyn Hinsen? Is he here?"

"Not right now."

"Good. And is anybody else here?" she asked, thinking of her aunt.

"Nuh-uh," the girl told her.

She didn't know whether to be relieved or disappointed. Hopefully, that meant Aunt Serene was safe. On the other hand, she wasn't any closer to finding out where she was. At the moment, though, she couldn't do anything about her aunt. However, with no one else around, she had a chance at freeing this little girl.

She made her mouth curve into a smile. "Guess what," she told her. "I'm going to get you out of here."

Raloria shook her head, edging backward. "I'm not allowed."

Jenna had heard of captives who'd been brainwashed by their kidnappers. Seeing this girl's allegiance to her abductor made her even more determined to get her free. "It's okay," she reassured her. "You don't have to do what he told you. I'll take you home. Do you know your address?"

"Home is a long ways away," she said solemnly.

Not helpful, but she'd deal with that later. First, though, she had to figure out how to free Raloria without touching her. She doubted the girl could untie the knots. Then Jenna remembered the knives she'd seen hanging in the study.

"Raloria, I need you to stand back, okay? I have to come inside so I can get you out." She stepped forward and slid her fingers under the edge of the window, pushing it higher.

Raloria hugged herself, frowning. "I told you already before. I'm not allowed to go!" She backed away until she bumped up against the mattress.

"You'll be okay. But we have to hurry and leave now before the man comes back."

Raloria threw herself down on the bed. "I don't wanna go with you!"

Jenna stopped moving. She was obviously frightening the girl.

"It's all right. I'm not going to hurt you. I have to cut you free, but you've got to be still, okay? I don't want you to touch me."

"I don't want you touching me either!" Raloria rocked back and forth, strangling her stuffed owl in terror.

Then Jenna froze as the black cap on Raloria's head...shifted.

Because it wasn't a cap at all. It was a pattern. Raised and intricate. Part tattoo and part scar—like the marks on Jenna's own arms.

Raloria was Charmed.

For so long, Jenna had thought she was the only one. But here was another.

The pattern on the child's head crawled, and a dozen thick black tendrils swirled out of the marks on her scalp, undulating in the air like Medusa's snakes. The tendrils lengthened and stretched toward Jenna.

She scrambled away from the window. "Stop! Raloria, stop!" she shouted. If the tendrils touched her, the girl would be infected with her curse. She couldn't let that happen. She held her hands up. "I won't do anything you don't want me to do, okay?" she said in a rush.

The tendrils hovered in indecision.

Jenna yanked the window nearly shut. "Look, I'm not coming in. Can you calm down for me?"

Raloria paused, sniffling, and the tendrils slowly retracted. She pressed Owly to her cheek.

If Thairyn was a member of the Council, it would explain why he was holding this girl. He would turn her over to them. And if Raloria was an abomination like Jenna was, it would be a death sentence.

She had to convince the child to come with her, but she needed to try a new tack. She smiled conspiratorially. "I want to show you and Owly something. Is that okay?"

Raloria didn't answer. She just stared intensely at Jenna.

Moving very slowly, Jenna moved nearer to the window. She tugged off one long glove and pushed up the sleeve of her jacket, revealing the patterns on her hand and arm. "See? I have Charms too. Just like you."

Raloria stepped closer, eyeing the marks with interest. She looked at Jenna, then thrust her stuffed owl forward. "Do you like Owly?"

Jenna gritted her teeth. This was taking too long, but at least it was progress.

"I like Owly very much." She paused and tried another angle. She leaned in, whispering, "Raloria, has he...are you hurt?"

The child blinked at Jenna. "Always. That's why I sleep in daytimes. In night-times I stay up just like Owly, and it doesn't hurt so bad."

Before she could respond, Raloria held the owl up to her ear. "Owly wants me to ask if you're the Kind Mirror Monster. If you are, you're not 'posed to be here."

Jenna shook her head. "The what?"

Raloria rubbed the back of her hand across her nose. "The Kind Mirror Monster."

The Kind Mirror Monster? Where was the child getting this from? "I'm just a girl. See?" She turned in a circle. "Not a monster."

Raloria took another step forward. "Owly hears him talking. Owls are excellent hearers." She petted her stuffed owl fondly. "He said the monster had Charmings. But not Charmings like mine, I don't think."

Jenna moved closer, trying to get Raloria to meet her eyes. "Look at my face. Do I look like a monster?"

Raloria shook her head sadly. "Owly says it's not a face monster. It's a blood monster. And your blood is sick, sick, sick. I can feel it. So does that mean you're the monster?"

I am a monster, Jenna thought. But to Raloria she said, "No, silly. I'm not a monster."

The child wrinkled her nose in confusion. "Can I see your Charmings again?" She pressed her forehead to the glass.

Jenna held up her arm obligingly, letting the girl study her Charms.

With no warning, Raloria doubled over and started screaming.

Chapter Twenty-Two

UNION DEPOT

The girl stumbled back and fell onto the bed, writhing in pain.

Jenna's breath caught, and her glove dropped to the ground as she sprang to the window. Were her Charms doing this to Raloria? How was that possible? She hadn't even touched her.

She splayed her hands on the glass. "What's wrong? Tell me what's wrong!"

"Go away, Monster," Raloria rasped between screams.

Jenna recoiled, stepping away from the window. She paced back and forth, desperate to help. But she couldn't touch the girl. She couldn't call for help. "Help" would treat this child like a lab rat if they discovered her.

"Go!" Raloria cried again, louder this time. She curled into a knot on the bed.

Maybe the girl knew something about her Charms that Jenna didn't. Maybe Jenna *was* the Kind Mirror Monster, and that's why she was hurting—even killing this child. And she didn't know how to stop it.

She didn't want to leave, but she couldn't stay. Not if she was making this happen. She returned to the window once more. "I'll get you out," she shouted.

From somewhere nearby, a police siren blared to life.

Raloria was shaking all over. "Go! Go, Monster!" she wailed.

Jenna backed away. With one last look at the pain-wracked girl, she fled.

The sound of sirens multiplied as she dashed to her car and slung herself into the driver's seat, heading back the way she'd come.

When she turned onto the main road, though, she realized where the din was coming from. A small Ford was crumpled into the side of a semi-trailer truck. Police lights flashed, blocking the highway off from traffic.

She detoured down the next road. The police sirens faded, but Raloria's screams blared inside her mind. She shivered. She'd get her out. Somehow.

But what could she do? She could confide in her mom and hope the stress didn't kill her, but she didn't want to risk that. And she didn't want to involve anyone in TOTEL. What could they do anyway?

Though she knew her aunt wouldn't pick up, she found the number on her dashboard and dialed. When Serene answered, Jenna was so surprised she nearly swerved off the road.

"Jenna! Thank god. Are you all right?" her aunt said. "I've been so worried about you."

Relief flooded Jenna—then anger. She pulled over. "I...I'm fine. But why haven't you been answering my calls?"

"I know. I know," Serene said quickly. "I'll explain everything. But first, tell me. Is your mom okay? Is she doing any better?"

Jenna's fury deflated a little. "She's a lot better, actually. She hasn't had even one episode since I started sneaking her the medicine you gave me."

Serene exhaled. "Thank goodness. I'm glad the pills are helping."

Jenna furrowed her brow, conflicted. Serene's pills had made a big difference, but that didn't explain her long absence. "Why haven't—"

"Wait! I know what you're going to say. But before you order my execution, hear me out, okay?"

Jenna pursed her lips, murmuring an agreement.

"The last time we spoke was at the park, remember? And you told me the man in the Mercedes was there—the man with the white tattoo. I realized he was working with the Council, trying to round up members of the Unbound. He must have hacked my phone, and he knew I was coming. So I had to leave town and drop off his radar. And I couldn't contact you because I was afraid I'd lead him right to you. I gave my phone to a friend to wipe it clean, and I just got it back today. I'm in town again now, and I think I've covered my tracks this time. But Jenna, if you hadn't warned me, I would have been a prize trophy in that man's collection." She laughed without humor.

"The man with the white tattoo was at the park looking for you?" Jenna asked, trying to process it all. "But then, why did he try to come for me?"

"He must have noticed the resemblance between us. If he thought you were related to me, that would explain why he was following you before. It's also possible he—" She stopped short. "It's not important now. He can't turn you in to the Council without proof of who you are—what you are. So don't give him any reason to question you. You haven't seen him since then?"

"No," she said. Then she made up her mind. There was no one else she could ask to help her. "I need to tell you something, Aunt Serene. Something important." Her mind swirled with the magnitude of everything she needed to say.

Jenna blurted it all out. "I know who the man with the white tattoo is and where he lives. He's keeping a little girl with Charms prisoner in his house. And this morning, I saw a dead boy. And also, Fore sent me a seed that dropped from an imaginary giant red flower." She paused, realizing how insane it all sounded, strung together that way.

But her aunt took it in stride. Her voice was firm. "Don't freak out. Are you freaking out? Listen, it's all going to be okay. Mindset, remember? I'll help you. First, tell me about the girl."

Jenna explained how she'd gotten Thairyn Hinsen's registration from the Mercedes and tracked down his address.

Her aunt stopped her mid-sentence. "I know the name Thairyn Hinsen." Her excitement thrummed through the phone. "He works as a bounty hunter for the Council, and that means the girl with Charms is in danger. But you said she's alone right now? Give me the address. I might be able to call on a couple of friends in the Unbound to get her out."

Jenna pulled up the screenshot she'd taken and read it aloud.

"Listen. I'm hanging up with you. But meet me as soon as you can in Parking Lot A of the Union Depot in downtown Saint Paul. Oh! And bring that seed. I think I know why Fore gave it to you. I'll explain when I see you."

That fast, Jenna was alone again. But it sounded like her aunt had a plan. She pulled back onto the highway, driving toward downtown.

When she arrived at the parking garage, she found a space and pulled in before realizing she was missing a glove. She must have lost it when she'd taken it off to show her Charms to Raloria. She dug around in the car's center console for a pen, which she used to bore a hole in the cuff of her sweater, and she pushed her thumb through. The material didn't cover her skin entirely, but at least it hid her

Charms. It was better than nothing.

She got out her phone and dialed her aunt again with no success. She waited. After almost an hour, she began to wonder if she'd misheard her instructions. But then Ian pulled up next to her in the white SUV.

Serene hopped out. She wore a long wool coat and skinny jeans, with a fuzzy, pale pink scarf wrapped around her neck. She had tucked her auburn waves into a low bun.

Jenna was surprised all over again at the resemblance between them. She'd done her own hair the same way this morning. Eagerly, she climbed out of the Corolla to meet Serene. She took the balaclava from her pocket, starting to pull it on, but her aunt stopped her.

"You won't need that. It's more important that we don't draw attention."

Jenna hesitated, then dumped the balaclava and shades in her car and locked it.

"You have the seed with you?"

"I do," she said, patting her jeans pocket.

Serene gave her a thumbs-up and leaned into the open passenger window of the SUV. "Call if there's any trouble," she told Ian. "Give me twenty minutes." She retrieved her coffee cup and motioned Jenna forward, taking off at a brisk pace and following the signs for Union Depot.

"We got the girl out safely," she said without preamble.

Jenna stopped in her tracks. "Raloria? You...she's safe?"

Serene glanced at her and smiled. "She's fine, thanks to you."

A feeling almost like pride swelled inside Jenna. For the first time in years, instead of ruining lives, she had helped save one. She rushed to catch up with her aunt, who was on the move again.

"We've got someone watching the house, waiting for Thairyn to return. The man's a technophobe, thank goodness. We didn't find any cameras set up, so he won't know you were there, but until we have him secured, I'm taking extra precautions. We need a crowd." She headed straight for the elevator that would take them inside the building.

Jenna winced. "Um...crowds are generally not a good idea for me, especially with uncovered skin."

They stopped at the elevator, and Serene punched the button to go up. "It's a necessary evil. If Thairyn realizes something is wrong, he'll suspect the Unbound, which means he'll know I was involved. Don't forget—he swore an oath not to harm someone without proof they've broken a Council law, so you should be safe. But he may be looking for me, and I don't want to put you at risk."

"I thought you said you have his house under watch."

She took a sip of her coffee. "We do. But the man's reputation is unbelievable. Supposedly, he's the most talented member of the Vigil—by a long shot."

The elevator door slid open, and three men in suits got out. Jenna reluctantly stepped inside. "The Vigil?" she asked.

Her aunt pushed the button for the main floor. "It's what the bounty hunters for the Council are called. And Thairyn is the best. He's a shark—able to smell one drop of blood in the water. Except his specialty is sniffing out anyone with Charms in their bloodline—people like you and me."

The elevator opened, and Serene led the way into a narrow corridor. She lowered her voice, and Jenna hurried to stay close enough to hear.

"Of course, it's not literally his sense of smell. But he can use his Charms to sense us. And, if the stories are true, he can tell where a Charmed person is—or isn't—from an impressive distance. I told you he followed you because of our resemblance, but he also might have sensed your magic. So we need a crowd to stay hidden in. It dulls his ability. I don't know how close he has to be to detect two people with Charmed blood, but I don't want to find out."

"Two people? But you're not Charmed, are you?" Jenna hugged the wall as a family of four passed them in the corridor.

"The Vigil can sniff out anyone with magic in their bloodline, even if the Charms are dormant. So, yes, he can find me if he gets close enough."

They stepped out of the narrow corridor, and Jenna ground to a halt. They were inside a colossal, multi-story space that put her in mind of the Gringotts Wizarding Bank from *Harry Potter*. The main part of the room was massive and wide open, but the perimeter was studded with thick, majestic columns of pink marble. Her eyes followed the columns up to a ceiling filled with skylights and surrounded by elegant chandeliers. She'd never been anywhere so grand.

Serene didn't give it a second glance. She marched straight through, and Jenna hurried to catch up.

In the middle of the room, they turned right and walked into a huge passageway with a tiled floor and a low undulating ceiling of interlocking terra-cotta. They passed an enormous artwork made of Lite Brites and then a life-size display of black-and-white photos showcasing the building's history as a train depot. Tourists and people with backpacks and suitcases milled about, and Jenna zigzagged to keep her distance from them all while trying to keep up with her aunt.

Serene didn't slow. They kept walking until the corridor opened out into an even more spectacular room. This ceiling was one expansive curve with arching skylights, and all Jenna could think about was King's Cross Station and Platform Nine and Three-Quarters. A series of thick wooden doors led to different gates for passengers taking trains and buses in and out of Saint Paul, and Serene made a beeline for one of these.

"There aren't as many people here as I'd hoped," she said. "In a couple of minutes, we'll head for the Skyway. We need to talk." She stopped at one of the wooden doors. "Can I have the seed? I want to show it to one of my colleagues. I think it's important."

Jenna fished it out of her jeans pocket and dropped it into Serene's waiting hand. Her aunt studied it, nodding as if in recognition. "This is fantastic, Jenna. Now wait here a minute."

Serene breezed into the hall, sipping on her coffee. She waved a ticket taker away, saying, "I don't need a ticket."

Unwilling to lose sight of her aunt, Jenna stepped into the hallway herself, but the ticket taker barred her path. She tried repeating the line Serene had just used, but the man only eyed her suspiciously and stood his ground. People were so biased against teenagers.

She blew out her breath in frustration and peered around him. Further down the passage, Serene was speaking quietly with a man in the shadows. He wore a hat and coat, and his collar was pulled up so high it hid his features.

She stepped forward, but the ticket taker once more moved to block her view. Then a young woman with purple hair shoved a brochure at Jenna. "I don't need this anymore. Do you want it?"

"Sure," she said, taking the Skyway map from the girl and opening it up.

Pretending to study the map, she edged closer, watching her aunt and the man surreptitiously. For a second, he glanced over his shoulder at her, the cut of his square jaw visible as he turned his head. She blinked and squinted, trying to see into the shadows. Then Serene passed him the seed, and he hurried off toward the train platform without another glance in Jenna's direction.

Serene returned, walking so quickly it was almost a run. "We need to go."

CHAPTER TWENTY-THREE

SEER AND SHARK

Jenna stuffed the map into her pocket. "Who was that?"

They retraced their steps. "A friend of mine in the Unbound. He's going to turn that seed into a cure for you and your mom."

Jenna no longer noticed the grandeur of her surroundings. Everything was a blur as her mind snagged on that one word—*cure*.

Serene glanced at her, smiling when she saw her expression. "When you mentioned a giant red flower and a seed, I suspected what it was. And my friend just confirmed it. It's from the Obru plant, and it has a powerful effect on people with Charms. I've seen documents copied from the Council library mentioning Obru, but I thought it was extinct. Fore found a way, though. She wanted us to have it. Remember, I told you the Unbound had already figured out a procedure we could use, and we knew the mages we would need, but the medicine was the key to the cure that we were missing. That seed was the breakthrough we've been waiting for."

"So I can stop going to Coldwater High School? We got what we needed?"

Serene's expression grew strained. "I don't mean to rain on your parade, Jenna, but it'll take at least a week or two before the cure is ready. And, no, you can't stop going."

"But why? If we already have—"

"Think about it. If Fore's only goal was to get you that seed, she would have made the plant grow inside your apartment. She wanted you in that school for a reason, and that's what I haven't worked out yet. You have to keep going, at least until we know more."

Serene pushed their pace until Jenna was huffing beside her as they turned into the Skyway.

From what she could see, it was a system of hallways that connected a lot of the downtown buildings. Part lobby and part mall, it meant you didn't have to deal with Minnesota weather to get around. She marveled as they used a glass pedestrian tunnel to cross over a busy city street.

After a few minutes inside, Jenna realized why they made Skyway maps. The path often changed levels and direction. For someone like her, unused to navigating, it was easy to get turned around.

Though the halls weren't crowded like they were at school, she was on high alert. The two of them twisted and turned through corridors filled with dozens of strangers. And she was conscious of every inch of exposed skin as she pushed her ungloved hand deeper into her pocket.

"Don't freak out," Serene said. "Are you freaking out? Try to stop. It makes it easier for someone like Thairyn to find you."

"What, freaking out?"

"Any kind of big emotion. It's like sending up a flare, so just try to breathe."

Easy for her to say. Jenna's area of expertise was taekwondo, not speed walking.

"With that in mind," Serene continued, "we'll have to be careful when we administer the cure. Even if it works perfectly, it'll be a shock to your system. I want you to take it inside the largest crowd we can find. Your mom is so weak, it won't make a difference, but you are another matter. I'm hoping we'll have Thairyn in custody by then, but you could still send up a beacon to every member of the Vigil in North America. Unless we have a crowd. I'll have to think of something."

"A crowd?" Jenna asked. "In around two weeks?" An image of Kelsea wagging her finger popped into her head.

"That'd be ideal, yes." Serene looked at Jenna's pursed lips knowingly. "What's your thought?"

"Well, there's the Winter Carnival," she suggested. "On opening night, the TOTEL group is meeting in Rice Park at 5:30 to hand out flyers." She frowned. "But how can I keep from being touched?"

"If you bundle up enough, chances are you'll be fine. And once I get there, you can sit inside my car, and then you'll be completely safe. I'm worried about your mom, though." Serene bit her lip. "First the crowd—then seeing me. I don't want to overwhelm her and send her into shock."

Jenna lit up as a solution formed in her head. "What if I take my dose first? I can do mine inside the crowd, and we'll test it out on me. Then, if it goes well, *I* can give it to Mom at home, so it won't be such a shock. Will that work?"

"That's perfect," Serene said. She nodded as she sipped her coffee. "We'll start with you at the Winter Carnival. And I can check out your TOTEL friends while I'm there, too. I want to see if I notice anything—off—about them. Maybe we can even get DNA samples. Then I'll know for sure if one of them is hiding a biomagical gift."

Jenna wrinkled her nose. "I don't know. It would be weird to—"

"You're right." Serene dismissed the idea with a wave of her hand. "And it would be tricky anyway with such a large group. How many are there, other than you?"

"Ten," she responded automatically. Then her eyes widened. "Nine!" she corrected. "Unless you count the ghost, Nardo." Her heart picked up speed.

Serene eyed her sideways, noting Jenna's uneasiness. "You need to calm down. Let's sit." She steered Jenna over to a white laminate table in a nearby food court. "You said on the phone that you'd seen a dead boy. Tell me everything."

Jenna folded her hands in front of her, staring down at the table so she wouldn't have to see her aunt's revulsion. The story spilled out, but Serene didn't seem shocked.

"I thought so," she said, drumming her fingers.

"What do you mean? Thought what?"

"Do you remember the first time we met? I told you your great-grandmother should have been an Artifex, and you should have been one, too."

Jenna frowned. She'd looked up the word *Artifex* that day. It meant someone who was creative. Someone crafty. But she couldn't even draw decent stick figures.

"The reason you're not an Artifex," her aunt continued, "is because there's another gift trying to come through in you as well. The gift of a Seer. Like your mom."

She sat stock still. "That's not possible."

"You'd be surprised what's possible. Maeby was your age when she started showing the signs. Check your scalp, Jenna. The Charms of a Seer are tiny—nearly invisible. But the hair that comes through those Charms turns white. I bet if you look at yourself closely, you'll find at least one white hair."

She swallowed hard. Her mouth had gone dry. "I plucked three this morning."

Serene nodded knowingly. "I thought so. I remember the first time Maeby dyed her hair to cover her white streak."

Jenna blinked in confusion. "Mom didn't have the streak until after my dad died. That's when she started having more and more of the spells."

"Either she stopped dying her hair then, or the dye wouldn't work anymore. Powerful emotions can do that—take a gift to another level. It's possible that after what happened with your dad she couldn't control it."

"I'm not a Seer, though," Jenna protested. "Trust me. If I could see the future, I wouldn't be blundering around clueless."

"Even Seers who see the past and the future—even they don't always know what their visions mean. Like your mom."

That made sense. Her mom had certainly never been all-knowing.

She thought of something else. The night her mom went comatose, she'd called Jenna's white hair the second sign. Maybe the marks on Jenna's arms were the sign of an Artifex, and the white hair was the second sign—the sign of a Seer. Did that mean her mom had always known this would happen?

Serene kept talking. "Your mom's visions are beside the point. Seers tend to specialize. Your mom sees visions, but you don't. That's not your specialty. What you see are spirits."

She froze, horrified. "I'm going to see dead people now?"

"Don't freak out. Are you freaking out?" She leaned forward across the table. "Think of it this way. You're not seeing a dead person. You're seeing something outside the normal range of vision—the way some animals see ultraviolet light. Nardo is outside the spectrum. The same thing was true of the fireflies and the butterflies you saw."

She sat bolt upright. "They were *dead*?"

"Again, not dead. Not...exactly. Outside the spectrum."

A wave of sickness pooled in her stomach. "So, I'm going to see people outside the spectrum all the time now?"

"Not people—person. Normally, Seers are linked to only one soul at a time. But...." She shook her head. "There's no telling with you. You said you couldn't hear Nardo when he spoke, but that shouldn't be happening. Your Seer gift isn't working the way it should. The problem is, you're not normal."

"Meaning what?"

"You're twice-Charmed, Jenna. When a person is born with two gifts, the Charms don't work the way they're supposed to. I think that's why your magic acts more like a curse. Your Charms are interfering with each other."

Jenna dropped her head into her hands. "My brain is exploding."

"Imagine two teeth growing through someone's gums in the same place—are you following me?"

"Yes," she groaned.

"The teeth push each other out of alignment. That's what happened to you. If you'd been born with one gift, you'd have been golden. Instead, the gifts are pushing each other out of whack, poisoning you."

Jenna shook her head. "So let's say, for the sake of argument, that I *am* a dysfunctional half-Seer. What am I supposed to do about Nardo?"

"Speak to him. Find out anything you can. Fore may have sent him as a messenger. And if you exert your will, you might be able to take control of your gift—even if it's just for a few minutes. It's mind over matter. Or, in your case, mind over spirit. Get it?" Serene grinned broadly.

Jenna raised an eyebrow, and Serene sighed. "Communicate with the boy. But first, you've got to change your mindset. Think of this new ability as a gift, not a curse."

Again, that was easy for her to say.

Serene's phone buzzed, and she answered. After listening for a few seconds, she hung up and leaped to her feet.

Jenna stood.

"We need to separate. There's still no sign of Thairyn, and that worries me. Can you find your way back to the parking garage?"

"I think so."

"Just to be safe, I'm ditching my phone again. I'll replace it and contact you as soon as possible, but if you don't hear from me, I'll see you on the first night of the Winter Carnival. Sound good?"

"I'll be there."

Serene looked as if she wanted to reach out and hug Jenna. "Take care of yourself, sweetheart. And with luck, the next time we meet, I'll have a cure."

She turned and rapidly headed off.

Jenna fished the Skyway map out of her pocket, grateful now that the girl with purple hair had given it to her. Using the map and the overhead signs, she made her way back to Union Depot and then Parking Lot A.

Her aunt had been right. It was all about mindset. As she drove home to Ashton Place, she tried to reframe everything in a more positive light. In some ways, things couldn't be better.

She only had a couple of weeks to wait, and then she and her mom would both be cured. A short time ago, she thought she'd have to live with her curse for the rest of her life, so two weeks was nothing.

Trying to talk to Nardo would feel strange, but once she had the cure, she'd leave the Seer gift behind. She'd never have to deal with anyone "outside the spectrum" again.

Also, she had to remember that today she had helped save a little girl's life. Raloria was safe now because of her. She gave herself a mental pat on the back.

School was awkward, terrifying, and exhausting, but she could handle it for two more weeks. The whole TOTEL group was crazy, of course, but also—they'd grown on her. A part of her would miss those lunatics.

And then there was Lane. She flinched away from the thought of him. But she had to face reality. Breaking it off had been the right thing to do. For one thing, even if she was cured, Lane would hate her forever once he saw her without the balaclava. He'd realize she'd been lying to him all along, and he'd never forgive her for it.

Besides, the cure could only get rid of her Charms. It couldn't change the things she'd done. She was a liar, a bad luck charm, and...worse. Lane deserved better than someone like her.

She finally made it home. She parked the car and trudged up the stairs, locking the apartment door behind her. She leaned back against it in relief. Sighing, she peeled off her one remaining glove. Then she shrugged out of the white jacket and hung it in the front closet.

All at once, she realized her mom hadn't said anything when she came in. She frowned and headed into the hall. "Mom?" she called. But there was no answer.

She knocked on Mae's bedroom door and, when she didn't hear anything, cracked it open. Then she sucked in a sharp breath and rushed inside.

Her mother was twisted sideways on the bed. Her eyes were closed, and a bright red streak of blood ran from the corner of her mouth onto the pale blue sheets.

She felt for her mother's pulse. It was weak but there, and she was burning up.

She tilted her mom's head back and looked inside her mouth, following the trail of blood. There was a small, circular puncture in the center of her tongue, and it was still bleeding.

What had happened?

She thought fast. She'd wrap an ice cube in a cloth and apply pressure to the wound. And then maybe she could get her mom to wake up.

She ran to the kitchen and was just reaching into the freezer when she heard a creaking sound in the hallway. It was the creak her bedroom door made when it opened.

She whipped around just as Thairyn Hinsen stepped from the hall into the living room.

"Don't move," he said softly. He lifted a gun and pointed it at her head.

Chapter Twenty-Four

VEROPHID

Jenna froze, her throat closing in fear. She couldn't have screamed, even if she wanted to.

"Sit," he hissed. "Now." With his free hand, he gestured at the living room couch. The pistol never wavered.

She thought about trying to run, but she couldn't abandon her mother. She'd find a way to distract and disarm him, she told herself. But her hands shook as she held them up, edging her way into the living room.

He waved the pistol again, silently commanding her to sit.

As she moved toward the couch, she glanced around, searching for a potential weapon, but there was nothing in reach that would work. Slowly, she perched on the edge of the faded beige sofa, watching the man warily.

He glided closer, a great white shark circling its prey.

She could see now that it was a dart gun he carried, not a regular pistol. But a poisoned dart could kill her as easily as a bullet. And no one would hear the thing go off.

A hint of madness lit Thairyn's light blue eyes. She hadn't been able to see it from a distance, but up close, his fury was as real and ragged as a wound.

How far would he go? He was capable of kidnapping children and breaking into apartments. And he'd attacked her mother, leaving her bloody and helpless. Rage surged through Jenna, momentarily overcoming the terror that was strangling her. "What did you do to my mom?" she demanded.

He ignored the question, stepping closer. "Where is she?" His voice was soft. Dangerous.

"I don't know who you're talking about," she lied.

His voice rose with anger and...something else. "You know exactly who I'm talking about. Raloria. Where is she?"

Jenna let her own fury spill out. It was the only thing holding her together. "That little girl is finally safe from you. That's all I know."

"Don't lie to me. I won't allow it." His hand shook as he reached into his coat pocket and removed a glass vial. He stepped closer.

There was something floating inside the tube, like a dead specimen suspended in preserving fluid. At first glance, it resembled a very small snake or eel, but its permanently open mouth had rings of teeth, like a...she searched for the word. Like a lamprey.

And then it moved.

It thrashed back and forth in the liquid, pulsing with eerie, strobing lights.

Instinctively, she shrank from the thing. *Why was he showing her this?*

Thairyn never took his eyes from her. "Do you know what this is?"

She shook her head.

"It's called a verophid. They're interesting creatures—exceedingly rare." Using his thumb, he popped the cork from the tube. "This will only hurt for a second."

She sucked in a breath and scrambled sideways on the couch, but Thairyn was already in motion. He flung the contents of the vial at her.

She threw her hands up, shrieking in horror, but she hadn't been fast enough. The verophid hit her on the neck and bit down, latching on. She grabbed at her neck to tear the thing free, but before she could reach it, searing pain stabbed through her entire body, paralyzing her.

Suddenly, the pain subsided, but Jenna could no longer feel her limbs. Unable to control herself, she slid downward onto the couch cushions, oozing like a melting candle. Her jaw sagged open, but her scream wouldn't come, even as the creature began to crawl up her neck.

It wriggled over her chin and disappeared into her open mouth, settling on her tongue. She wanted to gag, but her body wouldn't let her.

Then she tasted copper as the thing bit into the center of her tongue. Warm blood pooled and then spilled out the corner of her mouth.

The man with the white tattoo lowered himself onto the coffee table across from her and set the dart gun beside him. "It only takes a moment to penetrate."

Jenna was a prisoner in her own body. She could hear her own ragged breathing, smell the strange brine from the liquid that had splashed on her, and see clearly.

But she couldn't turn her head. Couldn't lift a finger.

The man watched her. Then his knuckles whitened as he gripped the edge of the coffee table, leaning forward. "Where is Raloria?"

Jenna's mouth felt numb and wobbly, as if she'd had a shot of Novocain. "I don't know," she rasped.

She was talking, but she hadn't meant to speak. Her body had simply responded to the demand for information, with no regard for what she wanted.

"You've met the woman, Serene, am I right?"

"Yes." Again, Jenna spoke before she could restrain herself.

"Was she involved in taking Raloria?"

"Yes."

"Are you working for her?"

"No," she said, and it was true—it just wasn't the whole truth.

"Are you a member of the Unbound?"

"No."

Thairyn's hands tightened into fists. "Then what does Serene want from you?"

She didn't want to say anything that could lead the man to her aunt. But she couldn't control her words. "She's going to cure me and my mom," she said through clenched teeth.

"Because...." He waited.

"Because she's my aunt, and she loves us."

Something flickered in the man's expression. "You should know your aunt's not as clever as she thinks she is. I slipped by her men today, and what do you think I saw outside Raloria's window? A glove, just like I've seen you wear. I know you were there. Why?"

"I was looking for my Aunt Serene. I thought you'd kidnapped her, but I found Raloria instead. She's the one you kidnapped."

Thairyn clenched his jaw tight, making his Charms turn an even brighter shade of white. A muscle ticked in his cheek. Then his eyes narrowed. "Has your aunt given you anything?"

"Pills. For my mom."

"Where?" he demanded.

"In the top drawer of my dresser."

He strode from the room, and Jenna heard him rooting through her dresser drawer. A tear escaped from the corner of her eye and rolled toward her ear.

The man returned, tucking the bottle of pills into his coat pocket.

She forced herself to speak again. "You...you can't harm me if I haven't broken one of your laws. You took an oath."

He raised his eyebrows, apparently surprised she'd spoken without being prompted. Then his mouth tightened into an ugly line. "You think I care about an oath? After this? There's nothing they can do that would scare me." He looked at her sharply. "Where is Serene now?"

"I don't know."

He cursed. Restlessly, he prowled the room. "Can you contact her?"

"No." That was true too. Her aunt had said she was ditching her phone. Jenna had no way to reach her.

"What about the Shepherd? He's known as Flynn. Do you know him?"

"No."

"And the Bear? Ian is his name. What about him?"

"I've met someone named Ian twice, but just for a few seconds."

"Do you know where he is?"

"No."

Thairyn slammed his fist down on the counter. Then he strode toward her aggressively. "When will you see your aunt again?"

She fought to stay quiet, fixing her gaze on the man's diamond earring. Maybe she could resist if she avoided his eyes. But the compulsion was too strong. "I'm meeting her at 5:30 on the opening day of the Winter Carnival."

"Where?"

"In Rice Park."

For the first time, a humorless smile lifted the corners of his mouth. "Very good. You're going to prove helpful after all. You'll lead me right to her, whether you want to or not."

"I won't," she ground out. She'd find a way to warn her aunt.

"You will," Thairyn promised. "You won't know you're doing it."

He picked up the dart gun from the coffee table. "This dart won't kill you, but it's loaded with a formula that will make you sleep a good, long time. Just like your mom."

Jenna eyed the gun warily, wanting to kick it from his hands. But the most she could do was stare.

"When the dart penetrates, you'll lose the last hour of your memory. So when you wake up, you won't remember this conversation. You won't even know I've been here."

She watched him with dawning horror. If she didn't remember, she couldn't warn her aunt.

His forehead creased. "Maybe I should have turned you over to the Council the moment I realized what you were. But I wasn't sure if you were working alongside them or if they were using you." He leaned over, his face inches from hers. "It turns out they were using you, but two can play at that game. I can use you, too."

He looked down at his gun, checking the dart. "The verophid and the dart will both dissolve within the hour, but try not to struggle, or you'll be sore in the morning."

He pointed the gun at her chest and pulled the trigger.

Her body jerked, but she felt nothing.

He strode to the kitchen and turned on the faucet. She listened to his footsteps as he went to Mae's bedroom. Then he returned and bent over Jenna.

He had wrapped a damp paper towel around the barrel of the gun. He used it to wipe the blood from her face, hiding the evidence that he'd been there.

She fought again to make her mouth move, but she could only choke out a single word. "Why?"

"Why?" His eyes were hard. "Because there are monsters far worse than verophids." He gave her another empty smile. "Monsters worse than me."

He spun on his heel, leaving the apartment. She heard the door close and a key turn, and as sleep sucked her under, she wondered how he'd gotten that key. She shivered.

She had to fight this, or she'd lead her Aunt Serene right into his trap.

"He knows," she repeated over and over in her head. Maybe, if she said it enough to herself, she would remember.

Her eyes closed, and she sank into dreams of the deep sea where she floated motionless through a swarm of tiny, pulsing eels.

Chapter Twenty-Five

SPEECHLESS

Jenna snatched the last sweater from her dresser, scowling.

She winced. Her tongue was still sore from where she must have burned it on Doc's apple cider on Saturday. She tossed the sweater onto her bed, alongside every other article of clothing she owned. She was staring down at an empty drawer. Again.

She fisted her hands on her hips, then shook herself and took a deep breath, remembering what Aunt Serene had said. It was all a matter of mindset. Everything was going to be okay, even if she couldn't find her mother's pills.

A cure was coming in a couple of weeks. Surely, her mom could make it until then. And after the Winter Carnival, she wouldn't need the medicine at all.

But worry rippled through her, despite her intentions. Changing her mindset wasn't as easy as telling herself that she should. She'd misplaced the pills and, deep down, it bothered her. She'd ransacked her room three times yesterday and again this morning with no luck. What had she done with them?

He knows.

Those words nagged at her as her brain played the phrase on repeat. She didn't know who *he* was or *what* he was supposed to know, but it was an earworm she couldn't shake. Was she losing her mind? She shoved her clothes back into her dresser, burying the thought.

Positive mindset. All she had to do was get through the next couple of weeks. Then her problems would disappear.

She gathered her things, told her mom goodbye, and headed for school.

By the time she reached the parking lot, though, her positivity had deserted her. She sighed and forced herself to get out of the car, but she couldn't trick herself into wanting to go inside. She had a long list of people she'd rather not see.

Brie was on the list, because Jenna was constantly offending the girl, no matter what she did. And now Lita was on the list, too. On Saturday, Jenna had made a tasteless joke about her dead brother—or that's how it had looked to Lita.

And Nardo was definitely on the list because...well, because he was dead. Or at least "outside the spectrum." Aunt Serene wanted her to talk to him, but it was hard to get excited about having a chat with a ghost.

And there was someone she wanted to avoid more than Brie or Lita, or even Nardo. And that was Lane.

She'd done the right thing, ending it with him—at least as Angel. But he'd sounded so defeated on the phone. Seeing him would be painful.

She attempted once again to change her mindset. After all, Lane wouldn't be upset with *her*. He couldn't be. He had no clue that the girl he knew as Mo, Rumpelstiltskin, and Jenna was the same person who'd just broken up with him. *Pre-broken up with him?* After all, they'd never officially gone out.

Still, *she* knew she had hurt him. And that made him number one on her list. She ducked her head against the bitter wind, reluctantly trudging forward across the slush-covered parking lot.

Suddenly, someone emerged from behind a dark gray Buick and stepped into her path.

Brent.

She stopped cold, her skin prickling in alarm. She'd been wrong. Her list had a new number one. And Brent ranked far above the others in people she did not want to see.

"It's not easy to get you alone," he said softly.

Quickly, she scanned the area. No one else was nearby. After Brent had watched her from the parking lot on her second day of school, she'd taken to parking away from everyone else near the unused tennis courts. But he'd found her anyway.

She fought her rising panic. "I'm not in the mood to play games with you. I need to go." She tried to step past him, but he moved sideways, barring her way.

He stared fixedly at her. "I remember."

She flinched. He could have been referring to the humiliation he'd suffered in the stairwell, but she didn't think so. There was an intensity in his gaze that hadn't been there before. What he remembered was the feel of her touch. Her Charms.

That day in the stairwell, his hand had wrapped around her jeans. The curse shouldn't have affected him through a layer of clothes—unless he was one of those rare, hypersensitive people. But Jenna didn't think he was.

She wondered, though, if she'd been wrong about the way her Charms worked. Maybe the curse *did* work through a layer of clothes. Maybe it worked slowly, over time, and Brent was just beginning to feel the effects.

A shiver worked its way up her spine.

He took a step toward her. "I asked you before to show me your face, and that's what you're going to do now. To start."

She stepped back. "I don't want to do this with you, Brent."

"None of your weird friends are here to stop me this time. You'll do this...and more." He continued to advance while she backed away.

Her thoughts spun, searching for a way out, but she couldn't take her eyes off his face. He looked so much like the other boy—Michael Stevens. She couldn't keep her mind from replaying that other day. When Michael had touched her, and then....

Brent's hand shot out, a cobra striking. He caught her arm and started to drag her behind the dark gray Buick.

The feel of his hand made bile rise in her throat, but she'd have to risk even closer contact now. She'd have to fight—even if it triggered the full effect of her Charms. He'd left her with no other choice.

She gritted her teeth, trying not to think about what she was doing. She let her training take over.

In one smooth movement, she wrapped her arm around his elbow, rolling to the outside. She twisted his arm up painfully and, before he could recover, she stepped through and behind him. With the pressure of her leg against his, she kicked out and forced him to the ground.

He grunted as he hit the frozen asphalt, then didn't move, momentarily stunned.

Jenna stood above him, panting, as she tried to decide what to do next.

Just then, brakes squealed, and a car came to a stop beside them.

Jenna stepped away from Brent. Relief flooded her as she looked up and saw the sky-blue Subaru Outback.

Doc was gazing worriedly at her from the passenger window.

Then Doc's dad, Mr. Lindgren, hurried out of the car.

Brent staggered to his feet, brushing the slush from his clothes. His nostrils flared and his fists clenched in fury, but he kept his distance from Jenna.

She let out a slow breath. The curse hadn't taken him fully, or he'd be charging at her now. Nothing else would matter.

But they'd made contact again—and for much longer. *Would that make the curse work even faster? How long did she have?*

A crease furrowed Mr. Lindgren's forehead. "Everything okay here?" he asked, looking back and forth between them. He turned to Jenna. "Is this boy bothering you? Anything you want to report?"

She hesitated. Mr. Lindgren meant well, but if she reported Brent, she'd be called in to the office to talk about what had happened, and she couldn't risk that kind of attention.

"Everything's fine," she lied. "I think Brent must have tripped. But I wouldn't mind hitching a ride with you to the teacher's parking lot. Is that okay?"

"You betcha," Mr. Lindgren said. Then he turned to Brent, still suspicious. "There's no loitering here. Go inside the building."

Mr. Lindgren gestured for Jenna to get into the back seat. He watched protectively as she climbed in. Then he eased himself into the driver's seat and they pulled away, leaving Brent trying to bore holes into the side of the car with his eyes.

Jenna shuddered. She'd have to be far more careful from now on.

"That was that same mean boy we saw on the stairs your first day, wasn't it?" Doc asked.

Jenna nodded wordlessly.

"I didn't know he was still bothering you. Good thing Dad and I always come the back way to the school, or nobody might have seen you."

"Would you like for me to pick you up and take you to school with us from now on?" Mr. Lindgren asked kindly.

"No, thank you, I'll be okay." She forced herself to smile reassuringly. "I'll just find somewhere else to park. Somewhere with more people." She scowled inwardly at the irony of that.

Doc leaned in close as Mr. Lindgren drove them around to the teacher's parking lot. She whispered, "I wanted to tell you.... After you left my house on Saturday, we talked to Lita. You know...about Nardo. And for the rest of the day, she only drew vines and spiders—not snakes and skulls. So that's good news, don'tcha think?"

"That's...fantastic."

"See, I told you everything would be okay," Doc chirped.

They parked in the faculty parking lot, and Mr. Lindgren led the way into the building through a side door. He gave Jenna a short lecture about staying safe and reporting any bullying to the administration.

She played along because there was no way she could explain what was really going on. This was far from a case of simple bullying. This was her curse. And she'd just have to hope that for the next two weeks she'd be able to dodge Brent.

In the hall, Doc waved Jenna off, telling her she'd be at the meeting after she fed Milly and Piglet.

Jenna made her way to the drama room, only slowing when she heard raised voices at the door.

Zinnia stood with her hands on her hips.

Markese blocked the doorway, waving a rag in her face. "I told you. Nobody gets in today without one of these. We are about to change up the energy in here. It's feng shui time, honey. Bad energy out. Good energy in. So make like Cinderella and get dusting."

He held a rag out for Zinnia to take, but she didn't move. "Where's Kelsea?"

"Kelsea can't help you," Markese told her. "She and Lita are in the auditorium, but Kelsea put me in charge. And I say this place needs cleaning."

"What are you talking about, Markese? This room is already clean."

"Then how do you explain the string of bad luck I've been having?"

"Oh, I can explain it. It's called imagination."

"Wrong answer," he said, crossing his arms over his chest.

Jenna came up beside Zinnia, and Markese swung to her next.

"Tell us the honest truth now, Aries girl. Don't you think this room has a serious case of the heebie-jeebies?"

"Well," Jenna said, glancing between the two of them.

But Markese didn't wait for an answer. "You know I'm right. I already feng shui'ed my house, but that didn't fix it. And I've been wearing my lucky necklace everywhere, but that didn't do it either. My bad luck is coming from somewhere, and this place is Spook Central. I can feel it."

Jose and Hampton emerged from the closet, carrying fake potted plants, and Jenna was relieved to see that there were no giant red flowers growing through the plastic leaves.

"Set those down and get more," Markese directed the twins.

Zinnia tried again. "You—"

He held his hand up, cutting her off. "The bad luck ends today, Zinnia. Did I tell you my little cousin came in fourth place at his spelling bee?"

The two girls exchanged glances.

"That was bad luck?" Jenna ventured.

He looked scandalized. "Fourth place? The number four? It's worse than heinous."

She blinked. The number four. Was Fore trying to tell her something? Was she pointing Jenna's attention toward Markese?

"I thought your unlucky number was thirteen," Zinnia said, unimpressed.

"Don't even get me started on thirteen now. But four is bad enough. First an alligator dream and now this? Oh no. Uh-uh. I'm not having it."

Zinnia raised an eyebrow. "So, you're telling us your cousin would have won the spelling bee if this room had been cleaner?"

He spluttered in indignation. "It wasn't just the spelling bee, Zinnia. Last week I asked out this hot guy, and he said no. Then I found out he was on the basketball team. And do you know what number his jersey was?"

"Number four?" Jenna asked obligingly.

"You better believe it." He grew more animated. "And this weekend, when I ordered the three-piece chicken tenders, do you know how many I got?"

"I'm going to take a wild guess and say four," Zinnia said dryly.

He pursed his lips in triumph.

She shook her head. "I'd call free food *good* luck, Markese. But I'm not gonna argue with someone who's already boarded the train to Crazytown."

"Choo-choo. You know what to do." He thrust the rag at Zinnia, and she snatched it, stalking away.

Jenna took a rag from Markese and followed. She glanced around, but no one else was here yet, just the twins and Zinnia. Hoping to stay out of sight and out of mind, she chose a spot at the prop shelves in the corner where she could dust in quiet seclusion.

She'd just started wiping down her first shelf when she heard Markese intercept Lane and Brie at the door. She whipped around.

Lane had pulled his hoodie up, masking his expression, but his steps dragged. Markese armed Brie with a can of WD-40 and sent her to oil all the door hinges. He handed a rag to Lane and pointed him in Jenna's direction.

She cursed as he plodded over.

He gave her the barest wave and then ducked his head, wiping down the set of shelves opposite her.

He knows.

The thought skittered across her mind, and her eyes widened. Had Lane figured out that she and Angel were the same person? Panic fluttered inside her chest. She moved closer and stole a glance at his face.

Relief washed through her. He was moping, not scowling, so he didn't know. And she could play her role here a little while longer.

Across the room, Jose spotted Brie spraying the closet door hinges with WD-40. He dropped the plant he was carrying and hurried to her side.

Lane's only reaction was a heavy sigh.

Jenna lifted an eyebrow. "Everything okay?"

He looked up and shrugged. "Sorry. Not my best day. I didn't mean to take it out on you."

She hesitated. Maybe all he needed was a change of mindset. She could talk him through this. It was the least she could do. "Anything on your mind?"

"Not really," he mumbled.

"Come on. I'm a good listener."

He glanced up. "I know, but it might be...weird."

"We're friends, right? Besides, who knows more about weird than me?"

He shrugged. "I don't know. See, it's about this girl."

"Ah."

"Too weird?"

"Oh no," she choked out. She waved her hand, hoping to look nonchalant. "You have this girl, and I have my...pen pal person. So not weird. At all. What's going on?"

"All right." He set his rag on the shelf and pulled his hoodie down, making his cowlick stand on end. "So—this girl." He ran his fingers through his hair. "I don't know what to do about her."

"Ah." Jenna nodded sagely. She reminded herself to play dumb. "Who is she?" she asked innocently.

"That's just it! I don't know. She's hardly told me anything about herself." Agitated, he squeezed the rag in his fist. "I call her Angel, but I don't even know her real name."

"Ah," she repeated. Then, feeling she needed to say more, she added, "That is weird."

"I know, right? But she's...she's...."

"A jerk?" Jenna volunteered.

"No. She's not a jerk." He gazed into the distance. "No, she's smart and charming. And beautiful."

She was so shocked she started coughing. "Wow." Then she couldn't resist. "Tell me more."

"Well, she has the most gorgeous red hair and full lips."

"Go on."

Dreamily, Lane moved his rag in a circle, dusting the same small spot over and over. "She's just exactly right, that's all. Everything about her. She's average height, maybe a little taller than you are, with these cute freckles all over her cheeks."

Her lip curled. "I've never been a fan of freckles."

"She makes you want to look at her again, you know? She's striking. Something about her face—her nose, maybe."

"You like her nose?" she asked, incredulous.

"It's just everything put together. And she's so funny and quick. You know, fun to be around, easy to talk to. She's outspoken and honest, too. I respect that."

She swallowed. "Honest? That's...I mean, honesty is all relative. What are you even comparing it to?"

"She loves dandelions. Isn't that amazing? Her favorite flower is a weed, and she's not afraid to admit it." He cocked his head, and a smile flitted over his lips. "Sometimes, though, she's so honest it borders on mean."

Her eyes narrowed. "Mean?"

He chuckled. "And she's kind of bossy. Definitely a control freak."

"Oh, okay. No, go ahead. Keep talking."

"She's stubborn, too. Like the most stubborn person who ever existed. She's like a mule."

Jenna tossed her rag down and crossed her arms. "A mule."

"Worse than a mule. If stubbornness were a superpower, she'd be like...Super-mule."

"Super. Mule. That's what you think?"

He laughed. "Oh—and she's kind of a klutz."

"A klutz?" She leaned forward, gripping the shelf. She'd watched Lane wipe out half a dozen times. But she'd only fallen in front of him once. Unbelievable. She tried to remain stoic, grateful for the balaclava that covered her face.

He paused then, and his eyes went distant. "None of that matters, though. I like being around her, talking to her." He ran his hand through his hair again. "The problem is, she doesn't want to be with me."

The outrage fled Jenna in a rush, and guilt pooled in the pit of her stomach.

"I've never been good at guessing what people are thinking. But she just says whatever's on her mind. That's one of the reasons I like her so much."

His shoulders slumped. "But I think she's in a bad situation, and she won't tell me what's going on." He thrust his hands into his pockets. "She won't trust me. And now she doesn't want to see me anymore."

Jenna's heart sank like a lead weight inside of her. She dredged up the only true thing she could tell him. "It sounds like she's nothing but trouble, Lane. You can do better. Try to move on."

He looked up helplessly. "I can't."

Maybe this whole conversation had been a mistake. Instead of helping him get past Angel, she'd made him dwell on her. "Well, if it's meant to be, it'll be," she said, attempting to wrap up their talk.

"You're right." A slow smile spread over his face. "And it *is* meant to be. I know it. It's like destiny, the two of us. It's just a matter of time."

"That's not what I...." She hadn't intended to encourage him, but he was smiling for the first time today, and she couldn't bring herself to crush his spirits yet again. "Sure. Destiny. If you believe in that kind of thing." She didn't. But Lane clearly did.

He picked up his rag once more, dusting with renewed vigor. "I do feel better, Mo. Thanks."

Her face burned. He had just thanked the girl who broke up with him for talking him through the breakup.

He flashed her a grin. "Let me know if I can ever return the favor. Anything you need to talk about?"

She paused. There *was* something that had been bothering her. "Can I ask you a weird question?"

"You're in luck," he said, leaning back against the shelves. "I'm only accepting weird questions today. I've set aside tomorrow for tedious questions and the day after that for annoying questions, but today is all weird, all day. What do you want to know?"

She hesitated. "Have you ever heard of a Kind Mirror Monster? I told you it was weird."

"You never disappoint." He hummed thoughtfully. "A Kind Mirror Monster? For some reason, it sounds familiar." He turned to the room and threw the question out to everyone. "Has anybody heard of a Kind Mirror Monster?"

Zinnia stopped pretending to dust the piano. "You mean a chimera monster? The one from Greek mythology that's made from different animals stuck together?"

Jenna's head spun. A chimera monster. That's what Raloria had meant. And the girl had been right. Jenna *was* a chimera monster—with the magic of an Artifex and a Seer melded together inside her.

"Actually, the chimera has a lion's head and a goat's body," Jose corrected. He glanced at Brie to see if he'd impressed her, but she was looking at her phone. He spoke louder. "The tail was originally a dragon tail, but now people draw it thinner, with a snake's head at the end. It's pretty cool." He seemed to be trying to gauge Brie's response. "If you're into that kind of thing."

When she still didn't react, he sidled closer. "What I want to know is, why are we talking about a monster when we have a goddess walking among us?"

Everyone groaned collectively, and Brie finally responded, rolling her eyes.

She moved toward Lane, reading from her phone. "It says here that the word *chimera* has other meanings, too. Sometimes in the womb, one twin will absorb the other, and the child that lives can have some of the DNA from the dead sibling. The living twin is a chimera because she has two sets of DNA." A smile spread across her face. "Wicked."

Markese stomped out of the closet, a broom in his hand. "You know what's wicked? The heinous energy in this room. Now stop talking and start cleaning."

But at that moment, Kelsea burst through the door with an armload of clothes. Markese threw his hands up in exasperation.

"I am a genius. The costume closet in the auditorium was a jackpot," she said, dumping the clothes to the floor. Then she tugged the whistle from under her collar and blew. "Front and center, people! Meeting time!"

Lita stumbled through the door next, carrying another pile of clothes, and Nardo trailed after her. His eyes went immediately to Jenna, and he darted across the room to her.

She braced herself, watching his approach with mingled fear and fascination.

He skidded to a stop, speaking and gesturing with animation.

But she couldn't hear a word. She concentrated, trying to will herself to hear him, but it didn't work. If mindset was the problem, she didn't know how to fix it. Then she tried reading his lips, but she wasn't any better at that. She spread her hands helplessly. "I can't hear you," she said. "Can you hear me?"

Nardo nodded.

"Loud and clear," Lane answered. "But I didn't say anything." Then he frowned. "Are you okay? You seem...distracted."

"I'm fine." She looked nervously between Lane and the ghost boy.

"Come on." Lane waved her over to join the group. "The meeting is starting."

Nardo reached for her arm as she moved away, but his hand passed right through her body, giving her a momentary chill.

She shrugged her shoulders, joining the other TOTEL members who had circled the pile of clothes. Nardo attempted to edge in beside her, but she turned to him and whispered, "Later."

He glared at her. Then he pivoted on his heel and went back to haunting Lita.

Kelsea had her gavel out. She smacked it once on the floor and then jammed it inside her pocket. "In the interest of time, let's fast forward through the formalities." She spoke quickly. "I will seek the truth, defend the defenseless, right the wrong, and stand up for—"

"Fairies," everyone chimed in over Kelsea. But she was so eager to start, she didn't even blink.

"Okay people, in two weeks we'll be handing out flyers at the Winter Carnival. Hundreds, maybe thousands of people will find out about our concert. But first, we need a name."

Zinnia groaned. "Not this again, Kelsea. Everybody already agreed. We're The Itchy Infinity."

"I refuse to be named by a computer algorithm."

Jose spoke up. "I still like my idea. The Earlobes. It's edgy."

Brie turned to him. "Seriously?"

"The...Toenails?" he tried again. "What's your favorite body part?"

"I have an idea," Doc said. "Why don't we put our suggestions into a hat and pick one, so we don't have to fight?"

Markese looked down his nose at her. "Yeah, and with my bad luck, we'll end up The Earlobes for sure."

"Or The Toenails," Hampton said.

"The Toenails of Death," Lita amended. "The Deathly Toenails."

Jose and Hampton fist-bumped her.

Markese spread his arms wide, appealing to the group. "See? This is what I'm talking about. Heinous."

Zinnia put one hand on her hip. "Well, then I think we should be called TOTEL CHAOS, because that's what these discussions always turn into."

Everyone went silent.

"TOTEL CHAOS," Kelsea breathed. "I love it."

"That is kind of cool," Lane agreed, and the others nodded.

"It's more...us," Doc said.

Before they could change their minds, Kelsea stepped forward. "I believe we have a quorum present. All in favor of our band being called TOTEL CHAOS, say *Aye*."

There was a chorus of agreement, and Kelsea banged her gavel to make it official.

Markese threw his hands in the air. "Hallelujah! We can stop talking about it."

"Indeed. Next order of business is costumes." Kelsea pointed to the clothes in the center of the circle. "Everyone will wear a costume to the Winter Carnival—and the flashier the better, people. It'll be great publicity. Speaking of which, Zinnia's friend Devonte will be there to write an article about us for the school paper."

Jenna glanced at Zinnia, one eyebrow raised, but she stared forward stoically, carefully avoiding eye contact.

Kelsea barreled forward. "This is Operation: Let's Get Attention, people. Pick your costume, or I'll do it for you."

Before everyone swarmed the pile, Kelsea swooped in and scooped up a big bundle of pink fabric. She marched over to Jenna. "I remembered what you said about needing space inside the crowd, so I pulled this dress for you. It has a hoop skirt. That should do the trick, right? Told you I was a genius."

Markese gasped. "You can be Glinda the Good Witch! Oh, and I have fairy wings and a wand you can borrow. OMG, I'm jealous now."

Jenna lifted the heavy pink skirt dubiously. "This will be"—*hideous*, she thought—"practical," she said aloud to Kelsea. "Thank you."

Before she'd made her plan with Aunt Serene, she would have done anything to get out of going to the Winter Carnival. But Jenna wanted this cure. And her mom *needed* it. The hoop skirt was ugly, but it *would* keep people at a distance. She could walk inside a crowd untouched.

"Try it on," Kelsea urged, then went to bully someone else.

Fortunately, the dress was big enough that she could wear it over her other clothes. But as she pulled it over her head, it got stuck for a moment. When she finally tugged the ruffled skirts down, Nardo was standing almost right on top of her.

She screamed in surprise, and everyone turned to look. "Mouse," she lied again.

"I thought I saw a mouse."

Lane made a strangled noise, and without a word, Hampton scooped him up in his arms.

Jose broke into a fit of laughter. "That never gets old."

Lane looked at Hampton levelly. "Dude. You've got to stop doing that."

Hampton nodded and set him on his feet.

Nardo recaptured Jenna's attention by jumping up and down and pointing at his sister. Lita was trying on a costume across the room, and Jenna sighed, squaring her shoulders. She did owe the girl an apology. She followed Nardo.

Lita had chosen a spandex skeleton suit that might have been one size too small for her. She struggled to shove her arms through the sleeves.

Jenna looked at Nardo. He was talking and gesturing wildly. Still, Jenna couldn't hear a thing.

When she turned again to Lita, the girl was watching her—half in and half out of the skeleton costume. "What do you want?" she asked morosely.

Jenna stepped forward. "I'm sorry about what happened on Saturday, Lita. I didn't know about your brother, and I certainly didn't mean to upset you."

Nardo moved to Lita's side and tried to take her hand. But his body passed right through hers. He hung his head in defeat.

Jenna's heart ached for him. He so clearly wanted to tell his sister how he felt. She couldn't translate his exact words, but she could relay his emotion.

She turned to Lita again. "If your brother were here," she said slowly, "I'm sure he would want me to tell you he loves you."

Nardo met her eyes and nodded.

But Lita's mouth tightened. "Nardo would never say that." She shoved her arms hard into the sleeves of the costume. The lime green watch she always wore in his honor popped off and skittered across the floor, smacking Jenna's sneaker.

She bent and picked it up.

"Duh. Of course, I wouldn't say it. She'd probably complain if I did. Doesn't mean I don't love her."

Jenna was so surprised she dropped the watch again.

Nardo went silent, like someone had pressed a mute button.

She snatched the watch off the floor and met Nardo's puzzled eyes. She didn't know why, but the watch was the key. "I can hear you," she whispered.

He goggled. "Whoa. You can hear me? I don't believe it! I need to—"

And then Lita grabbed the watch from Jenna's hand.

Nardo went silent again.

Jenna and the ghost boy stared at each other, speechless.

Lita re-wrapped the watch around her wrist. "This thing is always coming loose. I don't know why I put up with it." She moved past Jenna, trudging toward the costume pile.

Jenna raced to catch up. "If it's bothering you," she said, trying to act casual, "I could wear it for a while. Give you a break. It might feel good." She attempted her most winning smile, but Lita was appalled.

"You think it will feel good if I hand over my dead brother's watch to a stranger?"

Jenna backpedaled. "No. Of course not. That's not what I—"

"Get your own watch," Lita muttered, slipping away.

Jenna turned to find Nardo standing at her side once more. The watch was gone, and so was her only way to talk to him.

Chapter Twenty-Six

THE WINTER CARNIVAL

The next two weeks passed in a blur.

Nardo hung on Jenna's heels every time he saw her, waiting for another chance to speak. But she couldn't touch the watch without the danger of touching Lita. And that was too risky, especially with a cure so close at hand.

Eventually, she had to ignore Nardo's pouting and focus on making it through to the finish line—the Winter Carnival.

Her hopes climbed as the day of the carnival came closer, and she didn't have to work hard to have a positive mindset. Her mom was doing all right, even without Serene's pills. She'd stared into space once or twice, but it was nothing compared to the trances she'd had before.

At school, Jenna had been careful never to be alone. She'd spotted Brent watching her a couple of times, but if she was right and the curse was growing, at least it was growing slowly. He still had some self-control. And she wouldn't have to dodge him much longer.

Lane was a different problem. It had been a mistake to let him confide in her about his breakup with "Angel." Now her conversations with him alternated between hopeful delusions that Angel would come around and sulking because she hadn't.

She wanted to avoid school altogether, but she was afraid of jeopardizing the outcome of the carnival. Her job was to stay put and look for messages from Fore. But so far, there was nothing. She tried to see that with a positive mindset, too. No news was good news, right?

So she didn't complain—not even when Kelsea called for extra practices to get ready for their concert. And surprisingly, with every passing day, TOTEL

CHAOS sounded less like an out-of-tune fire alarm and almost—not quite—but *almost* like music.

She practically danced through the days, thinking about the cure that was coming. If all went well, she'd not only save her mother, she'd make everyone safe from her own curse, too. She and her mom could live a normal life at last.

When the day of the Winter Carnival arrived, the hours dragged. Jenna was laser focused on what would happen that night when she saw her aunt.

Everything was ready. In the trunk of her car, she had her costume—complete with hoop skirt, wings, a wand, and a strawberry-blonde wig Markese had insisted she borrow. It would look strange combined with her balaclava and shades, but after her weeks in school, she'd grown accustomed to looking bizarre. And it would provide a bubble of safety until she'd taken the cure.

She hadn't heard from her aunt since they'd made their plan in Union Depot, but she'd been expecting that. If there was a chance that Thairyn Hinsen could track them through a cell phone, it was better not to make contact. This was too important.

When it was finally time for Jenna to leave for the carnival, her hands shook with nervous excitement.

Her mom hadn't wanted her to go, of course, but Jenna convinced her she'd be safer outside in a hoop skirt than she'd ever been in the crowded halls at school. So Mae bit her tongue.

If her mom knew the real purpose of the outing, though, she'd be ecstatic. And it wouldn't be long before Jenna could tell her everything.

She opened the front closet and slipped on her white jacket and gloves. Then she put the balaclava in her pocket and went to kiss her mom goodbye.

Mae was in the living room, watering her fading lily.

Jenna stopped short when she saw her, though. Her mother's face was an ashen shade of gray. "Mom, are you okay?"

When she didn't answer, Jenna walked over and gently touched her arm.

Mae's head snapped up and her eyes glazed over. The ice blue plastic cup she'd been using to water the plant slipped from her fingers, splashing water across the drab carpet.

Jenna's stomach clenched. She recognized that look. Her mom was falling into one of her visions.

Mae's eyes fastened on her without seeing. "Jenna."

"I'm here," she said, even though her mom was staring right through her, deep in the trance.

Then Mae cocked her head to the side, listening. "Tell me," she said to the air.

Jenna glanced around hopefully. "Fore?" she whispered. "Are you here?"

But there was only silence. Her mother didn't move.

She tried again. "Fore, is there anything I should know about the cure? Like, take with water, or no food for an hour afterward? Anything? You can get Mom to tell me. You might not realize this, but giant plants and dead insects don't send a super-clear message nowadays."

When the silence stretched, Jenna sighed.

Suddenly Mae slid her hands over Jenna's cheeks, gripping her face. "I need you to know," she said. She gazed at Jenna as if she were a crystal ball.

Jenna held her breath. Here it was.

Mae's fingers tightened painfully. "Love is powerful."

"Okay." Jenna blinked. That wasn't what she'd been hoping for. "I love you, too, Mom." She tried to wrest her face from her mother's hands, but Mae's grip was iron.

"I don't understand, Fore," Jenna said. "What do I need to know about tonight?"

"Watch. Wait. Three," her mother whispered.

Three? Was there someone else in the room named Three now? Hopefully her mother was just delirious. Rambling.

Mae dropped her arms, thrown out of her vision. She stepped back and passed a hand over her eyes, swaying.

Jenna steadied her. "Mom, are you okay? You just had an episode."

Mae was silent for a moment. An odd expression crossed her face, but she waved off Jenna's concern. "I'll be all right," she said, "but you be careful tonight." She kissed Jenna on the cheek, then headed to her bedroom. "I'm going to rest. I'll see you when you get back."

Jenna let her go. She'd make her mother better. But first she needed the cure.

She put on her balaclava and shades, then slipped out the door and locked it.

She heard footsteps coming up the main staircase, so she headed for the narrow stairs at the end of the hall. She passed Mr. Cane's apartment and was nearly to the exit when the door to apartment 311 opened and Brent's little brother charged out.

She danced sideways, narrowly avoiding him as he raced down the hall. Then Brent stormed through the open door after him, slamming into Jenna from behind.

She gasped and stumbled forward, then threw a quick glance over her shoulder. Brent was pushing himself up off the floor.

Before he could get a good look at her, she dashed for the staircase. One more night. She just had to make it through one more night.

She flew down the stairs and then sprinted to her car. It wasn't until she was speeding away from Ashton Place that she breathed a sigh of relief. She was safe. But even so, she couldn't stop shaking as she drove toward downtown Saint Paul.

The streets thrummed with activity, and it took forever for her to reach the parking ramp near Rice Park. But her heart pounded with anticipation as she got out of the car.

She popped the trunk and, cringing only slightly, tugged the ruffled pink costume over her head. Then she slipped on the wings—one more barrier—and checked her balaclava and shades. She topped it all off with the wig Markese had given her. She looked like a lunatic, but it couldn't be helped.

Last, she hefted the star-tipped wand that was the size of a walking staff. She could use it to push people out of the way if she had to. Swallowing hard, she slammed the trunk closed and went to the elevator that led to the Skyway. She rode up to the next level and then crossed through the glass tunnel to the other side of the street.

Fortunately, the hoop skirt was working—keeping everyone around her at a distance. And as she walked, she noticed several women wearing burlesque saloon-style costumes. There was also a man dressed all in red, with a cape and a mask, so she wasn't the only person in costume. Maybe she didn't look as ridiculous as she felt.

She threaded her way toward downtown, where TOTEL CHAOS was meeting in front of the Ice Palace. Hopefully, her aunt would be able to find her there among all the people.

On another evening, she might have enjoyed her surroundings. There were white lights everywhere, twinkling in the twilight. Live music was playing, and the heady scents of corn dogs, cheese curds, cookies, and coffee wafted from nearby food trucks.

As she navigated the route to the Ice Palace, she passed enchanting ice sculptures bathed in neon light. One sculpture showed a phoenix rising from the ashes. Then she saw a seahorse, a dolphin, and a huge, malevolent dragon—all carved from ice.

But the sights and sounds of the carnival faded into the background when she caught sight of Lane's black jacket and bright red scarf in the crowd. She hurried to catch up, calling his name.

He turned, doubling over with laughter when he saw her costume. "Wow, Mo. Did Kelsea make you wear that?"

"Indeed," she said, imitating the girl. Then she eyed Lane up and down, and her jaw dropped with indignation. In jeans and his black jacket, he looked completely normal. "Where's your costume?"

"I'm a pirate." He reached under his beanie and slid an eye patch down over one eye. "Ahoy, Matey," he growled. Then he tucked the patch back out of sight.

"I hate you so much right now."

He laughed again, then strolled toward the Ice Palace. "Isn't this place incredible?" he asked. His eyes glowed. "It's like something from another world. Brie and I got here early, and I've been scoping everything out."

He pointed to the Ice Palace, an enormous structure with multiple towers like a fairy-tale castle. "It's seven stories tall and made from over four thousand blocks of ice. And there's a free ice skating rink over that way. But let's find everybody first."

She nodded, wondering how her aunt would find *her*.

Fortunately, Doc spotted them moments later. She looked adorable, wearing winter boots over fuzzy koala bear pajamas. The attached hoodie had eyes, ears, and a large koala nose—and it suited her perfectly.

"Change of plans," Doc said, leading them to a more secluded area near the vendor tents. "Kelsea wanted more space to get ready, so we're meeting over here."

Jenna wished Kelsea had picked someplace more visible. She craned her neck, looking for her aunt again, but there was still no sign of her.

As she caught sight of Kelsea, her worry faded slightly. In her UFO costume, Kelsea was hard to miss. She held a clear, domed umbrella with a ring of silver cardboard attached to the bottom. Dozens of blinking LED strips circled the umbrella and hung down to the ground, the flashing lights suggesting a rocket blasting off.

As the three of them walked up, Kelsea shoved the blinking umbrella into Doc's hands, removing her wire-rimmed glasses and pulling off the green alien mask she was wearing. "It's impossible to see in this thing," she said, replacing her glasses. Then she kneeled in the snow, mumbling about concert flyers as she rooted inside her backpack.

Beside Kelsea, Lita was drawing on Brie's face with an eyeliner pen. Nardo stood behind them in his Hawaiian shirt and shorts. As usual, he tried to speak to Jenna right away, but when she couldn't understand, he sulked and then disappeared. Hopefully that was normal ghost boy behavior.

Lane gaped at Brie, then turned to Lita. "What are you doing to her face?"

"Improving it." She didn't look up as she focused on her design—one that made Brie's face resemble a Cinco de Mayo sugar skull.

"But this isn't the Day of the Dead," he protested.

"Every day is the Day of the Dead," Lita said darkly.

At that moment, Jose sauntered over dressed in thigh-high boots, tights, and a cape. He bowed low to Brie. "Want to spend the evening with Prince Charming?" He winked at her cheekily.

"I'd prefer the Prince of Darkness over you," she said.

Jose swung to Lita. "Do me next. Make me into a devil."

"You're already a devil," she told her brother.

Hampton snorted with laughter. He carried a heavy silver flashlight, and he shone the beam right onto Jose's scowling face.

Hampton was dressed in camouflage pants and a matching camo jacket. And, as usual, he had his canvas sack slung over his shoulders.

Markese glided out of the crowd in a voluminous zebra-print coat and a sparkling tiara. "Shine that light over here," he directed Hampton.

"What are you wearing, Markese?" Kelsea asked.

"You said flashy. And I can do flashy." He whipped his phone out. "Selfie time!" He snapped a shot of himself. Then he leaned in beside Lane and Jenna. "Us-ie time! Everybody smile and say *Freaks*!" The camera on his cell phone flashed.

Zinnia and Devonte strolled up behind Markese, the last to join the group. Devonte was wearing his regular jeans and a hooded orange coat. Zinnia, though, wore a burlesque gown with a royal purple feather boa, like the women Jenna had seen when she'd first arrived. She looked amazing, and Devonte's eyes were glued to her heart-shaped face.

"You make a lovely Klondike Kate," Lane told her. He whispered under his breath to Jenna. "A lot of ladies dress up like her at the Winter Carnival. She's kind of a legendary character."

She nodded without understanding and suppressed a smile as she watched Devonte eating up Zinnia's new look.

Kelsea rolled her eyes, getting to her feet with a thick packet of papers in hand. "Hampton!" she barked. "We need the glow sticks. Let's get this show on the road."

Hampton thrust the metal flashlight at Jenna, who was standing next to him.

She took it, holding her wand in one hand and the heavy flashlight in the other. She aimed the light at Hampton as he unslung his brown canvas knapsack, rifling inside.

She used the opportunity to scan the crowd, searching for her aunt, but with no luck. If Aunt Serene didn't appear soon, she'd go back to the Ice Palace and search for her there.

"Jenna Getty," Kelsea barked, breaking through her thoughts. "Throw me that flashlight. I want to show everyone the flyer before we go." She clapped her hands impatiently.

Startled, Jenna tossed the flashlight to Kelsea, but it went off course.

Brie never saw it coming. She stood motionless as Lita drew on her, and the metal flashlight smacked her on the temple. She cried out and put her hand to her head. Then she pulled her fingers away, noticing blood.

Jenna gasped and immediately began apologizing.

Lane started toward Brie, a look of concern on his face, but Jose was already there. "Hampton, first aid kit!" he commanded.

Hampton dumped the contents of his canvas backpack onto the ground and grabbed the kit. He tossed it to Jose, who opened it and quickly found an iodine wipe.

"This is going to sting," he told Brie.

She sucked in her breath, wincing as Jose swabbed the wound.

Jenna watched with her hands pressed to her mouth. The sour taste of guilt climbed into her throat.

Jose eyed Brie's cut with clinical efficiency. Then he grimaced as he rooted through the first aid kit again. "Why are there no Band-Aids in here?"

Immediately, Hampton pulled off his camouflage coat and tossed it to the ground.

"What are you…why are you doing that?" Lane asked.

Then Hampton yanked his long-sleeve shirt over his head.

Lane held up his hand. "Okay, that's not…necessary. It's a tiny cut. She'll be fine."

Markese pushed forward to see. "Hush. Let the man work."

Hampton skimmed his white undershirt off, baring his chest to the winter cold.

"Dude. You don't need to—"

"Shush!" Markese said, waving his arms furiously at Lane.

Then Hampton hitched his pant leg up, revealing a calf holster with a knife tucked inside. He grabbed the brass handle, unsheathing the slim knife and slicing through the collar of the undershirt. He ripped it into long strips and tossed the pieces to Jose.

Jose gently wound them around Brie's head. Then he held his hand against her temple, putting pressure on the cut to stop the bleeding. "Are you good?" he asked her, serious for once.

"I'm…better." She met his eyes, confused, then looked away. Her gaze landed on Jenna, scorching her with hatred.

Lane held up his hands. "You're all overreacting." He turned to Hampton. "Will you please put your clothes on?"

Markese shot Lane a withering glare, but everyone else looked relieved.

Hampton sheathed his knife and shrugged back into his shirt and coat.

"I really am sorry," Jenna said. Then to herself, she muttered, "Another epic fail."

But Kelsea overheard her. "Don't say that," she said sharply. "There are no epic fails." She gestured to the group. "Everyone, tell Jenna Getty what I always say."

They exchanged blank looks.

"Come on, you know. What is it I'm always telling you? Jose, you know." She pointed to him.

He concentrated and then smiled. "Oh yeah. You always say 'What's wrong with you people?' right?"

Kelsea fisted her hands on her hips. "I never say that!" She pointed to Hampton. "Tell Jenna Getty what I always say."

He studied the sky. "You...you blow your whistle a lot."

"What's wrong with you people? That doesn't even involve words. No! I'm talking about a wise thing I say to you."

Markese piped up. "One time you said 'Be yourself. Unless you're a total jerk. Or at a cosplay convention. Or in a movie or something. Then be someone else. Otherwise—'"

Kelsea ground her teeth. "The thing I say is: *No failures. Only lessons.* Remember?"

"You've never said that," Zinnia pointed out.

"Well, I'm saying it now. *No failures. Only lessons.*" Kelsea breathed deeply and pushed her glasses up on her nose. She nodded to Jenna. "So not an epic fail. An epic lesson."

Jenna wasn't sure what lesson she was supposed to take from this. Don't throw flashlights? Or, more likely, stay away from other people. That sounded about right.

As Kelsea started handing out stacks of flyers, Nardo reappeared abruptly in front of Jenna. He mouthed something urgently, but she still couldn't understand him. This time, she was the one frustrated. She ignored him, searching the crowd for her aunt instead.

She didn't see Serene, but she did notice a young man in his twenties moving in her direction and carrying a cardboard box. He had long blond hair that he wore in a ponytail, and something about him tickled her memory. Oddly, she could have sworn he'd been watching her.

The next thing she knew, the man bumped into a woman walking a dog. Off balance, he stepped sideways and collided with Markese. The cardboard box slipped from his fingers and crashed to the ground in the center of their circle. The top split open, and to Jenna's horror, a swarm of hornets buzzed out.

But these weren't normal hornets. They were massive—like the hornet that had stung her that day in the park. The day she'd run from Thairyn Hinsen.

He knows.

Icy fear prickled across her body as the thought flashed through her mind. Did the man with the white tattoo know she was here? Had he sent these creatures?

Everything happened so fast, she had trouble taking it in. The hornets spread out, flying at the TOTEL members gathered nearby.

Markese twirled in a circle, swatting at one, and Lita and Brie swiped at each other as the hornets landed on them.

"Stop, drop, and roll!" Hampton shouted. He pulled Jose down with him, and the two of them rolled in the snow, trying to smash the creatures.

Beside her, Lane hopped up and down. He flapped his jacket to dislodge a hornet that had landed on his back.

Jenna waved her star wand at it, hoping to shoo it away, but it was too late. The hornet was stinging.

Shouts went up all around the circle. Then, as quickly as they'd emerged, the hornets flew off. The man with the blond ponytail was nowhere to be seen.

Aside from Nardo, Jenna was the only one unscathed.

"Now that was an epic fail," Kelsea said, righting her glasses.

Everyone rubbed sore spots where they'd been stung, and Jose searched the first aid kit for a cream that would help.

"Do you see now what I've been talking about?" Markese demanded. "Heinous with a capital H." He grabbed his lucky necklace, muttering to himself.

"What were those things?" Zinnia asked.

Jose and Hampton exchanged glances. "Too big to be yellowjackets or paper wasps," Hampton said.

"Wicked," Brie said, and shivered. "But not wicked cool. Wicked evil. Did everyone get stung?"

They all nodded, and Jenna kept her mouth shut. Why hadn't she been stung, too?

Nardo looked at her, troubled. Then he vanished.

"Maybe the guy who dropped the cardboard box was an exotic animal breeder. I've never seen insects like that," Doc mused. "They have to be illegal."

"He sure got out of here quick enough," Devonte said in his ultra-low voice.

"Heinous," Markese grumbled again.

Just then, Serene walked up, smiling. She wore a quilted pink coat with a high neck and a ruff of fur, and she sipped coffee from a steaming thermos. She was the picture of comfort, and a wave of relief swept over Jenna.

"I've been looking all over for you," Serene said, not even batting an eyelash at Jenna's strange attire. Then her face fell as she took in the expressions of the TOTEL members. "Is everybody okay?"

"Indeed," Kelsea said breathlessly.

"Wrong answer," Markese objected. "But we're alive, if that's what you mean." Everyone else murmured in agreement.

"But if somebody collapses, call 9-1-1," Zinnia added.

Serene looked confused. "I'll do that."

"It's hard to explain," Jenna told her. "We just had an incident with a bunch of bees or wasps or...something. Anyway, it's not important." She changed the subject, introducing the band members to her aunt.

Serene lifted an eyebrow in amusement when Jenna pointed out Lane, but the expression was subtle enough that she hoped nobody noticed.

"Nice to meet you all," her aunt said. "Tell me, are any of you with the Council?"

When no one spoke up, Jose asked, "Is that the name of another band?"

"You could say that," Serene agreed. "Now don't let me interrupt your meeting, but I have to steal my niece away for a while. I've got something I need to give her." She looked meaningfully at Jenna. "She'll catch up with you when she can."

Jenna waved goodbye and was about to follow her aunt when Nardo appeared, motioning wildly. She tried to ignore him, but he got right in her face, pointing to the ground.

Lita's lime green watch was lying in the snow. It must have come loose when she was swatting at the hornets.

Jenna scooped it up and closed her hand around it before anyone could notice.

Nardo's voice switched on suddenly. "Whoa! That was crazy. Okay, I've got to tell you something big."

She hurried after her aunt. "I'll tell Lita you love her later," she said under her breath. "I'm doing something important right now."

Behind them, Kelsea was already issuing orders. "Let's clear out, people. I don't want to be here if those hornets decide to come back. Plus, we have work to do."

Nardo walked backward in front of Jenna, refusing to be ignored. "This is about your aunt."

She nearly tripped over her own feet. "What about my aunt?" she asked defensively.

Ahead, Serene was leaning into the open passenger window of an SUV, speaking in a low voice with Ian.

Jenna wondered how in the world they had scored a parking spot alongside the food trucks and other vendors.

"She's going to try to get you in that car," Nardo said. "But trust me—you don't want to do that. If you get in the car, that guy in the driver's seat is planning to shoot you with some kind of tranquilizer dart. Your aunt told him to a little while ago. I heard her."

"What are you talking about? My aunt is here to help me." But the tiniest doubt squirmed to life inside of her.

Her aunt waved her over. "Climb on in. This is the moment we've been waiting for." Then she noticed Jenna's face and frowned. "Is something wrong? You seem...distracted." She looked around suspiciously. "Are you seeing that boy again? The one who's outside the spectrum?"

"Who, him?" Jenna shook her head dismissively. "I only saw him that one time," she lied. "Like you told me, I don't think my Seer gift is working the way it should." She forced herself not to look at Nardo.

"What's wrong, then?"

She had to stall. "It must have been that bee incident. I've got a migraine coming on, and I'm a little nauseous. If I can sit by myself in the cold air for a minute, I'll feel better."

Serene frowned, but she was already scanning the area. She led the way to a steel park bench near the street. A family of four was sitting there, but Serene didn't hesitate. "My niece is sick. She needs this seat," she told them, and the family hopped up, vacating the bench.

"I'll stay right here with you," Serene said.

"No!" Jenna scrambled for an excuse. "I don't want you in range if I throw up." She put her fingers to her temples, selling her story. "Please, just give me a minute to myself."

Serene frowned, then nodded. "I'll bring you some juice. Maybe a little sugar will help. I'll be right back." She walked toward the SUV, glancing over her shoulder to check on Jenna.

Jenna put her head in her hands, covering her face so her aunt couldn't see her mouth moving. "Spill it," she told Nardo. "I want to know everything."

Chapter Twenty-Seven

HE KNOWS

Nardo leaned in.

"So that guy with the cardboard box of horrors—the hornet thingies—his name is Flynn, and he was here talking to your aunt earlier. I saw him. He said something about DNA samples, and he showed her the insects, and she told him to go ahead. She said she'd pick the group up later if they tested positive for...something. Sounded like biology, but that doesn't make sense."

"Biomagy," Jenna whispered.

Nardo clapped his hands. "That was it! Biomagy. Weird, right?"

At Union Depot, Aunt Serene had talked about getting DNA samples from the people in TOTEL. Jenna had objected, and she'd thought her aunt had given up on the idea.

But what if she hadn't? And what if the hornets didn't just sting—what if they used their stingers to draw blood? It would explain why Jenna hadn't been targeted tonight. A hornet had taken her blood weeks ago. Serene already had her DNA.

"You know what's even more weird?" Nardo asked. "That creepy critter guy—Flynn—he's parked in a Jeep Wrangler around the corner. And after those wasp things stung everybody, they flew over to him, and he put them inside, like, an aquarium in his Jeep. Oh, and he has a dog and a bird in the car, too." He grimaced. "Heads up. Your aunt is incoming."

Serene walked over with a paper cup in her hands. "I brought you some juice," she said kindly.

Jenna resumed her sick act. "Thank you," she said weakly.

"Are you doing any better?"

"I think so. The cold air helps. But I need a little longer."

"Sure thing, sweetheart. I'll be right over there when you're ready." She returned to the SUV, glancing over her shoulder at Jenna with a look of concern.

Jenna waved at her reassuringly and sipped her orange juice, using the cup to hide her mouth. "What else?"

"Well, this crazy lady named Fore told me I needed to keep my eyes open, so I went poking around."

"Wait a minute. You talked to Fore?"

"I know, right? She just appeared a couple of weeks ago, like La Llorona or something, and I was like, whoa, I'm the ghost here. How am *I* being haunted?"

"Nardo, focus! What did Fore tell you?"

"She said you were draining her energy or whatever and she couldn't stay this time, or in this time—something about time. I don't know."

"I'm draining her energy? How?"

He shrugged. "I'm a ghost, not a mind reader. But I do know she said it was up to me to keep watch."

Jenna gaped at him. "You couldn't have told me this before today?"

"You couldn't hear me, remember? How was I supposed to tell you?"

"Oh, gosh, let me think. Holding up four fingers would have been a good start!"

"Whoa. Like charades or something. You are totally blowing my mind right now."

"Nardo, you—never mind. What else do I need to know?"

"Oh yeah. So tonight, I got the feeling that something was up, so I broke into your aunt's car to check it out."

Jenna shot him a look. "You broke in?"

"Figure of speech. I guess I morphed in. Is that better?"

"Okay, okay. Whatever." She took a long swallow of orange juice to calm herself. "You got in. Then what?"

"Oh yeah, well, in the back of the SUV—get this—there's a little girl all tied up. She's like, drugged or something. And I was like, whoa. Would a normal person do that? Tie up a little girl? I don't think so."

Dread pooled inside of her. "What did she look like?"

"Small. Maybe five or six years old, with, like, huge anime-size eyes. Oh, and she was bald, but her whole head was tatted up or something. She was kind of a freak show."

Jenna's throat grew tight. She'd been so sure she'd saved Raloria. She'd pictured her reuniting with her family and happily playing with her stuffed owl. But then, why was she drugged and bound in the back of an SUV?

"Anyway, that's when I heard your aunt talking to the driver, saying that once you were in the car, he needed to shoot you with the tranquilizer real quick and that he should make sure not to touch you."

Through her fingers, Jenna saw Serene watching her intently. She sat up and tipped most of the orange juice into her mouth, hoping to keep her aunt appeased a little while longer.

Then Serene turned away, answering her cell phone.

"Nardo. Can you find out what she's saying?"

He studied the distance. "It should be inside my spookosphere."

"Your spookosphere?"

"That's what I call my bubble." He waxed enthusiastic, happy to be communicating at last. "Picture my anchor—like my watch—in the center of a circle, and it's attached to an invisible leash I can't go past. Didn't you ever wonder why I never haunted you at your house or anything? My spookosphere is like a hundred feet or something. But, yeah, I think I can get over there. Be right back."

Jenna watched from the corner of her eye. After a moment, Serene hung up. Then she leaned inside the car window, speaking to Ian.

Nardo blinked into existence in front of Jenna. "Uh, do you want the bad news or the way worse news?"

She groaned. "The way worse news, I guess."

"Well, you need to hightail it out of here. Your aunt was on the phone with the critter creep, and he said some guy named Thurston—"

"Thairyn?"

"Thairyn. Yeah. He took the bait, but then he got away. And now he's coming for you. They're trying to figure out how to get you into the car if you won't come willingly."

She swallowed. "And the bad news?"

"Serene says she put some kind of extract in your drink. Don't know what that means, but it sounds shady."

"The Obru extract," she breathed. "It was in the orange juice." She stood, crumpling the empty cup in her hand. She walked toward the white SUV and pitched the cup in the trash along the way. "Follow my lead, Nardo. I don't know what the Obru is going to do to me, but I don't want my aunt around when it kicks in."

"Gotcha. What's your plan?"

She jammed a pleasant expression on her face. "Time to do some acting."

Serene looked relieved to see her return. "I'm glad to see you're feeling better. Now, let's get you cured of your curse! Hop in."

Jenna grinned. "I can't believe this is happening!" She put her hand on the door handle, then stopped short and smacked herself on the forehead, feigning realization. She pulled Lita's watch from the sleeve of her gown where she'd stuffed it. "I forgot. I have my friend's watch. Let me just run and give it to her. Be right back."

Before her aunt could protest, Jenna dove into the crowd, moving as fast as she could in her hoop skirt. "Did she buy it?" she asked Nardo.

He blinked away and then back. "Yeah, I think she bought it. But she also got on the phone to Flynn and said Rusty should keep an eye on you. Who's Rusty?"

"No idea." She walked faster, making her way out of the park. She passed the ice dragon sculpture and almost ran right into Lane.

"Mo!" he said happily. "I waited around, hoping I'd run into—"

"Sorry," she called. "Something's come up."

Nardo blinked away, but she kept pushing through the crowd.

Lane followed. "What's wrong? Is everything okay?"

"Kind of hard to explain," she said, not even looking at him.

Nardo reappeared by her side. "Bad news. Flynn is on our tail, and he's got his dog with him. A beagle, I think. Better pick up the pace." He left again.

Keeping a firm hold on the watch, she scooped up the front of her skirt and ran in the direction of the parking garage. "Talk to you later, Lane!" she called.

Lane trailed after her, jogging to keep up. "No. You'll talk to me now. What's going on?"

Nardo popped in for an update. "Flynn's like three hundred feet behind us."

"Isn't your spookosphere only one hundred feet?" she whispered.

"What am I, Einstein? You don't become a genius when you cross over, you know."

"Never mind," she said, and he blinked away.

"What did you say?" Lane asked. He scurried to keep up.

She glanced behind her and then changed direction, hoping to throw off both Lane and the man with his dog.

But Lane wouldn't let her out of his sight. "Tell me what's wrong, Mo."

She grunted in frustration. "I robbed a bank, and the police are after me. Run while you still can."

"Very funny," Lane said. "Tell me the truth."

A man carrying a carton of kettle corn stepped into her path, and she narrowly missed him. Kernels flew like confetti, startling a red-tailed hawk from the branches of a tree.

"Come on, Mo! The truth. Tell me!"

She crossed the street, skirting a large group of women wearing feather boas. "You won't like the truth."

"Tell me anyway."

"Fine," she said, rolling her eyes. "A ghost just informed me that a man and his dog are hunting me down, probably because of my magic."

He threw his head back and laughed. "That's hilarious. Now be serious. Are we being filmed? Is this a YouTube thing? TikTok?"

She had to stop herself from screaming. "I'm in trouble, okay? Is that what you want to hear?"

His jaw tightened. "I knew it. It's just like what happened to the girl I told you about—Angel. Is someone following you? Don't worry. I'll help."

At his mention of Angel, her cheeks burned behind the fabric of her balaclava. He was coming too close to the truth. "No time to explain," she shouted. And she ran faster.

Nardo was back. "FYI, he's almost on you now. I got right up to his phone to listen to your aunt, too. She knows you're running, and she asked if Rusty is watching, and he said yes. But she's saying she's gonna hack your cell phone location too, just in case."

"Turd burgers." Jenna glanced around. There was no sign of this Rusty person, but Flynn was much closer now, his hound pacing at his side. The sight of the man's blond ponytail gave her pause once more. She'd seen him before tonight, but she still couldn't place him.

As she passed the skating rink, she veered toward a trash can and tossed her cell phone inside, trying not to flinch. Then an idea occurred to her.

She broke into a sprint, racing for the rink. She vaulted over the barrier and kept moving—half running, half skating across the ice in her sneakers.

Lane nearly slipped and fell as he leaped over the barrier after her, but he pulled himself upright and followed.

Flynn and his dog went over the barricade too, but the beagle's claws couldn't find purchase on the ice. Its feet splayed, and it spun flat on its belly, knocking the man off balance.

Jenna ignored the annoyed shouts of skaters as she and Lane cut across the rink. She clambered over the barricade on the other side and then passed beneath the branches of a tree decorated with white lights.

She slowed, and something made her look up.

A red-tailed hawk perched above her, watching. Hadn't she startled one from a tree just a moment ago?

Her suspicion grew.

The hornets. Flynn's dog. And now the hawk—Rusty, perhaps? She knew so little about other people with Charms. Could some of them use their gifts to control animals?

Her intuition told her she was right. The bird was spying on her. She had to get out of the open.

Just as Lane caught up with her, she took off again, pelting down the street. She visualized the map of the Skyway she'd gotten in Union Depot. There should be an entrance just ahead, and the hawk would have a hard time keeping tabs on her once she went indoors.

She turned the corner and saw the sign for the building she needed. She burst through the stately front door, slowing just long enough to check the Skyway signage. Then she hooked her arm around the rail post, changing direction, and pounded down a flight of stairs.

Nardo looked confused about where they were going, but she couldn't explain with Lane there.

"Isn't this the tunnel under the park?" Lane asked breathlessly. "The one that leads up into the Skyway?"

"That's the one." Then she heard it. The baying of a hound. Flynn had found her again.

Nardo disappeared.

She rounded another corner, picking up speed as she entered a long corridor with shiny, waxed floors.

She glanced behind her. She could see the beagle now. It was off the leash, bounding down the hall.

Nardo appeared as they passed an intersection. "That way!" he said, pointing left.

But that was just a different hall, and she knew she couldn't outrun the dog. Just ahead of her, though, she'd spotted an elevator. She hurtled forward, punching the button frantically. She watched in horror as the hound closed the distance between them.

The elevator dinged open, and they scrambled inside, hitting the "Close Door" button. The doors slid shut a second before the dog reached them, and it bayed in frustration as the elevator rose.

Their breaths came fast in the enclosed quiet.

Careful not to lose her grip on the watch, Jenna turned her back and seized her chance to get rid of the extra layers that were slowing her down. She unstrapped the wings and yanked the hoop skirt over her head. The wig, crown, and wand soon joined the pink ruffles on the elevator floor. Once again, she was wearing her "Jenna" attire, with her white jacket, shades, and balaclava.

"Now can you tell me what's going on?" Lane asked.

"I've got no clue, man," Nardo answered, as if Lane had been talking to him. "And her aunt's out of my spookosphere now."

Jenna ignored Nardo, shrugging her shoulders. "I don't know what they want with me." At least that wasn't a complete lie.

"We need to call the police," Lane said, getting out his phone.

"No!" she said forcefully, and he frowned, surprised.

The elevator door opened, saving her the effort of inventing an excuse. She leaped out, dodging a group of people waiting to get on. Then, with Lane hard on her heels and Nardo at her side, she sprinted along the hall and down a set of stairs.

"Where are we going?" Lane asked, panting.

"I've got to get to my car. It's an emergency."

Following the signs, they reached the Skyway exit for the RiverCentre parking ramp. Nardo disappeared again.

The stitch in Jenna's side was becoming unbearable, but she pushed forward, racing through the glass tunnel that crossed the road. She was nearly there.

She ignored the elevator this time, bounding down the stairs to get back to the street. Then she bolted toward the parking ramp and up another set of stairs until she reached the level where she'd parked.

She pulled up short, though, when Nardo reappeared in front of her, waving his hands. "Whoa. It's Flynn. He must've known where you were going and beat us here. Not sure where the dog went."

Jenna ducked behind a van, motioning Lane down with her.

Her stomach dropped. Of course, Flynn had known where she was going. She'd been naïve to go back to her car. If the hawk had been watching her all night, Flynn knew exactly where she'd parked.

Lane's brows knitted in confusion. "What's happening?"

"That man is here," she whispered. "I think he's over by my car." She pointed, and Nardo nodded, confirming her suspicion.

"Don't worry," Lane said quietly. "I'll distract him. When he comes after me, make a break for it. Be safe out there, Mo."

"Lane, please don't—"

But he was already moving, crouching low to remain hidden behind the cars. When he was three aisles over, he stood up and shouted, "Jenna, follow me!"

He ran, and Flynn took off in pursuit.

She waited until their footsteps died away. Nardo nodded at her, and she dashed toward her Corolla. But as she fumbled for the keys, she lost her grip on the watch. It slid across the concrete and disappeared under a red Corvette.

Nardo went silent.

She cursed and dropped to her knees. Stretching her arm beneath the Corvette, she patted the floor in search of the watch. Suddenly, the car alarm went off, and she reeled back, startled.

She gritted her teeth against the noise and pressed herself against the freezing pavement again, peering beneath the car. But she couldn't see the watch anywhere.

Then a car roared by, and plastic crunched beneath its wheels. She darted out into the feeder lane, and there on the concrete were the broken shards of a lime green watch.

Nardo was gone. She stood there in shock.

Then a voice spoke behind her. "Don't move."

She whipped around. Flynn was so close, he'd overtake her in a moment if she tried to flee.

He had one hand tucked inside his jacket, and he opened the flap to show her the pistol he held. "This way." He motioned her forward, and she walked stiffly beside him as they retraced their steps through the parking garage.

Jenna's mind raced. Flynn had found her. Her aunt had betrayed her. And she could no longer see or talk to Nardo. She'd apparently been draining Fore's energy, and her mother didn't have the first idea what was happening. The TOTEL group was clueless, too.

No one could help her.

Then her eyes bulged. Lane was creeping along beside her, crouched behind a row of cars. She looked in the other direction, trying not to give him away. He must have returned for her when he realized Flynn was no longer trailing him.

Thinking quickly, she stopped and angled her body so that Flynn's back was to Lane. "I'm not going any further until I know what you want from me," she bluffed.

Behind Flynn, Lane tiptoed nearer.

Jenna spoke loudly, trying to mask the sound of his approach. "You can start by telling me where you're taking me."

Then Lane stopped, engrossed by the shiny Ford Ranger beside him.

He was geeking out over a truck *now*? She ground her teeth.

"Serene will explain what you need to know," Flynn said. "Get moving."

"I'm not going anywhere," she said stubbornly.

Flynn opened his jacket, laying his hand on the gun.

At the same time, Lane reached into the bed of the truck and picked up a plastic bottle of motor oil. As he twisted the cap open, the sound alerted Flynn.

The man whirled just as Lane sprang forward and splashed the oil in his face.

"Go!" Lane screamed at her.

Flynn groaned and grabbed at his eyes.

But Jenna couldn't leave Lane here. He didn't even realize Flynn had a gun. And the man was already wiping the oil from his face.

He lunged, tackling Lane to the ground. The gun clattered to the concrete as they struggled, and Lane and Flynn both clawed for it.

Jenna eyed the gun. Something about it bothered her. It wasn't a pistol, she realized. It was a dart gun. She thought she'd seen one like it before—she just couldn't remember where.

Then she put the gun out of her thoughts. With Flynn and Lane flailing around, she couldn't get close to it—not without being touched.

Instead, she rushed to the bed of the Ford Ranger, hoping to spot something she could use. She gave silent thanks as she noticed a short wooden board buried beneath a pile of bungee cords. She grabbed it and dashed back to the two men wrestling on the concrete.

Flynn had pinned Lane to the concrete.

Jenna circled behind the man and raised the board. She brought it down on his head—aiming to knock him out, not kill him. He sagged forward, crumpling on top of Lane.

Lane shoved him aside. He checked to make sure Flynn was still breathing. Then he scrambled to his feet, beckoning to Jenna. "We've got to call the police now."

"I told you, we can't!" she said, backing away.

Suspicion flickered in his eyes.

Then Jenna looked past him. The hound was barreling toward her.

It knocked her backward, and her shades clattered to the concrete. She flung one hand up to cover her face and neck, rolling onto her stomach.

The beagle bit down, shaking its head back and forth. She struggled, trying to dislodge it, but the hound's teeth had locked into the fabric of her balaclava.

Then a quiet thud echoed through the garage, and the dog went limp, the heavy grip of its jaws relaxing. Frantically, she pushed it to the side. It was alive but unconscious, a dart protruding between its shoulders.

Jenna looked up.

Lane was standing above her with the dart gun still in his hand.

And he was frozen in shock, as if he'd been carved from ice.

The hound had torn away Jenna's balaclava, and her bun had come loose. Her hair spilled down around her shoulders in a tangle of red. Lane was no longer looking at Jenna.

He was looking at Angel.

Their eyes met, and she couldn't breathe. For so long, she'd feared he would discover her deception. But the reality was worse than anything she'd allowed herself to imagine.

Emotions flickered across his face, one after another. Shock, confusion, hurt, and then anger. He backed away from her, his jaw clenched. "Why?"

She shook her head, trying to find the words to explain.

"What was all this? A setup? A joke?" His voice was a knife. "I thought I knew who you were. I thought—" He choked off, unable to speak.

"Lane, I'm sorry. Let me explain—"

"Don't talk to me." He balled his fists. "I should have known. This whole time, you were lying to my face. Everything about you was a lie. Everything we were."

She closed her eyes, not wanting to see the raw intensity of his pain.

Then his voice went cold—quiet. "I don't know what you're mixed up in or what you were using me for, but you can count me out. I'm done with you."

"Lane, wait!" she called.

But he turned his back on her and strode from the parking garage.

Jenna slumped on the freezing concrete, too numb to move.

The seconds ticked by.

She was cold and hurt. She was in danger. But she couldn't make herself care.

Someone would come by any minute and find her with the unconscious man and dog. She knew she needed to get out of there—before someone called the police. Before her aunt discovered where she was. Still, her body refused to move.

Then something penetrated her haze.

She had to warn her mother.

She'd screwed up everything else, but she could make sure her mom was safe. And her mother would know what to do.

A searing pain shot through her temple, and she clutched her head, groaning. Stars danced in her vision, and her hands started to shake. Was this the Obru extract taking effect at last?

She couldn't pass out here. She had to get to her mom. Jenna heaved herself to her feet and stumbled forward.

She was nearing her Corolla when tires squealed, and a car roared toward her. A silver Mercedes.

Thairyn slammed on the brakes, skidding to a halt. His window was down, and his diamond earring glinted in the eerie light of the garage. His voice was hushed and urgent. "We don't have much time," he said. "Get in."

PART THREE

Chapter Twenty-Eight

TRAPPED

Jenna's heart slammed against her ribs. She turned to run.

But Thairyn called out to her. "They've already got my granddaughter Raloria, and now they're coming for you."

She stopped short and spun around, reeling. "Your granddaughter?"

Through the window, he tossed her a pistol, and Jenna caught it against her chest. It was a loaded dart gun, just like the one Flynn had carried. Her vision blurred once more, but she forced herself to concentrate.

"Fire on me if you have to," Thairyn said. "But get in."

An image flickered in her head—something about Thairyn's dart gun. But the thought wouldn't crystallize.

She leveled the gun at him. "What do you want from me?"

"It's what I don't want. I don't want you to become a weapon for Serene. If I was trying to kill you, I could have done it already. Isn't that true?"

She paused. She didn't know if she believed him, but she needed information. And he had thrown her the pistol. Besides, she couldn't be sure if Serene was tracking her Corolla.

She opened the back door of the Mercedes and slid inside. "Take me to Ashton Place. I have to warn my mother. You'll answer my questions on the way." She kept the gun pointed at his head, ready in case he tried anything.

"I'd advise against going home right now—"

"You can't talk me out of it."

One look at her face told him she meant it. He nodded and jerked the car into gear, careening through the parking ramp and out into the city streets. "At least the hawk won't be watching for us. Not until Flynn's back in commission."

Her head was no longer spinning, but pain pounded behind her eyes. She ignored it. She wouldn't lose this chance to find out everything she could.

"How could a hawk be watching for us?" she asked. "I don't understand."

He glanced at her in the rearview mirror, and his diamond earring flashed again in the streetlight. "Flynn is a Shepherd."

She heaved a breath in frustration. "I don't know what that means."

He shifted in his seat. "It means his Charms help him communicate with animals. Especially the ones he's trained. The hawk is his creature, and he can use it as a second set of eyes. But that isn't the worst you have to worry about with Flynn."

"What do you mean?" she asked, sitting forward.

"His real talent is breeding animals. Rumor has it he's made monsters. Dogs that climb trees, lizards with gills. That kind of thing."

"Hornets with stingers that can draw blood?"

He shot her a piercing look. "Council laws are meant to control what the Shepherds do, but Flynn and the others in the Unbound only obey the laws that suit them." His lip curled. "They don't see right or wrong. Only power."

Jenna shook her head. "But what do they want with me? I'm not powerful."

His mouth tightened. "You *are* powerful. People in the Vigil—people with Charms like mine—can sense power. It's part of how we keep law and order inside Haven. We can't have mages—especially powerful ones—fighting duals."

"Duals? What kind of duals?"

"I'll give you an example. If Flynn and another Shepherd were to each give a dog a different command, what would the dog do?"

"I guess it would obey the mage who's stronger."

"Yes, basically," he said. "But the struggle can also burn both mages out."

"How?"

"It's like a power surge. An overdose. If two mages with the same Charms go off at once...well, imagine using a lightning bolt to power a toaster."

"I see."

"The Vigil tries to keep that from happening." He squinted at her in the mirror. "Now you, your Charms are powerful, but they're odd. It's biomagy I've never seen. Whatever is inside of you is massive. That's how I found you tonight, even with the crowd."

"You can...feel my magic?"

"I can feel all magic if it's close enough. But yours is especially strong. On a normal day, you light up like a sparkler. Tonight, you went off like a volcano. That usually only happens when someone comes into their magic for the first time—or when a mage feels a powerful emotion. It amps up the gift. That's how strong your signal was."

A powerful emotion? she thought. Yeah. You might say that.

Then she cringed, embarrassed. "It could have also been...well, my aunt gave me something to drink a little while ago," she confessed. "And it had something in it—Obru extract, I think. Do you know what that will do to me?"

"I don't," he said, frowning. "But you're alive. Be grateful for that. And I'm lucky to be alive, too. Tonight was a setup, and I walked right into it. If I hadn't noticed that hawk, they'd have taken me for sure. Should have known it was a trap, with her leading me into a crowd. Thought I could follow Serene and find my granddaughter."

Then Jenna narrowed her eyes as she realized Thairyn's story didn't add up. And she wasn't going to tell him anything about Raloria until she was certain it wouldn't make things worse. Again.

"If Raloria's your granddaughter, why was she tied up in your house?" she demanded.

His mouth thinned. "You don't know what it means to have healing Charms, do you?"

She shook her head, and he grunted.

"Healers feel what others feel. It's what makes them so good at their work—their sensitivity to emotion. To pain. But the more powerful the Healer, the more sensitive they are. And Raloria's the most powerful Healer born for generations. Pain affects her deeply."

"That doesn't explain why you had her tied to a bedpost," she pointed out, her voice hard.

"Let me finish." He turned onto a side street, moving out of heavy traffic at last. He picked up speed.

"Raloria is so sensitive, her parents—my daughter and her husband—had to move out to the country to be away from others. They tried to get Raloria to sleep during the day when her pain was the worst, but even then, she'd sleepwalk. One time she got out of the house, fast asleep, wandering toward a car that had crashed a mile from home."

Jenna suddenly recalled the car accident she'd passed after leaving Raloria. She'd thought her Charms were causing the girl's agony, but maybe she'd been reacting, not to her, but to someone who'd been hurt in the accident.

"At first, my daughter locked Raloria in her room to keep her from sleepwalking," Thairyn continued. "But the child wound up injuring herself trying to get out. So they tied a stretch of stocking to her wrist instead. That way, when she was awake and alert, she could just undo the knot."

Jenna nodded thoughtfully.

"After my daughter was—" His voice caught, and he cleared it. "My daughter and her husband were killed, and I took the girl in."

Jenna remembered the awful moment she'd found out her father was dead. Her chest clenched. "I'm so sorry," she told him.

He stared straight ahead. "I left the Vigil and moved Raloria to my old homeplace. With no near neighbors, I thought she'd be safe there. And I bound her when she slept just like my daughter had done."

His shoulders slumped. "I shouldn't have left her alone, but what else could I do? I couldn't bring her with me when I went out for supplies—she was in too much pain. And she attracted attention. She couldn't help it."

"I believe you," Jenna whispered.

"And who could I ask to sit with her? A babysitter would have noticed that something was wrong and reported it." He glanced in the mirror at her, then away. "We were alone in the world."

She could relate to that. For years, it had just been her and her mother.

His hands gripped the steering wheel hard. "When I came home that day and she was gone, I knew members of the Unbound were behind it. But when I found your glove outside the window, I thought you were working with them. You might know where they'd taken her. So I used a skeleton key to break into your apartment, and then I used a verophid on you and your mother. I had to know."

A verophid.

The word brought the memory back in a flash—the glass vial, the leech-like creature, the unhinged look in Thairyn's eyes.

Because his granddaughter had been kidnapped. It made sense now.

"You're the one who took the bottle of pills," she said, realizing.

"I knew if Serene gave them to you, they were dangerous."

"But my mom's symptoms went away on the pills," she protested. "She didn't have a single vision while she was on them."

"That's probably what they were for. To keep your mom from seeing. Serene was afraid one of your mom's visions would reveal what she was doing, and the pills prevented that from happening. She didn't want to make your mom better. She wanted to make her blind."

Jenna swallowed hard.

"I underestimated Serene from the start," Thairyn said with disgust. "I should have taken precautions—set up cameras or a security system to keep Raloria safe, but I've never been good with technology. With my Charms, I didn't think I needed to be."

"So you weren't the one who put a tracker on my car?"

"Why would I need a tracker? With the amount of power inside you, if I'm in the same city, I can feel where you are, or close enough to track you down, anyway."

She bit her lip. Her aunt must have been the one tracking her. Maybe she'd been worried Jenna would tell her mom the truth, and they'd leave town. Instead, Jenna had kept her aunt's secrets and blamed this man. She'd gotten everything wrong.

"What did you want with me that day in the park?" she asked. "I thought you were coming after me. But you could have found me any time. Why didn't you?"

"I'd been following you off and on ever since you and your mom got into town. It was impossible not to sense your power when you were flaring—both of you. I wasn't sure exactly what I was dealing with."

He grimaced. "Eventually, I realized you didn't even know what you were. You had Charms, but you never used them. And you weren't a part of Haven, but I couldn't connect you to the Unbound either."

He shifted in his seat. "I was supposed to report you, but you hadn't broken any Council rules. That day in the park, I felt another magic besides yours in the area. I almost warned you. I tried to approach you—more than once. But then I thought better of it. If the Council found out I'd revealed our existence to you, it would violate my oaths and draw their attention."

He hesitated. "With your strange magic.... There are strict laws about what kinds of biomagy are allowed to...exist. And you have freckles like my daughter had." He blinked, leaving the rest unsaid. "So I let you go." He trailed off again and gazed out the window when they stopped at a red light.

Jenna was too overwhelmed to speak. By choosing not to report her to the Council, Thairyn had been trying to save her life.

"What does my aunt want with Raloria?" she asked.

"I wish I knew."

She sat forward suddenly, deciding to trust him. "I need to tell you something. Serene has Raloria tied up in the back of her SUV. She's alive but drugged."

Thairyn flushed red, and the white Charms along the side of his face went even more pale. "You saw her?" he demanded.

She hesitated, then spit it out. "I didn't see her myself, but I'm friends with a ghost boy who told me."

"You're a Seer," he breathed.

"And an Artifex, according to my aunt."

"Two gifts," Thairyn said, frowning. "You're a chimera. That would explain it."

"Raloria called me a Kind Mirror Monster—or a chimera monster—that day we spoke."

"There have been rumors. She must have overheard me talking. But it's Serene who's the monster. She wants power, and I don't think she'll stop until she has it."

"I'm sorry I didn't—hawk!" Jenna cried out, spotting the bird as it swooped beneath a streetlamp.

He cursed. "Give me the pistol."

She scrambled to hand the gun back to him.

He rolled the window down, biding his time until he stopped the car. The hawk perched on the edge of a roof, its silhouette visible in the dim lamplight.

Quickly, Thairyn whipped out the dart gun, took aim, and toppled the hawk backward onto the roof.

He set his jaw. "That'll take care of the bird for a while," he said. "But it means Serene and the others will be here any minute. I need you to hide in case they take me."

"I don't want to hide," she protested. "Maybe I can help."

"You can help by not being taken," Thairyn growled. He made a quick turn into a parking lot and stopped the Mercedes again. Then he opened the glove box and took out a dart, reloading his pistol.

"Get down on the floor," he told her.

When she did, he reached behind her and pulled on a knob, swinging the back seat down. There, between the seat and the trunk, was a false compartment about a foot wide. "I had this built so I could move Raloria without anyone seeing her. It'll be tight, but you'll fit."

"But if—"

Thairyn swung the pistol around, aiming it at her. "I'm sorry, child, but I don't have time to argue with you. Get inside."

She swallowed and climbed into the narrow space. Then she turned to face him. "If anything happens, I can—"

He shot her.

"If anything happens, you won't be able to move."

Her body went slack. She attempted to crawl away, but her limbs wouldn't obey. Unable to speak, she stared at him in shock.

"You don't understand what your aunt is capable of. Believe me, this is for the best. The drug I gave you causes paralysis for about an hour, but it'll leave your memory intact." He glanced through the back window. "They're coming. When you can move again, run. Hide. But don't go home."

He heaved the seat shut, leaving her helpless in the sudden dark.

A car pulled up beside the Mercedes and, faintly, she heard her aunt's voice through the open window. "At last, I meet the famous Thairyn Hinsen."

"Where is Raloria?" he snarled.

Serene ignored his tone, sounding almost chipper. "You know, the girl would be upset if anything happened to you. So, for her sake, try to be cooperative. Now get out slowly."

There were muffled sounds, and car doors opened and closed. Then Serene's voice came again. "Ian, check the Mercedes."

More doors opened and shut. The Mercedes rocked as Ian popped the trunk and leaned in, looking inside. "She's not here," he said.

Serene's voice had an edge to it. "Where's my niece? Tell me."

"I was headed to her apartment so I could warn her about you."

Ian spoke. "Don't forget what his Charms can do. He may be lying."

"I know that," she said thoughtfully.

Thairyn spoke again. "I want to see my granddaughter."

"You're in luck," she said. "She happens to be in my car, and I'd love for you to join her. Have a seat." A car door opened, and Jenna strained, trying to piece together what was happening. Then, almost too quietly for her to hear, Serene said, "Shoot him."

There was the soft thump of a dart gun being fired.

A car door closed. "We'll grill him later if we haven't found Jenna by then," Serene said.

"What about her mother?"

"Flynn's going to take care of it. He's not at his best, but I think he can handle one sick woman."

A tremor shuddered along Jenna's spine. What were they planning to do with her mom?

Ian asked, "How long before the dose you gave your niece is out of her system?"

"Twenty-four hours. But I'm not worried. We'll drop these two off at the lab, and if Flynn hasn't found her by then, I'll come back. Even without her phone, I'm sure I can find her. It's not like she's been able to make friends. There are only so many places she can be. She might go see that Lane boy, but I know where he lives, and I'll deal with him if I have to. And if she goes back to her car, we'll pick her up there. She can't get far."

Jenna couldn't move, but her stomach twisted.

"Let's go," Serene said. "Flynn will be right behind us."

Car doors slammed, and then came the sound of Serene's SUV pulling away. Jenna was alone.

She had to reach her mom. But if Thairyn's estimate was right, she had an hour to wait before she could do anything. She was trapped inside her own body.

Suddenly, the Charms that twisted along her arms began to burn. The pain took her breath as it blazed through her. She was catching fire, and there was nothing she could do to stop it. She stared into the darkness, counting the seconds until she was free.

Chapter Twenty-Nine

GHOST GIRL

By her count, it had been more than an hour since Thairyn had shot her with the dart.

But she still couldn't move. She could hardly breathe. Pain was a living thing, clawing her insides to shreds.

Had Serene's drink done this to her? Or maybe the dose in Thairyn's dart was too much for her system. She tried to stay calm, but she was frantic to see her mother.

Thairyn had told her not to go home, but that wasn't an option. She had to get out of this trunk and help her mom.

She lost track of the minutes.

Much later, feeling eked back into her limbs. The inferno inside her dimmed, and only her Charms continued their slow burn.

Gritting her teeth against the pins and needles, she stretched her fingers and found the mechanism to release the seat from the inside. She pulled the latch and spilled into the back seat of the Mercedes.

She opened the door and tumbled from the car to sprawl on the ground. She lay on the pavement, panting and gathering her strength. Another sharp pain seared her Charms, and she crawled to a bank of snow piled at the edge of the parking lot. She ripped off her gloves, plunging her arms into the slush until the spasm passed.

After a few seconds, she took her arms out and brushed the snow from her skin. But something strange caught her eye. It could have been a trick of the streetlight, but her Charms looked different. The last of the three Strands that wound through the pattern had turned from gray to ebony black.

Her throat constricted, then itched. She hauled herself to her feet, tugging down the collar of her jacket. She stumbled back to the Mercedes and studied her neck in the side-view mirror. An ugly red rash stretched from her collarbone almost to her jawline.

Maybe the Obru extract had inflamed her throat from the inside out. But there was nothing she could do about it now. She had to get to her mom.

She slid her gloves back on, orienting herself. Fortunately, she recognized this parking lot, and she was only a couple of blocks from Ashton Place. She left the Mercedes behind. It would be too easy for Serene to track her in it. Trying to walk as normally as possible, she headed for home, hoping she wasn't being watched by a hawk or another of Flynn's animals.

When she neared the building, she approached more cautiously, looking for her aunt's white SUV or Flynn's black Jeep, but they weren't there. She went through the back door and dragged herself up the stairs. Her muscles ached as if she'd been beaten, but she made it to the top and crept down the hall.

When she found her apartment unlocked, her hackles rose. She eased the door open, but nothing was out of place, and the apartment seemed deserted. She tiptoed to her mom's bedroom, hoping she was asleep. But it was empty. Flynn must have already been and gone.

He'd taken her mother, and Jenna didn't know how to even begin searching for her. She was too late.

Numb, she wandered back to the living room. She was so weary, it was an effort just to stand. She gazed out the window, trying to decide what to do next. Her aunt had mentioned a lab, but that could be anywhere.

Then she heard a whisper of sound. She spun around, but there was no one there.

Beside her, she noticed her mother's half-dead peace lily plant. A new shoot was growing up through the center of the plant at lightning speed. Then, just like the enormous Obru plant that had grown in the drama room, her mother's houseplant formed a bud that opened into a beautiful red bloom. It was a miniature version of the plant she'd seen before. In seconds, it grew to the size of an amaryllis, and suddenly the flower withered.

Inching close, she held out her hand, and a tiny black seed dropped into her palm. She tucked it carefully into her jeans pocket.

Behind her, she heard the door open. She turned in anticipation, hoping it was her mother.

But Brent stood there, watching her with empty eyes—eyes that stared but didn't see. The same eyes that had looked out of Michael Stevens's face years ago.

He was fully in the grip of her Charms now. Maybe their last brush in the hall had taken him over the edge. He must have recognized her when they touched, and he'd been watching for her ever since, waiting for her to come back.

He stepped inside the apartment and closed the door.

She held up both hands, glancing around for a weapon she could use against him. But there was nothing within reach heavy enough to do damage.

On any other day, she'd have trusted her training and her skills to fight her way past him. But her body was a wreck, and her movements were sluggish. Right now, she was no match for Brent.

He advanced slowly, no emotion on his face. There was no anger—no gloating. And that chilled her more than anything else could have. Before the Charms had taken hold, he'd been awful. But she'd rather deal with the old Brent than deal with...this.

She circled, keeping the couch between them. If she could distract him, maybe she could make a break for it. "Have you ever wondered why you can't stop thinking about me?" she asked him.

He kept pace with her, waiting for his chance.

"You don't know me, but I'm in your head. Doesn't that strike you as odd?"

A small frown creased his forehead.

She saw her advantage and pressed it. "You're risking yourself for someone who's not important to you. Does that make any sense?"

He came to a standstill.

She stopped, too, studying him. Had she gotten through somehow? "Ask yourself, Brent—why are you doing this?"

He stared at her, unmoving. His voice was lifeless. "Because you're mine."

Without warning, he lunged across the couch at her.

She cried out, throwing herself backward, but not fast enough. His hand caught the tail of her jacket, twisting. She went down hard, crashing into the coffee table as she fell.

When she hit the carpet, she rolled over, pulling her elbows toward her ribs to keep him from gaining control of her arms. But her movements were too slow.

He dove on top of her, seizing both her wrists and forcing her hands above her head.

She cried out, flinching away from his touch. Panic flooded her, and every defensive move in her arsenal scattered from her mind.

His feverish eyes hovered inches above her own. "You're mine," he whispered, and his grip on her wrists tightened.

Adrenaline spiked through her, fueling a surge of renewed energy.

She set her jaw, moving her foot to trap one of his legs. Then she arched her hips and sent him rolling to one side. She landed a sharp jab to his nose as she got to her feet and raced to the apartment door.

She grabbed the bowl they used for keys and heaved it at him. It slowed him just enough for her to get out into the hallway. Hearing footsteps on the main staircase, she paused. What if Flynn or her aunt was returning for her? She pelted toward the stairs at the end of the hall.

Brent followed, fast on her heels.

She hurtled down the stairs and nearly crashed into Mr. Cane.

He was making his laborious way back from the lobby mailboxes, shuffling along with his cane at about the speed of a tree sloth. He stopped in astonishment when he saw Jenna and Brent barreling toward him.

She tore past, calling out an apology. She threw a look over her shoulder just in time to see Mr. Cane slide his walking stick to the side.

Brent tripped and face-planted on the landing, and Mr. Cane gave him a whack with his walking stick for good measure.

She skidded to a stop, looking back in disbelief.

Brent was out cold.

Panting, she turned to Mr. Cane. "Thank you," she said. Her forehead creased. "But why...why did you help me?"

He tilted his head. "Why wouldn't I help you? You appeared to be in some distress."

Just then, she noticed movement through the large bay window in the landing.

On the opposite side of the street, a red-tailed hawk had just perched on the streetlight. And a white SUV was pulling into the driveway of Ashton Place.

She ducked away from the glass. "I...I have to go," she told Mr. Cane. "Thanks again!"

"Stay safe," he called after her, as she bolted down the stairs. "And come say hello sometime."

Thinking fast, she hurried to the basement hallway and into the laundry room. The little hopper window there opened out the side of the building. If Ian and Serene were watching the main doors, they wouldn't see her leave.

But what about the hawk?

She looked around and heaved a sigh of relief when she spotted the paisley umbrella still leaning in the corner where she'd put it after she'd taken it back from Lane's house. Hopefully, it would be enough.

She grabbed it and then clambered on top of the same dryer she'd hidden inside all those weeks ago. She opened the narrow hopper window and climbed out onto the wet pavement, dragging the umbrella with her.

Out of sight of the hawk, she popped it open and hurried along the sidewalk, hidden from view beneath her paisley shield.

She had to get away from Serene. But, more importantly, she had to warn Lane.

Her aunt had said she knew where he lived. Briefly, she wondered how long the hawk had been watching her movements. But if her aunt knew where to find Lane, he was in serious trouble. Serene had said she'd "deal with him" if she had to, and Jenna didn't know what that meant.

The trip to his house seemed to take ten times longer than usual. Probably because she'd rather get a root canal with no pain killers than face him again tonight. He'd told her he never wanted to see her again, and she would respect that. Starting tomorrow.

Finally, she crawled through the row of low hedges outside his room and crouched below his window. She dropped the umbrella and knocked. She waited, then she knocked again.

She cried out in surprise when, a few seconds later, the window next to Lane's opened and Brie leaned out, dressed in her pajamas. "He wants me to tell you to leave. And by the way, he told me what happened, and I hope you realize how messed up your lying was." She shot Jenna her most scathing look and started to close her window.

"Brie, wait!" She scurried over. "Please. I know you don't like me. With good reason," she added. "Even *I* don't like me. But your brother is in danger, and I need him to know."

"You just can't stop lying, can you? Angel...Jenna—whatever your name is—he's not going to talk to you. Ever. So go home." She went to close the window again.

"Please, Brie. Please. Can I...can I talk to you?"

She hesitated, frowning. "You want to talk to me?"

"That's how important this is!" Jenna scream-whispered. "Yes. If I have to. I'll even talk to you."

They regarded each other silently.

"I can't believe I'm doing this," Brie sighed, but she opened the window wider, motioning her inside.

Unlike Lane's drab room, Brie's bedroom exploded with color. She'd painted the walls a sunny shade of yellow. And dozens of movie posters, magazine pages, and pictures of rock bands were tacked up everywhere.

"You've got five minutes," Brie said, flouncing down on her bed. "Sit." She pointed to a fuzzy pink pouf in the corner, and Jenna lowered herself onto it.

She bit her lip, trying to decide what to tell the girl and what to keep hidden.

Brie crossed her arms. "Four minutes and counting."

Jenna took a deep breath. There was no way to sugarcoat this. "Here's the thing," she said. "Something weird is going on, and my aunt is responsible. You know those hornet things we saw at the Winter Carnival? That was her doing. Also, she's kidnapped more than one person, including my mom, and I don't know where they all are now. And I can't go back to my apartment because she's looking for me there. I even had to throw away my cell phone so she couldn't track it. But a little while ago, I overheard her say something about dealing with Lane. So, if she shows up here, he needs to be careful, because she's dangerous. Basically, I'm in a lot of trouble here, Brie, and I really don't want Lane to get mixed up in it!"

Brie narrowed her eyes, considering. Then she sat forward. "You are certifiably crazy, you know that?" She shook her head. "I met your aunt tonight, remember? And she was perfectly fine. I think this is all some story you've cooked up to—"

The doorbell rang, and Hercules barked. They could faintly hear Mr. Phillips's voice as he opened the door. "Can I help you?"

Serene answered. "I'm looking for someone named Lane. Get him for me."

The blood drained from Jenna's face, and she rose to her feet. "Aunt Serene," she mouthed to Brie, then motioned her to silence.

Mr. Phillips went to Lane's door and knocked. "There's a lady here to see you, Lane."

Jenna unplugged the ceramic lamp on Brie's dresser and hefted it. She wanted a weapon in case she needed to charge in and help.

Brie sat up, skeptical but quiet, as Lane walked past Brie's room and went to the front door. "I'm Lane," they heard him say. "You wanted to see me?"

"You're going to answer my questions as quickly as possible," Serene said without preamble. "Do you understand?"

"I understand," Lane answered, his voice oddly stilted.

"When and where did you last see my niece, Jenna Getty? Tell me the truth."

"I last saw her a couple of hours ago in the RiverCentre parking ramp."

"And you haven't spoken to her since then?"

"I haven't spoken to her since then," he said flatly.

There was a pause, and Brie and Jenna exchanged looks. Lane didn't sound like himself, and they both knew it.

"Do you know where she might be?"

"She might be at home, but I don't know where she lives. She lied to—"

"Spare me the details." Serene heaved a sigh. "This is my number," she said. "If Jenna makes contact, I want you to find a private place and call me as soon as possible. Is that clear?"

"That's clear."

Brie stood up, a flicker of doubt in her eyes.

"You won't tell Jenna or her friends that you've spoken to me. And as soon as you've called me, you're going to forget all about it. Will you do that for me?"

"Yes."

A troubled frown spread over Brie's face.

"Tell your father I was here to return a flash drive my daughter borrowed from you. Go now."

The door closed.

Jenna and Brie stood together, listening.

"What was that all about?" Mr. Phillips asked Lane, as he went back into the living room.

"She was here to return a flash drive her daughter borrowed from me."

If there was more to the conversation, Jenna and Brie didn't hear it.

"That was not...normal," Brie said, her eyes wide. "I know Lane better than anybody, and he would never act like that. It was like he was hypnotized. The way he repeated what she said—the way he lied to Mr. Phillips as if it was nothing." She shuddered.

"I tried to tell you." Jenna put the lamp back on the dresser. Her aunt was definitely looking for her, but at least she hadn't hurt Lane. "You should both stay away from her if you can. Keep an eye on your brother for me." She turned and lifted the window so she could climb through.

"Where do you think you're going?" Brie demanded.

Jenna paused. "I have no idea, actually. But I'll figure something out."

"You idiot. No, you won't." Brie pushed the window back down. "You're staying here, obviously."

"What are you talking about?"

"Do you even have a plan? A place to hide? A place to sleep?"

"Well...no, but—"

"Then this is the safest place for you." She went to her closet and pulled a sleeping bag off the shelf. "Your aunt was just here, so she'll rule our house out."

"But I thought you hated me. I lied to your brother."

"I do hate you. But I've lied to my brother, too. It's one of his imperfections—his perfection. He expects too much of people, and nobody's perfect. Especially you." Brie tossed her the sleeping bag. Then she went to her bed for an extra pillow.

"Why are you doing this?"

"Haven't you been paying attention during TOTEL meetings? I swore an oath to defend the defenseless. That's you." She threw the pillow on the floor.

Jenna scowled. "I'm not defenseless. I can—"

"You're a baby bird in a fox's den. It's obvious to me because I was in a bad situation, too, once. And I also refused to ask for help. You're not alone, you know."

"Maybe not. But I should be. It's what I deserve."

"Because you're such a terrible person? Because of all the horrible things you've done?"

"Well...yeah."

"Who hasn't? You've got to get over it at some point. Like Kelsea said tonight—there are no failures, only lessons."

She took the sleeping bag from Jenna's hands and spread it on the floor. "Here's what you're going to do. In the morning, you'll apologize to my brother. You'll tell him the truth. Then you'll let the rest of us do what we can to help."

"I can't—"

"You know what I think?" She sat back on her heels. "You told Lane you were an angel, but in reality, you're a ghost."

"What?"

"You're a ghost. You're haunting your own past—hung up on what you did and what you didn't do. You've gotten good at fading away and not actually connecting to anyone. Lying to yourself and everyone else. I've seen you. Let me spell out the situation for you." She leaned forward. "The past is past. Do you hear me?"

Jenna stared at her, shocked.

"I said, 'do you hear me?'"

"I hear you," she snapped. "The past is past."

"And the future isn't promised." She stared Jenna down, until, exasperated, she repeated that phrase too.

"There is only now. Don't waste it." She stood up. "That's what my grandfather always used to say." Brie let the words hover in the air. "It's time you came back from the dead and started living. And if there's anyone in the world you can trust with the truth, it's my brother."

"If he'll listen," Jenna mumbled.

"Leave that to me."

"Just a few minutes ago, you told me he would never talk to me again. Ever."

She sniffed. "If you give up that easily, you don't deserve him. Listen, ghost girl. If you care about my brother at all, prove it. Try."

Brie crawled under the fluffy covers of her bed. "Now take your shoes and coat off, get in the sleeping bag, and shut up. And if you can't sleep, plan. Do something useful. But don't wake me up." She leaned over and switched off the light, leaving Jenna to stew.

And, much later, to plan.

Chapter Thirty

LOCKED INSIDE

Jenna woke the next morning to a pillow in the face.

Brie stood over her. "Rise and shine. Lane and I are about to catch the bus. It's best if he never finds out you were here. Kelsea's coming to pick you up in a few minutes."

Jenna sat up, rubbing her eyes. "Kelsea?" she asked blearily.

"She'll take you to school, unless you have a better plan." She arched one perfect eyebrow.

Jenna did have a plan, but unfortunately, it involved talking to Lita. And that meant going to Coldwater High. On the plus side, Serene probably wouldn't try to abduct her from inside of a school. But Brent was a different story. He'd find her if she went to classes as usual.

"If it helps," Brie said, tapping her toe impatiently, "for *my* plan to work, I need you to play hooky. I have a safe spot in the school where you can hide."

That *was* helpful, actually. If she could hide out during the school day, she might avoid both Serene and Brent. "Okay. Thanks," she said.

Brie tossed something at her, and she caught it.

"I safety-pinned a scarf to my beanie. It's the closest I could come to your face thingy."

"A balaclava," Jenna said, relieved. Her own was still on the concrete floor of the parking ramp.

"And you can borrow my shades, too." Brie pointed. "Leave through the window, and don't forget to close it behind you." She grabbed her backpack and strode from the room.

Jenna went to the mirror and tried to make herself look presentable. Overnight, the few strands of white hair she hadn't bothered to pluck had become a full-fledged streak. She shrugged. She had bigger problems.

According to plan, she hid out until she heard the AH-OOO-GAH of Alex-Vander's horn. Then she clambered through the window and closed it behind her. Luckily, there was no sign of a white SUV or a black Jeep. But she wished she had a less conspicuous ride to school than the tie-dyed eyesore.

She climbed into the passenger seat of the camper van, blinking when she noticed a second set of glasses Kelsea was wearing over her regular wire-rimmed frames. They had two round lenses in front and another two on the sides, near her ears. And inside the lenses, a half-inch of blue liquid sloshed back and forth.

"They're for motion sickness," Kelsea said, answering Jenna's unspoken question.

She closed the door. "You get motion sick?"

Kelsea merged onto the street. "I don't, but I wish I did. These glasses are spectacular."

Jenna sighed again and tuned Kelsea out for the rest of the ride. It was easy. She was gushing about TOTEL's amazing success handing out flyers at the Winter Carnival last night. Jenna sank lower in her seat, wishing she could forget last night altogether.

When they arrived at Coldwater High, she glanced around anxiously, but she didn't see Serene, Flynn, or Brent. She followed Kelsea to a part of the building she'd never seen.

Kelsea pulled out a key and unlocked a heavy blue metal door.

"Is this the auditorium?" Jenna asked as she trailed the girl into a dark hall.

"Indeed. According to Brie, you need somewhere to hide, and I have the perfect place."

They moved through the backstage area toward an open doorway with light spilling through.

Brie stood inside talking to someone. She waved silently to Jenna, motioning her forward. "It's up on the top shelf somewhere. Keep looking," she directed.

Jenna joined Brie inside a prop storage closet about the size of most bathrooms. Three of the walls were lined with shelves, and Lane was feeling around on the top shelf, his back turned.

"Now!" Kelsea said.

Brie leaped out of the closet, and the two of them slammed the door.

Lane wheeled around and froze. His eyes locked on Jenna's.

Outside the closet, there were muffled voices and then loud banging sounds.

For a moment, Lane and Jenna could only look at one another. Then they heard the distinctive sound of screws being drilled into wood.

"Crap!" He bolted for the door, turning the knob and pounding on it, but it wouldn't budge.

"Sorry, Lane, that won't work," Brie called merrily. "Not only did we screw in a two-by-four to block the door, I'm barricading it for good measure."

Lane's back stiffened. "What? Why are you doing this?"

"You two need time to talk."

Kelsea chimed in, "Ms. Chester won't notice that her keys are missing until the end of the day, but we'll check on you at lunch. If you've made progress, we might let you out."

"Lunch?" Lane was aghast. "I've got classes to go to."

She continued as if she hadn't heard. "Also, don't forget that it's Friday. We could leave you here all weekend if necessary."

"You can't be serious." He slammed his hand on the door. "I'll call for help!"

"No one is using the auditorium today," Kelsea told him. "I checked. Nobody's going to hear you."

"And I took your cell phone this morning," Brie added.

Lane's hand went to his empty jacket pocket, his eyes wide.

He glanced at Jenna, but she shook her head. "I threw mine in the trash at the carnival, remember?"

"We're leaving now," Kelsea sang. "We've got a TOTEL meeting to go to. Hope you kids can work it out."

Lane pounded on the door. "Brie! Kelsea! Come on!" But there was no reply.

Warily, he turned to look at Jenna.

She gave him an awkward wave. "Um, hi."

Lane sprawled dejectedly on the floor in front of the locked door, bouncing a tennis ball he'd taken from the prop shelf.

The space wasn't big enough for either of them to get comfortable, and Jenna sat across from him with her knees pulled up to her chin, her back pressed against the shelves.

"So stupid," he mumbled.

It was the first thing he'd said all morning. The couple of times she'd tried to start a conversation, he'd refused to engage with her. So this was progress. She watched him, waiting.

He sighed and rolled the ball from one hand to the other. "Here I am playing the fool again today. I fell for Brie's trick—hook, line, and sinker. I may be the dumbest person on the planet."

"Don't say that."

"It's true," he protested, still not looking at her. "When Brie was living with my mom, I was too stupid to see she was in trouble. You'd think I would have learned from that. But I didn't. I was too stupid to see through you, too." He clenched his jaw.

She wanted to reassure him, but she wasn't sure how. "Remember what Kelsea said," she pointed out. "'No failures, only lessons,' right?"

"Yeah. Except that I'm incapable of learning." He rolled the ball again, snorting in derision. "You were lying to me every day, and I never saw it."

She winced, and the silence thickened once again.

He studied the ball in his hands. Then he sat up. "You don't need that mask anymore. I know you're not sensitive to light, because you didn't cover your skin when you were pretending to be Angel." He glanced at her with disgust. "You can cut the act now."

She squirmed.

"You know what? Forget it." He dropped his head back against the door. "It's just that I can't think of any reason you would lie to me like that. I guess you wanted a good laugh."

"That wasn't it."

He looked at her hard. "Why then? Why pretend to be two different people? Why tell everyone you have a disease and wear all this stuff to school?" He shook his head. "I just don't get it."

She shifted. "It's complicated."

His laugh was harsh. "Well, cell mate, we're not going anywhere for a while. We have time for *complicated*." He dared her with his eyes. "Try me."

Her heart raced. "You wouldn't believe me."

He looked at her sadly, the anger leaching out of his voice. "That may be true, but we won't know unless you tell me."

She'd spent so many years fighting to protect her secret, the thought of confiding in someone about her Charms made her choke.

At the same time, she wanted to tell him. She wanted him to understand why she'd lied. To understand her. And maybe Brie had been right—if anyone in the world was trustworthy, it was Lane. She took a deep breath. "You have to keep this between the two of us."

"I can do that."

"I'm serious. My life depends on it."

The tennis ball dropped from his hands and rolled across the floor toward her. "Okay?" he said, a question in his voice. Then he frowned and sat forward. "It won't leave this room. I promise."

She picked up the ball and squeezed it between her own palms. Then, trying not to think about it, she took the plunge. "I do have a disease. Just not the one I told you I had." She set the tennis ball down beside her and took off the shades Brie had loaned her. Then she pulled off the makeshift balaclava.

His eyes turned quizzical.

She ran a hand through her tangled hair and then shrugged off her oversize coat. "It's not that I'm sensitive to light." She swallowed and tugged off her gloves, revealing the Charms that crisscrossed her skin. "It's that I can't touch anyone. Ever."

He looked silently from her face to her hands and back again, waiting for her to continue.

She forced herself to go on. Keeping her eyes focused on the area above his head, she said, "If I touch someone, or if they touch me, it makes them feel, uh…desire." She took a breath. "And it's so strong they become obsessed by it…or by me, I guess." She risked a glance at him.

He was unmoving, his features locked in confusion. "You're serious?"

"I've never been more serious."

Seconds ticked by.

He put on his gentle face. "Have you talked to a counselor about these ideas?"

Anger flashed through her. "Don't you use that 'I'm talking to a crazy chick' tone with me!" She picked up the tennis ball and chucked it at him. Hard. But the ball smacked the door beside him.

"Hey! You almost hit me."

She turned and plucked the first thing she could reach off the shelf, a dog toy. She hurled it at him, and it squeaked as it landed near his head.

"I'm sorry, okay?" He held his hands up in front of him. "But you've got to realize how that story sounds."

She deflated suddenly, slumping against the shelf. "I know how it sounds. But it's the truth."

He let out a slow breath. "Why don't you start from the beginning? Tell me why you think this about yourself."

So she did. She went all the way back to age twelve, when her Charms had first appeared. She explained everything her mother had told her—how the sickness ran through their bloodline and what would happen if she touched anyone besides her mom.

Her hands shook when she talked about leaving home and about her father's death. But she clasped her fingers and pushed on.

He listened without interrupting, and she let it all pour out. She told him about years of being on the run. Then she told him about how she'd seen the fireflies, and then Fore. About finding his wallet in the snow and taking on the role of Angel.

She leaned toward him earnestly. "When you helped change my tire a couple weeks later, it surprised me when you didn't recognize me."

"You should have told—"

She waved her hands. "I know, I know. I should have told you who I was right away, but I never thought I'd see you again. And I didn't want you asking questions that could get me and my mom in trouble—especially after I had the fake medical excuse on file. I didn't know then that I could trust you, but I do now, and I'm sorry."

"That helps," he said, considering.

"And the longer the lie went on, the harder it was to undo. I thought if I told you, you'd hate me—which, you have to admit, was pretty accurate. And how could I tell you the rest of it?" She sat back. "I've never done this before." Her momentum left her at once, and she watched him closely, waiting for his response.

He blew out a long breath. Then he ran his hand through his hair. "I'm glad you told me." He hesitated. "I have a few questions, though." He held up one hand. "I'm not criticizing, okay? Just asking." He paused. "But first, will you promise not to throw anything at me?"

"I promise," she grumbled.

"I would feel safer if you moved away from that shelf."

She scooted forward. "Happy?"

"Relieved, actually."

They were close now, and she could see the jumble of emotions that played across his face.

"From what you've said, your mom was the one who told you about being Charmed. So, no offense, but how do you know it's true?"

Her anger flared again. She held up her arms, flashing her marked skin at him. "How else do you explain these?"

"I don't know, okay? But couldn't there be some other explanation besides what your mom said? You could be ruining your life for nothing. Where's the proof?"

Her breath caught. She didn't want to tell him this. He'd never look at her the same way. But unless she gave him the full story, he wouldn't believe her.

She looked down, twisting the hem of her jeans as she spoke. "I don't need proof because I saw the curse infect someone I touched. His name was Michael Stevens, and he died when I was fourteen."

Lane was silent for a moment. Quietly, he asked, "What happened?"

She stared at her shoes. "I had zero friends, so I went online to find people to talk to. Most of them didn't live anywhere close to me, of course, but then I found Michael. He lived in my neighborhood, and that made him seem special."

A thread had come loose at her hem, and she pulled on it. "He said he was fifteen, although later I found out he was twenty. We talked online for months, mostly while we were gaming, but he wanted to meet. There was a duck pond with a path around it near where we lived, and I figured it would be safe outside—with plenty of room."

She bit her lip. "It was a hot day, so I wore shorts and a T-shirt. I didn't want to look weird in front of him." She glanced up at Lane. "But when I got there, it was...awkward. I didn't know him at all. Not really. And I didn't know what to say. We walked around the pond once, and there were these long silences. And then—I think he did it to be funny—while we were standing at the edge of the pond, he pushed me in. The water wasn't deep there, but I fell over and got soaking wet."

She paused, swallowing. "When I stood up, he was looking at me with the strangest expression on his face. His eyes were...empty. And that's when I knew."

"If this is too hard to talk about, you don't have to," Lane said softly.

She took a shuddering breath. "I want to. You need to know." She leaned her head back against the shelf. "My mom had told me that if I touched someone, what happened next would depend on the other person. The curse could take a while to take hold, or with some people, it could happen fast." She winced. "For Michael, it was an immediate change. He grabbed me by the arm and started to drag me into the trees."

"What did you do?"

"I didn't do anything at first, even though I could have. Mom made me take self-defense classes when I was little, so I could have gotten away. But I was in shock. And I was afraid of hurting him. He was my friend." She unraveled more of her hem. "I tried to talk to him as he was dragging me, but it was like he wasn't there anymore, you know?"

She closed her eyes and spoke almost in a whisper. "He pulled me down behind a bush. And that's when I knew I had to do something. Nothing I could say was going to make any difference. I fought him then, and I thought I'd kicked him hard enough to knock him unconscious, but it was like he was possessed. He got up and came after me again."

Her hands clenched into fists. "I was running, heading for the street, and he was right behind me." She flinched. "I didn't see the car. The driver swerved to miss me, and he hit Michael instead."

Her throat constricted. "I heard the car hit him, but I kept going. When I did look back, the driver was on his cell phone calling for help. I just ran and ran until I got home. Mom and I left town that night. A few days later, I went online and found Michael's obituary."

Lane moved closer to her. "I'm so sorry."

"Do you see now why I didn't want to get you involved? I'm like a black hole, pulling people down into disaster. And you don't even know everything yet."

"There's more?" he demanded, eyes wide.

She laughed sarcastically and then told him about her Aunt Serene and Flynn. When she got to the part about Nardo, he stood up, shell-shocked.

"The Winter Carnival makes a lot more sense now," he said dryly.

She sighed. "I told you. I'm a mess."

He paced back and forth in front of the door. "What's your plan?"

She pressed her lips together. "Well, if I can get Lita to give me something of Nardo's, I can talk with him again. Then I'll let my aunt kidnap me. She'll lead me to the others, and Nardo and I will figure out the rest on the fly."

He stopped and stared at her. "That's your plan?"

"Yes. What's wrong with that?"

"Um, only about a billion things. No, I'm not letting you do that. But we need ideas." He crouched down in excitement. "We need to crowdsource this thing."

She dropped her head into her hands, groaning. "Please tell me you're not thinking what I think you're thinking."

"Indeed," he said, grinning. "It's time for TOTEL CHAOS."

Chapter Thirty-One

SIREN

When Jenna had fled Doc's house three weeks ago, she'd never expected to come back.

But today, Lane had asked Kelsea for TOTEL's help, and so here they were. Again.

Jenna wasn't convinced this was a good idea. Everyone would think she was having a mental breakdown. Or they might try to prove she was wrong by touching her. Anything could happen.

But she was out of options. She needed to talk to Nardo, and maybe the others could convince Lita to help her. Also, Fore had connected her to this group of people more than once. That had to count for something.

Still, her head whirled with the speed of it all. This morning, Lane had hated her, and Kelsea had actively boarded them up inside a closet. This afternoon, Lane was her ally, and Kelsea had worked wonders to get the word out about the last-minute TOTEL meeting. Doc had stepped up, too, volunteering her house. And everyone had driven out to the country on short notice just to hear what Jenna had to say.

She took a steadying breath, glancing at Lane. He sat near her on the floor of Doc's wood-paneled den. He'd folded a fortune teller from a piece of notebook paper, and he was trying to distract her while they waited for everyone to get settled.

"Otter, lion, dolphin, or dog?" he asked.

Doc's Saint Bernard, Pudge, lumbered over and parked himself on Jenna's other side, somehow sensing her need for comfort. "Pudge votes for dog," she said, reaching out to pet him with a shaking hand.

"D-O-G," Lane spelled, opening and closing the fortune teller three times. "Now pick a number." He held the fortune teller up for her inspection.

Sighing, she picked the number four. Hopefully, that would give her some luck.

Lane opened the flap and read, "Today you will find your destiny." He grinned. "Good pick! See, you've got nothing to worry about."

She grunted.

Kelsea began pounding her gavel. Wearing both sets of glasses, she sat cross-legged on top of Doc's desk once more. "I call this emergency session of TOTEL to order. Pledge time," she said. "Devonte, you can join in if you want."

Devonte, who was wedged between Zinnia and Markese on the couch, shifted uncomfortably. "I'm good."

Kelsea counted down on her fingers, and everyone mumbled together. *"I will seek the truth, defend the defenseless, right the wrong, and stand up for fair—"*

Kelsea spoke over the group before they could fill in the rest. "Jenna Getty has an urgent announcement she needs to make. So sit up and shut up, people. Jenna, you have the floor."

Lane nodded encouragement, and she rose awkwardly, looking around at everyone's expectant faces. Her mouth went dry.

"Get it over with," he whispered.

She swallowed. It was true. The faster she went, the sooner it would be done. "I want to start with an apology," she began, "because...well, because I've been lying to all of you." She took off her shades and balaclava.

"OMG, she's a redhead?" Markese gasped. "*And* a fire sign?" He pursed his lips as Zinnia shushed him.

Jenna peeled off her gloves. Then she pushed up her sleeves, turning her arms so they could see her Charms.

Her words tumbled out. "The truth is, I don't have a disease. I have magic, and it's dangerous to touch me. But not too long ago, a magical glowing creature named Fore appeared, and she kept leading me to you all. She showed me giant butterflies and seven-foot flowers when I was around you—things that were invisible to the rest of you." She took a deep breath. "The last time we were here, I realized I could see Nardo, but you couldn't. Because he was dead, obviously.

Um, outside the spectrum, my aunt would say. And the animals could see him, too. They were acting up because Nardo was messing with them." She giggled nervously, surveying their blank expressions.

When no one said anything, she pushed on. "So now my aunt is trying to find me. I don't know exactly why. And there's this guy who can control animals who's working with her. They've kidnapped my mom and Thairyn and his little granddaughter, who's also magic, with, like, tentacles that come out of her head." She ground to a halt as the blank expressions changed to looks of horror.

The room was silent. Even the animals seemed to hold their breath.

Then Kelsea demanded, "Are you on drugs, Jenna Getty?" She looked to Lane for help. "Are we having an intervention right now?"

Lane stepped forward. "I know it sounds crazy, but she explained it all to me this morning, and I think she's telling the truth." He turned to her. "Is there a way to prove it? Maybe tell them something you can't know unless Nardo tells you?"

She looked around nervously. "Unfortunately, Nardo isn't here right now." She moved toward the armchair where Lita sat.

The girl regarded her with crossed arms. "Lita, do you have anything with you that was Nardo's? A necklace or a bracelet, maybe?"

"You want me to give you something that belonged to my brother?"

"He needs an anchor. That's what he told me. If *you're* touching the anchor, I can see him, but that's all. But if *I* touch the anchor, I can hear him, too. So, do you have something?"

Lita's voice was a mixture of anger and sorrow. "After I lost his watch, I was afraid of losing anything else. So, no. I don't have anything on me."

Jenna turned to Jose in desperation. "What about you? Any chance you have something in your pocket besides a hand buzzer? Something of Nardo's?"

"I don't," he said. Then, just for her ears, he added, "If this is a prank, it is off the charts. Bravo." He leaned closer. "If it's not a prank, you have very successfully creeped me out."

Doc tugged on Zinnia's arm, whispering, "Do we need to get her help?"

"Help!" the parrot, Gandalf, repeated from Doc's shoulder. She shushed him with a treat.

"I've got something!" Hampton piped up. He slung his canvas pack to the floor and reached all the way to the bottom. After a moment, he pulled out a plastic baggie with a very dead and very brown object vacuum-sealed inside. "It's beef jerky," he said. "Nardo and I made it together three years ago. It's at least half his."

Lane snatched the bag from him, holding it out to Jenna. "What about that—will it work?"

She took the bag, looking around for Nardo, but he didn't appear.

"Maybe you have to eat it to get the full effect," Hampton suggested.

Zinnia shook her head. "You're taking your life in your hands, eating that junk."

"She should probably be in a hospital anyway," Doc said. "Maybe it's for the best."

"Does somebody else have an object of Nardo's?" Jenna asked the group. "Anybody?"

When no one spoke up, she squared her shoulders and turned back to Hampton. "I'll try anything at this point."

"Yes!" he said enthusiastically. He grabbed the bag from her and unsheathed the knife he kept in the holster at his calf. Then he sliced open the seal, carved off a bite-size piece, and handed it to her.

She took it from him, careful not to touch his fingers with her ungloved skin. She glanced once more at Lane for moral support. "Down the hatch." She chewed and swallowed. And waited.

"How long before we know if it works?" Nardo asked. He was suddenly sitting next to Lita, perched on the cushioned arm of her chair.

Gandalf the Grey squawked and flew across the room to land on his perch. Pudge barked once at the dead boy, then settled down to sleep.

Jenna blinked. Unlike every other time she'd seen him, Nardo was faded and translucent—a shadow of himself. He looked like...well...a ghost.

She stepped toward him in excitement. "I can see and hear you."

"Oh yeah!" he said, leaping to his feet. "Back in business, baby."

"He's here?" Lane asked, and she nodded.

Everyone else in the room exchanged uncomfortable glances.

She waved her arms at Nardo. "Quick, tell me something that will make them believe me."

He pursed his lips sagely and held up one finger. "I've got it. You can say.... Huh." He frowned. "Tell them...." He sat back down on the arm of the chair, scratching his head. "Whoa. This is tough."

Lita glared at Jenna. "You're telling me that my brother is in the room with us right now?"

Jenna clenched her fists in frustration. "He is. But he can't think of anything to prove it to you."

"Wait! I know," Nardo said. "Her favorite color is black."

Jenna relayed his answer.

"Uh-uh. Too easy," Markese said, wagging his finger. "It's the only color she ever wears!"

She looked at Nardo again, listening. Then she returned her gaze to Lita. "He says you used to like pink."

A murmur went through the group, but Lita remained unconvinced. "I bet eighty percent of little girls go through that phase. I have a better test. Where did we hide our secret candy stash from Jose?"

"Hey!" Jose protested. "You had a secret candy stash?"

Lita kicked her foot up and down, waiting.

"Nardo says it was inside the plastic head of your doll."

Lita's foot went still. She shifted in her seat, and everyone else sat forward. "That's right, but I bet that's common, too." She snapped her fingers. "How about this? No one knows this but me. And Nardo, if he really is a ghost. What's my favorite epitaph?"

"Epitaph?" Jenna asked. "Like on a grave?"

"Not a grave. A tombstone," Lita said, rolling her eyes.

Jenna listened again, then answered. "Your favorite epitaph is three graves down from where Nardo is buried. He says that, after you visit him, you always stop by that headstone and read it aloud."

Lita's face blanched white. She stood up. "That was a guess. A lucky guess. What does the tombstone say?" she demanded. "You can't know that."

Jenna hesitated, then recited the words Nardo fed her. *"Stranger, as you're passing by, as you are, so once was I. As I am, so shall you be. Prepare for death, and follow me.*"

Lita's jaw sagged, and a hush fell over the room. "That's right," she whispered.

"Tell them about this," Nardo said. "I used to do it when things got too serious. It'll lighten the mood."

"What?" Jenna turned to Nardo, then looked quickly away again. "I don't think that's appropriate, even if it will lighten the mood."

Lita's voice was raw. "What's he saying?"

Jenna faltered, looking between Lita and Nardo. "It's not so much what he's saying as what he's doing."

"You tell me right now, Jenna Getty!"

It was the loudest she'd ever heard the girl speak. Jenna raised her eyebrows and cleared her throat. "Nardo is...twerking. Badly."

Doc gasped, covering her mouth with her hand, and the gavel dropped from Kelsea's fingers, clattering onto the desk.

Lita sank into her chair. "Twerking? It really is him," she breathed.

He stopped twerking and gave Jenna a thumbs-up.

Zinnia was the only one who was taking it calmly. "If Nardo is real and in this room, does that mean everything else was real, too? The little girl with magic tentacles and the strange glowing woman? All of it?"

Markese leaped to his feet. "Holy hell in a handbag—fairies are real? Ghosts are real? OMG—that is crazy heinous!" He collapsed onto the sofa again and started rubbing his lucky necklace, rocking back and forth.

Kelsea stood up. "What's wrong with you people? Pull it together. Jenna Getty needs our help." She turned to Jenna. "What's your plan?"

"Uh, I thought I would let my aunt kidnap me, and then Nardo and I can figure out the rest."

"I told you she was an idiot," Brie said. She sighed. "But she's our idiot, and I have a better plan. We let her aunt come to kidnap her, but meanwhile we're all in hiding, and we spring out and grab the woman—get her to tell us everything."

Kelsea clapped her hands together in excitement. "Now that is a shiny, sparkly, exceptionally stupendous idea, Brie! I love it." She turned to Doc. "We need weapons."

"We can't kill anybody!" Doc said, aghast.

"No," Kelsea said, "but we can bash people and then tie them up. What can we use?"

Doc hesitated. "There are some things in the barn that might work."

"Perfect!" Kelsea said. "Jenna and Lane, go to the barn and bring back whatever you find."

"I'm going, too," Brie chimed in.

"And me," Jose said.

Kelsea pointed. "Brie, yes—Jose, no."

He scowled at her.

"The rest of us will figure out the details. All right, people, get into Thinking Stations! Let's brainstorm great locations for an ambush. Go!"

Lane, Jenna, Nardo, and Brie ducked out, hurrying to the barn—the same place they'd practiced playing their instruments the last time they were here.

Jenna shivered. In the excitement, she'd left her gloves and balaclava behind in the living room, and it was hovering at around forty degrees outside. That was balmy for winter in Minnesota, but she felt exposed without her usual layers on. She shoved her hands deeper into her pockets.

When they reached the barn, they pushed open the heavy wooden door, and Brie climbed into the loft. "There's some lumber up here that might work," she called down.

Lane, Jenna, and Nardo wove through the section of the barn filled with power tools. They were looking for anything that might incapacitate but not kill, but everything seemed either too unwieldy or too deadly. Finally, Lane picked up a cordless sander. "What do you think? We could tickle her feet until she talks."

"Or what about this?" Jenna asked. She held up a drill. "Too much?"

"Lane. Jenna. There you are," Serene said, entering through the open barn door.

Jenna's drill clattered back onto the workbench.

They whirled to face her, and in the loft above, Brie dropped out of sight.

Jenna shot a quick look at Nardo, but he put his hands up innocently. "Nobody told me I was on lookout duty!"

Serene walked forward, with Ian trailing behind her. "Time was running short, and I was just starting to worry." She shook her head. "I never thought it would take you so long to call, Lane, but you came through in the end. And without your excellent directions, we might never have found this place."

Lane stiffened. "I don't know what you're talking about. I didn't call you."

"You don't remember calling me," Serene corrected. "But you did. Around three o'clock, I'd say. Maybe at the end of the school day?"

"That's when I got my phone back from Brie," Lane said in a strange voice.

"Don't beat yourself up about it," Serene told him. "You were just following orders. You couldn't help yourself." She looked at Jenna. "We've got to get on the road. The Obru mixture will only be in your system for another hour or two, and it could take months before I can get more. I need you to come with me now."

From the corner of her eye, Jenna noticed the side door of the barn. If they made a run for it, maybe they could reach the others before Ian and Serene caught up. She swung around, motioning to Lane. "Come on!" She dashed away, and Lane spun to follow.

"Stand still, Lane," Serene said.

He froze mid-run.

Jenna skidded to a halt, realizing he was no longer behind her. She turned, and her eyes went wide.

Lane was like a statue. He couldn't run—couldn't move. But he could talk.

"Keep going—get out of here!" he told Jenna.

Jenna stared at Serene with dawning horror. "What are you doing to him?"

She shrugged. "I'm a Siren. I speak—he listens."

"What's a Siren? Is that...are you Charmed?"

"I'm one of the lucky ones," she said, smiling. She pulled down the rose-colored scarf she wore to reveal a light pink pattern of raised lines that ran up and down her neck.

Jenna glanced at Lane. He hadn't moved an inch.

Serene continued. "People with Siren Charms are named for these fascinating chicks from Greek mythology with voices people couldn't resist. Like mine."

Jenna edged closer to Lane. Maybe she could find some way to release him.

Nardo circled him, too. "This is the weirdest thing I've ever seen," he said. "And that's coming from a ghost."

Lane's eyes pleaded with her. "Run," he whispered. Every muscle in his body strained, but he still couldn't budge.

"Your Charms work through touch, but mine work through sound," Serene explained. "Watch this." She pivoted to Lane. "Walk over to that table saw."

Lane obeyed, immediately walking toward the saw.

Jenna followed, watching with growing dismay.

"See?" Serene shrugged her shoulders. "He does whatever I tell him. Lane," she said again, "cut yourself on the blade."

In the center of the table was an exposed, circular blade. Lane reached out, but Jenna dove forward and covered the blade with her own hands. "Stop!" she yelled.

At the same time, Serene said, "Be still, Lane," and he stopped moving.

But it was too late.

Lane's fingers had bumped against Jenna's skin—just for a moment.

Instantly, she jerked her hands away.

He was frozen in front of her, arms poised above the exposed saw blade, but it was his eyes that had her attention now. Something in them shifted—darkened. His breath came quickly, even though he was standing still.

The curse was taking him and taking him fast.

Her pulse raced. She'd touched him, and she couldn't undo it.

"Jenna!" Serene's voice was sharper. "I told you, we're in a hurry."

Luckily, Jenna's body had blocked her aunt's view. She hadn't seen the slight touch of their skin. What would she do to Lane if she knew?

Serene sighed, turning to Ian. "Well, now I'm glad I brought him along. Get him from the car."

Jenna couldn't look away from the strange intensity in Lane's eyes. She didn't want to leave him this way. But she couldn't stay either. As soon as he could move, he'd come for her. "I'm so sorry," she whispered.

He blinked, and for just a moment, his eyes cleared. "Why are you still here?" he growled at her. "Run!"

"I've got him," Ian said.

Nardo stepped in front of Jenna. "You're not gonna like this."

"Jenna, sweetheart," her aunt said. "You've had a tough couple of days, and you're not thinking straight. Please don't force me to do something neither of us will like. You remember Brent, don't you?"

Jenna spun around.

He was standing between Serene and Ian, his empty gaze fixed on her.

"When I went to your apartment to look for you, guess who I found? I thought he might be useful, since he can handle you without…well, I mean, he's already cursed, isn't he?"

Brent lurched toward Jenna, but Serene stopped him with her voice. "No! I told you, you can't touch my niece unless I tell you to."

Brent stopped, but his body shook with effort as his desire battled with the power of Serene's words.

"Brent can escort you to the car if that's what it will take. I'd use a dart on you, but I don't want to risk putting another chemical in your system right now. So what's your pick? You can come willingly, or I can choose for you."

Jenna closed her eyes. She was outnumbered. Outsmarted. And for Lane's sake, she should probably put as much distance between them as she could. Hopefully, if she went far enough away, the curse would weaken. "Be safe out there, Lane," she whispered. Then she turned on her heel and went to her aunt.

Nardo walked by her side, wringing his hands.

"Wait here," Serene instructed, pointing to a place beside Ian. Then she strode to Lane. "Listen to me, Lane," she said. "Five minutes after I leave, you'll be able to move again. Here's what you're going to do."

She stepped closer. "You will tell your friends that Jenna's mom came for her. She's taking her to a hospital where they can make her better. Reassure them that everything's all right. You won't mention me or anything that happened in this barn. You won't try to follow us, and you won't raise the alarm that anything's wrong. Do you understand me?"

"I understand," he repeated.

"Good lad." She turned, motioning for the rest of them to come along as she headed to the SUV.

Jenna glanced back at Lane one more time, and her stomach clenched in self-disgust. Once again, she'd hurt someone she cared about. And the only thing she could do to help was get as far away as possible.

She set her jaw and trudged after her aunt.

Chapter Thirty-Two

DISTANT

In the back seat of the SUV, Jenna pressed herself against the car door. She wanted as much space as she could get from Brent.

Nardo was busy climbing all over, checking for a potential weapon or a way out.

But this was no ordinary car. There was a glass panel that separated the front from the back, like a limousine. Serene was driving, and Ian sat up front with her, occasionally turning in his seat to make sure Jenna and Brent weren't making trouble.

Unlike a limousine, though, there were no controls in the back. She couldn't even roll down her window or open her door. It was a prison cell masquerading as an SUV.

Nardo climbed right through the glass panel. He shook his head as he returned to the back seat. "No luck," he told her. Then he began peering inside all of Brent's pockets.

She looked away—partly because it was disturbing to watch Nardo's face go straight through Brent's jacket and disappear, and partly because Brent's eyes were still fixed on her with that obsessive, vacant gaze.

She shivered.

"This guy's got nothing on him but a pack of cigarettes." Nardo gave up and sat down between Brent and Jenna. "He couldn't at least have a lighter? Now that would have been useful."

"Great idea," she said sarcastically. "Set the car on fire."

Nardo disappeared suddenly, and Jenna blinked. Had she hurt his feelings? Then, in the rearview mirror, she saw her aunt frown.

Serene's voice floated through an intercom. "Jenna, sweetheart, I don't want to hear you talk like that. There's no need to set anything on fire."

She froze. She hadn't realized her aunt could hear her through the glass. But maybe this was a good thing. She could use her time in captivity to get some answers. She sat forward. "Where are you taking me?"

"You know, if you would just relax and cooperate, everything would be much easier."

"That doesn't answer my question."

Serene sighed heavily. "We're going to a little cabin Flynn has in the woods. There. Are you satisfied?"

A cabin in the woods. It came back to her in a flash. After Lane had found the tracking device on her car and she'd thrown it out onto the frozen pond, the black Jeep she'd followed to the cabin in the woods had been Flynn's Jeep, and it was Flynn's cabin she'd investigated.

Images flooded back. The aquariums and cages in the living room. The squeaks and chirps she'd heard coming from the back room that had made her skin crawl.

Something else clicked in her head. Thairyn had told her that Flynn experimented with animals—breeding. "Is Flynn's cabin also a lab? Is that where you're holding my mom and Thairyn and Raloria?"

"Don't make everything sound so nefarious," Serene scolded. "Yes. They're all there." She exchanged a look with Ian and then glanced over her shoulder at Jenna. "I need you to change your mindset. All of this is for the best, so stop freaking out."

"Is that a command? How do I know you're not using your Siren Charms on me right now?"

She snorted. "I wish. No, nothing about you works the way it should. If it did, I'd have just told you what to do a long time ago." She paused, smirking. "Mae used to hate it when I used my Charms on her."

"You used your Siren trick on my mom?"

She gave a low laugh. "I was around your age when I came into my gift, and at first Maeby didn't even know I was doing it. I was a natural, and I was stronger than she was."

Jenna's forehead creased in confusion. "But you were sisters. I didn't think

Charms worked on close family members."

"Mae wishes." Serene smiled and then sighed. "No, Jenna. Family doesn't matter. It's only power that matters."

"Then how can my mom touch me without being cursed?" she asked. "I know the curse is real because, well...." She glanced over at Brent's fixed, expressionless gaze, and then away. "I've seen it happen." She swallowed. "More than once."

Through the mirror, Serene regarded her with serious eyes. "I remember. You told me his name was Michael Stevens. I looked him up." She shook her head. "I don't know why your mom can touch you. Like I said, you're a wild card. But you'll notice I haven't risked it. Mae might be a special case because she carried you in her womb. I don't know. Nothing about you makes sense."

Jenna pursed her lips. Then she leaned forward again. "You said you used your Charms on my mom. What did you do?"

She shrugged. "Silly stuff, mostly. I would make her buy me an ice cream or loan me her earrings. One time I made her watch a horror movie marathon. You should have seen her face." She laughed aloud, and then her expression grew thoughtful. "But Mae changed. After I left home and joined the Unbound, she lost her sense of humor. I wanted her to help us. We were doing important work—trying to make this world better for everyone. But your mom was scared."

Her mouth grew pinched. "I worried she would turn me in—that she'd turn all of us over to the Council. So I had to Charm her. I told her she could never mention the Unbound, and she couldn't tell anyone who I was or what I could do." She glanced at Jenna. "It's why she never mentioned me to you—she couldn't. I'd Charmed her." She sighed again. "But after I did that, she broke off contact. Moved away." Sadness flitted across her features. "I probably could have found her if I tried, but your mom is stubborn. It wasn't worth the trouble."

Dread pooled inside Jenna's stomach. "What do you want from her now?"

"She's going to help me. All of you are. I finally have everything I need. See, I wasn't lying to you when I said I'd cure you of your Charms."

Jenna cocked her head, confused.

Serene gripped the steering wheel, barely containing her excitement. "I'm going to transfer the Artifex Charm from you to me—add it to my own power. After today, I won't just be a Siren. I'll be a Siren and an Artifex. I'll be a chimera."

Brie stayed flat on the floor, hidden in the loft of Doc's barn. She listened, waiting until Serene got into her car and pulled away—taking Jenna with her. Then Brie scrambled down the ladder, only sparing a moment to gape at Lane.

He was still frozen with his hand stretched over the blade of the table saw.

"Be right back!" she yelled, bolting for the house.

Moments later, she returned with the other TOTEL members. She held her arm out, presenting Lane to the group as if he was Exhibit A. She walked in a circle around her brother. "What did I tell you? It's like she turned him to stone. For another minute or two, anyway. Then he's going to come unstuck and try to convince us that nothing's wrong. And Jenna's aunt did this with only her voice! I saw the whole thing."

Doc crept closer to Lane, peering up at him. Gandalf the Grey perched on her shoulder, wearing a red harness and a leash that was strapped to her wrist. Pudge stayed close at her heels. "That's awful," Doc said and turned away, shuddering.

"That's awful!" Gandalf repeated, and Doc shushed him, bending down to pet Pudge.

"Not awful. Heinous," Markese muttered, and Zinnia patted him on the back.

Kelsea stepped forward, but before she could get a word out, Lane started moving.

He rounded on the group and instantly launched into the story Serene had given him. "Jenna's mom came to take her to a hospital where they can make her better. Everything is going to be all right."

Brie held up a hand. "Ignore him. He can't help himself."

"Okay, people," Kelsea said. "It's up to us now. We've got to rescue Jenna!"

"But how do we find her?" Zinnia asked. "We don't know where they went."

"I told you!" Lane insisted. "Her mom took her to the hospital."

"Shush," Brie said.

"Ideas, people. Quick!" Kelsea shouted, but she was met with silence.

Then Lita waved her arms, excited for once. "We can ask Nardo for help."

"That's true," Jose said, frowning. "We could ask him, but nobody here can see him except Jenna, so how does that help us?"

Zinnia's eyes narrowed. "Actually, somebody can see him." She looked at Doc.

"Me?" Doc squeaked. "I promise you I can't—"

"Not you. Your animals," Zinnia said. "Remember the last time we were here? You couldn't get the animals to calm down. Jenna said it was because Nardo was messing with them. They can see him."

"But Zinnia," Markese broke in, "Nardo isn't here right now." He frowned. "You're not here, are you, Nardo? Please tell me you're not here."

"Markese has a point," Devonte said. "He has to have an anchor. That's what Jenna told us. And we don't have one."

Hampton swung his canvas bag around to the front and reached into the pocket. "Who's up for some beef jerky?"

Lita thrust her hand out. "Give it to me."

He cut off a slice, and she chewed and swallowed. "How long—"

Pudge barked, and Gandalf flapped his wings.

"It's him!" Doc said.

"Whoa. Like whoa." Nardo staggered around, putting one translucent hand to his forehead. "I'm totally being pulled two ways right now. Do you guys know what I'm talking about? It's like going downhill on a roller coaster. When your stomach goes up and your body— " He broke off as he realized no one could see or hear him.

"Minor problem," Jose said. "Does anyone speak dog? Or parrot?"

"We don't need to," Kelsea said, grinning. She took Doc by the arms and swung her around, so she was facing one way and Pudge was facing the other way.

"Let's see if this works," Kelsea said, rubbing her hands together. "Nardo!" she yelled. "Are you here with us now? Answer Parrot for yes and Dog for no."

Nardo's forehead wrinkled in confusion.

"Can you hear me, Nardo?" Kelsea yelled louder. "If you're in here, make Gandalf speak."

Understanding dawned, and Nardo leaped into action. He ran to face the parrot, dancing and flapping his arms.

"Fool of a Took!" Gandalf squawked.

Kelsea turned to the group smugly. "Everybody, say hello to Nardo."

"A chimera?" Jenna asked Serene.

Her aunt was driving the white SUV farther and farther from the Twin Cities, heading down a two-lane highway surrounded by a patchwork of open fields and dense woods. Jenna remembered it from the last time—when she'd followed Flynn down this same road.

Now she barely registered her surroundings. And she purposely avoided looking at Brent, who was still staring at her with that eerie, absorbed expression. She frowned, studying her aunt. "Why would you want to be a chimera like me? You told me that's what made me cursed. Having two gifts."

"You're right. But your gifts are twisted because there was nothing to stop them from fighting against each other—from poisoning you. But it'll be different for me. I have two things you never had." She glanced at Jenna in the rearview mirror. "One—I have Raloria. And even as young as she is, she's the most powerful Healer alive. When she transfers your Artifex Charms into me, she should be able to heal them."

Jenna's eyes narrowed. "That's why you took her."

Serene nodded. "She's a handy gal. But it's not just her. The second piece—the Obru plant—is just as important. I thought it was extinct, so when you told me you'd been given a seed, I freaked out."

Jenna blinked, then furtively patted her jeans pocket, where she still had the tiny seed that had dropped from her mom's houseplant. She wouldn't let Serene get her hands on it.

"Once we had Raloria and the Obru, I knew we were in business. I gave my partner the seed at Union Depot, remember? He's working to propagate more of the plant because, as a chimera, I'll have to keep taking the Obru on a regular basis. But it's a small price to pay."

She shot Jenna a meaningful look. "You threw a wrench into everything last night, though. I thought you were coming with me, so I gave you half the Obru extract. I even brought Raloria along so she could Delve you on the spot. That way, she'd have time to rest before the procedure. Now I'll have to push the girl to do the Delving and the procedure back to back."

Ian grunted, and Serene let out a long breath. "The important thing is, I found you before the dose was out of your system. But we have to hurry if we're going to keep you from dying of withdrawal when I cure you."

"Withdrawal? This cure might kill me?"

"What, you think a Healer can just remove Charms like you'd clip a fingernail? It doesn't work that way. The magic is like blood that runs through you. If you lose too much too quickly, you die. It's a shock to the system to lose the magic—like going through withdrawal—unless you have the Obru inside you."

"That's why you gave me the drink."

"The transfer won't work if you're dead, Jenna. And I have to have the Obru inside me, too. Gaining too much magic at once is like having an overdose. But the Obru numbs your magical immune system and keeps your body from self-destructing."

Serene shifted in her seat. "Unfortunately, I don't have enough Obru extract to give you a second dose. I won't for months, and we can't wait that long. Things are already in motion. I think we still have time, but we had to guess on your dosage. All we had to go on was one blood sample." She pressed down on the gas pedal, speeding them faster down the highway.

"So it was you, wasn't it? You had Flynn use that hornet to take my blood in the park."

She clucked her tongue. "Reality check, Jenna. I couldn't just ask you for blood. It would have sent up all kinds of red flags. Anyway, you're fine, aren't you? And it was necessary. A means to an end."

"And the black cat—did you send it, too? Or was that Fore?"

"I don't know what you're talking about."

Suddenly, Nardo reappeared in the seat between Brent and Jenna.

She almost jumped out of her skin, but Nardo didn't notice. He turned to her, speaking and gesturing rapidly, but she could no longer hear him. And he looked even more faint than the last time she'd seen him. Maybe it had been a mistake to eat the beef jerky—because now, apparently, she was digesting it. Her connection to Nardo was fading.

She shook her head, trying to interrupt his silent rant, but he didn't notice. "I can't understand you," she finally blurted out in frustration.

Nardo's jaw dropped open, and she saw him mouth a single word. "Whoa."

"It's not that you can't understand me," Serene said, thinking Jenna had spoken to her. "It's that you refuse to see the truth." She tapped her finger on the steering wheel. "What I'm doing is important. The Council is corrupt and self-serving. I'm going to change that."

"Uh-huh," she answered, half listening.

Nardo pointed outside the window. Then he traced a giant question mark in the air between them.

She eyed him quizzically.

Then he pointed ahead and repeated the question mark.

It dawned on her. He wanted to know where they were going. Why—she wasn't sure. It's not like he could help. No one else could even see him except her. But he seemed adamant, so she bit her lip, thinking.

"If I become an Artifex," Serene continued, "I'll be the first person in generations who can really challenge the Council. Do you understand what I'm saying, Jenna?"

"I think so," she said. She looked at Nardo hard. "You're saying that with the Council in charge, things will just continue the way they are, maybe for another thirty miles or so—"

"Miles?" Serene asked.

"Not miles," she forced a laugh. "I meant years." But she shot a meaningful look at Nardo. "It's like the Council is crooked, but we need to go straight. Straight for a long time. And then one day we'll pass a big red silo."

"A silo?"

"It's a metaphor," she said, shaking her head at Nardo to negate her words. "Because the Council has stockpiled all the power. Like in a silo. Am I right?"

"I'm not sure I get the metaphor—"

"The important thing is, we have to choose. We have to turn away from the silo and choose what's *right*," Jenna said, emphasizing the word, and Nardo finally nodded in recognition. "But even after we've chosen what's right, we still have to go down a path that's less traveled by, you know?"

Serene and Ian exchanged glances, and Serene studied her in the rearview mirror, a concerned expression on her face. "How much sleep did you get last night?"

Jenna turned to Nardo to see if he'd understood, but he was gone.

"Is this necessary?" Lane asked.

"It is," Brie said. She hopped down from the workbench in the barn, coming over to inspect Hampton's work. "Tighter," she told him.

Hampton cinched another coil of rope around Lane's middle, pinning his arms to his sides.

Lane grunted, and all the TOTEL members winced sympathetically.

Jose fed more rope to Hampton, who continued looping, trapping Lane's legs as well.

Brie tested the rope, nodding. "We can't take the chance that Serene's orders will make you sabotage us."

"I would never do that."

"Oh really?" Brie asked. "Who was it that called Serene and told her where we were?"

He scowled.

"See?" she said. "It's necessary."

"And highly entertaining," Markese put in.

Zinnia elbowed him and turned to Brie. "I don't understand why Serene's spell didn't affect you, too."

"I was wondering that too," Devonte said thoughtfully.

"She didn't know I was there. And when she gave Lane instructions, she directed her commands only at him. That's my theory."

"But he'll be okay once we get there?" Doc asked.

"Serene said he wasn't supposed to try to follow her. *Try*, get it? That's the key word. So, if we *make* him come along, he's not trying—he *has* to follow. And once we're there—he won't have to try. He'll just be there. Problem solved."

"He'll be normal again?" Doc asked, unconvinced.

"He'll be an overprotective granny-man, but if you call that normal, then, yes,"

Brie said. "He'll be normal."

"My ears still work," Lane grumbled as Hampton tied the last knot.

Outside the barn, Lita opened the back door of AlexVander. "Kelsea, do you want me to unload some equipment so we have more room?" she called.

Kelsea swung down from the loft ladder, where she'd been hanging upside down, thinking. She adjusted her wire-rimmed glasses, and a wide grin spread over her face. "I've just had a shiny, sparkly, exceptionally stupendous idea. Leave the equipment where it is."

She turned to the others and raised her voice. "Let's get this show on the road, people! Everybody, pile inside AlexVander!"

Lane looked at Hampton and sighed. Trussed up the way he was, he couldn't walk.

Hampton nodded wordlessly and picked him up. Then he heaved him inside the van, dumping him into his seat. "You good?" he asked.

"Good, dude. I'm good." Lane's face was beet red.

Brie squeezed in beside her brother and closed the door. "Ready, Kelsea!"

Kelsea looked to Doc, who sat up front with her, Gandalf on her shoulder. Then she turned in the driver's seat and checked with Lita. "You have Pudge with you in back?"

"Got him!" Lita called.

Kelsea pulled to the end of the driveway. "It's up to you now, Nardo," she said to the air. "It's Pudge for left and Gandalf for right."

There was a moment of tense silence, and then Pudge began to bark.

"Woo-hoo!" Kelsea yelled triumphantly. She thrust her hand into the back seat. "Hands into the middle, people. It's Operation: Let's Get Jenna!"

She counted down and everyone chorused, "Let's Get Jenna!" and lifted their hands in unison.

"Jenna," Lane said. His eyes glazed over.

Brie gave him an odd look and waved her hand in front of his face.

But Lane's eyes had gone distant. Empty.

"Um...Kelsea?" Brie said. "We may have a problem."

Chapter Thirty-Three

A Shock

The deeper into the woods Serene drove, the further Jenna's spirits sank.

They rolled silently through the tunnel of trees. Even if she could have opened her window to scream, no one was close enough to hear.

Nardo had flickered in and out once more during the drive, but he was almost too transparent to see. He'd disappeared quickly, and he hadn't returned. She was on her own.

At a bend in the road, the dark wooden cabin came into view. With its rotting door jamb and missing shingles, it radiated an air of neglect. But maybe Flynn kept it that way on purpose. Who paid attention to a rickety old house in the woods?

Serene parked the SUV in the garage alongside Flynn's Jeep. She turned in her seat. "Brent, take Jenna into the cabin and wait for me. Touch her only if I tell you to move her—unless she tries to run or fight." She glanced at Jenna. "I hate to do things this way, but you've forced my hand." She climbed out and headed inside.

Jenna glared at her back.

Ian let Brent out and came around to open the car door for Jenna. Before she could get out, though, Brent dragged her from the SUV. It took all her willpower to stop herself from lashing out at him. Before she acted, she needed to know what she was facing.

After the bright light in the garage, she had to squint when Brent pushed her into the darkened cabin. There was a small mudroom just inside the door, and a dog in a crate growled at her. It was the beagle that had followed her at the Winter Carnival, she realized. No wonder it was growling.

Brent kept her moving into the main part of the house, where faded brown curtains were drawn over every window. The massive room was lit by only a single lamp and the dim flicker of the fireplace.

She passed shelves filled with cages and aquariums, and this time she was close enough to see the huge hornets buzzing inside the glass tanks. There were lizards, too. And a few cages held hamsters and even ferrets. But all the creatures looked...off. They were too large or small, or they had odd colors or appendages.

But she didn't have time to study them. Serene had stopped with Ian in the kitchen, and she waved Brent past. He shoved Jenna forward, dragging her to a halt again in the center of the room.

She glanced around, assessing the situation. Her mother was drugged or asleep on the plaid sofa, her hands and feet bound with rope. Her skin was drawn, and her chest rose and fell unevenly. But at least she was here and alive.

In another corner was a twin bed with a metal frame. Raloria crouched on top of it, half-hidden under the covers. Her huge, lemur-like eyes peered out above the sheets. She was tied by one thin wrist to a bed rail, but when she saw Jenna, she leaned forward. "I can't heal Granddaddy," she said sadly, her features twisting in pain. "Or Owly either." She held up her stuffed toy, rubbing the spot where one ear had come off. "Can you help them?"

Jenna shook her head and followed the girl's gaze to the foot of the bed. A man was curled up on the floor, handcuffed to the steel bed frame. He was bruised so badly it took her a moment to recognize him. Thairyn.

He woke at the sound of Raloria's voice, using the bed rail to pull himself into a sitting position. When he saw Jenna, he went perfectly still.

The severe line of his mouth made her remember why she'd feared him in the first place. The light from the fireplace glinted off the diamond in his earring, matching the diamond-hard coldness in his eyes.

Raloria dove under the sheets as Serene approached, sipping from the thermos she'd taken from the kitchen. "Come on out," she said.

Raloria pouted, even as she compulsively obeyed the order.

Serene looked over her shoulder at Ian. "Bring the girl water. She needs to hydrate before the Delve."

He closed the refrigerator door, cracking a raw egg into his mouth. Tossing the shell in the garbage, he went to get a cup.

"You found Jenna," Thairyn said, drawing Serene's attention. His voice was deceptively lazy. "So the rumors are true. You've been working to become a chimera." He barked out a humorless laugh. "You must have thought you hit the jackpot when you realized your niece had Artifex Charms. With that gift, you can create an army to do your bidding."

Serene regarded him coldly. "I'll do what it takes to overthrow the Council."

Jenna looked between her aunt and Thairyn, confused. "Create an army? What does that mean?"

"Thairyn is being melodramatic," Serene said, crossing her arms. "Most Charms are inherited. But some can be created—by an Artifex." She paused and shot a look at Jenna. "The only other Artifex alive is under the thumb of the Council. But if I have Artifex Charms, I can recruit people loyal to the Unbound—and I can give them magic of their own. It wouldn't be an army so much as a new block of voters. Either way, though, the old Council would be finished."

"What makes you think you could wield Artifex Charms?" Thairyn demanded. "It takes years of training to learn to use them."

"Normally, yes. But I'm not starting from scratch, and these Charms can't be that different from my own. I'm not worried."

Ian walked up with the cup of water, and Serene returned her attention to Raloria, dismissing Thairyn. "You have a big night ahead of you, Raloria, and you're going to start by Delving my niece. So drink up. I need to know how much Obru is still in her system."

Raloria took the cup from Ian with shaking hands, but she drank deeply.

"Stand back," Serene ordered Brent.

He dropped Jenna's arm and stepped away.

"Take off your jacket and pull up your sleeves," Serene told Jenna. "It's easier if Raloria touches your Charms."

She balked. "Raloria can't touch me! I'll infect—"

"You won't," Serene interrupted. "Raloria's Strands are...different—not truly a part of her. So don't freak out. You won't infect the girl."

"It'll be okay," Raloria whispered.

Reluctantly, Jenna took off her white jacket and tossed it on the bed. She rolled up the sleeves of her blouse. She'd already left her gloves behind at Doc's house, and she felt exposed now without her layers of clothes.

Raloria looked straight at her. Then her eyes unfocused—as if she were looking *through* her—*inside* of her.

The pattern on the girl's head unspooled into the thick black tendrils Jenna had seen before. The Strands stretched toward her, coiling around her wrists. And to her surprise, they were pulsing and warm—almost as if they were alive.

But as soon as the Strands touched Jenna's skin, Raloria gagged, doubling over in pain. "Her Charmings are so, so sick."

Thairyn strained at his handcuffs, watching his granddaughter. "Stop this, Serene! Can't you see it's hurting her?"

"I want to heal her," Raloria rasped.

"No." Serene's voice was firm. "You can't touch her with your hands. We'll do the transfer soon, and then you can—"

"Resist her orders, child," Thairyn told Raloria. "You have to try!"

Serene nodded at Ian, and he sprang forward and struck the man so hard he slumped sideways to the floor, alive but unconscious.

Raloria screamed, grabbing her head in the same place Thairyn had been hit.

Serene moved to the girl's side. "Concentrate now," she said, blocking her view of Thairyn. She pointed to the Strands that were still wrapped around Jenna's wrists. "Is there enough Obru extract in her blood to do the transfer?"

The girl rocked back and forth, her knees pulled up to her chin. Her face twisted in pain, but she gritted out one word. "Yes."

Serene patted her shoulder. "Good. Rest now. Sleep."

The long black Strands retracted into her scalp, and Raloria dove under her blankets. Almost instantly, her soft crying changed to the rhythm of troubled sleep.

Jenna wheeled on her aunt. "Did you have to do that?"

"Raloria will be fine. It was just a difficult Delve because of your Charms."

"And what about Thairyn?"

Serene snorted. "The man can't keep his trap shut. Lucky for him, he's useful. He cares too much about his granddaughter to watch her suffer. Eventually, he'll tell us all we need to know about the Council."

"But why hit him? You could have just done your Siren thing."

She laughed. "Unfortunately, Charms like mine don't work on members of the Vigil. I had to resort to other methods."

Jenna remembered being trapped in the trunk of Thairyn's car. He'd lied to Serene, even after she demanded the truth from him. She looked at him again now, seeing his injuries with new understanding. The only way her aunt could manipulate him was to use force—force and his love for his granddaughter.

"He brought this on himself," Serene said. "Don't you dare feel sorry for him."

"And what about my mom?" Jenna stabbed a finger at Mae's listless form on the couch. "Have you Charmed her asleep, or did you have to resort to *other methods*?"

Mae moaned, as if she was unconsciously aware of their attention.

"Flynn put her under very gently," Serene said, "and she's been asleep ever since. It was the humane thing to do, Jenna. She doesn't have long."

The words went through her like an electric shock. "What does that mean—*doesn't have long*?"

"I've never misled you. I told you your mom was dying the first time we met."

"You also told me you could cure her."

"And I will tonight. But her last weeks would have been agony without the pills I gave you for her. It was the least I could do. This way, she had some peace at the end."

The fine hairs on the backs of Jenna's arms rose in warning. "The end?"

Serene's face grew very still. "I need you to understand. What we're doing here is bigger than any of us. Do you see that? Tonight could change the course of human history. Every wrong in the world—we could right it. It's why I've worked so hard to accomplish this. There's nothing more important."

"What about my mom—your sister? She's not important?"

"It's time for you to face the facts, Jenna. Your mom is already too sick for Raloria to heal. And even if I had enough Obru—which I don't—she's not strong enough to survive the withdrawal process. Look at her."

"So there was never any cure." She shook with rage. "You lied to me about everything."

"I never lied. I'm going to cure your mom. It's just that her Charms were killing her slowly. The cure will kill her fast—it's a kinder death."

Jenna stared at her in horror.

Serene turned to Ian. "Get Flynn. And tell him to bring Dot." She returned her gaze to Jenna. "Your mom would want it this way. Her last act will be to help us test the transfer process. She'll help usher in a better future for everyone. Her death will have meaning."

Jenna yanked free from Brent and leaped to her mother's side. "Mom, wake up!" Frantically, she shook her mother's limp arms. "Please! You have to wake up now. Your sister is trying to kill you!"

—ele—

Pudge barked loudly and Gandalf squawked at almost the same moment.

Kelsea frowned. "You're confusing me, Nardo. We're on a dirt road. Either way I turn, I'll crash into a tree."

Zinnia leaned forward. "I think he wants you to stop. We're here."

Kelsea pulled off the road, parking behind a large stand of evergreen trees. "Verifying. Nardo—are we in the right place? Pudge for no and Gandalf for yes."

"Fly you fools!" Gandalf called.

"Indeed." She nodded in satisfaction. "This is it, people," she said, turning in her seat to address the group. "We're moving on to stage two. Time for the pledge."

Everyone chorused, *"I will seek the truth, defend the defenseless, right the wrong, and stand up for fairies."*

"Fairness!" Kelsea corrected automatically.

Markese raised his voice. "Nardo," he called out to the empty air, "you'd better warn us if something heinous is coming, you hear me?" Then he turned to Lita. "Eat another one of those jerkies, girl."

On the ride over, they'd had to pull over two times because the animals wouldn't respond to Kelsea's questions. The worst part was, they didn't know if Nardo was even there. After it happened a second time, though, Lita started eating a chunk of beef jerky every fifteen minutes just to be on the safe side.

Kelsea pointed to Hampton. "Go scout the area. Make sure this is where we're supposed to be. We'll wait here for you."

Hampton clambered out, and an awkward silence descended on the van. Everyone avoided looking at Lane.

He was sitting stiff as a rod in the backseat, staring ahead at nothing. "Lane, we're here. Do you understand?" Brie whispered.

But Lane was silent. She hadn't been able to get a word out of him the entire ride. It was unsettling. They all took turns calling his name, but he never even blinked.

Five minutes passed. Then ten.

Finally, Jose climbed forward to crouch in front of him. He cocked his head. "Is there a full moon tonight? Because he could be changing into a werewolf. Is that possible?"

Markese covered his mouth with his hand, horrified, but Zinnia rolled her eyes. "No, Jose. That's not possible."

Lita appeared behind Jose. "Have we ruled out a zombie attack? He looks more like a zombie than a werewolf to me."

"He's going to be fine," Brie said with forced confidence. "Whatever it is will wear off once we get him out of the van and moving."

"We're almost out of daylight, though, and Hampton's not back yet," Devonte commented in his ultra-low voice. "Should I go look for him?"

But at that moment, Hampton emerged from behind a cedar tree and climbed into AlexVander. "The cabin is a half mile ahead, down this dirt road," he told them. "There's cover the whole way, but this is the perfect spot to set up. Nardo was right."

"Did you hear that, people?" Kelsea said. "All signs point to yes. It's Go Time!"

As everyone got out, Brie motioned Hampton over. "A little help here?"

He nudged Jose aside and plucked Lane from the van, lifting him easily. He stood him on his feet outside and unwound the rope, tucking the cord into his pack.

Everyone gathered around to watch.

When Lane was free, his head swiveled back and forth as if he was looking for something, but the eerie expression never left his face.

"What's wrong with him?" Doc asked softly.

Markese was rubbing his lucky necklace. "I'll tell you what's wrong with him. He's possessed, that's what. Just when I think I know what heinous is, a new heinous comes along and makes the old heinous look cute as a cupcake."

Brie shook Lane's arm. "I need you to wake up, okay?"

But he just stood there, dazed and unblinking.

"Snap out of it!" Brie said, shaking him harder. "You pick now of all times to zone out? I have half a mind to smack you!"

Helpfully, Hampton hauled back and slapped Lane across the face. Hard.

Lane cried out, staggering backward. "What the...?" He put a hand to his cheek, blinking rapidly as he looked from face to face. "Where am I, and what just happened?"

"We're in the woods getting ready to rescue Jenna Getty," Kelsea said matter-of-factly. "Hampton had to slap the turd burgers out of you because you'd become a space cadet."

Lane swallowed. "I think I know what's going on. And it's not good."

"What is it? Something that woman said to you?" Brie asked him.

"It's not Serene. It's, uh...Jenna." He shook his head to clear it. "Never mind. I'll figure out something." Then an idea struck him, and he swung around, looking for Jose. He grabbed the boy by the shoulders. "The first time we met, you shocked me with a hand buzzer. Do you still have it?"

"Never leave home without it," Jose said, pulling it from his pocket.

Lane snatched it and gave himself a quick shock. "That's better." He looped the metal ring of the buzzer over his middle finger, cradling the gadget in the palm of his hand. "Hopefully this will be enough," he muttered.

"Can you walk?" Brie asked.

He stepped forward experimentally. "Yes, I think so."

Brie grinned in relief. "Told you guys he'd be okay once we got here. That lady should have been more careful with her word choice."

Kelsea went to the back of the van, grabbed a plastic tub, and set it in the center of the group. She popped the top off. "Everybody, grab a headset." She rubbed her hands together in excitement. "We can use these to communicate. If Serene gets close, we'll turn the volume up and drown her out. If we can't hear her, she can't control us, right?" Kelsea looked to Lane for confirmation.

He nodded slowly. "You know, that might actually work."

"Indeed," Kelsea said. "It's my shiny, sparkly, exceptionally stupendous idea." She motioned the group into a huddle. "Okay, people. Here's the plan. Lane, Jose, and Hampton will go get a closer look at the cabin. Markese, you're with me. Everybody else knows what to do?"

Heads nodded, and Markese kissed his lucky necklace.

Kelsea thrust her arm into the center of the circle. One by one, each person added a hand to the pile. "Okay, people. It's time we show these sickos what TO-TEL CHAOS is all about. This is Operation: Let's Get Jenna! Three-two-one...," she counted.

"Let's Get Jenna," everybody echoed and lifted their hands in the air.

CHAPTER THIRTY-FOUR

POISON

Mae's eyes fluttered, and Jenna shook her harder.

She grabbed at the rope that bound her mother's wrists, trying to loosen it. "Mom! Mom, you have to—"

Serene said something to Brent, and he pounced, prying Jenna away from her mother's side.

She fought back, struggling to get away, until Ian pulled a pistol from his sport coat. She froze. The gun was only loaded with a dart. But if she was unconscious, she wouldn't be able to help her mom at all.

Mae pushed herself up weakly onto one elbow. "Where am I?" she asked, glancing around. Her eyes widened when she saw Jenna. "Are you all right?" she demanded.

"Mom, Aunt Serene is trying to kill you! She wants to transfer my Artifex Charms to her, and she wants to use you to practice. But I don't think you'll survive the withdrawal from your magic!"

Mae's gaze shifted to her sister, and she went still.

The two women studied each other.

"I never meant for you to suffer, Maeby. I was hoping you'd sleep through all this," Serene said quietly.

Mae's eyes narrowed. "What are you playing at, Serene? What do you want with my daughter?"

"I'm giving Jenna her life back. She's twice-Charmed—you know that, don't you? It's what's causing her curse. If I take her Artifex Charms away, her Seer gift will work normally."

"Don't pretend you're doing any of this for her. This is about you, Serene.

You're using my daughter to further your own agenda."

Serene balled her fists at her sides. "Why do you always think the worst? I'm helping Jenna. More than that, I'm helping everyone. Don't you understand? If I become an Artifex, I can change things for the better. So, yes. I'm doing what needs to be done. Something you could never do."

A wave of pain rippled through Mae, and for a moment she couldn't speak. She panted, then gritted out, "It took me too long to see what those people were doing to you. The Unbound. And now you don't care who you hurt, as long as you get what you want." She collapsed back onto the sofa as pain shot through her again. Her eyelids fluttered, and she hovered at the edge of consciousness.

At that moment, Flynn came in from the hall. He'd washed the oil and blood from his blond ponytail, and he didn't have a scratch on him. Raloria must have healed the man after Lane and Jenna had attacked him in the parking garage.

Her gaze slid past Flynn, and her jaw went slack. There was an enormous snake following at his heels like a pet dog. It was at least ten feet long, with dark splotches along its back. When its mouth opened wide, it bared rings of concentric teeth, and a flash of light strobed through its body.

She took a step back. "Is that...a verophid?"

"That's Dot," Serene said, as Flynn led the creature closer. She glanced knowingly at Jenna and raised an eyebrow. "So Thairyn used a verophid on you, did he?"

When she nodded, Serene continued. "What Thairyn would have used was actually a verophid hatchling. But Dot," she said, reaching out to pet the thing, "is an adult. Not only that, she's a hybrid. Flynn calls Dot a verothon. He's been crossing verophids with pythons, breeding them bigger."

"Why would he do that?"

"Verophids are special. Charmed people have been using them in Council ceremonies for generations. They're not like other animals because they can connect to our power. A regular verophid—even an adult—isn't large enough to hold Charms itself. But Dot is. She can store the power in her body, and we can test to make sure the transfer process works." She spoke aside to Flynn, "Bring us a chair."

He nodded.

Serene strode to Raloria's bedside. "The child has never taken someone's gift, and Dot's going to give her the chance to practice."

Flynn retrieved a chair from the kitchen and placed it beside the sofa.

Jenna glanced at her mother. Mae was contorted with pain, lost to the world around her. "You're going to take the Seer gift from my mom and put it into that...verothon?" she asked incredulously.

Serene ignored her question. She pulled the covers away from the sleeping child. "Time to wake up, Raloria."

The girl woke, cringing when she spotted Serene.

"Go sit there," Serene instructed her. "Ian, get Mae ready for the transfer."

Raloria tottered to the chair, rubbing her eyes sleepily. Halfway there, she dropped Owly and broke into tears.

Flynn and Serene frowned at the girl, while Ian bent over Mae.

While everyone was distracted, Jenna scanned the room, searching for a weapon. Her eyes fastened on an iron poker beside the fireplace. She acted fast, directing a sharp kick to Brent's shin.

He cried out, releasing her in surprise.

Then she lunged for the poker. She grabbed it, bringing the iron rod down across Ian's exposed back.

But instead of knocking the man to the ground, the poker ricocheted off his flesh, as if she'd struck an armored car, not a person. His muscles bulged, and he swung around to face her.

Raloria whimpered, and Jenna hugged her arm to her body as pain lanced from her wrist to her shoulder. The man hadn't even flinched. What was he made of?

Ian grinned and pulled the collar of his shirt down to reveal the dark lines that ran across his chest.

Charms. A kind unknown to her.

He plucked the poker easily from her hand. "Should I use the dart gun on her now?" he asked Serene.

She huffed in exasperation. "No. I want nothing but Obru in her system. Get the rope."

He went to the kitchen and pulled a length of cord from a drawer.

Serene leveled a disappointed look at Jenna. "If you insist on acting like a wild animal, you'll be treated like one." She nodded at Brent. "Tie her down."

Jenna's heart pounded as Brent took the rope from Ian and shoved her onto the bed. Ian stood guard, the fireplace poker in hand, watching as Brent bound her wrists to the bedrail.

She was out of ideas, and her mother was barely conscious. Her breath came in shallow gasps.

Brent finished securing the rope, and Ian returned his attention to Serene.

She nodded. "Let's get started. My sister's finally going to volunteer for the cause, whether she wants to or not."

Lane, Hampton, and Jose approached the cabin cautiously. They darted from tree to tree, watching for any signs of movement in the gathering dark.

When they were close, Lane paused and gave himself a thorough shock with Jose's hand buzzer. Then he nodded, and the three of them sprinted to the side of the house.

Lane was wary of hearing Serene's voice, but he took a chance and pulled off his headset, pressing his ear to the wood siding. He could hear voices, but they weren't clear enough for him to understand words. He crouched low and motioned for the twins to follow.

They crept along one wall, peeking into windows, but dark brown curtains were closed over every single one. One window, though, made them pause. Water dripped between the panes of glass. And behind the curtains, something was making strange squeaks and chirps.

A chill went up Lane's spine. He exchanged glances with the other two, and all of them hurried past.

They found a screened porch at the rear of the house, and Lane crawled over to investigate, leaving the twins hidden behind a bush. He poked around and then raced back, excited.

Everyone pulled their headsets off, and Lane spoke in a whisper. "The porch has a tin ceiling. My granddad had one like it, and there was empty space above it. If I can get up there, I can use a joist to crawl from the porch attic into the main house. Hampton, can I borrow the rope you used to tie me up?"

Hampton dug inside his backpack and handed it over.

Working methodically, Lane tied a large knot in the rope every foot or so. Then he wound it into a loose coil and ducked his head and arm through, wearing it like a sash. He frowned. "I'm also going to need to cut through the screen and maybe the ceiling drywall."

"Take my knife." Hampton pulled up his pant leg and unstrapped the holster from his calf.

"Right," Lane said. He strapped the holster onto his own leg, over his jeans, while Jose looked on, nodding his head conspiratorially. Lane took a deep breath. "Follow me."

They scurried to the porch, and Lane cut a slit in the bottom corner of the screen. They crawled through, grateful for the growing darkness.

He pointed at the large tin tiles above them. "I'm going to need a boost," he whispered. "Once I'm in, you guys hide in the woods with your headsets."

"Got it," they said in unison.

"Now, let's get Jenna!" Suddenly, Lane went stock still. His eyes glazed over, and his head turned, searching.

Jose muttered a curse and grabbed Lane's wrist. He forced Lane's fingers to close over the hand buzzer, shocking him out of his daze.

"Thanks, dude," Lane said, and Jose saluted.

Hampton squatted and clasped his hands together, making a sling.

Lane caught Hampton by the shoulders and put his foot into the larger boy's hands. He took a deep breath.

"Don't worry—I'll spot you." Jose stretched his arms out as if to catch him.

Lane nodded at them both, and Hampton slung him upward with all his strength.

Lane held his hand above his head to knock the ceiling tile out of the way as he rose. He quickly caught hold of a joist before he could fall into Jose's waiting arms. He hauled himself up onto a large beam, balancing so he wouldn't crash through the flimsy tin ceiling.

Taking out his cell phone to use as a flashlight, he inspected the attic space and sighed in relief. An opening between the porch and the main house would allow him to cross through.

He leaned down and waved Hampton and Jose out of the porch. He replaced the tile he'd knocked aside and made sure his headphones were secure around his neck. He'd need them later, but right now he had to listen for Jenna.

Holding the phone with one hand, he got down on his belly and crawled along the beam. He ignored the dust and cobwebs as he set his jaw and pushed forward. He'd get Jenna out of here somehow. But first, he had to find her.

Jenna tested the rope that bound her hands to the bed, but Brent had been thorough. He stood near her now, watching her with that vacant expression in his eyes.

She looked to where her mother lay, weak and panting. She had to do something—she just didn't know what that something was yet.

Serene beckoned Flynn close.

The man with the blond ponytail kneeled in front of the plaid sofa, facing Mae. He lifted Dot onto his shoulders, and it opened its mouth, showing off its multiple rings of teeth.

Raloria cringed and clutched Owly to her chest.

Jenna studied the room desperately. Her gaze snagged on Thairyn, crumpled on the floor. She hid her start when she saw his eyes blink open and close again. He was feigning sleep.

Serene cried out, "Wait! She's having a vision. It could be a message from Fore!" She stood up, excitement vibrating through her.

Her aunt was right. Mae had gone rigid with that deep focus that meant she was looking at something beyond them all.

Ian and Flynn exchanged glances, unnerved, but Raloria only tilted her head to the side in curiosity.

Then, just as suddenly as it had come, the vision left Mae. She relaxed, sinking back onto the cushions.

"What did you see?" Serene asked.

Jenna smothered her gasp as Nardo appeared at her mother's side. He sat on the edge of the sofa and took both of her bound hands in his. He leaned close and whispered in her ear.

The faintest smile lit Mae's lips, and she tightened her hands around Nardo's.

Jenna's jaw dropped. Apparently, her mother could not only see and hear Nardo, she could *feel* him too.

Nardo looked over at Jenna and disappeared again.

"What did you see? Tell me," Serene demanded, louder this time.

But Mae just lay there with that Mona Lisa smile on her face.

Ian's brow furrowed. "I thought you said your Charms worked on her."

"They do." Serene stepped closer. "Tell me now, Mae! What was in your vision?"

Mae ignored her.

Serene's eyes blazed. "How are you doing this? When we were younger, you could never resist me."

Mae locked eyes with Jenna. "I wasn't a mother then. Love is powerful."

Serene's mouth tightened. "So you refuse to tell me what you saw?"

Mae remained silent, and Serene's lip curled in contempt. "That just proves your selfishness." She gazed down at her sister, regret written across her features. "I'm sorry it had to end this way, Maeby. I really am. But if you're not with us, you're against us. And anyone who won't put their gift to good use doesn't deserve to have it."

She moved to Raloria's side. "Tether to them," she commanded, pointing to Mae and Dot.

"Mom!" Jenna cried out. She struggled frantically to free herself from the rope.

Raloria's Strands whipped out, attaching to Mae's Charms first, where the streak of white hair emerged from her scalp. Then another group of Strands shot toward Dot, wrapping around the creature's body.

"Give Dot a few drops of the Obru so we don't kill her," Serene directed Flynn. She handed him the thermos she'd been drinking from, and Flynn dribbled some of the liquid directly down the verothon's open maw.

Jenna had assumed her aunt had been drinking coffee. One more thing she'd gotten wrong.

Serene put her hand on Raloria's shoulder. "Start the transfer."

The child flinched, but she had to obey. Her Strands pulsed with light, blinking to life like a bioluminescent squid.

And the white streak in Mae's hair began to darken. At the same time, the black splotches on Dot's back leached color, and the verothon flared with light.

Mae jerked awake, convulsing as the beginnings of withdrawal blasted through her.

"Mom!" Jenna called out. She fought her ropes, but her struggles only tightened the knots.

"Is the transfer working?" Serene pressed Raloria.

"Yes," the girl ground out through clenched teeth.

Flynn petted Dot, soothing the animal as it writhed in either ecstasy or pain.

Jenna watched, unable to stop it. If she could get free, maybe Raloria could reverse the process—put the Charms back inside of Mae and give her more time. There had to be a way.

Finally, Raloria's Strands retracted into her scalp. "All done," she said in a small voice. She rocked back and forth, hugging her knees to her chest and whimpering softly. Tremors wracked her thin frame, mirroring the seizures still gripping Mae.

Serene crouched down in front of her. "Thank you, Raloria. Mae won't have long to suffer now."

Jenna's chest clenched, and her throat felt tight. Her wrists were raw from the bite of the rope. Her panic had transformed into a dull ache that threatened to wreck her. Tears burned at the back of her eyes.

She hung her head, unable to watch her mother any longer.

Then, out of nowhere, music blasted from the woods nearby, and everyone in the room jumped.

It was the worst, most cringe-worthy rock music Jenna had ever heard, but her heart leaped wildly as she recognized it.

TOTEL CHAOS.

She didn't know how. She didn't know why. Against all odds, her friends had come for her.

Ian and Serene rushed across the room to look out the window, and Brent followed.

Raloria put her hands over her ears and moaned.

"What is that music?" Ian asked.

Serene's lips thinned. "Trespassers. Probably locals who don't even know we're here." She turned to Ian. "The child is having trouble focusing as it is."

Out of the corner of her eye, Jenna saw Thairyn sit up and motion to her. In her panic, she'd forgotten he wasn't unconscious.

She looked closer. They had cuffed only one of his hands to the bed. If she could get close enough, maybe he could use his free hand to untie her.

With Brent and the others distracted by the music, she put her feet on the floor and inched closer, ready to spring into action if he could loosen the knot.

Thairyn put his hand to his ear, and she realized he wanted to tell her something. She leaned over the rail, trying to catch his words over the earsplitting music.

The man's features were cut from ice—his jaw set. "I'm so sorry, child," he told her. "But Serene will bring us all to ruin. You're better dead than a weapon in her hands."

Light glinted off something in Thairyn's fingers, and she felt a sharp sting on the top of her foot.

Across the room, Raloria screamed.

Serene whirled around, her eyes wide.

Thairyn's voice cut through the din. "It's over. Your niece won't live long enough to serve you now."

Serene approached him slowly. "What are you talking about?"

Jenna's foot was going numb. With her bound hands, she hitched up the leg of her jeans. Something had pierced the thin material of her sock, drawing blood. And she recognized it.

A diamond—Thairyn's earring.

He sagged against the steel bed frame, his eyes hollow. "It's a fast-acting poison," he told Serene. "I crafted that earring years ago to hold the chemical and inject it—in case I needed a quick death." His lips were grim. "I can't let you use the girl."

Serene went rigid with rage. She motioned to Ian. "Shoot him."

Ian took the gun from his coat pocket and fired the dart at close range. Thairyn toppled sideways against the bed, unconscious.

Raloria screamed again. Then she passed out, too, sliding bonelessly to the floor.

Serene cursed. "It must have been too much at once for her." She bent beside Raloria, examining her. "She's dehydrated. Flynn, take her to your lab and get fluids into her. We need to do the transfer immediately. It won't work if Jenna's dead. Hopefully the poison isn't as fast-acting as Thairyn believes. If he's had it for years, it shouldn't be as potent."

Then Serene pointed to Ian. "Go take care of that noise. I need every bit of Raloria's focus now." She looked at Brent. "And you. Take Jenna to the lab and strap her to the bed."

Jenna looked down at the diamond again, seeing the tiny facets catch the light. The music from TOTEL CHAOS sounded suddenly distorted, and the room began to spin.

So, this is what it's like to die, she thought, as she pitched forward into Brent's arms.

Chapter Thirty-Five

POLICE

Ian padded down the dirt road in the moonlight, seeking the trespassers.

It was almost certainly a group of teenagers—mischief-makers who thought they could party unnoticed in the empty woods. Well, he'd send them packing. And if they gave him trouble, he was prepared. He patted the dart gun in his pocket.

Darkness had fallen, but he didn't use the light on his phone. He didn't want the kids to know he was coming.

He was tempted to put his hands over his ears, though. The music was as terrible as it was loud. He could feel a headache starting in his temples.

Suddenly, there was a bright flash in the woods to his left. "Smile and say *Sleazebag*," a voice called over the racket.

He frowned. He wasn't fond of games. Ducking under a tree limb, he left the path and crept slowly through the undergrowth in search of the prankster. His head swiveled from side to side, studying the brush.

There was another flash. "Smile and say *Creep*!" the voice called merrily.

He took the dart gun from his jacket pocket, holding it at the ready.

Directly in front of him, a petite teenage girl with wire-rimmed glasses swung down from a tree limb, hanging upside down by her knees. "People so rarely think to look up," she said.

Before Ian could react, she blasted him full in the face with a can of pepper spray.

He staggered backward, dropping the dart gun as he reached up to swipe at his eyes.

Markese dove for the gun and took aim. He let loose a dart that sank into the man's neck.

Ian's muscles bulged, swelling until his sport coat nearly burst at the seams, but his strength did him no good. The dart had already penetrated, and the man went down in a heap, muscles deflating again as he lost consciousness.

Kelsea climbed out of the tree, pushing her glasses higher on her nose.

"OMG," Markese said. "Why didn't we get this on video? My YouTube channel would be blowing up right now."

Kelsea ignored Markese, talking into her headset. "Lita, are you there? We took care of one of them. Ask Nardo if Serene is on her way." She paused, listening, then pulled the headset down and spoke to Markese. "Nardo says no. What do you think—time for Plan B?"

"Plan B it is," Markese agreed. "Bigger, bolder, and better than ever."

Jenna came awake in Brent's arms as he carried her down the hall.

She'd blacked out—but only for a few seconds, she thought. Trying to clear her head, she continued to feign unconsciousness, watching through her eyelashes. Her stomach twisted, though, as she remembered the poison working its way through her.

But TOTEL CHAOS was still playing their painfully awful music outside, and the sound gave her hope. Even if her own life was ending, there was a chance her friends would rescue her mom and Raloria.

Brent pushed a bedroom door open and stepped inside, and Jenna was momentarily stunned. A suffocating wave of heat made her itch all over as her pores popped with sweat.

Or maybe her skin was crawling because of what was in the room.

More than a dozen cages were filled with rats. Worse than rats. They were rats Flynn had been...experimenting on. They were monstrosities. And the squeaks and scurrying of the animals sent an uncontrollable shiver along her spine.

This was Flynn's lab, she realized, and a heater worked on high to keep the temperature almost tropical. Half the space was dedicated to the animals—with an enormous glass tank in one corner for Dot. The other half housed bulky machinery that looked like it might have come from a hospital. Beakers, syringes, cotton bandages, and microscopes lined a long counter, and a rolling office chair was tucked underneath. In another corner was a metal hospital bed covered in the waxy, waterproof paper she associated with doctors' offices.

The antiseptic smell in the air made her want to gag. As Brent swung her around, a wave of dizziness washed over her. He strode toward the bed, and she knew she couldn't delay any longer.

She moved suddenly, striking Brent's chin with the heel of her palm.

He grunted and dropped her as his hand went to his face, but she was ready to land on her feet.

The problem was, her feet weren't cooperating. Her legs went out from under her, and she couldn't stand. *Was the poison working that quickly?*

Brent scooped her up from behind, pinning her with her back against his chest.

It was a hold she knew how to escape—if her legs were obeying orders. She struggled, but her dizziness surged, and she forced herself to be still. She didn't want to risk passing out again.

Serene hurried through the door, taking a huge gulp of Obru extract from her thermos. She stopped short, though, when she saw Jenna crushed against Brent's chest. "What's going on here? Brent, I told you to strap her to the bed."

He froze, and Jenna felt a ripple go through his body as the curse inside him warred with Serene's words.

Her aunt stepped closer, narrowing her eyes. "Listen to me, Brent. Put her down."

There was a moment's pause.

"Now!" she shouted, and he dumped Jenna unceremoniously onto the hospital bed.

Serene gestured to the counter. "Take those strips of gauze and strap down her ankles as well as her wrists this time. Be quick about it."

Jenna wiggled her toes, wondering if her feet would bear weight. But the pins and needles she felt only expanded when she tried to move. She couldn't make a run for it.

Brent returned, cotton gauze in hand. She turned her face away as he tied one wrist and then the other to the metal rungs of the bedframe. Then he moved to her ankles, repeating the process.

Flynn came in, carrying a sobbing Raloria over his shoulder. The massive snake-like creature glided at his heels. Flynn grabbed the rolling chair and set Raloria down in it. Then he opened the glass door of the empty tank, allowing Dot to slither inside.

"Get the IV fluid ready," Serene directed him. "I'll talk to the girl."

He nodded and removed a plastic bag full of fluid from a cabinet over the counter.

Serene crouched down, taking Raloria by the shoulders. "Stop crying now."

Her sobs choked off instantly, but she shuddered as she glanced around. "It's too much hot in here. And scary. I don't like it."

"Mr. Flynn needs it warm for his experiments," Serene explained. "You'll be fine."

Flynn rolled the IV pole toward the girl, and she flinched. "What's that?"

"It will help you stay healthy while we do the transfer," Serene told her. "Because I don't have anyone to heal you if things go wrong. So I want you to take a deep breath and focus."

Raloria breathed deeply, and Serene gave her an encouraging pat on the shoulder.

But at that moment, the rock music TOTEL CHAOS was playing amped up another notch. Raloria pressed her hands over her ears. "Too much loud!"

Serene exchanged a glance with Flynn. "Don't worry. Mr. Ian is putting a stop to it right now."

Then, as if Serene's wish had been granted, the noise outside stopped abruptly.

Jenna's heart lurched. What had happened? Had Ian taken the TOTEL members prisoner or convinced them to go home? She closed her eyes, hoping they were safe.

"Finally," Serene muttered. She returned her attention to the girl. "Look at me, Raloria," she said, compelling her.

Raloria stared.

Flynn stretched a band around the girl's upper arm and then slid a needle into her vein.

Raloria cried out, but Serene was ready. "Focus on me. You're going to Delve

Jenna and answer my questions. Do you understand?"

She nodded. "Understand." The Strands whipped out of her skull obediently, but the child gasped in pain once more when they wrapped around Jenna's wrists. "Her sick is so strong now," she said.

Serene leaned forward intently. "Can you cure her of the poison without touching her?"

"No," she panted.

"How long before it kills her?"

"Not long," Raloria said, shaking with the effort. She doubled over in agony.

"Let go!" Serene commanded.

Raloria's Strands retracted, and Serene had to reach out to steady her.

"What does *not long* mean?" she pressed. "How many minutes?"

"I don't know minutes," Raloria said, starting to sniffle. She wiped her nose on her sleeve. "Maybe two SpongeBobs."

Serene stared at her blankly.

Flynn spoke up. "One SpongeBob cartoon lasts fifteen minutes—so she means Jenna has about half an hour left. But Raloria needs to be on the IV for at least five to ten minutes before you try the transfer, or I think she'll pass out again."

"If I can get her calm enough, she'll be fine."

Without warning, police sirens started to wail. "We know you're in there. Come out with your hands up!"

Everyone jumped, and Raloria clamped her hands to her ears and sobbed.

Lane crawled along the beam on his belly, careful not to break through the thin drywall on either side of the attic joist. He'd been moving randomly, listening for voices, but it was difficult to hear over the racket TOTEL CHAOS was making.

Abruptly the music stopped, and all he could hear was the creepy squeaks and chirps coming from that strange room. He crawled in the opposite direction. Before he got far, he almost leaped out of his skin as sirens suddenly blared nearby.

And then he heard the crying. Unfortunately, it was coming from the same place as the chirping.

There was no help for it. What if it was Jenna? He set his jaw and went back.

When he'd come as close as he could, judging by the sound, he slid the knife from the holster Hampton had given him.

Carefully, he pushed it into the drywall, slicing open a triangle barely big enough to see through. He grabbed the piece of drywall before it could fall through, and then he put his eye to the hole.

He almost fell off the beam.

The room below was lined with cages and cages of rats. That's what those strange chirps and squeaks had been.

His heart nearly beat its way through his chest, and he broke out in a cold sweat. He looked up, trying to breathe.

Digging his fingers into the wooden beam to steady himself, he peered through the hole again. He avoided looking at the cages, scanning the rest of the room, and saw Jenna. She was lying on a hospital bed in one corner. The moment he saw her, the curse began to fight for control. Quickly, he gave himself a shock with the hand buzzer, grateful the sound of crying disguised the noise it made.

He forced himself to look away from Jenna.

The person crying was a small girl with enormous eyes. She sat in a rolling office chair with her palms pressed to her ears, upset by the noise of the sirens.

Serene was at the window, trying to see out into the dark. But the panes of glass were impossibly fogged. She couldn't see anything.

Suddenly, an incredibly deep voice boomed out over a speaker. "We know you're in there! Come out with your hands up!"

Serene blew out her breath in frustration. "What has Ian done?"

"Somebody must have called the cops," Flynn said.

Serene studied Raloria, her lips pressed together. "We can't start with the child in this state. I can only make her stop crying. I can't force her to truly focus." She turned to Flynn. "You and I will take care of the police while she hydrates."

"I'll bring Rusty," he said.

Serene spun to Brent. "Roll the child and the IV stand into the other room and lay her on the bed. But don't let her get disconnected from the IV. Then keep watch." Serene took a step toward him. "Brent, you will not touch Jenna again unless she's trying to escape. Do you understand?"

His eyes lingered on Jenna, but he nodded vacantly and rolled Raloria and her IV pole from the room.

"What about your niece?" Flynn asked so quietly Lane had to press his ear against the hole to catch the words.

Serene snorted. "She's not going anywhere."

They hurried out into the hall and shut the door behind them.

Balancing carefully, Lane took the headset from his neck and fitted it back over his ears. He turned it on and found the correct channel. Then he swung the microphone into place.

"Hampton—Jose, can you hear me?" he whispered.

"Ten-four," Jose answered. "Whatcha got?"

Lane took the knotted cord from his shoulders and looped one end of it around the attic joist. "Serene and another dude are leaving the cabin. Can you let the others know?"

"On it."

"This guy Brent, though. He's still inside." He tied the rope securely, tugging to check the knot. "Any chance you two can cook up something to lure him out?"

"Leave it to us," Hampton said, and Jose chimed in, "We got this, boss. Over and out."

Lane squinted through the hole in the ceiling. "I'm coming, Angel," he whispered. "Hang in there."

Chapter Thirty-Six

PIRATE

"Keep the sirens coming," Lita told Zinnia. She aimed her cell phone light toward the equipment they'd set up near the van. "If possible, we want them to think a full SWAT team is out here."

Lita had hooked the sound system up to her laptop, and Zinnia was playing the police siren sound effects they'd downloaded earlier.

"And Devonte, you're doing great! Your imitation is spot on." Lita clapped her hands with excitement, and Zinnia and Doc exchanged shocked glances. They hadn't seen this much energy from her in years. Even Brie knew her well enough to be surprised.

Zinnia shrugged and added another siren.

"Ready, Devonte?" Lita asked. "I'm taking your mic live again. Here goes."

Devonte put the microphone to his mouth and boomed, "I repeat: come out with your hands up. We have gun power, and we're not afraid to use it!"

Lita gave him a big thumbs-up. She whirled to Brie. "Cue guns."

Brie picked up her drumsticks and then lit into the drum kit, simulating the sound of gunfire.

"Those were warning shots," Devonte said into the mic. "The next shots we fire will be real."

"Great!" Lita whispered. Then she motioned for Doc to bring Pudge over. "Okay, Nardo," she said. "If you can hear me, will you help Pudge play his part?"

Suddenly, the dog bolted into the woods as if he were chasing something—or someone. His heavy barking echoed through the trees, sounding—they hoped—like a police dog on the scent.

Lita smiled and gestured to Devonte.

"Surrender now and no harm will come to you," he said. Then he covered the mic with his hand. "What now?"

"Now we hope Plan B works," Lita said. "Because there is no Plan C."

—*ele*—

Brent stood with his feet planted in the front room of the cabin, keeping watch over Mae, Thairyn, and Raloria.

There was a loud knock at the door, and Brent frowned. Serene hadn't told him what to do if someone came knocking.

"Who's there?" he called. When no one answered, he went to the front door and yanked it open.

A drone hovered in the air at eye level, a piece of paper taped to the underside.

Brent looked around, then hesitantly pulled the paper off and read the note aloud. *"Here's something special, just for you."* The drone buzzed away.

Brent looked confused. He turned the paper over. Someone had traced a hand with the middle finger extended.

His fury blazed, and the vacant look retreated from his expression. He crumpled the paper and threw it to the ground.

The area around the cabin was lit only by the moon. He narrowed his eyes, trying to see into the dark. "Who's there? You think you're funny?" When there was no answer, he turned and went inside, grumbling.

A moment later, there was another knock on the door. Grunting low, he went again to answer it.

The drone was back.

Brent smacked the thing to the ground and snatched the paper. He read, *"Roses are red, violets are blue. This drone is brainless, and so are you."*

He balled the paper up and threw it into the woods. "Come say that to my face!" he yelled into the trees.

When no one appeared, he stormed inside, slamming the door behind him.

The knock came again.

This time, he flew to the door and flung it open.

About fifty feet away, Jose stood with his back to the cabin. He said something into his headset. Then he dropped his pants and mooned Brent, wiggling his butt back and forth.

Brent took off after him, and Jose broke for cover, yanking his pants up as he ran.

Then Hampton called to Brent from the other side of the yard. When Brent turned to look at him, Hampton mooned him, too.

Brent changed directions and chased after Hampton instead.

Hampton fled into the woods, and Jose joined him. Both boys sprinted at top speed, leading Brent away from the house and Jenna.

Jenna cursed her own helplessness, twisting her wrist to try to free it from the gauze binding. But her arms felt as thick and clumsy as her mind. She was out of ideas.

TOTEL was still out there, of course. She'd recognized Devonte's resonant voice as soon as he'd spoken, pretending to be a police officer. But she also knew Serene was on her way to confront them—and the Take Over the Earth League was no match for her aunt. Hopefully, they'd escape unharmed.

She closed her eyes. She was so tired of ruining lives.

Suddenly, Nardo appeared at her bedside. He was barely visible, but he was talking a mile a minute, even though she couldn't hear him. Fisting his hands on his hips, he jabbed his finger toward the sky and then blinked out. Probably for good.

She wondered if he'd been pointing to Heaven, urging her to go to the light. Although with her track record, she wasn't sure she'd be heading in that direction.

Maybe she'd join Nardo in some kind of limbo existence where her only hope of communicating was to meet a Seer. She'd wander the earth unseen, watching the devastation she'd left in her wake—unable to apologize.

Earlier tonight, she'd seen the curse take hold of Lane when she'd touched him. Would the curse end with her death? She hoped so. It bothered her that the last time she'd seen his robin's egg–blue eyes, they hadn't been his own.

She turned her head to the side, trying to banish the image.

That's when she noticed Dot.

Serene had given Flynn an order while he was closing the door to Dot's tank. He'd been interrupted before he'd latched it properly, and now the verothon was poking its head through the gap. It paused as if scenting prey, then swung toward Jenna, baring its rows of sharp teeth.

She froze as it curled sinuously around the glass door and spilled down onto the floor. With eerie grace, it slithered toward her.

Suddenly, a strange sound caught her attention—a sound like somebody sawing wood. She looked up, then cocked her head to the side.

The poison was making her hallucinate.

A knife was sliding up and down through the ceiling, as if someone was carving a large circle in the drywall above. Then the circle dropped to the floor.

Lane's face appeared in the gap, a headset looped around his neck. He met her eyes, then immediately slapped his forehead with one hand. He shook himself. "Don't worry," he told her, sticking his arm through the hole for her inspection. "I have a buzzer."

She could only stare in wonder. In her last moments of life, her brain had conjured a vision of Lane.

Dream Lane poked his head further down into the room. "Remember at the Winter Carnival when I told you I was a pirate? Well, I'm here to rescue you, matey." He tossed a length of rope through the hole, letting it dangle to the ground.

Jenna marveled at the strange way her mind worked.

He looked confused by her silence. "Your line is— *'Oh, Lane, you're my hero!'* And then maybe you could throw me a kiss or something."

He fumbled the knife he'd been holding, and it plummeted down, landing on the wooden floor with a heavy thunk.

Jenna started in surprise. This was no Dream Lane. This was the Lane she knew—clumsy, geeky, stupidly protective Lane—who was grinning down at her. "You idiot!" she said. "What are you doing here?"

"That's more like it! I knew you were in there somewhere." He took a deep breath, wiping sweaty palms on his jeans. "Quiet now. I've got to concentrate." He began to climb awkwardly down the rope.

She lifted an eyebrow. "Your eyes are closed. Didn't you lecture me about that once?"

"I know my eyes are closed. I'm trying to pretend that this is not a descent into my own personal hell, thank you very much."

"What are you talking about?"

"The rats. I'm talking about the rats. If I close my eyes, I can almost imagine those squeaking sounds are the delightful chirps of songbirds in the trees outside."

The rats. Jenna had forgotten them.

And then she remembered Dot.

Quickly she glanced around, but there was no sign of the creature. "Lane, wait a minute—"

"Don't thank me. Without Brie, none of us would have known what happened to you. So, all thanks go to her. Oh, and to Nardo, of course. Although it was Zinnia who first figured out...well, it was everybody, really."

He had come about halfway down. With his eyes squeezed shut, he searched with his feet for the next knot in the rope.

"Lane, there's a huge—"

"Don't distract me, Angel. I've got this. How far am I from the ground?"

"Only three or four feet."

He cracked one eye open, peering down. Then he looked at Jenna. He immediately had to let go of the rope with one hand and buzz himself on the forehead. Twice.

He jumped the last few feet, and she pretended not to notice his wobbly landing.

He swept her a low bow. "Milady."

"Lane, there's a problem. Several problems."

"Ah, I see." He picked up the knife and strode to her side, slicing the gauze that bound her ankles.

"That wasn't the problem I was talking about."

He leaned over her and cut the ties around her wrists.

"This problem is much more...massive than that."

"We'll figure it out," he said, glancing down. He abruptly stopped moving, his face hovering inches above her own.

Jenna's breath caught as his stare went distant. The curse was taking hold.

Suddenly, Lane was yanked off his feet. The knife skittered across the floor and came to rest beneath one of the heavy pieces of equipment on the other wall.

Dot's tail tightened around Lane's ankle, and she dragged him, kicking and punching, under the bed.

In a panic, Jenna reached down to her heels. She managed to tug off one shoe with her numb fingers. Her legs still weren't working, so she tucked her arms into her sides and rolled off the bed.

She landed hard, but she was so numb it was painless.

Lane fought to pry the verothon loose, but it tightened its coils and began to drag him back toward the glass enclosure.

With her shoe, Jenna reached out and struck Dot as hard as she could in the face.

It released Lane, swinging its head toward her. The verothon slithered forward, and Jenna used her arms to haul herself backward across the wooden floor.

Lane scrambled up. He grabbed a wooden branch from inside the terrarium. Then he whacked Dot's tail from behind, making the creature change course once more. "I'll cover you!" he shouted to Jenna. "Run!"

"I can't!" she screamed at him.

"What do you mean, *you can't*?" Lane swayed from side to side, trying to keep Dot's attention fixed on him. The verothon seemed torn, unsure which of them to attack.

"You'll have to leave me here," she told him. "I was poisoned, and now my legs aren't working. Lane, I...I'm dying."

His jaw went slack—then hard. "Well, you're not dead yet. And I'm no quitter. I'm getting us both out of here! I have an idea."

Resolutely, he turned to the wall of rats. "This isn't real, this isn't real, this isn't real," he repeated like a mantra. One by one, he went to each cage and opened it, dumping the rats onto the floor.

They scurried around his feet, unsure what to do with their newfound freedom.

"This is just a terrible, *terrible* nightmare," he told himself. His face was a mask of determination. "I'm going to wake up in my bed any minute now."

Finally, Dot seemed to become aware of the scurrying behind her. The verothon turned away from Jenna.

Lane was dancing, desperately trying to avoid the rats. "This is not happening!" he shouted. Then he spotted an air vent in the floor. With sudden inspiration, he hurried over and pried up the cover.

The rats sensed Dot's approach. As one, they scurried toward the vent and fled into the ductwork, and Dot followed them down.

When the last of the verothon's tail disappeared down the hole, Lane thrust the cover back over the opening and rushed to Jenna's side. "Let's get out of here."

"Leave me!" she insisted. "Save the others—they're in the front room."

"Whatever you say. Except for that part about leaving you here to die. Here we go!" He gave himself a quick shock with the hand buzzer and then bent down and picked her up, cradling her in his arms.

She tried to resist, but her limbs felt strange and rubbery. And then her bare wrist brushed against Lane's warm neck.

He froze.

His gaze swung down to her face.

"Lane?" she whispered.

A shadow passed over his blue eyes, like an eclipse of the moon. His grip tightened. Abruptly, he pushed her against the door, holding her up with the weight of his body. The hand buzzer clattered to the floor. "I want you," he said, his voice ragged.

The words blazed through her, a match to tinder.

Lust darkened his eyes, and she could feel every inch of him pressed against her.

She sparked to life at his touch, and liquid fire pooled low in her stomach. Her awareness burned down to a single thought. Him. His clean scent. His hard body. The pressure of him pinning her there, melting her resistance.

He looked into her eyes. "I need you now," he whispered. Then he dipped his head and claimed her lips with his own.

Chapter Thirty-Seven

TRUTH

Desire shot through her. She wanted to press herself closer to him and twist her fingers into his hair.

But then her eyes fluttered open, and she realized at once that this wasn't her Lane. His eyes were too vacant, too alien. He wasn't choosing to kiss her—the Charms had chosen for him.

But her Lane was in there somewhere. And if she was almost out of time, there were a few things she should tell him. She pulled her lips away from his. "You're my best friend," she said quietly.

He went still, his mouth inches from hers. He didn't move.

Had she gotten through to him? "Come back to me," she said, searching his eyes. "Please. I need you here."

A flicker of recognition ran across his face, and she seized on it.

"Lane, do you remember who I am? It's me, Jenna. Or Mo, or Rumpelstiltskin, or Angel. All those people are me."

His jaw clenched as he struggled against the curse. "Angel," he ground out.

"Yes!" Hope ignited inside her. She spoke faster. "The day we met, I told you I was your guardian angel, and I gave you your wallet back. The next time I saw you, you helped me with my flat tire, remember?"

A tremor went through him. "I remember." He picked her up again. "Keep talking."

"We went to Doc's house one Saturday and invented crazy song lyrics, and you folded my napkin into a parrot and made it speak in Pig Latin."

He blinked and then nodded, shifting her to reach for the doorknob.

"Another time you took me to your back yard and showed me the quinzee you made from snow. That was the day I found out your favorite flowers are peonies."

"And yours are dandelions," he said. His voice was slurred but stronger. "More." He opened the door and carried her across the threshold.

"Today you dropped out of the sky and tried to save me again, and I want to say...." She swallowed. "You know the truth about my Charms, but I never told you the truth about how much I like you." She rushed on before she could lose courage. "I mean, what's not to like? You're funny and brave and—"

"Dashing. Don't forget dashing."

Her lips quirked. He was nearly back. "Yes, you're very dashing," she allowed. She met his eyes. "You told me once that you wanted to be with me. And the truth is, I want to be with you, too. I always have."

He stopped, gazing down at her.

"Lane, I remember every single second I've spent with you because...." The words caught in her throat.

"Because...." he prompted, his face serious.

She took a deep breath. "Because you're my best friend. But you're more than that, too." Her cheeks heated. "I want you to be more than that. I want—"

"Put her down. Now."

Jenna's head snapped up and awareness crashed back into her.

Brent stood silhouetted in the front door, his chest heaving.

Quickly, Lane slid Jenna onto the kitchen island next to him. He'd carried her to the front room, and she hadn't even noticed.

She glanced around. Her mom was still lying on the sofa, shivering with withdrawal. And under the covers of the twin bed was a Raloria-sized lump. The girl was hiding, one arm connected to an IV bag. Thairyn lay on the floor near her, chained and unconscious.

She tested her legs, but she couldn't move them at all. It was all she could do to sit up.

Brent kicked the door closed behind him as his murderous eyes swept possessively over Jenna and then moved past her, pinning Lane. "I should have known you put those two morons up to their stunt. But now it's just me and you."

Lane braced himself, watching Brent with grim determination. "Okay. Me and you," he repeated, sighing.

Brent charged, a ram eager to butt horns. Lane was taller, but Brent was more solidly built. He pushed Lane backward as they grappled, slugging him in the gut.

Lane bent double, but he recovered and delivered a glancing strike across Brent's jaw.

Raloria peeked out over the covers, groaning with every hit.

Jenna felt helpless watching them. She had to do something, but her self-defense skills were useless. She glanced around desperately.

Brent crouched low and rushed toward Lane, fists swinging.

Lane absorbed blow after blow, unable to gain the leverage for another punch.

Jenna's search was futile. The countertop was empty. And even if she could lay hands on something, she wasn't sure she could throw it. The only weapon she had left was her Charms.

She whistled loudly, drawing their attention.

Both of them swung around to look.

"Aren't you forgetting something?" she said in a low, husky voice. She ran her hand seductively through her hair and let her fingers trail down her neck to her blouse.

Pain erupted in her wrist where the rope had rubbed her skin raw, but she clamped her jaw against it, giving them an enticing smile. Slowly, she undid her top button.

Both guys froze.

Brent ignored Lane entirely, his gaze fastened on Jenna, and Lane's eyes inflated like balloons.

Her fingers traveled down to the second button. "Do you want to see more?" she asked, her voice warm and inviting.

In a daze, Brent moved toward her.

She cut her eyes to Lane with a look that said, *"Any time now, buddy."*

He shook himself.

Brent was closing in, reaching for Jenna, when Lane caught him by the shoulder, hauled back, and punched him square in the face.

Brent lost his balance and staggered backward into the side of the bed.

Immediately, Raloria's Strands swirled to life and encircled Brent's wrists. She studied him quizzically. "You need healing," she said. Then she reached out one hand and laid it on his face.

He sucked in a sharp breath, shaking, as Raloria's gaze went into and beyond him. When she finally pulled her hand away, Brent toppled onto the bed beside her, unconscious.

Lane looked at Jenna, eyes wide with shock. Then he nodded at Raloria. "Now *that* was a shiny, sparkly, exceptionally stupendous idea."

"What does that mean?" Raloria asked.

"It means you're wicked smart!"

"Owly too." She held up her stuffed owl, and the ghost of a smile flitted across her drawn face. Then she gazed at Lane intensely. "I can heal you, too."

He took a step back. "Later! Right now, I'm getting you guys out of here."

"Actually, you're not," Serene said, swinging the front door open. "Stand still, Lane," she commanded.

Lane froze helplessly, and all at once, Jenna realized she hadn't heard the police sirens for some time.

The TOTEL members marched inside behind Serene, like ducklings following their mother—every one of them compelled by the Siren Charms.

Jenna looked from face to face. They were all there—even Jose and Hampton had been rounded up and forced to join the grotesque parade. None of them could speak, but she could read the agony in their eyes.

At the rear of the line, Flynn closed the door firmly behind him.

"Your friends didn't factor in Flynn's hawk," Serene said, answering Jenna's unspoken question. "We had Rusty scout the area ahead of us. After that, it was just a matter of singling out one of them. I spoke to her, and the rest were easy. Those headsets saved me so much time in gathering everyone up."

"Now," Serene directed, moving into the center of the room, "I want everybody who came here in that crappy van to stand still. And remember, I don't want to hear a peep out of any of you."

Every TOTEL member was rooted silently in place.

Serene noticed Brent lying unconscious on the bed. Her lips twisted in annoyance. "No matter. I don't need him anymore." She swung to Lane. "I have you. If Jenna resists, I'll have you strap her down instead."

Jenna opened her mouth to speak, but her aunt cut her off.

"I don't have time to argue with you now. But here's the good news. If you cooperate and work fast, I can take the Artifex Charm quickly, and there might still be time for Raloria to heal you from Thairyn's poison." She stepped closer. "Do you understand what that would mean? With only the Seer gift, your curse would be gone. And that would mean you could take back your freedom. Your touch wouldn't hurt anyone, and you'd have the life you always wanted."

"Or," Serene continued ominously. "If you won't cooperate, I will do what I have to do." She looked meaningfully at Lane and the others. "I won't let you ruin everything I've worked toward. Either way, you'll do the transfer. But if you make it difficult, you'll only be hurting yourself. And your friends. Do we understand each other?"

Jenna sat up as tall as she could, trying to look like someone who was strong—unintimidated. The opposite of how she felt inside. Her own strength was leaking away. She couldn't walk—she could hardly move. And it was already too late for her mom. But what were her aunt's plans for her friends? Jenna had to bargain for their safety.

She crossed her arms over her chest. "The transfer won't work if I'm dead. You need me to cooperate, but I'll only agree if you let my friends go," she stated boldly.

Serene put one hand on her hip. "Are you crazy? I'm not letting them go. Those kids attacked Ian. They tried to attack me. No. They can stay stuck. At least until the transfer is done. But," she said, a hint of a smile crossing her face, "if you play nice, I'll have Raloria erase the memory that they were ever here. That way, they can't make trouble for us. And after the procedure, they can all go about their little lives again. I give you my word. Do we have an agreement?"

Jenna had no alternative. She couldn't exactly force her aunt. She'd just have to trust that Serene would honor the bargain and let her friends go. "Deal," she said.

Serene motioned to Flynn, and he lifted Raloria from the bed and set her in the rolling office chair once more. He wheeled the girl and her IV pole close to the kitchen island where Jenna was sitting with her legs dangling over the side.

Eagerly, Serene shrugged out of her jacket and scarf, taking one last swig of the Obru extract from her thermos. She nodded to Raloria. "Let's start."

Chapter Thirty-Eight

STAND

The Strands unfurled from Raloria's scalp.

One Strand circled Jenna's wrist, and another wound lightly around her aunt's throat.

Serene nodded to Raloria, and light began to pulse through the girl's Strands, flowing from Jenna to Serene.

And Jenna felt...weird. As if an animal had been asleep beneath the skin of her arms, and now it was awake and swimming. Fascinated, she watched as the thickest of the three black Strands that twined along each arm began to fade away.

Aside from a slight burning sensation, she had no symptoms of withdrawal as the power left her. Maybe she still had enough Obru in her system to ward off the sickness. Or maybe she felt nothing because she wasn't losing her Charms entirely. She'd still be a Seer when the transfer was done.

And if Raloria could heal the poison, she could live the normal life she'd always dreamed of. She looked down at her arms again, transfixed by the steadily vanishing line. There was virtually no pain. Her Charms were being erased. For years, this was all she'd wanted.

But if that was true, why did she feel so gutted?

She'd never pictured it like this, that was for sure. She'd thought the day she lost her curse would be the happiest of her life.

Instead, her mother was dying, and the safety of her friends depended on the honor of a pathological liar.

Serene had given Jenna her word that the members of TOTEL could leave after this, but she'd lied before. And she'd already used Flynn's hornets to draw blood from them. Serene had no intention of letting them go. Not if there was a chance she could use them.

Her aunt said she wanted to make the world a better place for everybody. But she treated the people in her life like they were nothing. She was willing to hurt anyone and everyone to get what she wanted.

And with Jenna's magic added to her own, she'd be unstoppable. Thairyn said she planned to create an army of mages she could control. That would make her the most powerful person in history.

Her mouth went dry. Was she going to let that happen?

She looked down. The thick center line of her Charms was nearly gone. And that's when the realization hit her. She had to fight.

Of course, she wouldn't win. She couldn't even move from the counter.

But she had to try to keep her Charms—if only to stop her aunt from getting them. It would mean she'd always be cursed—if she survived at all. And she'd never be able to touch anyone—to have a genuine relationship. But none of that mattered. Even if there wasn't a shred of hope, she had to try. It was the only choice she could live with. The only choice she could die with.

She looked up at her aunt. "I won't let you have my Charms."

Serene's head bobbed in surprise, and she laughed out loud.

"I won't let you have them," Jenna repeated, louder this time. She pushed away her self-doubt, focusing on what she wanted to do—what she had to do.

Then suddenly, she felt something...shift. She glanced down at her arms, and her eyebrows climbed in surprise.

Her Charms had stopped fading, and the pulsing lights in Raloria's Strands stood still.

Her eyes widened as she met her aunt's gaze. She wasn't sure which of them was more shocked.

"What did you do?" Serene demanded.

Jenna had no idea what she'd done. But she was going to keep doing it. She squared her shoulders. "You can't have my Charms!" she said again, and the central line on her arms began to fill back in.

Serene's surprise turned to unease. "How are you doing that?"

The lights pulsing through Raloria's Strands changed direction, flowing toward Jenna now. Then the lights pulsed faster, and in seconds, her Charms were as thick and whole as they had ever been.

She couldn't believe it had worked.

She frowned. But *why* had it worked?

Her eyes fastened on Serene's throat—on the raised pink rash that stretched from her collarbone to her jaw. She'd seen that rash somewhere before.

And then it struck her. Her hand flew up to her own throat, and she pushed her hair away, feeling the raised lines of pink.

Last night at the Winter Carnival, Serene had dosed her with the Obru extract. When she'd been trapped in the back of Thairyn's Mercedes, her arms and throat had burned like never before. And when she'd looked in the car's side mirror, the pink rash was there. Something in her had changed—or been freed.

She looked down again at the Charms on her hands and arms. There were three Strands intertwined. Artifex, Seer, and—was it possible?—Siren.

She felt numb all over again. "I'm a Siren, too," she breathed.

Serene's face went purple. "That's not possible."

"It's true. You thought I was cursed because I was born with two Charms. But it was worse than that. I was born with three. All three gifts run in our family, and I inherited all of them. But the Siren Charms never showed themselves until last night when you gave me the Obru. Aunt Serene, you unblocked my gift."

Serene's lips tightened into a hard line. "Then I would be very careful if I were you. The Siren Charms are a responsibility. Think about it, Jenna. Even if you do have the gift, can you be trusted to use it? I mean, with your track record? I'm sorry, but you're not a Siren. You're a train wreck."

Jenna winced.

Her aunt stepped forward. "Look at the decisions you've made. Look at what happened to your father when you cut him off. Look at what happened to Brent—and to that poor boy Michael. He was your friend until you got him killed."

Her aunt's words were like a slap in the face. Everything she was saying was true.

Serene saw her advantage and pressed it. "There's no way you could use the gift wisely. Your whole life has been a series of failures."

Jenna's attention snagged on that word—*failures.*

There was truth in what her aunt was saying. She'd faced failure after failure. But that wasn't the whole truth.

She took a shaky breath, and for some reason, the TOTEL pledge floated through her mind. *"I will seek the truth,"* she whispered.

Serene had been right about one thing—Jenna needed to change her mindset. She met her aunt's eyes. "They weren't failures," she said. "They were lessons."

Her thoughts were racing. If she and Serene were both Sirens, this would come down to the two of them. The strongest mage would win the day. And Jenna had to be stronger. Everyone was depending on her. Serene was fighting for theoretical people. Jenna was fighting for real ones. Lane. Her friends. Her mother.

A memory came to her—her mother standing in the living room, her hands grasping both sides of her face. Love is powerful, her mother had told her.

And later, the plant her mom had been watering had dropped a seed.

The realization went through her like a lightning bolt. Her hand went to her jeans pocket, and she pulled out the tiny black Obru seed.

She glanced over at her mom again. She was shivering—mouth open and gasping for air as she struggled for life. Defenseless.

Jenna clenched her hand around the seed and willed herself to be strong enough. She cried out, *"I will defend the defenseless!"* Then she narrowed her eyes. Nothing else existed but the seed and her target.

She wound her arm back and launched the seed across the room. It sailed through the air, straight as an arrow, and landed inside her mother's open mouth.

In her whole life, it was Jenna's one and only perfect throw.

Mae coughed, choking. Then, instinctively, she swallowed.

Jenna swung to Raloria. "Help me! Tether my mom—quick!"

"Don't listen to her!" Serene commanded, but her compulsion didn't take. Jenna's did.

Raloria twisted around in her seat, and another of her Strands whipped out and attached to Mae's scalp in the place where her white streak used to be.

Serene whirled to Flynn. "Do something!"

He rushed forward, but Jenna pointed a finger at him. "Stop right there!" she commanded.

The man froze mid-stride.

Then Jenna turned once more to Raloria. "I need to give my Seer gift to my mom, do you understand?"

The child nodded enthusiastically, and the pulsing lights inside her Strands flowed from Jenna toward Mae.

Her scalp burned. Quickly she grasped a handful of her hair and pulled it in front of her, watching as her one white streak returned to auburn red.

Across the room, Mae's honey-brown bob regained its familiar snowy stripe, and she woke up, coughing but restored.

Jenna faced Serene once more.

"You're making a mistake, I promise you," Serene said coldly. "You're cursed. And no matter what you do, you will always be cursed. You're dangerous, Jenna."

"That makes two of us."

And suddenly, she knew what to do. There was a cure, after all.

Ever since the day she'd discovered her dreadful Charms, her touch had been cursed. Worse than that, she'd thought she was a curse. Today, though.... Today—she was going to save the world.

"I will right the wrong!" she sang out. She turned to Raloria, whispering, "Help me!"

The girl nodded, clutching Owly tight.

Jenna gritted her teeth and began to push her gift—her Siren gift—toward her aunt.

"What are you doing?" Serene asked with dawning horror.

"Thairyn told me that when two mages with the same power duel, they can burn their power out—like a lightning strike that fries your TV. You wanted my Charms, Aunt Serene, and I'm giving them to you."

She gaped. "You don't know what you're doing! We'll both lose our power!"

"That's the idea." Jenna set her jaw and concentrated on forcing her magic toward Serene.

"Stop it!" Serene lunged at her, hands reaching for her throat.

But Jenna caught her arms, channeling every ounce of her strength and holding her aunt at bay. All those self-defense classes were still paying off.

She focused on pressing the Siren Charms into her aunt, letting her body work instinctively to fend off the physical attack. They strained against each other, neither of them able to get the upper hand.

Beside them, Raloria whimpered softly with the effort. The push and pull of their magic was taking its toll, and sweat beaded the girl's forehead.

Then Serene leaned forward, using her body weight to gain the advantage.

Jenna realized that, if she didn't stand, her aunt would overpower her, toppling her backward onto the counter. And then Serene's hands would find her throat.

Blocking out everything around her, Jenna summoned every remnant of her strength and slid her feet to the floor.

She didn't know if her Siren Charms could work on herself, but in case they did, she spoke aloud. "Stand up, Jenna. Just for a minute. Stand up for yourself, for your friends, for the people you love. Your legs will hold you. This is your moment—time to stand up!"

Her legs straightened and held. She tilted her body forward, crying out as she shoved the last of her Siren gift into Serene.

Then her neck caught fire.

At the same moment, the Charms on her aunt's throat vanished. Serene screamed, clutching the place where the marks had been. She crumpled to the floor, sobbing and powerless. In a single second, all the fight went out of her.

Exhausted, Jenna lifted her fingers to her own neck, feeling the smoothness of her skin. Her Siren Charms were gone.

"Angel!" Lane cried, rushing toward her. He and the others were moving again, freed from Serene's spell.

Jenna's legs finally collapsed beneath her, and the last thing she saw was Fore. The otherworldly woman loomed silently above her, glowing softly. And though her face never changed expression, Jenna could have sworn she was smiling.

She smiled back. *"I will stand up for fairies,"* she whispered.

And then her world went dark.

Chapter Thirty-Nine

MAGIC

Someone was calling her name. A lot of someones.

Jenna's eyes flew open.

Mae leaned over her, clasping Jenna's hands in her own. "She's awake!" she cried exultantly.

There was a chorus of cheering.

Jenna blinked, trying to clear her thoughts.

Lane's face appeared above her, his forehead creased with worry. "You were asleep so long after Raloria healed you, I was afraid.... Are you okay?"

It all came back to her in a rush, and she sat up abruptly. Her mom and Lane were on either side of her, and the TOTEL gang was gathered around her in a loose circle. Suddenly the room swam, and Mae pressed her gently back down on the counter. "Not so fast."

But she needed to know. She pushed up onto her elbows, searching her mom's face. "You're all right?" When her mom nodded, she glanced around at the others, afraid of what she might find. But everyone had come through unscathed.

Finally, she allowed her gaze to land on Lane, and she let out a breath she didn't know she'd been holding. It was him—not the awful, Charmed version of him—but the Lane she knew and cared about.

He stared back at her with his robin's egg–blue eyes, and a slow smile spread over his face.

Mae pushed Jenna down once more and wheeled on the group. "Everybody, shoo! Give her a few minutes to rest, and then I'm sure she'll be happy to see you."

Reluctantly, they dispersed. Lane gave her one last look over his shoulder before he went to find Brie.

Mae helped her sit up slowly.

"You're really okay?" Jenna asked. "You're not dying?"

"Not anytime soon, I hope. When you gave me your Charms, it saved my life. I'm a Seer again—but with the Charms of a seventeen-year-old. I won't have to worry about my new gift making me sick for a long, long time."

Jenna heaved a sigh of relief, really seeing her mother for the first time since she woke up. Even with the white streak in her hair, she looked more energized—more herself—than she had in years.

"I knew everything was going to turn out for the best," Mae told her. "At least I did after my vision from Fore."

"What did you see?"

She smiled mysteriously. "Let's just say, Fore showed me enough to make me stop worrying."

Jenna nodded. "And Lane is okay? He's not cursed anymore?"

"No, he's not cursed."

"Brent too? The curse is gone?"

Doubt flickered across Mae's face. "It's gone, but there is something you should know." She glanced toward the plaid sofa, where Brent sat alone, apparently in a daze. As they watched, Doc approached with Pudge at her heels. She coaxed Brent to stand up and, holding him by the arm, she guided him outside.

Mae turned back to Jenna, her expression carefully blank. "Raloria...she's so young. She thought she was helping him. When she tried to heal him, she said she found something...sick...inside of him. So she erased the memories that were causing the sickness." She heaved a sigh. "The long and short of it is, Brent can't remember who he is."

Jenna gaped at her. "Are you saying he has amnesia?"

"I'm saying we had to tell him his own name." She shook her head. "I've never seen anything like it."

"Will his memory come back?"

"It's impossible to say. We'll have to wait and see." She brightened. "But your friend Lane seems to have made a full recovery."

Jenna felt her cheeks grow warm. "I'm glad," she said as casually as possible. Then another thought struck her. She sat up in alarm. "What about Serene? And

Ian and Flynn?"

Mae was already nodding. "They're in the other room, safely bound and gagged. Ian's still out cold from that shot with the dart gun, and even Serene won't be able to do any damage after today. You burned her magic out of her, but she's still alive because of the Obru she drank." Her expression grew sorrowful. "She's changed so much. We were close once."

"I liked her," Jenna said. "At first, anyway. I'm sorry she tried to use us both."

Mae nodded sadly. "Thairyn is with Serene and the other two now. After we leave, he'll contact some friends he has in the Vigil, and they'll turn them over to the Council—along with all of Flynn's...pets. The verothon won't have gone far, and they'll look for it, too. The Council won't want it out there in the wild, that's for certain."

"Won't the Council come after us?"

"Raloria did her memory wiping trick on all three of them—just not as severely as with Brent. She erased about a month of memories, so Serene, Ian, and Flynn won't recall even contacting us."

Jenna let out a long breath. "It'll be like none of this happened." She tilted her head. "And what about Thairyn and Raloria?"

"I spoke to Thairyn. He won't say anything, and he'll keep Raloria from talking, too. Even though he worked for the Council, he won't allow them to harm you, Jenna."

She raised an eyebrow. "I'm pretty sure he tried to kill me with a poisoned earring just a little while ago."

Mae sighed. "He explained it to me. He didn't think you'd survive the procedure. And if you were going to die anyway, he wanted to make sure Serene couldn't use your power to hurt even more people."

"I guess I can understand that," she agreed reluctantly.

"Look on the bright side," Mae said, lifting Jenna's hands into view. "You don't have to worry about your Charms anymore."

She froze. Then she quickly shoved her sleeves up, inspecting her unmarked skin. Where the three twisting lines had been, there was only a faint bruise. Her voice caught. "You mean I'm cured?"

"Close enough," Mae told her. "You gave your Seer Charms to me, and you burned the Siren Charms out of you and Serene both. Only the Artifex Charms are inside you now."

Jenna's stomach dropped. "I'm still an Artifex?"

Mae took her by the shoulders. "Yes, Jenna, but you're not cursed. Raloria Delved you. She said the Artifex Charms are all that's left, and they aren't fully formed. And according to Thairyn, the current Council Artifex had to train for years before getting access to the gift. It's most likely too late for you."

"Meaning...."

"Meaning, you're basically a normal young woman now."

"Normal," she repeated. "So I can touch people and they won't...."

"No. Your Artifex Charms can't hurt anyone."

She closed her eyes. She'd thought the hope of a cure was gone, and then, suddenly, she was fine. It was almost impossible to believe.

Mae touched her arm. "If you're feeling better, I need to go check on Thairyn. I think he has a concussion. Are you okay here?"

"I'm good. Go help Thairyn."

Her mom left, and Jenna stared down at her hands, marveling at her unmarked skin. For the first time in years, she wasn't a danger to anyone else. She was just a boring, ordinary, run-of-the-mill person. It was a dream come true.

A giggle made her look up. Jose and Hampton sat on the twin bed with Raloria sandwiched between them. Jose had taken Gandalf from Doc, and he was imitating the parrot's voice, pretending to have a conversation with Owly. Raloria was delighted.

Hampton reached into his bag and took out the hacky sack he'd been crocheting. He unraveled part of it and then tied it off, making a little cap for Owly that he tugged over its head, hiding the torn ear. Raloria squealed in pleasure and hugged the owl closer. Then she noticed Jenna watching and made Owly's tiny wing flap hello.

Jenna waved back and got down from the counter, wanting to check on the others. She grabbed her jacket and went outside, looking up at the moon and enjoying the clean, cold air on her skin, the crunch of snow underfoot.

Lita was leaning against the trunk of a birch tree nearby. She'd positioned her cell phone to throw light on her arm. And once more she was drawing on herself with a Sharpie.

She didn't look up as Jenna walked over. "You can't see him now, can you?" Lita asked. Her voice was flat and scratchy.

Jenna didn't need her to explain who she was talking about. She was decorating her arm with Nardo's name, adding—not snakes and spiders—but hearts.

Jenna shook her head sadly. "I'm not a Seer anymore. I won't be able to see him again. But I'm sure if Nardo were here, he'd want to say that he—"

"Are you Lita?" Mae asked, striding over to the tree. She turned her head as if speaking to someone beside her—someone invisible. "You're going to have to be more patient." Then she pointed to Lita. "There's a spirit here who says his name is Nardo. He wants me to tell you he loves you, but—and I'm quoting him now—you need to do like the chick in the movie and let it go." She eyed Lita carefully. "Does that message mean anything to you?"

Lita blinked.

Jenna put her hand on her mother's arm. "Mom, you can see and hear Nardo? How? Did you eat the beef jerky?"

Mae looked at Nardo, confused. Then, after pausing to listen, she nodded in understanding. "You're forgetting," she told Jenna. "Your Seer gift never functioned normally. How could it? It was competing with two other Charms for magic." She sighed. "No, unfortunately I can see and hear him."

Lita's face had gone slack. "He's here now?"

Mae turned to Nardo, irritated. "No, I'm not doing that. Absolutely not. I have to draw the line somewhere."

Lita stood up straight. "What's he saying?"

"He wants me to imitate him. To show you a...a...dance? He says it's a dance, but...."

"He's twerking!" Lita said happily. She laughed out loud. "So typical, Nardo." She rushed toward Mae. "Can you tell him from me that—"

Jenna slipped away to let Lita have her privacy.

Kelsea and Markese came out of the woods, followed by Zinnia and Devonte. They carried the bins of headphones and the sound equipment they'd used.

"Let me get this straight," Kelsea said, trudging through the snow. "Serene wanted Jenna's power so she could take over the world?"

"That's right," Zinnia told her.

Kelsea shook her head in disgust. "What a sicko!" She hopped into the back of the van to redo their packing job.

Markese stared after her in disbelief. He turned to Zinnia. "Does she not realize she's the founder and leader—the so-called presidempress—of the Take Over the Earth League?"

Zinnia shushed him. "Move on, Markese. Just move on."

Markese gestured to Devonte. "Are you hearing this?"

Devonte grinned. "Listen to the woman, Markese. Move on."

Kelsea poked her head out of the van, noticing Jenna's approach. "Ah! Jenna Getty. Welcome back! I know why you're here, but there's no need to thank me for saving the world. It's all a part of my job as presidempress of TOTEL. It makes you stop and think, though, doesn't it? It was my unparalleled genius that came up with the morning pledge, and without that, tonight would have been a disaster. So, you're welcome."

"I'm sure that's why Jenna came over here, Kelsea. To give you all the credit," Markese said sarcastically.

"I just said that, Markese. Try to keep up. Anyway," she said, returning her attention to Jenna, "I expect you'll be fully recovered for our concert next week. We're resuming Operation: Let's Get Our Groove On. How many tickets can you sell?"

"Um...I don't really know anyone except for you guys. Although...." She paused as an idea occurred to her.

"You're too late," Kelsea told her. "I already asked Thairyn. He and Raloria are both coming."

Markese rolled his eyes. "Kelsea, when someone tells you they might make it, that means they won't make it."

"Actually, I was thinking of someone else," Jenna interrupted before Kelsea could respond. "I'd like to invite my next-door neighbor. I owe him a favor, and I think he'd enjoy the company."

"Do you hate your neighbor?" Markese asked. "Because our band is a hot mess."

Kelsea fisted her hands on her hips. "TOTEL CHAOS has an eclectic sound,

Markese, that's all." Then she ignored him, turning to Jenna. "We'll find a place for your neighbor."

Markese sucked his teeth. "Kelsea girl, unless you plan to pay people to show up, he may be the only one in the audience."

They continued bickering as Jenna smiled and walked away. Then she noticed Doc and Brent sitting together on a fallen log with Pudge at their feet, and her smile fell.

Doc spoke to Brent using the same quiet voice that had soothed countless animals. He sat at her side like a lost child, petting the big Saint Bernard dejectedly.

A chill went up Jenna's spine. It was Brent sitting there, but also—it wasn't. And she didn't know how to feel about that.

Just then, a snowball hit her on her arm. "No frowning allowed," Brie said. "This was a good day." She walked toward the van, carrying one of her drums.

Jenna ran to catch up. "Lane told me that none of this could have happened without your help. I want to thank you. For today, and for last night, too. It meant a lot."

"You know what you can do if you really want to thank me?" Brie asked.

"What's that?" Jenna asked eagerly.

"Stop thanking me." She shuddered. "I'm in sugar shock over here. What runs through your veins, blood or maple syrup? I may gag."

Jenna sniffed. "Okay then, I won't thank you. I take it all back. Is that better?"

"Yes! I can feel my insulin levels returning to normal."

Jose and Hampton came out of the cabin at that moment, and Jose called out to Brie. He scurried over, Hampton trailing behind.

Brie exchanged glances with Jenna and crossed her arms, bracing herself.

Jose skidded to a halt and gazed adoringly up at her. "Greetings, Lady Fair. In the moonlight, your unparalleled beauty is even more entrancing. Will you do me the honor of sitting beside me in the van?"

Her expression never changed. "I would rather wear a bacon bikini and swim with sharks." She turned on her heel and joined the others.

Jose looked at Hampton and beamed. "That was the shortest one yet." He waggled his eyebrows. "Bacon bikini! I think she's warming up to me." He raced over to the group. "Hey, you guys," he said, "I think Operation: Let's Get Jenna was a ginormous success. Now who's up for Operation: Let's Get Tacos?"

They all shouted in agreement, and Jose stretched out his hand, an expectant look on his face. Zinnia beckoned Jenna over to join them as everyone piled on, one hand at a time.

Jenna hesitated only a second, then added her hand to the center of the circle.

"Three, two, one—Let's get tacos!" everyone said in chorus and flung their hands in the air. They broke into excited chatter, but someone was missing. Jenna noticed Lane hovering at the edge of the trees.

He motioned her away from the crowd, and she followed him into the deeper calm of the woods. The moon was nearly full, casting just enough light to see by as they wove through the winter trees. They walked side by side until they found a small glade out of sight of the others.

It was suddenly too quiet.

Lane stopped and cleared his throat. He met Jenna's eyes. "I have something I want to—" But as he stepped closer, he slipped on a patch of ice and skidded forward.

She reached out and caught his arm, steadying him. Her breath hitched as she looked at her hand on his arm.

She had touched him. She was touching him now, holding him without fear. Without guilt. And it was fine.

It was more than fine. It was amazing.

Overwhelmed, she thrust her hands into her pockets and looked down at her feet.

That's when she noticed the impossible green leaves. They were growing too rapidly, pushing up through the snow. She pointed. "Lane, can you see those, too?"

He followed her gaze and gasped.

Stems unfurled from the jagged leaves, and they began to bud. In seconds, the plants burst into bloom, and Jenna recognized her favorite flower—dandelions. Hundreds of tiny yellow suns dotted the clearing. Then the yellow flowers closed again, reemerging as delicate white balls of fluff.

"How?" Lane asked. "How is that possible?"

"Maybe it's Fore's way of saying thank you." A black-and-white chickadee perched on the branch above them and began to sing.

She bent down and picked two dandelion stems. "You can't say I never brought you flowers," she said, holding one out to Lane.

He took it wonderingly. Then he cocked his head. "What will you wish for?"

"Easy," she said. "Everybody knows you wish for more wishes." She blew the dandelion fluff into his face and darted away laughing, kicking up more of the fuzzy seeds.

He gave an indignant shout and chased after her, catching her hand and bringing her around to face him.

His smile melted. "There's something I want to give you, too," he said softly. "Close your eyes and hold out your hands."

She raised an eyebrow.

But he was peering at her intently. "Trust me, okay?"

She did as he asked, curious what he was up to. She waited, hardly daring to breathe, but her hands remained empty.

"I'm very tempted to peek," she told him.

"Don't you dare."

She wrinkled her nose, trying to place the faint whispering sound she knew she should recognize. What was he doing?

Then, without warning, he dropped something lightly into her palms. "You can look now."

She opened her eyes and gasped. In her hands was a paper flower he'd folded out of a dollar bill.

She stilled.

Not a dollar bill. A two-dollar bill.

She swallowed and looked up at him. She remembered the story he'd told her about his grandparents' love for each other—two who were one. In their memory, he always carried a two-dollar bill in his wallet. And now he'd given it to her.

She was at a loss for words. "It's beautiful," she finally told him. And she tucked it carefully into her pocket.

He reached his hand out for her again, and she took it, intensely aware of the warmth of his fingers wrapped around hers.

They walked further into the woods, and as they walked, Jenna noticed a tiny orange butterfly flitting across their path. She blinked in wonder, and then it was gone.

Lane stopped abruptly. He released her hand and turned to face her. "Listen, I just want to say that I...I know you aren't used to being touched."

She waited, confused.

"I know it's too soon now. You've been through a lot, so we can go super slow, okay? That's all I'm saying. I don't want you to feel pressure or anything. If you're even interested at all...in...whatever. Do you understand what I'm talking about?"

"Not remotely."

He ran a nervous hand through his black hair, making his cowlick stand on end. "So, the thing is...." He dove in. "The thing is, I really, really want to kiss you. Really, really, really. But as myself, you know? No Charms involved."

Over Lane's shoulder, a firefly sparked to life.

He risked a glance at her. "And I really, really hope that maybe, someday, you'll want to kiss me too." He looked down at her and blushed.

"I'm glad you said that," she told him.

"You are?"

She took his hand, twining her fingers in his. "Yes. Because right this very moment, I'm really, really, REALLY going to kiss you."

He sucked in a surprised breath as she reached up and pulled his head down to hers, meeting his lips with her own.

He laughed and drew her closer.

Her wait was over. Jenna finally let the heat inside of her ignite.

And in the air all around them, fireflies sparkled, lighting up the night with magic.

The End.

THE MAGIC CONTINUES...

To connect with me online, please visit EllySmithton.com and sign up for my mailing list—I would love to hear from you! When you sign up, you'll receive a bonus short story featuring TOTEL CHAOS as well as Lane and Jenna's first date, and I'll keep you informed about the release of the next title in the series.

Also, please consider taking a moment to leave a quick review for this book—just a line or two would be great. It makes an enormous difference in helping people find this story. Thank you so much!

Hope to hear from you soon,

Elly

Acknowledgements

We are magicians, you and me.

I can put words on the page, but the stories only come to life when you rouse them from slumber. It is such a curious sorcery, this connection between us, Reader—across time and space. Thank you so much for reading, for creating with me the only real magic I know.

But before the words came to you, Reader, they needed taming. Thank you to Cyndi Sandusky of Sandusky Editorial Services for helping me craft the best version of this story that I could write. Cyndi's expert eye and editing fingers were invaluable.

Thank you, too, to friends who read and wrangled very early drafts. Helen, thanks for your honesty. I needed it. And Elizabeth, your thoughts were, as always, insightful and thought-provoking. Can we have another Creataway soon?

Thanks also to all of my family members for their moral support over years. Mom, this book is dedicated to you. I'd need another whole book to list the reasons, but the simplest is this: you shared your love of reading with me—and that has powerfully shaped who I am and who I want to be. Thanks, Mom.

I want to especially thank my brother, David, who has taken this writing journey with me. Thanks, Dave, for all of our long talks, your hilarious memes, and your sincere encouragement. It meant so much.

And to my wonderful husband, Peter—I wish I could give you the thanks you deserve. Ink isn't good enough. There should be flowers and fireworks. There should be music and dancing. There should be pastries and parades, confetti and clapping—skywriting, at the very least. But all I have are these two words: thank you. A million times, thank you. For reading, suggesting, cajoling, consoling. For all the joy you bring me. Thank you, Peter.

About the Author

 Elly Smithton is an author, book lover, podcast fanatic, and ballroom dancer. After exploring many wonderful cities, including Saint Paul, Minnesota, she now lives in her home state of South Carolina. Elly would like to claim she is a parasailing champion or at least a world-renowned yodeler. Truthfully, though, her idea of a good time is puttering in the garden, walking with her husband Peter, birdwatching, or even—gasp—daydreaming. Get in touch at EllySmithton.com.